"FLANNERY IS A HELL OF A STORYTELLER!"*

"*Moving Targets* is a Cold War brain-twister with devious layer piled on devious layer, and lots of punch and grimy atmosphere in Moscow and Washington....There is no question that Sean Flannery is a hell of a storyteller."
—New York *Daily News**

"Full of intriguing, fully drawn characters from both sides of the Cold War...Clever and thoroughly believable painting of inter-agency warfare, diverted loyalties, and political confusion in our time. Quite good."
—*Kirkus Reviews*

"Characters and subplots abound....One can't be certain of the ending until Flannery's skillfully drawn climax."
—*Chicago Tribune*

"*Moving Targets* is a genuine blockbuster, a chilling and breathtaking story of the KGB at its most desperate and ruthless. With this novel, Sean Flannery takes his rightful place among such masters as Tom Clancy and Clive Cussler and provides a terrifying scenario of what may yet happen in today's New Russia."
—Ed Gorman, *Mystery Scene*

NOVELS BY SEAN FLANNERY

WRITING AS DAVID HAGBERG

SEAN FLANNERY

MOVING TARGETS

TOR

A TOM DOHERTY ASSOCIATES BOOK
NEW YORK

This is a work of fiction. All the characters and events portrayed in this book are fictitious, and any resemblance to real people or events is purely coincidental.

MOVING TARGETS

Copyright © 1992 by David Hagberg

Cover art by Paul Stinson

A Tor Book
Published by Tom Doherty Associates, LLC
175 Fifth Avenue
New York, NY 10010

www.tor.com

Tor® is a registered trademark of Tom Doherty Associates, LLC

ISBN: 0-812-51013-5
Library of Congress Catalog Card Number: 91-33310

First edition: January 1992
First mass market printing: November 1992

Printed in the United States of America

0 9 8 7 6 5 4 3 2

This novel is for my eldest son, Kevin Hagberg, with the certain knowledge that the other children could not possibly take offense that I singled out one of them. I love you all.

— PROLOGUE —

AN EARLY FALL EVENING

VALENTIN YAKOVLEVICH ZIMIN SAT STARING AT A COMPUTER screen, his eyes glazed by lack of sleep. His staff of four were busy at other terminals. They occupied a large room on the fifth floor of a nondescript office building on Volkhonka Street near the Pushkin Museum, and the only security they'd been provided was an electronic interface between the lock on the door and their equipment. If the lock were ever to be forced, the memory within the central processing unit of their IBM system would be instantly destroyed, and along with it the machine's entire store of memory. It was not a comforting thought, but with the way things were going these days in Moscow, the precaution was necessary.

He and his assistants had been busy at their task fourteen days, working thirty and forty hours at a stretch before catching a few hours of sleep. Only Zimin had been outside in all that time. He had to make his reports in person every twenty-four hours, at three in the afternoon. This special operation, classified Most Secret, was simple in concept, but so far had proved to be much more difficult than any of them had imagined. Zimin and his people were trying to break into the KGB's main computer network without detection. Because of the coup and the aftermath, paranoia ran high in the Kremlin and the Russian Parliament, so a failure here would almost certainly mean death, at the hands of what were being called "vengeance squads."

He'd come upon another interlock which showed as a red rose on his full-color screen. The symbol was a new one to them, but its meaning, like the other blocks they'd managed to sidestep, was clear. At this point the user was not only supposed to come up with a coded sequence, such as a password or a series of numbers, but was also supposed to ask a question that would display the knowledge that an authorized user would be expected to possess.

Two days ago Zimin had successfully entered into First Chief Directorate territory and had roamed at will for the most part through many of the directorate's still closely guarded programs. At various stages he'd been required to come up with passwords and a display of knowledge that his contact had been able to provide for him.

Not this time, though, he told himself, staring at the screen. He was there, at the entry to the territory he'd been sent to search—namely, the most secret financial records of the former Komitet. The rose signaled a way through a liaison channel between the First Chief Directorate (which always had been and still was the biggest user of foreign currencies) and the KGB's powerful Finance Directorate, which was one of the unnumbered divisions. But he was going to be stopped for the time being because of lack of knowledge. And now that he had finally gotten this close, he did not want to blow his chances.

It was two-thirty when he logged out his terminal with his personal code, got his coat and cane, and hobbled out of the office without saying a word to the others. They were absorbed in their work and wouldn't have bothered looking up in any event. It was pleasantly warm outside, and it felt good to Zimin, who turned right and headed up toward Red Square.

* * *

At precisely three o'clock Zimin was ushered into the office of Konstantin Ivanovich Malakhov, a Kremlin deputy secretary.

"What progress this afternoon, Valentin Yakovlevich?" the deputy secretary asked. He was a large, boisterous man, and in appearance he looked very Western. He'd been completely cleared of any complicity in the August coup, but in some minds there was still some doubt.

"We've made it into First Directorate files, and I've actually uncovered a link between that series of programs and the Finance Directorate. But we're using telephone lines, of course, and progress is slow."

"I understand," Malakhov said, beaming. "But this is excellent news. Really splendid news. Are you ready to find out what we need to know?"

"Not quite, Comrade Deputy. There is one final security lock to be breached, for which I will need some help," Zimin said. He was a computer expert, of course, but he was also a wizard at macroeconomics. A powerful combination in the use he had been put to.

"Tell me."

Zimin quickly went over everything he'd managed to find to date, finally coming to the rose symbol. "This one I have no wish to tamper with. If I cause an alarm, an investigation will be made and our work will be discovered."

"I agree," Malakhov said. "There is someone who might be able to help us." He buzzed his secretary. "Ask Deputy Mukhin to join me for a few minutes," he said.

"Yes, sir."

"Mukhin is an assistant foreign affairs adviser to the President, but before that he worked for the KGB. In the Finance Directorate."

"Is he to be trusted?" Zimin asked. His own career, and possibly his life, were riding on the integrity of this investigation.

"Completely," Malakhov assured him.

* * *

Two hours later, and eight time zones to the west, Nancy Perigorde, who worked as a night duty shift supervisor at the National Security Agency's Communications Intercept complex at Fort Meade, Maryland, turned in her security badge at the door and ten minutes later stopped at a service station, where she filled up her bright red Nissan Sentra. Finished, she parked off to the side and used the pay phone to dial a Washington, D.C., number. A man answered on the first ring.

"Hello."

"It looks as if they're about to make a breakthrough," she said.

"What directorate are they after?"

"Finance."

"I see. Keep me posted."

Three other seemingly unconnected events that fall heralded what could be argued as the watershed of relations between the various spy agencies of the East and West. A last hurrah of the dying cold war. A last spasm before the corpse was finally laid to rest.

In Riga, the capital city of a newly emergent Latvia, a thin, desultory rain had been falling all day from a deeply overcast sky. A raw wind blew off the Baltic Sea, temperatures all week had never gotten above ten degrees Celsius, and as if to add insult to injury, the city had been plagued with a spate of electrical outages to go along with the endemic shortages Latvians had always suffered. Moscow had severely limited the flow of natural gas into the republic, and Soviet warships including a guided missile frigate of the Krivak III class were patrolling the gulf, barely eighty kilometers from the city center.

The Aeroflot direct flight from Bucharest touched down at Riga's Spilve Airport a few minutes after nine in the evening. The sun was still shining above the overcast, lending a foreboding grayness to the city and the choppy waters of the bay, an odd flattening of perspective that the assassin who deplaned hardly seemed to notice.

He was short and totally unremarkable in appearance and build, with the small paunch of a man who was probably in his mid to late forties. His hair was graying and he'd gone bald in the back. His shoulders sloped, and his face could only be described as forgettable. He wore a reasonably well cut dark suit, decent shoes, and the single bag he'd passed through customs with diplomatic papers was leather and handmade, though not ostentatious because it was fairly well battered by long use.

In Bucharest, where he'd spent the last four years of his life under cover as a secretary in the consular section of the Soviet Embassy, his name had been Nikolai Stepanovich Noskov. Before that, in Afghanistan, it had been I. F. Skripov, and before that, in Africa, it had been R. A. Markov.

Here, the Estonian passport he'd presented to the customs officials identified him as Vladimir Ivanovich Privalov. None of those names was his real one, of course. And it had been so long since he had used his own name that had someone stepped out of the crowded airport terminal and called it, he would not have responded.

Outside, he joined the queue at the taxi stand, unprotected from the wind and rain. But he didn't mind. In fact, it was good to be back in the field, though he sincerely suspected that this would be his last assignment, no matter what his control officer had told him.

"You have languished here for all but eight months of your posting, Nikolai Stepanovich," his control officer, Yuri Krivtsov, had told him, his voice gently, patiently understanding.

They were having an early dinner of *cotelet Valdostana*, which was a hearty veal dish, and the specialty of the Cina Restaurant, where they were meeting downtown, very near the Athenaeum.

"There has been no need for my . . . services," the

assassin said. He glanced across the crowded dining room toward the garden café in the rear. With the fall of Ceauşescu everything had changed here, as it had throughout the rest of eastern Europe, and as it still was in the *Rodina*.

"On the contrary, there has been and continues to be a great need for you. And now it is time for you to go to work."

The assassin looked sharply at Krivtsov. "This has been directed by Moscow?" He was, among other things, a pragmatic man. He didn't want to be caught in the middle of some harebrained operation that one of the new Kremlin power brokers might have cooked up. Great Russians were notorious for their love of scheming and intrigue.

"*Da.*"

"By whom?"

"Come now, this is not necessary. Not amongst old friends." They went back nearly eight years together.

"Who?"

"I can't tell you . . ."

"Then I will not accept this assignment."

Krivtsov stiffened slightly. He did not want a scene here. He could not afford it. His instructions had been very concise. Besides, despite their old friendship, he was slightly fearful of the man.

"It comes from very high up," he said.

"A name," the assassin insisted point-blank. He watched his control officer's gray eyes so that he would know if the man was lying to him. It was a talent he'd been born with in Yakutsk and had used to good advantage in Moscow. It was a talent that had saved his life on more than one occasion, and a talent that had been a root cause of his becoming what he was.

He'd studied to become an engineer. He wanted to build dams. It was to have been his ticket out of the Soviet Union. More than anything he had wanderlust. He wanted to see faraway lands. In his last year of school he was engaged to a girl in one of his classes. The same night they met, they went to bed with each other and life suddenly took on a new, exciting meaning to him. They were to be married in the summer, as soon as they both graduated. But in April he caught her in a lie. He'd seen it in her eyes. She'd told him that she was tutoring another engineering student, when in reality she'd been sleeping with the boy. The assassin had killed her the moment he found out, and forty-eight hours later the KGB had recruited him out of jail. That had been in 1971, at the height of the cold war. He had killed twenty-seven men and one woman in that time, and he remembered every one of their names and faces. Especially their faces at the moment of their deaths.

"Lavrushko," his control officer whispered.

"General Lavrushko?" the assassin asked sharply.

Krivtsov nodded nervously. Lavrushko was a deputy director of the GRU—the Soviet Military Intelligence Service. If it was true, his name was a gold passport. No matter what happened, it would be a way out. Insurance.

"Prove it."

Krivtsov took a sealed envelope out of his pocket and handed it across. "Don't open it here," he said. "If your decision to take this assignment depends only on proof of that one thing, then do so. If not, the contents will be of no value to you. Believe me in this."

The assassin did. It was in the man's eyes. There would be no need to open the envelope. "What is my assignment?"

"We want you to kill a man in Riga. A Latvian union leader by the name of Ergi Janjelsgau. Do you know this name?"

The assassin did. Janjelsgau was Latvia's Lech Walesa. "He will not be guarded?"

"Not all the time. In three days he meets in secret with what is being called the Committee for October First. It's the date they have planned for an armed revolt."

"Against his own government?"

"Yes. But just now it's in our best interests to keep the present government in place. We have some control."

"Where will they be meeting?"

"In a warehouse in Pardaugava on the left bank."

"There'll be others with him, I presume."

"Of course."

"Am I to kill them all?"

"Only Janjelsgau. A taxi will pick you up at the airport and the driver will take you into the city. He will let you off one block from the warehouse. You will kill Janjelsgau and then walk back to your taxi."

"And afterward?"

"You will be given instructions."

"Will I return to Bucharest?"

Krivtsov looked at him and shook his head after a moment. "I don't know," he said.

He'd been lying, the assassin thought as he climbed in the backseat of a taxi. He gave the number of a street on the right bank of the Daugava River, which split the city in two, and as the cab pulled away he sat back in his seat and took the nine-millimeter Beretta automatic pistol and silencer from his bag and loaded it.

But that lie hadn't mattered. He knew he could not return to Romania. He never returned to the posting from which he was dispatched on a kill. It just wasn't done. The question, of course, was where he would be sent after this.

He levered a round into the pistol's firing chamber, his heart beginning to quicken. He would not return to Russia either. That part of his life was over. Only the CIA cowboys fielded assassins. That had been the line ever since Khrushchev had made such a big deal out of Francis Gary Powers. And it had become terribly more important after Oswald had assassinated Kennedy to keep Russian hands as clean as possible . . . at least in the world public's eye. It was a long-standing policy that was finally beginning to bear fruition. No, he would not be welcomed home.

He closed his eyes for a long moment or two, drawing deeply of the cool night air. Tension began to build in his body, strengthening not only his muscles but his resolve as well.

In Switzerland, in Belgium, and on the Channel island of Jersey he maintained secret bank accounts far from the prying eyes of the KGB. When it was time to run, and after tonight it might be, he would have no financial worries. Over the years he had secreted in excess of three million pounds sterling, in large part from the assets of those victims he'd first gotten close to.

They crossed the river into Pardaugava twenty minutes later, the night finally dark, and the driver took them down a series of narrow streets, finally passing a four-story warehouse across from which railroad tracks ran away from the river to a switchyard.

"There," his driver, a slightly built Latvian, said, and he continued around the block, where he parked in the shadows. He shut off the cab's headlights, but he did not switch off the engine, nor did he say another word.

The assassin got out of the cab, and holding the pistol loosely at his side, his thumb on the safety catch, walked back the way they had come.

Outwardly he appeared calm, a man in complete control of himself. Inwardly, however, he was sweating. His heart hammered in his chest. His breathing was rapid and shallow. He felt flushed, sweaty, twitchy.

At the corner he stopped in the darkness. From here he was forty meters from the front door of the warehouse. It was too far.

Easing around the corner, he walked the rest of the way down the block, stopping in a doorway just across the tracks. A few seconds later a black Chaika limousine, its hubcaps missing and its right fender smashed, pulled up across the street.

The assassin switched the Beretta's safety catch to the off position. A warmth began to build in his groin, and he began to feel a sexual power. It was the same at each kill.

Nothing seemed to happen for a full minute, but then a light appeared in the doorway of the warehouse, and six men came out. Only one of them was dressed in a business suit, and he towered over the others. His profile was very reminiscent of De Gaulle's, with the large nose. He was

Janjelsgau, and even from across the street the assassin could feel the charismatic power emanating from the man.

A second automobile, this one a Soviet-made Lada, pulled up behind the limousine. The drivers of both cars got out and hurried around to open the doors.

The assassin stepped out of the shadows and walked rapidly across the street, his penis erect and pressing almost painfully against the material of his trousers. His blood was singing, his breath came even more rapidly, and he was on the verge of orgasm.

No one across the street spotted him; they were too intent on what Janjelsgau was saying to them. The assassin raised his pistol at the same moment the Latvian union leader looked up, and he fired two shots, the first hitting the man in the face just below the bridge of the nose, and the second in the chest, driving him backward.

The assassin ejaculated as he turned and walked back into the shadows and around the corner, pleasure coursing through his body as if he had just made passionate and satisfying love to a beautiful woman.

No one followed him in the confusion.

Reaching the cab, he climbed in the backseat, and the driver pulled away, switching on the headlights a block away.

"It's done."

"Good," the driver said. "There are new orders for you. Another assignment. This time in the West. America."

The surest way of ruining a trip home was to conduct a joint intelligence service briefing, Richard Sweeney thought, approaching the lectern. It was nearly dinnertime and his stomach rumbled. Kay was waiting for him at the hotel, and he wanted nothing more than to get back to her and fix himself a decent drink . . . an American drink.

The auditorium was small by Pentagon standards, with less than fifty seats, most of them taken this evening. Besides the military intelligence establishment contingent, the civilian complement included the CIA's deputy directors of intelligence, Chris Roberts, and operations (Sweeney's boss),

Richard Adkins. Allen Young had come over from the FBI's Special Investigations Division, as had the second assistant directors of the National Security Agency and Defense Intelligence Agency.

"Good evening, gentlemen," Sweeney began. "It's good to be home, even if it's only for a few weeks."

There were a few polite chuckles from the audience. Sweeney worked for the CIA as assistant chief of station at the U.S. Embassy in Moscow. He'd been recalled to Washington for update briefings on the current political thinking of this administration. It was common for returning CIA officers to help conduct such briefings as these in turn. The theme of this evening's meeting, at which Chuck Markham from NSA and Dennis Warner from the State Department had already spoken, was "Intelligence Gathering for the '90s."

"Chuck and Dennis have both promised you no surprises," Sweeney said. "It's business as usual for them. Or very nearly so. But I'm afraid I can't be quite so sanguine."

A few men in the audience shifted in their seats, and Sweeney grinned and held up his hand. He was a large man. Strongly built, with a thick waist, a bull neck, and massive shoulders. He loved to fish and hunt, and in high school and college he'd been a hell of a lineman. His wife of twenty years called him "Ernie" in private. Short for Ernie Hemingway. "A man's man," as she put it.

"This is not the usual field officer paranoia talking here, although I suppose I've developed my share of that occupational hazard."

There were a few more good-natured chuckles.

"What I'm talking about tonight are the changes that have and are taking place in Moscow. And we all know what some of those are. I'm not telling tales out of school in this room when I remind you that the CIA's budget has been slashed by nearly sixteen percent over the past year and a half. No new hiring at Langley. Nearly every research project our Technical Services Division had going has been put on hold . . . some permanently. And there've already been drastic cutbacks at all but a few of our key stations.

"Germany, for instance, is in near shambles. The only real work of any consequence we're doing there is being done out of our Bonn Station.

"Hungary, Romania, Czechoslovakia, Poland, all the former hot spots have been shut down for all practical purposes. At the Photo Reconnaissance Laboratory and the National Security Agency, and our own Satellite Surveillance Division, it is business as usual. I agree. But from where I sit, I see a different picture. A painfully different picture, gentlemen."

Sweeney glanced at Dick Adkins, who gave him a slight nod. It had been decided that he was to be the bearer of this particular message. Coming from a field position in Moscow, just now, his words would carry some weight.

He agreed, though he didn't like it. He was a field officer, not a politician.

"Part of the job, Richard," his boss had told him. At Langley he was Richard, and Adkins was Dick. It saved some confusion.

"ELINT—electronic intelligence—gathering will continue to play a vital role, of course. But these days it behooves us to know the Russian government's intent. Which means we must return to the basics. People spying on people. It's as simple, and as complicated, as that."

"The Russians will be doing the same damned thing," someone muttered loudly enough for Sweeney to hear.

"Exactly," Sweeney said. "The comment has been made that the Russians will be doing the same thing. Well, gentlemen, they've already begun. Not that they ever really stopped. And now it is up to us to do what we can, and to stop them. They've still got the weapons and the delivery systems. It's up to us to make certain we always know what their real intentions are. Stimson was wrong. Gentlemen *must* open other gentlemen's mail, if we are to survive. And now with everything over there changing so rapidly, intelligence gathering has become even more important than before."

The night was brilliant. A star-flung sky competed with the brilliant carpet of lights that swept up from the Black Sea and the lights of an occasional ship in the inky darkness toward the horizon. The city of Odessa was thirty kilometers to the southwest. From the balcony of the villa perched on the seaside cliff it was only a glow in the distance.

Moscow, fourteen hundred kilometers to the north, was nothing here except for the brief telephone warning the man had received.

He was not large, but he was compactly built, his skin dark from exposure to the sun, or a sunlamp. He stood on the balcony looking out to sea. A glass of white wine sat on the low rail. He smoked a cigarette in the American fashion, holding it not between his thumb and forefinger, but between his forefinger and middle finger. He wore nothing more than a white towel around his slim waist, not cold at all in the gentle sea breeze.

"Where are you?" the woman called from inside the house.

He didn't answer for a long time, preferring his own solitude for just a few moments longer. The struggle was coming much sooner than he'd hoped for. They were not ready. But there was no help for it. They would have to move now, or the opportunity . . . the golden opportunity of a lifetime . . . would be lost, and with it the KGB. Vanished into thin air. Dissipated like smoke on the wind.

"Here," he said at length.

The woman came across the bedroom and joined him on the balcony. She was nude, her skin nearly iridescent in the starlight, her long legs ending at a narrow swatch of dark pubic hair, her breasts firm, the nipples already erect. Here was a . . . child, who had never had children. She was almost thirty, perhaps, but she was a child still, with no real memories of her own. She was like putty, ready and even willing to be formed.

"I got lonely," she said in Russian.

"In English, please, Marinka," the man said, using the diminutive of the name they'd given her.

"What are you thinking about out here?" she asked, but he put a finger to her lips to silence her.

"Tomorrow you return to Moscow."

"Already?" she asked, a look of alarm crossing her face.

The man nodded. He brushed his fingertips across her breasts and she shivered.

"So soon?"

"Yes."

She leaned into him and took the nipple of his left breast into her mouth, running her tongue lightly in circles. He smiled and flipped his cigarette out into the night, sparks trailing all the way down to the water.

Together they went into the bedroom, where he took off his towel and lay with her on the wide bed, caressing her flanks, taking her long, dark hair between his fingers as he entered her dark, warm body.

"You will be my banner, my love," he whispered into her ear.

"Forever," she replied.

1

THE WINTER

THE RUSSIAN EMBASSY WAS FIVE AND A HALF BLOCKS NORTH OF the White House on 16th Street between L and M streets. Like virtually every embassy in the world, business as usual included cocktail receptions. This one celebrated the appointment of a new deputy undersecretary to the ambassador to the United States, Igor Mikhailovich Lubiako, a tremendously charming man whose English was so idiomatically perfect that he could have been mistaken for an American anywhere. In Iowa they would have figured him to be from the East, Boston perhaps. In California he'd be from Minnesota, and in Boston from out West somewhere.

Richard Sweeney and his wife, Katherine, had been invited to attend. In the morning they were returning to Moscow.

"Hell of a way to spend our last night home, Ernie," she'd complained good-naturedly on the way over. But she was a good sport. She'd always been the perfect wife for an intelligence officer: Smart, cool under pressure, and when it came to politics, especially the world view, she definitely had her head on straight. No bleeding-heart liberalism for her. Of course she'd been raised that way. Her father had graduated in the top ten of his class at West Point. As a child she'd been a tomboy. As a teenager a standout in high school and college swimming and soccer. She'd grown up to be a pleasant-looking if not beautiful woman with a good body, wide pleasant eyes, and thick, sensuous lips.

"We're showing the flag," he told her in the cab on the way over from their hotel.

"There're plenty of eager hands in this town to take care of that job nicely, thank you."

"Not many of them are special assistant to the ambassador in Moscow."

She looked closely at her husband. They'd been married long enough for her to understand when he was telling her to back off. They'd never had children, and they both believed that they were closer to each other because of it . . . not necessarily better off, just closer in many respects.

He caught her looking at him and grinned. "Just keep your ears open."

"Around whom?"

"Lydia Lubiako," Sweeney said.

"Ah, the wife. Could be the new deputy undersecretary is a spook?"

"Sister. He might be."

"Maybe it's her . . . she?"

Again Sweeney had to grin. "Just keep your ears open and your mouth shut. Deal?"

"Deal," she said in mock disappointment.

They often played these little games with each other, mostly to relieve the tension. On this trip back to the States, their stay had been too short for them to open their house in the Maryland countryside, located just outside of Lexington Park about sixty miles south of Washington. They owned twenty-five wooded acres of what had once been a part of a horse-breeding ranch. From the house they could see the Chesapeake Bay eight miles away. It was a beautiful spot that they both loved. "Peace in a world of turmoil," she'd once said.

"Yes, isn't it?" he'd replied, holding her, knowing what was coming next. The cold war was still going strong.

"But when the bombs fall on Washington it won't be such a great spot."

"Won't happen."

"No?" she asked, looking up into his eyes.

"Not if I can help it."

Washington had received a couple of dustings of snow since they'd arrived, but it still seemed like the tropics to them after Moscow. They'd already spent two and a half years in the Russian capital; two long winters, this their third. They'd definitely acclimatized. At least physically.

The cabbie dropped them off in front of the Russian Embassy a few minutes past five-thirty. They were fashionably late, as were a number of other guests, and they had to queue up just inside the vestibule, where their invitations were examined before they were allowed inside. In the old days they would have been subjected to a metal detector search. The Gorbachev regime had put a stop to that, and in that respect, nothing had changed since.

"This new openness will survive," a well-known Russian journalist had written, although Sweeney had his doubts. The Russian distrust of foreigners and anything foreign went back a long way . . . even before Stalin, back to the time of the czars. It was in the national spirit, the people's psyche.

"Be friends with the wolf," the old peasant proverb said. "But keep your hand on the ax." After all, America's loss of life in the Great Patriotic War had been measured in tens of thousands, while the *Rodina*'s losses had been measured in tens of millions!

The reception was being conducted mostly from the main hall and the state dining room on the ground floor, though the string quartet played on the second-floor balcony overlooking the stair hall. A number of people had gone up to listen, and to talk.

There was a muted hum of dozens of conversations among the more than one hundred guests. At this party the caterer was American and the canapés and other hors d'oeuvres were excellent.

Katherine accepted a glass of typically sweet Russian champagne from a passing waiter, while Sweeney took a small cognac. They would drink their first drink, and would accept a second in due course, which they would not touch. An oft-used trick was serving the first drink undoctored, but the second drink, after the guest's taste buds were numbed, could be safely spiked. No one could taste the chemical.

"Mr. and Mrs. Sweeney, I believe," a Russian said as they started across the hall into the dining room. Sweeney turned around.

"Yes," Sweeney said, extending his hand. "Nice party."

"Thank you, but frankly it's easier to do here than at home," the Russian said, shaking hands. "I'm Yuri Truskin, embassy chief of protocol." He was a short, stocky man with thick black hair.

"Pleased to meet you. Maybe I can help change all of that, you know. Now that your President is opening up the country to foreign investment again."

"Investments, not loans," the Russian said.

Sweeney smiled broadly. "Ah, but then, my friend, on the world market there's hardly a difference."

"Except that one has to be paid back, the other not."

"Not always necessary."

Truskin turned to Katherine. "I see that you're drinking our champagne. How do you like it?"

"Sweet, but very good," Katherine said, with a little giggle.

"Some Americans are beginning to acquire a taste for it. A small market has been developed."

"Don't forget your vodka," Sweeney interjected. "The yuppies are all drinking Stoli and grapefruit, or Stoli and a mix of orange and cranberry juices. Sells like gangbusters. Good for your balance of trade."

Truskin's smile broadened. "It's incredible, isn't it? Good vodka and . . . cranberry juice?"

Sweeney looked beyond him toward the dining room. "What I'd really like to see in Moscow would be a Ford or GM plant. Could employ a lot of people. Pump a lot of money into the economy."

"That may be a dream . . ."

"Actually we're returning to Moscow in the morning. Who knows, maybe we can work out such a deal, Mr. Truskov," Sweeney said, deliberately mispronouncing the man's name.

Truskin smiled pleasantly. "Then I'll wish you a good trip."

"Thanks, but we just stopped by to offer our congratulations to your new deputy undersecretary. I understand exactly what he's up against."

Again Truskin smiled. "I'm sure you do, Mr. Sweeney."

Sweeney took his wife's elbow. "Nice chatting with you," he said, and he steered his wife toward the dining room.

"Nice fellow," Katherine said as they crossed the room.

"Yes," Sweeney said. The embassy was bugged, of course, so they had to watch what they said.

Katherine wore a low-cut white cocktail dress that they'd bought in Paris on the way back to the States, for what she'd thought at the time was a ridiculously high price. Considering the looks she was generating now as they crossed the room, she would have gladly paid double. She and Richard were the same age; at forty-three a girl took her compliments where she got them.

Sweeney steered her toward a knot of people near the head of the large room. The huge dining table had been removed for this occasion, and the gilded walls were lined with the chairs. Waiters bearing trays of cocktails and hors d'oeuvres circulated in and amongst the groups.

He recognized Lubiako from the photographs he'd studied at Langley. At over six feet, the man was very tall for a Russian. His complexion was fair, and his hair dishwater blond. With a tan he could have passed as a southern Californian.

Lubiako was a relative newcomer. A 1974 graduate of Moscow University, he had spent one year at Cambridge, in England, and eighteen months at Harvard. He did not drink, he didn't smoke, and although he'd never married, so far as the Agency could determine he wasn't a homosexual (it would have been highly unusual if he had been). He was clean. Adkins called him "Snow White." And Sweeney wondered if the Russian had his seven dwarfs lurking somewhere nearby; Truskin was one, were there six others?

Two men speaking with Lubiako were Americans. One of them tall and craggy, the other heavier and much older. They turned as Sweeney and Katherine stepped up.

"Richard Sweeney. Just stopped by to offer my congratulations, Mr. Deputy," Sweeney said to Lubiako. They shook hands.

The Russian grinned, the expression seemingly open and guileless. "I'm sorry, but I don't think I know the name."

"I'm stationed at our embassy in Moscow as a special assistant to our ambassador."

"I see. In what capacity, may I ask?" Lubiako asked.

"Developmental loans," Sweeney said, watching the man's eyes. "It's a job."

"And why are you in Washington?"

"Oh, the usual instructions and conferences and all that at the State Department."

"We keep them busy," the tall, craggy American standing next to Lubiako explained to the Russian. "I'm Walter Miller, State Department, Economic Affairs," he explained to Sweeney. "I recognize your name, but I don't think we've ever met."

"No, sir," Sweeney said, shaking hands with the American. His legend was good with the State Department.

"May I add my congratulations, Mr. Deputy?" Katherine said sweetly.

"Mrs. Sweeney, I presume?" Lubiako said. "*Enchanté, madame.*"

"Oh, thanks," Katherine twittered. When need be she

could play the part of a mindless American wife very well. The Russians accepted it.

The other American introduced himself and shook hands with Sweeney. "Omar Ward, State Department. We've met."

"Yes, sir," Sweeney said. "Indeed we have." He'd never seen the man in his life.

A horse-faced woman who looked to be in her late forties or early fifties, but who was probably not yet forty, came up.

"Good evening," she said in English, her Russian accent extremely thick.

"May I present my sister, Lydia Lubiako," Lubiako said, and he introduced the others.

"Pleased to make your acquaintance."

Miller and Ward again offered their congratulations, and excused themselves.

"Is there a powder room here?" Katherine asked the woman.

Lydia Lubiako hesitated, but her brother stepped in. "Show Mrs. Sweeney to the ladies' room, would you be a dear?"

"Of course," the woman said, and she and Katherine left.

When they were gone, Lubiako eyed Sweeney with some amusement. "So, are you finding good opportunities in Russia?"

"You can't believe how good, Mr. Deputy. I just love it over there. Especially now. It's exciting and interesting."

"And what exactly is it you do?"

Sweeney laughed out loud. "It's my job to make millionaires."

"Pleasant work," Lubiako said.

"Yes," Sweeney replied. "It's good that we're finally friends again."

"I see you two are getting along well," Yuri Truskin said, coming up behind Sweeney. "There is someone who wishes to speak with you," he said in Russian to Lubiako.

"It was a pleasure meeting you, Mr. Sweeney," Lubiako said. "But I'm afraid duty calls."

"Perhaps we'll meet again," Sweeney said.

"Perhaps."

Sweeney sipped his drink as he watched them cross the big room. There was something about Lubiako that had been irritating. It was as if the man were condescending toward Americans. Often it was an affliction of very good spies who began to believe that they were invincible and therefore above everyone else. In some respects Sweeney was almost sorry that the cold war was over. His father would have called him an anachronism for not keeping up with the times. "I know, because I was one," the old man would have said. He'd been a case officer in Cuba and then in Mexico in the late forties, fifties, and early sixties. His car had been blown apart by a bomb thirty-six hours after he'd arrived in Saigon in 1964.

His father had not trusted communists. His son had limited his distrust to the Russians.

"What was that all about with Truskin when we first came in?" Katherine asked her husband in the cab on the way back to their hotel. It was nearly nine in the evening. The cocktail party had run over, as most parties these days in Washington did.

"He's Yuri Fedorovich Truskin. Intelligence has got him pegged as the KGB's Washington *Rezident*."

"Does he suspect who you really work for?"

"We don't think so," Sweeney said. "But I'd rather not spend a lot of time talking with him. He's a sharp bastard, no telling what he might pick up."

"Did he seem interested?"

"No. Now, what about Lydia Lubiako?"

"She's either the most incredibly stupid woman I've ever met, or the best actress. But I haven't a clue which."

"Are they actually brother and sister?"

"I don't know."

"Why's she here in Washington? Did she give you any idea of at least that much?"

"I don't know."

"Katy, what the hell did you talk about?"

Katherine looked at her husband. "It was scary, Dick. Trust me. She talked, and then I talked. She talked again, and I answered. Sometimes I asked a question and she answered. And after all was said and done, the woman had said nothing. *Nada*. Absolutely nothing."

The purpose of a language was to communicate. The purpose of civilization was to protect us from the beasts in the night. Sometimes, however, he thought that he'd been listening to gibberish all of his life, while trying to keep a candle lit in a monster-ridden night in which a hurricane wind always blew.

"Twelve months," he said at length.

Katherine smiled wanly. She reached out and squeezed his hand. "I was having the same thought," she said.

His assignment to Moscow had only another year to go. He'd already declined an extension. In twelve months they would be coming home. Two years on the Russian desk, and then . . . ? They'd make that decision together depending upon what his next assignment might be.

Time enough, Sweeney thought. In the interim he had to be careful. The ship at sea was safer than the ship returning to port after a long voyage. That's when the real disasters happened.

It was nearly midnight by the time Yuri Truskin entered the *referentura*'s screened room in the embassy basement where top-secret KGB work was usually done. Like the screened rooms in U.S. embassies abroad, this room was safe from all kinds of eavesdropping, electronic or mechanical.

All, that is, Truskin thought wearily, except for the human kind of eavesdropping . . . using the oldest piece of spy equipment known, the ear.

It was morning in Moscow. In another hour he would use the encrypted circuits to make his report. In the meantime he would enjoy his solitude, something he had come to appreciate more and more the older he got.

Loosening his tie, Truskin sat down at one of the desks in

the large room and lit a Marlboro. Blended whiskey and Marlboros, the two vices he had picked up here, would kill him sooner or later, according to his wife. Sometimes he wondered how she meant that.

The Kremlin coup notwithstanding, the cold war was over for now, and world peace was assured. Yet there were still enough nuclear weapons in existence to annihilate all human life on the planet a thousand times over. Who to trust? More important, who to distrust? The answer had always been easy for him: Simply never trust any nation that has the power to destroy the *Rodina*.

But as the Americans were fond of saying, things were getting a little flaky around the edges these days. In the first place there were vastly too many members in the nuclear club. And secondly the role of a spy in this new era was not clear.

Especially not clear, Truskin thought morosely, when Russians were practically tripping over themselves in the rush to change the old ways, no matter the cost.

Stalin had said, kill them all. Khrushchev had said, jail them all. Brezhnev had said, send them all to mental institutions. And Gorbachev had said, let them all leave, if they wish.

No matter what, Mother Russia had lost. And continued to lose.

"Welcome home, Mr. Privet," the customs officer at Washington's Dulles International Airport said.

The assassin, who was traveling on a U.S. passport that identified him as Vincent Privet, born in Milwaukee, smiled pleasantly and nodded. "Thanks a lot, it's good to be back."

"Been gone long?"

"Heavens, yes," the assassin said. "Far too long. Business, you know."

"Well, we all have to make a living."

"Isn't that the truth."

"Anything to declare, sir?" the customs officer asked.

"A carton of French cigarettes and a couple of bottles of

cognac," the assassin said. "I wrote it down on my customs declaration." It was always better not to come in clean. Less suspicion was generated.

"Right," the customs officer said. "Have a safe trip home, then."

"Will do," the assassin said, picking up his single bag. He stepped through the barrier and walked down a short corridor into the arrivals and departures hall, where he headed directly across to the main doors.

Another international flight had come in a few minutes before his from Paris, so the terminal was very busy just now. As they landed he had spotted the familiar tail shape of an Ilyushin jumbo jet on the ramp. It would be the Aeroflot flight for Moscow. Seeing it gave him a slight twinge for home, but only slight. Whatever it was he'd been called here for would surely mean that he could never go back. Never.

The struggle between the United States and Russia continued despite recent events. Yet here he was, on U.S. soil for the first time in his life. It made him shiver to think of the consequences.

Outside, he was lucky and got a cab almost immediately, giving the driver an address in Georgetown. As they pulled away he sat back in his seat as if he were indifferent to the countryside. But he was not. This was the United States. Not different from and yet very different from western Europe.

Wider; the single word came to him. It seemed that the horizon was farther away here than anywhere else.

The sky was overcast and it had begun to snow again by the time they crossed the river on the Key Bridge into Georgetown, so he'd been unable to see much of the city proper after all. The cabbie dropped him off at a charming brownstone on Dent Place near 34th Street.

After paying the driver, he let himself into the building and on the third floor knocked at the apartment door. A tall, well-built man with an expensive haircut and very well cut clothes opened the door. His name was Vsevolod Sergeevich Radchenko, and he was the assassin's control officer.

"You're right on time," Radchenko said, looking beyond

Privet into the corridor before he stepped aside. "Come in."

Privet stepped into the apartment, put his bag down beside the door, and took off his coat. "Are we alone here?"

"Yes, and the place is clean. Any trouble coming through passport control or customs?"

"None. I was supplied with very good documents."

"Fine," Radchenko said. He was nervous. "You'll be comfortable here. There's food in the kitchen, no liquor though. Clothes and other things in the closet and in the bathroom."

"When do I begin?"

"Not yet. I don't know when. When I'm told, I will tell you."

"In the meantime?"

"You wait," Radchenko said. He grabbed his overcoat from a chair and pulled it on. "I jotted down a number you may call here in Washington if there's trouble. You're to ask whoever answers if Uncle Harold is back."

"What about you?" the assassin asked. "Are you clean in this city?"

Radchenko looked startled for just a moment. "I think so," he said. "Or at least I'm as sure as I can be in this town."

"The FBI?"

Radchenko nodded. "They're very good, and of course they've been jumpy since August."

"Anyone in particular I should watch for?"

"All of them," Radchenko said, going to the door. "I'll contact you when it's time."

The assassin went into the kitchen without a word and looked for the tea things. He never heard the door shut behind his control officer.

The wide-bodied Il-86 Aeroflot jumbo jet took off from Dulles International Airport on time. Their flight over the north pole to the Soviet Union would get them into Moscow at seven in the morning, Moscow time. The trip was a grind that no one liked.

"We just got here," Katherine Sweeney lamented as she watched the city of Washington drop behind them.

"Twelve months," Sweeney replied absently. His thoughts were still back at Langley. These next twelve months would be the most important of his career. He'd gotten that directly from CIA Director Robert Vaughan. "The General."

"Novikov tells anyone who'll listen that we're still spying on each other," Vaughan had said at one point. They were meeting in the director's seventh-floor conference room adjacent to his office. Yuri Novikov was the new KGB director.

"Hell, General, the Israelis are our friends and they spy on us," the Agency's deputy director, Alastair Whitehead, said. "Why not the Russians?" He'd been born in England, and had not become a naturalized U.S. citizen until he was nearly twenty-five. He'd risen higher in the CIA than any other person who'd not been born in the States.

"Nobody's saying we're closing up shop, Phil," Vaughan said. Whitehead's middle name was Philip. "But we cannot ignore the cogent facts here." He turned to Sweeney. "Fact one is Congress has done a shabby number on us, cutting our budget now, of all times. Fact two is the admiration the average American still has for Gorbachev, which means if you're caught, your ass will be out in the wind to dry. Loving Gorbachev will get you nowhere. Fact three, nobody has much control over there. No one is really in charge."

Sweeney looked at his wife, who was still watching out the window. And facts four, five, six . . . ad infinitum were that Russia was still so fractured, so beset with internal problems not only with its republics but within its military-industrial establishment, within its intelligence services, and among the labor pool, the farmers, the factory workers, the miners, everyone . . . that the country was ripe for upheaval into the twenty-first century. Violence would become a way of life.

Considering their vast arsenals of nuclear weapons, most of them aimed at the United States, it was more than imperative that we know their intentions.

"Imperative, that is, if we don't want to be caught with our pants down," the DCI said.

2

THE ANCIENT RADIATOR IN DICK SWEENEY'S OFFICE HISSED AND clanked, seemingly on the verge of exploding. He'd opened his window, which looked down into the courtyard behind the embassy, and although it was minus thirty degrees Fahrenheit outside, his office was a sweatbox. It was Moscow.

His telephone rang. It was Sam Varesco, chief of records. "We're ready whenever you are, Mr. Sweeney," he said.

"Thanks, Sam, we'll be right up." Sweeney gathered the half dozen files he'd been studying and went across the narrow corridor to Kelly Pool's office, knocked once, and let himself in.

The chief of Moscow Station, thin and effete-looking, was in almost every respect the direct opposite of Sweeney—mentally, physically, and emotionally. He was just finishing on the telephone and he hung up. "Are you set for me?" he asked.

"Sam just called. We're ready to fly."

Pool shook his head as he got to his feet and reached for his jacket. "Not ready to fly, Dick," he said petulantly. "Not yet. Not until I see what you cooked up back in Washington."

"Figure of speech, Kelly," Sweeney said.

"In the meantime I'm still in charge," Pool answered, coming around his desk, and together they went into the corridor and took the stairs one floor up to the fourth.

Pool was due to rotate out as soon as a replacement for him was found, a job Sweeney had turned down because it would have meant at least two more years here, and probably three. But the MOHAWK briefing had fallen to Sweeney because of his senior position, and because he would be here long enough to at least see the operation through its opening stages. In the meantime Pool had become irascible. That, countered by the fact that he probably knew Moscow better than anyone currently on the Agency's payroll, made for a difficult situation.

Varesco, a thick cigar clamped at the corner of his mouth, had set up the projector in the screened room, and was waiting for them along with Roy Rodgers, who directed the station's countersurveillance efforts, Tony Havlachek, the embassy's general counsel, who was an expert not only on international law but on the ever-changing vagaries of Russian law as well, and David Zuckerman, special assistant to the ambassador, actually liaison between the ambassador and the CIA.

"Is this everybody?" Varesco asked.

"Yes," Sweeney said. "We'll start with Kaplin."

"Right."

Pool started to protest. He'd thought he was going to look at a few slides. He had no idea that the others would be present.

"Just bear with me for a half hour, Kelly, and you'll understand."

Pool looked at him bleakly, but then nodded and took his seat. The others noted the exchange. There was little doubt who, in actuality, was in charge here.

Sweeney went to the lectern at the head of the room, the lights went out, and a photograph of a Russian man with a long, scraggly beard, long hair, and Rasputin-like eyes was projected on the screen.

"His name is Anatoli Stepanovich Kaplin," Sweeney began. "He is a radical, he is a sometime dissident, he is a Jew, and he is one of the best analysts that the KGB has on its payroll."

The only sounds in the conference room were the whirring of the projector's fan and the slight buzzing of the electronic countermeasures devices in operation to keep them secure.

Sweeney dropped his bombshell. "Kaplin is ours. Has been for the past two months, although to this point he has been an unused asset except for two very isolated test runs. Gentlemen, welcome to MOHAWK."

"Why wasn't I told about Kaplin as a resource?" Pool demanded.

"Because I wasn't sure of him. I wasn't sure of his value. His duties at the Lubyanka do not include reviews of Western interests. So far as I understand, he deals mainly with the Middle East issue."

"What about MOHAWK, Dick? Your idea?"

"No, someone on Chris Roberts' staff apparently proposed the idea and Phil Whitehead went along with it. The first I knew that anything was afoot was in Washington. Adkins took me over what they'd come up with, and I spent two solid weeks going through the drill."

"I can still stop it if I don't think it will work here," Pool grumbled. "Get on with it."

The fact was, Sweeney thought, Pool could not stop the project. It had gone beyond that already.

"The problem that has been identified is twofold. The first is Russia's nuclear arsenal. The National Photographic Interpretation Center, along with the NSA's latest SKYBIRD project, will continue to provide us with real-time data on nuclear warhead movements within Russia itself. The Navy's SOSUS network will give us a pretty fair idea of Russian submarine movements. And the DIA will input data to the MOHAWK Control in Langley about Russian troop and equipment movements.

"In other words, we're going to continue to have a damned

good idea where the hardware is located, better than we've ever had before. But simply knowing that the man in the dark corridor has a loaded pistol doesn't mean much unless we know if he means to use it."

"That's why we're here," Zuckerman, the ambassador's liaison man, said.

"Which brings us to the second part of the problem. Since the Kremlin coup, who speaks for Russia?"

"There may be no real answer to that question, at least for the moment."

"Exactly, Mr. Zuckerman," Sweeney said. "And that's the problem in a nutshell."

Pool was intrigued, and so were the others, despite the fact that they were being told nothing new. "What about MO-HAWK?"

"We need information about the intentions of the Russian government. The intentions of the people whose fingers are on the nuclear triggers, and the people who direct them. But with no realistic central control—or at least a central control that would be of questionable stability if an international crisis were to arise—we need to gather our intelligence from a wide range of sources."

"Hell of a mouthful," Rodgers said.

"Kaplin is our starting point," Sweeney said. "He is willing to provide us with information about Russia's intentions in the Middle East, which in itself is important enough. But Comrade Kaplin has a major fault. He is a gossip."

"What?" Havlachek asked, confused.

"Let him finish," Pool said.

"He knows everyone within the KGB, or practically everyone. He's smart, he listens with a sympathetic ear, and he's a problem solver. Doesn't mind taking on other people's problems."

"Unusual for a Russian," Pool said.

"Damned right he is," Sweeney replied. "In himself a gold seam. But in combination with what he can tell us, and the people he can steer us to, who will in turn steer us to others,

I think we have the makings of the largest spy network in the history of the business."

"If the man is legitimate," Rodgers cautioned, his accent East Texas. "Hell, Dick, it's one of the oldest scams in the book. We've all used it at one time or another. Beware the resource that seems too good, because it probably is."

"I agree," Sweeney said. "Since Kaplin will be our starting point, we've come up with a safeguard. A watchdog. A known quality against which we can measure his performance."

Sweeney nodded to Varesco, and Kaplin's image on the screen was replaced by that of an attractive young blond woman. She was dressed in a bikini, and stood knee-deep in water just off what appeared to be a tropical beach.

"Her name is Larissa Dolya. She was born and raised in the States, but she has lived and worked in Paris with Russian and Ukrainian émigrés for the past three and a half years. She'll be arriving in Moscow with a spotless record, so far as the Russians will know, within the next day or two."

"I don't understand," Zuckerman said.

"I do," Pool snapped. "But I'm going to query Langley about her. We don't do those kinds of things, Dick."

"Would someone mind explaining to me what the hell is going on?" Zuckerman said.

"Kaplin is a ladies' man," Rodgers snorted, and he turned back to Sweeney. "What else have you got for us, Dick?"

"Plenty," Sweeney said, and he continued with his briefing, liking it even less than Pool did, but understanding the necessity nonetheless.

Transmission on the encrypted telephone link with headquarters at Langley was perfect. "I don't like it," Pool said.

"We're not paid to like what we do," Richard Adkins replied.

"Come on, Dick, this is me you're talking to. We go back a long way together. For Christ's sake, a tunnel into East Berlin is one thing . . . and remember how that turned out . . . but a wholesale shopping expedition like this is bound to have serious repercussions. Political repercussions once it gets out."

"It's already been decided, Kelly."

"And this woman you've got coming in from Paris. The moment the Russians get hold of her it'll blow everything wide open. It'll be worse than Francis Gary Powers."

Adkins was silent for several beats, and when he came back on the line, Pool could almost hear the resignation in his voice. "Not these days. No one cares about things like that now."

"Shit."

"But even if they did, MOHAWK is of overriding importance to us. Surely you can see that, especially now."

"But when it falls apart . . ."

"We'll have to do everything within our power to make certain that it doesn't."

Albert Tyson's oak-paneled study was mostly in darkness, the only light coming through the open door to the stair hall, and what filtered in through the French windows overlooking Georgetown's Montrose Park. From where he stood, he could just pick out the Naval Observatory a few blocks to the northwest, through the trees, and he thought how peaceful it was here and now at just this place and time. Unlike an earlier age he'd lived through.

He was a lanky man, bony, with a lot of planes and angles. He'd been a track and field man, and still these days tried to run at least fifteen miles a week, though sometimes with his busy schedule it was difficult if not impossible.

In his left hand he held the letter from his oldest daughter. He'd just finished reading it and his eyes had become moist. *Daddy*, she had written, *it's so awesomely rad standing where those students were gunned down by the National Guard. I guess I can sort of feel how you must have felt then. Sort of sad and scared and angry all at once.*

She was in her third year at Kent State University, his alma mater. He'd not actually been there when the shots had been fired. That had come later. But he'd been one of the first campus protestors against the escalating war in Vietnam. And when he'd seen the reports on the television news, he had wept, as he was on the verge of doing now, for such a terrible waste of lives. Senseless. Useless suffering. It made no sense to him then and it still did not.

"Al?" His wife, Kit, called for him from the hall.

"In here," he said, turning.

"Dinner's about ready," she said, appearing in the doorway. She was a petite, good-looking woman, still in excellent shape, though ever since she'd turned fifty the year before last, her mood swings had become bad. When she was up, she was flying, but when she was in one of her black periods, she was an unreasoning terror. Her doctor wanted to start her on hormones, but she'd staunchly refused.

"Be right there," Tyson said.

She started to leave, but then turned back, a sudden concerned look on her face. "What are you doing in here in the dark?" she asked, but then she saw the letter in his hand. "Is that one from Debbie?"

"Yes," he said. "It made me think. Brought me back."

"Not such good memories," Kit said. "At least not all of them." She was graying, but it was hard to tell because she was blond.

"No," he agreed. "They were terrifying times. I often wondered if we'd live through them . . . I mean as a nation, if we could survive."

"We did," she said gently. "In part because of men like you."

"I wonder about that sometimes too."

"You mean if what you did was worthwhile?"

"Or if it had any effect. I mean, after August it seems in some ways as if we've taken a gigantic step backward . . . toward anarchy."

Kit came the rest of the way into the study and held him for a long time, tears finally slipping down his cheeks.

"Just look around you, darling. Look at the last summit. Look at eastern Europe. Here at home." She leaned back and looked into his eyes. "Can there be any real doubt, Al? Was there ever any doubt?"

"Maybe not," he said. "But I get frightened sometimes . . . about everything. It's as if someone or something is catching up with me."

She smiled softly. "Then remember not to look behind you."

They parted and she mixed a brandy and soda at the sideboard and brought it back to him. "You have exactly five minutes to wallow in your past, Mr. Tyson, and another three to clean up for dinner. Don't be late."

"No, ma'am," he said, and when Kit was gone, he downed most of his drink in one swallow and went back to his desk, where he sat down and switched on the lamp.

He took out a pen and a piece of stationery that was marked, "The White House, From the Office of Albert F. Tyson, Second Deputy Assistant to the President for National Security Affairs," and began his letter to his daughter.

I clearly remember those days in the sixties and seventies, and yes, they were "awesomely rad" and yes, I was sad and scared and angry all at once.

But I was also young, and so sure that I could make a difference in the world that I was not intimidated by anything or any person. My voice would count, as yours will . . . must, my darling daughter.

He put his pen down and looked at what he had written. It was a start, enough for now. He would finish it later. He got up and went into the bathroom, where he splashed some water on his face and then looked into the mirror. At fifty-four his face was not so terribly weathered and lined that he could be considered old. Not yet, though that would come. Sooner than he'd hoped.

There was a man who had showed up on campus. No one knew anything about him, except that he was old, probably in his late twenties or perhaps even thirty, his name was Joseph, he had taught at some small college or other on the West Coast, and now he was traveling the universities in an effort to find an honest man. He was a modern-day Diogenes. His light, he'd told them, was the truth in a world gone terribly wrong.

The arguments he'd used on them, so old and trite now, seemed new and excitingly fresh in those days. Joseph had been melodramatic enough to attract them all, and Tyson remembered listening to him in reverence. They were in church, hearing the Messiah's messenger foretell the coming of the end.

Joseph had left as mysteriously as he had come, though someone thought they'd heard about a man named David at the University of Wisconsin in Madison who fit his description. But no one bothered following it up, because it didn't matter. He'd come and he'd left his message. There was nothing else.

After drying his hands and face, Tyson flipped off the light and went to the kitchen. So much had happened since then. God, had it actually been thirty years? More than half of his lifetime ago?

After graduating with a degree in political science, he had enlisted in the Army, completing OTS in ninety days, and was commissioned second lieutenant. A year later he was in Vietnam serving on General Westmoreland's staff as number three behind the G2. By the end of his tenure, he was captain, and headed the G2 . . . he had a knack for the business of intelligence gathering.

In the subsequent heady years he had joined the CIA, had risen briefly to the position of deputy director of intelligence, before transferring to the National Security Agency as its assistant director. Eighteen months ago he had been appointed number two man behind the President's national security adviser, Robert S. Harms. Two months ago Harms had suffered a near-fatal heart attack, and Tyson had been filling his shoes ever since.

He had never thought he would come this far, and yet now that he was here it wasn't what he had expected it would be.

"What do you want to drink?" Kit asked him.

"Milk," he mumbled.

"Open a bottle of Beauj. We're not going to waste a *coq au vin* by drinking two percent."

He blinked and looked at his wife, really looked at her. What in God's name was he doing? he asked himself. What in God's name had he been doing?

"Come on, shake a leg," Kit said before he could answer himself, and he went to open the wine.

The cold was bone-numbing, and the Muscovites Sweeney encountered downtown seemed listless, as if they were resigned not only to the weather but to the shortages of consumer goods that had deepened after the coup and subsequent shakeup.

It was coming up on ten in the evening, and he was tense, nervous, as he always was out in the field. Especially here in Russia. In his mind nothing much had changed since the Brezhnev days, at least not when it came to the KGB, although the central government was trying to control the spy agency by mounting purge after purge. Still, there were a lot of hard-liners in hiding.

He got off the subway across from the Warsaw Hotel on Oktyabrskaya Square and walked the last long block over to Gor'kiy Park, which would not close until eleven, despite the weather. Before he even entered the park he could hear music coming from the loudspeakers around the skating rink. Moscow had snow on average 164 days a year. People here were not put off by the cold, only by the indifference of their own government toward them.

"Perhaps we will still bury you," Kaplin had told him at one of their first meetings. "If we can kick the Kremlin in the ass hard enough to wake those bastards."

"I'm not after conquest here," Sweeney had said foolishly.

Kaplin laughed. "You're for world peace, and Mother Teresa and the fucking Nobel Prize, I know. In the meantime it's your fervent desire to place a McDonald's restaurant on a corner of every city in the world."

They'd met at a trade fair at the university. Kaplin had approached Sweeney, who was at the fair as a representative of the embassy . . . this time as a legitimate representative.

"We need manufacturing equipment, not TVs and VCRs," the Russian had said.

Sweeney, who'd been talking with a salesman from a small California computer firm, looked up. "What you need is foreign exchange so that you can live. Real money."

"It would take a war for that."

"I wouldn't know about such things," Sweeney had said coolly.

"I do," Kaplin had said, but instead of launching a pitch as Sweeney had expected, the man had turned and walked off.

Back at the embassy, it took Sweeney less than three hours looking through their file photographs of known KGB and GRU operatives to find Kaplin's file, and he had begun his cautious recruitment the next day. They met three more times at the trade fair and then in various other places around the city. "This is very dangerous for me, you know," Kaplin had said at their last meeting.

"I'll see what I can do to help alleviate the problem," Sweeney had promised, but Kaplin had just laughed.

"You still don't get it, do you?"

"Get what?"

"Next time," Kaplin said. "We'll see what you've come up with."

Away from the skating rink and the amusement area, footpaths crisscrossed the woods that skirted the embankment above the Moscow River. It was very dark back here, and although he was out of the wind, he pulled up his coat collar against the cold, his breath thick in the night.

At one turn lights from the Ferris wheel cast his long shadow across a clearing, but then he was back in the woods, his thick-soled boots crunching on the snow.

"How was Washington?" Kaplin said, coming up behind him.

Though Sweeney knew it was coming, he was startled nevertheless. He kept walking without turning around.

"A hell of a lot warmer than here, I can tell you that much."

"But then you go to Bermuda for the weather, not Moscow."

"You have been legitimized," Sweeney said.

Kaplin laughed ruefully. "It will make my mother happy to know that her son is real, and has been certified so by the U.S. government."

Sweeney looked at him. Kaplin wore no hat; his hair and beard flew everywhere in a jumbled mass of reddish brown. His eyes were wide and ebony, and extremely intelligent. Here was a man who could see right into your soul. He looked like a hypnotist.

"Your mother is dead, so is your father. Only your sister is alive in Leningrad."

"You don't believe in God?" Kaplin asked. "My mother knows." He laughed again. "My father, on the other hand, was a wastrel. He never knew or cared about anything or anyone."

"Are you married?"

"A man like me never marries. I would break the poor woman's heart. But then you know this too. I am legitimized. May we get to work now?"

"You told me that these meetings were dangerous for you. Can you tell me exactly why?"

"Those Special Investigations pricks. They still watch us. And this you know as well, Mr. Richard Sweeney." Kaplin had stopped and he was looking directly into Sweeney's eyes.

"The last time, when I told you that I might be able to help alleviate your problem, you told me that I didn't get it. Get what?"

"It's cold out here."

"Get what?"

"What have you done for me, to alleviate my problem?"

"That can wait," Sweeney said mildly.

"I might just turn around and walk away."

"You might."

"Or I might just report you. At the very least you would be asked to leave the Soviet Union."

"You might do that as well."

Kaplin looked away for a moment, and Sweeney thought the man was diminished somehow just then. The set of his shoulders wasn't as proud as it had been.

"Your CIA once had an acronym to explain why men like me do this to their countries," Kaplin said. "Why we turn traitor to our own people." He smiled wanly and shook his head. "MICE . . . money, ideology, conscience, and ego. It fit in a rather tidy package, and there is nothing that you Americans love more than fitting things into tidy packages. You must classify everything, typify it, put it in its niche. Maybe you learned more from the Nazis than you thought you did, fighting us. Trouble is, this tidy package contains mostly bullshit.

"I am doing this for my country. Not for that Kremlin bunch and its bullshit public relations campaign. Not for Yeltsin and his dreams of power. Not even for the Union. I am doing this, you American bastard, for the people. For my people. For the *Rodina*, which is a concept you cannot possibly understand."

"You're probably right. But I've yet to meet a Russian who has the faintest notion of what freedom is. You'd all rather be led around by the nose, as long as your leadership gives you enough bread and sausages and makes the trains run on time."

Kaplin threw back his head and laughed out loud, all the way from his gut. "In Japan the trains run on time; here it's a wonder they run at all." He was shaking his head, steam rising off his neck as if he were a locomotive in Siberia. "Now, fuck your mother, what's this surprise you have for me?"

Sweeney had to laugh too, but he'd never felt more alone, more cut off from the real world . . . from his real world in the West . . . or more in mortal danger than he did just now. But then it was a job, after all. And he sure as hell hadn't come to Moscow for the weather.

"Come on," he said, turning and heading back the way he had come.

"Where are you taking me?"

"I got us an apartment. A safe house where we can meet, and where you can go if you need to run, or just relax. It's not far from here. All I ask is that you be careful you don't lead anyone to it."

"Don't worry, I won't shit in my own nest," Kaplin said. "Besides, your people are watching the place, right?"

Sweeney didn't answer him, and the Russian didn't press the issue.

The apartment was a half dozen blocks from the park's north exit, on Dobryninskiy 1 Pereulok, one of four side streets of exactly the same name (just different numbers), near the Moskovsko-Leninskiy department store. The building was an ancient yellow stone structure of three stories, and the room that embassy housekeeping had found for them was on the top floor at the front. From the apartment they could keep tabs on what was happening below in the street, and if someone were to come in the front door, they had a good chance of escaping across the roofs.

It wasn't foolproof, but then nothing was in Moscow, not even these days.

The apartment was poorly furnished and very poorly lit, but it had running water, a tiny gas water heater above the tin sink in the kitchenette, and a gas ring to heat tea water. There was no refrigerator or icebox, but this was winter, and besides, there would never be enough food in the place to spoil. Heat came mostly from up the stairs, which meant they had to leave the door open if they didn't want to freeze, although someone at housekeeping had thoughtfully provided a Finnish-made electric heater. The cushions on the back of the couch could be removed to convert it into a bed, and there was some bedding stuffed in a cardboard box in one corner. The place smelled of unflushed toilet. The bathroom was at the end of the short hall.

There was a Metro station on the corner, but Sweeney cautioned Kaplin against ever using it. "Give yourself at least four blocks to make sure you're coming in clean. If you're ever in any doubt, even the slightest doubt, do not try to come in. This place could save your life one day."

"And yours," Kaplin said, going to the single window and slightly parting the filthy curtain. He studied the street for a few seconds, then let the curtain fall back as he turned around.

"We'll be reasonably safe here for a while. Later, perhaps, we'll have to move."

Kaplin smiled. "I think that if you treat all your spies this poorly, you might not be in business much longer."

"It's not the Radisson, but this isn't a lawyers' convention either," Sweeney said. He went into the kitchenette, got two glasses down from the shelf over the counter and a bottle of good vodka from beneath the sink, and from a wooden box propped against the wall took out a cardboard tray containing bread, some pickled fish in a small box, a few grams of caviar, and a tiny piece of good Swedish cheese. Russians could not drink without eating something.

He brought the stuff to the small, rickety table in front of the couch and motioned for Kaplin to take a seat. As the big Russian came away from the window, he stepped on a loose board that creaked, and he froze. For a long five seconds or so he stood listening, but when the building remained quiet he came to the table and accepted a glass of vodka.

"I'll remember that one," he said.

"No one lives beneath us," Sweeney said. "No problem."

"Ah, but here you always watch your floorboards as well as your friends . . . either can betray you when you least expect it."

"Which is what we're going to talk about, Anatoli Stepanovich, your friends."

"How long have you been in the business?" Kaplin asked after his third glass of vodka. He'd eaten some of the bread, all of the fish, and most of the cheese.

"A long time."

"How long?"

"Fifteen years." Kaplin had not mentioned the CIA, but they both knew what they were talking about.

"University?"

"Minnesota, and then MIT for my master's."

"Subject?"

"Physics, mathematics. Double major."

Kaplin looked at him with renewed interest. "A smart boy. Why didn't you get your doctorate? Why didn't you stick with it?"

"I wasn't interested," Sweeney said, which of course wasn't the truth, and Kaplin chuckled. "I got married."

"Still married to the same girl?"

"Yes."

"Do you love her?"

"More now than on the day I married her."

Kaplin poured himself another vodka. "Vitali Konstantinovich Boyarov, Igor Greshkinovich Gremiakin, and Mikhail Lukich Mukhin."

"Who are these people?"

"Friends, acquaintances."

"KGB?"

"They work for the government," Kaplin said, cautiously. "They . . . feel as I do."

"Have you met as a group?"

"No."

"Have you spoken with these men individually, then, recently?"

"Yes."

"About me?" Sweeney asked.

"Ah, well." Kaplin hesitated. "About you, yes. But by name? No. Only by principle. We have always talked merely principles. You understand, Richard, that this is a very big, very important step for these three."

Sweeney nodded. "Are there others?"

Kaplin looked startled. "There could be."

"Will you tell me about these men?" Sweeney asked. He wasn't familiar with any of the names. They could have been anyone—even a figment of Kaplin's imagination. It was one of the things they'd discussed with him at Langley. A staff psychologist who was an expert on why men became traitors to their country had cautioned that Kaplin could be insane.

"He might be suffering from what I call the Napoleon complex," the psychologist had said. "He thinks he's somebody he's not, willing to give you information that he doesn't have. It won't necessarily mean he's stupid, just that he might be insane."

"How do I tell?"

"You don't, at least not immediately, but you must be on your guard for it."

"Not only could he be a KGB ringer, he could be nuts," Sweeney said.

"Interesting, huh?" the psychologist said.

Not very, Sweeney thought.

"Boyarov works in the Special Service II Branch of the Komitet's First Chief Directorate."

"The counterintelligence division?"

"Yes. Gremiakin is the executive secretary of the direction of School One."

School One was the KGB's training base outside of Moscow, very much like the CIA's Farm at Camp Peary outside of Williamsburg.

"What about Mukhin?" Sweeney asked, holding his excitement in check. If this was true, they'd hit more than a gold seam; this was the fucking mother lode.

"Mukhin is an assistant foreign affairs adviser to the President."

CIA Director Robert Vaughan, an intense look on his square-jawed face, was just leaving the Oval Office when Tyson got off the elevator. "Morning," he mumbled in passing.

Tyson had noticed the Agency limousine at the west portico at nine. That had been a half hour ago. This morning's intelligence briefing had run longer than normal.

The President's appointments secretary, Ray Geller, stepped out of his office, a harried look on his pinched accountant's face that turned to one of relief when he spotted Tyson.

"I just tried to call your office. He wants to squeeze you in right away. He's got a nine forty-five that's a must."

"What's up?" Tyson asked.

"I don't know," Geller said.

Tyson knocked once and entered the President's study. The President, a tall, distinguished man with a quiet voice, was pouring himself a cup of coffee from a silver service. "Morning, Al, coffee?"

"No thanks, Mr. President," Tyson said, crossing the room. The Oval Office had come as a surprise to him the first time he'd seen it. It was small. He didn't notice now.

"Robert brought this over this morning," the President said, handing Tyson a buff-colored file folder marked "Top Secret" top and bottom. "Read it. Tell me what you think."

Tyson sat down and opened the folder to the first page of a brief, three-page report titled "MOHAWK." The list of signatures on the promulgation page was very short.

He read it in five minutes. When he was done he closed the folder and looked up. He was impressed, but troubled. The President read that from his face.

"It hit me that way too. But what do you think their chances are?"

"It's dangerous. If the CIA screws up over there, you'll end up the villain, and what relations we've managed to salvage will be irreparably harmed."

"We can't ignore it."

"No, Mr. President, that we cannot do. The question is, how far do we want to take this?"

"What happens if the Kremlin does turn up the heat?" the President asked. "Not because of this, but because of something else? Where would that place the information we'd get from MOHAWK?"

"At the head of the class," Tyson said without hesitation. "If there's any further fracturing of the Russian government, we'd need that information in a worse way."

"Exactly my point, Al."

"Yes, sir."

"Our only real problem, then, as I see it, is making sure the operation goes without a hitch."

"What have you got in mind, Mr. President?"

"Who have we got to send over there for a quick look? It would have to be someone bright, someone reliable, someone who wouldn't stick his nose in where it didn't belong."

"Without first apologizing," Tyson said. "Roland Clark. He's on my staff. Used to work with me over at the Agency, so he knows the business as well as anyone."

"Do you trust him?"

"Completely, Mr. President," Tyson said.

"Keep your distance," Radchenko warned his driver, Viktor Yakunin. They had just turned onto Pennsylvania Avenue from 19th Street and had come to within forty or fifty meters of the assassin, who was on foot. They had been tailing him since Georgetown. So far as Radchenko could tell, no one else was following him.

"Where is he going?" Yakunin grumbled half under his breath as he pulled over to the side of the busy street.

"I wouldn't be a bit surprised if he was going to see the White House. This is his first trip to the States."

"The bloody fool," Yakunin said.

Radchenko looked sharply at his driver. "Do you know who that man is?"

Yakunin shrugged. "Another field officer."

"He is an assassin, Viktor Vladimirovich. And from what I am told, a very good one."

Yakunin glanced at Radchenko. "What, that one? He looks like my uncle Dmitri."

"That one has killed more than twenty people in his career. I think I would not want him to hear me call him names."

Yakunin glanced from Radchenko to the nondescript-looking man on foot ahead of them. The assassin had stopped and was admiring the passing traffic.

"We don't do that anymore," he said.

Radchenko started to laugh, unable to help himself, and a woman in a passing car, seeing him that way, smiled.

It was well after midnight and Zimin's legs ached as they often did if he sat in one position for too long. He'd been here forever, it seemed, and he needed sleep. But he thought they were finally getting close.

The key past the Finance Directorate's rose was Tchaikovsky's Violin Concerto in D Minor. The first ten notes which defined the concerto's theme were entered by the standard digital values used in most music synthesizers. Zimin had pirated one of the programs from the University of Moscow's music department. He pushed the enter button.

WELCOME TO DIRECTORATE ONE FINANCE ACCESS
STATE YOUR MENU CHOICE
ALARM SEQUENCE IN PROGRESS

Zimin stared at the screen for a moment. Fuck your mother, but he was in! At least this far. Mukhin's information was accurate.

"Once you're in you'll have ten seconds to secure your entry or you'll be locked out, an alarm will sound, and they'll put together an access review board immediately. You'll never get back in. And sooner or later they'll catch up with you. So you'd better be careful."

Zimin entered the next sequence:

PAYMENT GREEN GRASS
FIRST FISCAL QUARTER 1992

Green Grass was the old name the KGB had used for its foreign currency transactions. Mukhin wasn't sure that the program by that name was still in existence. But he thought it would be a starting point.

RESTRICTED ACCESS
BETA LEVEL AND ABOVE
IDENTIFICATION PLEASE

No alarm sequence now. He was in, but only just, still with no access to anything useful.

WITHDRAW REQUEST
LIST AUTHORIZED USERS BETA LEVEL AND ABOVE

The computer replied almost instantly:

RESTRICTED ACCESS
BETA LEVEL AND ABOVE

A moment later the rose appeared on the screen, and Zimin sat back. The KGB was hiding something, and it was very big. Even authorized users of Finance Directorate records were locked out. Beta level and above, whoever they were, held this little secret close to their vests.

No doubt they would kill to protect themselves, Zimin told himself. It was time to move with even more care now than ever before.

3

"THE BALL IS IN OUR COURT," SWEENEY SAID TIREDLY. HE'D been going steadily for the twenty-four hours since he and Kaplin had met in Gor'kiy Park. "We're going to have to come up with a list of prioritized questions that won't reveal the gaps in our knowledge, and get them to Kaplin. It'll be up to him to pass them on to his people, and get their replies."

"Or the answers that the KGB will manufacture for us," Pool said.

"Naturally we'll include some tag questions to which we already have the answers . . . but answers they don't know we have."

Pool shook his head. "It's their game, Dick. Hell, they practically invented it."

"Then we'll have to be extra careful," Sweeney said. They were alone in Pool's office. It was after ten in the evening. "But this is just the start, the tip of the iceberg. Kaplin's is only the first name on the list. There are others I'm going to try to develop. We can't let this opportunity pass."

"Something you've already taken care of," Pool said. "I never thought this would happen. Not of you."

"I have my orders too, Kelly."

"I'm talking about your cable report to Langley last night before I had a chance to even read over your shoulder."

"I tried to get to you, but you were gone, goddammit. What the hell was I supposed to do, sit on the biggest find to come along since . . . God knows when?"

"You could have made more of an effort, is all I'm saying," Pool said petulantly. "It's all I've ever asked of my people, besides loyalty: that they make an effort."

Sweeney was suddenly sorry for his old friend. The man, like so many before him, had lost touch. Either it was Moscow or it was the business itself. Either way a lot of intelligence officers left the service burned out.

"I'm sorry," Sweeney said.

"Am I being cut out here?" Pool asked bluntly. "It's all I want to know. Have you been given instructions . . . ?"

"No, of course not."

"Then if this is still my station, I want to make something perfectly clear. That is, we're going to have to move with caution, and I don't give a rat's ass what Langley has to say about it. They're not out here in the field like us. First off we're going to make damned sure that your feed to Kaplin is exactly what you say it will be. We're not going to throw out the baby with the bathwater. And secondly, we're definitely going to hold off with your other contacts until we get a good handle on Kaplin and his crowd. It's the only way that makes sense from where I'm sitting."

"I agree," Sweeney said.

"Even a small percentage of something is better than one hundred percent of nothing."

The analogy didn't work, but Sweeney nodded. "You're right. We'll get the committee together and work out the scenario. Langley will have to be put in the loop, though."

"I know that," Pool said. "Tomorrow. Right now it's late and you look like hell."

"I can't look half as bad as I feel. I think I'll go home and get a few hours' sleep."

"I don't want to see you back here until noon. I'll set our first meeting for then."

"Yes, sir."

Sweeney got up, but at the door Pool stopped him. "It's too hard a business to go it alone, Dick. Just remember that."

"Yes, sir," Sweeney said, and he left the office.

When Roland Clark was nearly four years old, and had not yet spoken his first word, everyone was concerned that there was something the matter with him; either he was retarded or his vocal cords had somehow been damaged at birth. But one afternoon his father had looked down at his young son and asked him why the hell he hadn't said anything yet. Roland replied in a clear, strong voice: "I've got nothing to say, Daddy. Nothing at all."

In the intervening thirty-five years, Clark had not changed very much in that respect. If he had nothing to say, he said nothing.

The most disparaging comment he'd ever made about a fellow intelligence service officer was that when the man could no longer baffle everyone with his intellect, he tried to dazzle them with his bullshit.

There was absolutely no bullshit in Clark's lexicon.

"What can I do for you, sir?" he asked Tyson.

Tyson handed him a copy of the MOHAWK brief. "Nothing in there leaves this office under any circumstances. Clear?"

"Yes, sir," Clark said. And he quickly read through it. When he was finished he looked up, absolutely no change in his expression.

"What do you think?"

"Looks good if they can pull it off. Who's Sweeney?"

"Richard Sweeney. Assistant chief of Moscow Station."

It wasn't what Clark had meant, and Tyson suddenly realized it. "From what I've been able to find out so far without shaking the tree too hard, he's good. Solid without being dull. If he can keep his mouth shut—it's his only apparent fault—he'll go a long way, even though he has no connections, family or otherwise. No ax to grind, no skeletons. Wife is first-class. I'm told she'd make a good field officer in her own right. No children, no divorces, no affairs, no legal troubles, no relatives in a foreign land."

"Who's his sponsor?"

In the CIA, and in fact in most government service, any sort of real advancement was almost impossible without a big brother, a mentor, a sponsor in the vernacular.

"Adkins."

Clark said nothing, waiting for Tyson to continue. He'd often sat across from the man's desk like this; first in the CIA, for a short time over at the NSA, finally here in the White House. Clark was a handyman, a fixer, sometimes a gofer, an extension of Tyson.

"This is important to the administration. We want no fuckups. I want you to get over to Moscow, take a quiet look around, and report back here to me personally. I want to know what MOHAWK's chances are. If it falls apart there'll be hell to pay. I want to know about Sweeney and the people he has to work with at the embassy, as well as Kaplin."

"In attempting to get close to the Russian, we could screw the pooch."

"You won't go that far. If it looks as if your presence is changing the balance of things, you're to withdraw immediately."

"Has Sweeney or the chief of station been informed that I'm on my way?"

"Not yet, but they will be before your actual arrival. If there is any sort of a problem, have them call me. If need be, the President will talk to them."

Clark wasn't impressed. He never was. A fact was nothing more than a fact.

"When do I leave?"

"This afternoon. The regular Aeroflot flight out of Dulles. Problem?"

"No, sir. How long do you want me to stay?"

"As long as it takes," Tyson said. "I want some answers. Assurances if I can get them. A lot depends on this turning out."

"How much?" Clark asked gently.

Tyson hesitated a moment before answering. He never lied to Clark. He never held back from the man. It would be like holding back on a hammerblow and still expecting the nail to penetrate the wood. Impossible.

"Very much," he said at length.

"Shall I take my pistol?" Clark asked.

"I don't like it, but it's your ass on the line, so it's your decision."

At four in the afternoon Tyson asked his secretary to send a brief message to the embassy in Moscow requesting that Mr. Roland Clark be met at Sheremetyevo Airport, and be given every courtesy during his stay.

"Say that he is on a fact-finding mission for the President's national security adviser, and that his security clearance level exists to top secret," Tyson said.

"Yes, sir. Anything else?"

"If there are any questions, I'm to be queried directly," Tyson said. "Oh, and as soon as that's off, get me Mrs. Tyson on the phone."

"Very good, sir," his secretary said.

While he waited, Tyson stuffed a few papers in his attaché case and locked the rest in his office safe, spinning the dial past zero twice and then checking to make sure it was locked. He'd been security conscious all of his adult life. It was part of the business.

Kit was on the phone a few minutes later. "Don't tell me you're going to be working late again," she complained. It had been a frequent occurrence lately.

"You haven't got dinner on already, have you, sweetheart?" he asked.

"Not yet."

"I've got to go up to Camp David this afternoon. In fact,

I'll be leaving the office in a few minutes, and I won't be back until morning."

"Doug and Janet are coming over tonight. I thought the four of us might go out later."

"Sorry," Tyson said. "But don't say anything to them about this."

"Of course not," Kit said. She was a good wife and understood that what her husband did at the White House remained at the White House. "How about lunch tomorrow? Will you be back in time?"

"Probably," Tyson said. "I'll call you later in the morning."

"Take care," she said.

"You too," Tyson replied, and he hung up, his brow wet with sweat. He thought for just a moment about his daughter's letter to them, and the answer he'd started last night. He made a mental note to try to explain to her that contrary to popular belief, the world was a much more frightening place these days than it had been in the sixties and seventies. There were more fingers on more nuclear triggers than ever before. And irresponsibility seemed rampant on every continent.

But then he put that happy thought out of his head, put on his coat, and, attaché case in hand, left his office. He instructed his secretary that except for a national emergency he would be out of touch until morning. Sealed in an envelope he'd given her six months ago was a telephone number to be used only at that time.

He left his car in the Executive Office Building parking lot west of the White House and walked a couple of blocks up G Street before he caught a taxi. It felt good being out in the fresh air. It seemed as if he hadn't been outside in months—since the last backyard barbecue in October, when Debbie had surprised them by showing up unannounced for the weekend.

He wanted to remember his past as happier and simpler days. But it wasn't true. The last twenty-five years of his life had been one series of complications after another. And he saw no end in sight.

But the choices he had made were all his. He'd never been forced into anything. Somehow, that made things worse just now.

"Where to?" the cabbie asked him.

"Columbia Island Marina," Tyson said. "It's in Johnson Park, across the river."

"Right," the cabbie said, and Tyson sat well back in the seat so that no passersby might see in and recognize him.

He'd met Toni Wagner about ten months ago at a cocktail party at the British Embassy, and he'd been smitten at first sight. Actually she had sought him out, she admitted later, because "you looked hungry, and vulnerable, and I was damned lonely just then."

She worked in the Washington office of the Internal Revenue Service's Public Information Division. But what she actually did there was never quite clear in his head. She always seemed to have as much time off as she wanted. If Tyson could sneak off for a day or sometimes even two during the week, she never had a problem being with him. After a while he stopped thinking about it.

She was tall, with long dancer's legs, no ass, a very flat stomach, and tiny breasts. Her eyes were large and vivid green, her nose was so tiny it was almost pug, and her mouth was very wide, her lips thick.

"It's my flaws that you like," she told him once. "If I were perfect I would be just ordinary." She smiled. "You know that I'm a witch."

"A good witch or a bad witch?" he'd actually asked.

Her smile widened. "Guess."

The most startling thing he learned about her the first time they'd gone to bed, besides her sensuality and her intelligence, was her perfectly bald head and perfectly hairless pubis. She shaved both every day.

"My hair is mouse brown, frizzy and horrible, top and bottom, so I got rid of it."

Tyson had been flabbergasted. He still was. He had never met, or even imagined, a creature like her. That she existed, and that she found him attractive, was nearly beyond his comprehension. But then, he was thinking through his dick, had been from day one. He was fifty-four and she was thirty-four. It was a volatile match for his ego.

They were discreet, sometimes meeting out of town, and once at an apartment in the Watergate, but mostly at her houseboat moored on the Boundary Channel in the marina, never in the city. Never in public.

In the first month of their relationship he had fallen in love with her, or thought he had, and was thinking about leaving Kit. But Toni had talked him out of it.

"I don't want to marry you," she said. "I don't want to marry anybody. I just want to fuck you. If you screw up your marriage and your career, you won't do me or yourself any good. Think about it, Al. I mean really think about it."

"What do you get out of it? You've never asked for money."

"The same thing as you."

"What do you mean?"

"You're here because you think I'm attractive, and you like the kinky sex whenever you can get it. Or at least kinky on your terms. Well, I'm the same. So if you want to get all emotional and screwed up over it, then let's break it off here and now."

Every man's dream, he'd thought at that moment . . . his last rational thought concerning her. She couldn't be real.

The cabbie dropped him off at the far end of the marina well away from the office. It was just starting to get dark, and the first lights were coming on. When the cab was gone, Tyson crossed the driveway onto the docks and stepped aboard the large houseboat at the end of a finger pier, letting himself in with a key.

The Tchaikovsky violin concerto was playing softly on the stereo, and the main saloon was mostly in darkness, the curtains drawn. The smell of incense wafted out to him from the bedroom aft.

He laid down his attaché case and tossed his coat over it. Loosening his tie, he went into the kitchen, where he poured a stiff drink, and then, kicking off his shoes, walked back into the bedroom.

As he walked across the tarmac from his plane to the terminal at Moscow's Sheremetyevo Airport, the air was so intensely cold it hurt Roland Clark's lungs. It reminded him of Thule, Greenland, where he'd been stationed in 1962 with the Air Force. It had the same smell, the same feel. The elemental forces of the Arctic, inimical to human habitation.

Nature was the only force that Clark respected. And he thought, My God, this is only Moscow. What is it like in Siberia?

He'd never been to Russia before and his first impression was of old-fashioned shabbiness. Everything seemed dirty and frayed. The entire country needed a coat of paint.

He had no problems going through customs because his single bag had been sent as diplomatic cargo, nor did he have any difficulty with the passport control officials, because of his diplomatic status, and because the embassy had pulled a few strings. Still it took nearly an hour before he stood on the other side of the barrier in the main terminal with David Zuckerman, who'd come out with a car to pick him up.

"How was your flight?" Zuckerman asked as they started across the arrivals and departures hall.

"Long," Clark replied. "I'd like to speak with Kelly Pool and Richard Sweeney this morning."

Zuckerman shot him a look. "You don't fool around, do you? We'll get you registered at your hotel and drop off your bag first."

"I'll stay at the embassy."

"Not such a good idea, Mr. Clark. That is, if you want any freedom of movement. The Militia is still keeping a very close if low-key eye on anyone coming or going from the embassy."

"The hotels are not watched?"

"Not as closely."

They had come outside, the cold air again taking Clark's breath away. Zuckerman grinned.

"Welcome to Moscow, Mr. Clark. I hope you find what you're looking for here. Not everyone does."

They got into the embassy car, a Russian contract driver behind the wheel, and headed into the city. Clark said nothing. He'd glanced at a briefing booklet before he'd left Washington, meant for government personnel about to be stationed in Russia. Automobiles, the booklet warned, that American diplomatic persons used were very often bugged, as were most hotel rooms used by Westerners.

"I think you'll like the New Russia," Zuckerman said conversationally. "The people here are open, friendly, enthusiastic, and even charming when it's called for. The weather isn't so great, but hell, it's no worse here than it is in upper New England or Minnesota. Where are you from?"

"California," Clark lied.

"Ah, the land of movie stars," Zuckerman replied without much of a reaction, indicating to Clark that the man didn't know very much about him. He had evidently not done his homework.

Zuckerman was like a lot of other diplomats Clark had met in his career. "Don't make waves" seemed to be the occupational credo. But Clark hadn't been sent to Moscow to follow the herd. He'd been sent to find out something. The sooner that was accomplished, the sooner he could get the hell out. Already he was beginning to feel claustrophobic.

"What hotel have you booked me into?" he asked.

"The Radisson. You'll like it."

"I want to check in at the embassy first."

Zuckerman looked at him sharply. "I don't think . . ."

"The embassy, Mr. Zuckerman, if you please," Clark said, and he settled back in his seat and looked at the drab countryside they were passing through, dismissing any further protests.

After a second or so, Zuckerman instructed the driver to take them directly to the embassy, and then he too settled back in silence. Thirty minutes later they arrived, the Militia guards on duty passing them through without stopping them to check their papers.

"They know this car and my face," Zuckerman explained as they went inside. "Now they know yours."

Clark registered with the marine guard on the ground floor and Zuckerman took him directly up to the third, where he had to register with another guard. This time he was subjected to a body search with a metal detector. When they fluoroscoped his bag, the pistol showed up.

"I'm sorry, sir, but you will not be allowed to carry your weapon beyond this point," the marine said respectfully. His name tag read "Armstrong."

Zuckerman was startled.

"Check with your superiors," Clark said. "It comes with me."

"Not here," Zuckerman sputtered.

Clark said nothing.

The marine guard was clearly nervous. He had his orders, but he suspected he was in over his head here.

"Call Mr. Pool," Zuckerman finally said. "Ask him if he would step out here."

"Yes, sir," the marine said, and he made the call.

Pool came out of his office a minute later. "Clark?" he asked.

"Yes," Clark said, and they shook hands.

"Let's go back to my office, and I'll see what I can do for you."

"Sir," the marine said, "Mr. Clark is armed."

"It's not advisable to carry a weapon around Moscow," Pool said. "But no matter, just leave it here, and you can pick it up on your way out."

"No," Clark said evenly.

Pool glanced at Zuckerman and then back at Clark. "I can assure you that you will be in no danger up here."

"Mr. Tyson is standing by in Washington for your call, if there is any problem."

"That's not necessary. But . . ."

Clark stood impassively.

"No matter," Pool said after an embarrassed silence. "It's all right," he said to the marine guard.

"Sir, I'll have to ask that you sign my log taking responsibility for Mr. Clark."

"Why didn't you say so in the first place, Armstrong?" Pool said peevishly. He scrawled a quick note in the log.

"Sir, if you'll just sign that," the marine said.

Pool seemed to want to challenge the young man, but he signed his name. "That ought to keep you out of trouble."

"Thank you, sir," the marine said.

"If you'll excuse me, then, I'll get back to my office," Zuckerman said.

"I'd like you present as well," Clark said. "And are Sweeney, Rodgers, and Havlachek here in the embassy this morning?"

Pool's eyes narrowed. "I think we can round them up."

"Then we can get started," Clark said. "I have a lot to do."

Kit's mother had gotten ill and Kit had flown out to Salt Lake City to be with her, giving Tyson a second opportunity in the same week to spend a night with Toni. He'd not been able to get away from the White House before ten because the President had scheduled a news conference for eight in the evening. Castro's government in Cuba was coming apart at the seams now, and the American public wanted to know what was happening down there, and what we were prepared to do about it. It gave him an odd feeling knowing that Kit was probably watching television and had seen him come in with the President.

Since it was dark, and he planned on leaving by six in the morning, he drove directly down to the marina in his own car, parking in the shadows well away from the parkway. A raw wind blew off the river as he hurried, head bent, across the parking lot, out onto the pier and then aboard the houseboat.

He let himself in and then leaned back against the door, letting out the pent-up breath he'd been holding. He was glad and yet disappointed that he was here. A part of him was excited, and yet another, deeper part of him wished that somehow he could extract himself from the mess he was in.

Something heavily classical was playing on the stereo. Tyson didn't recognize the piece, but instinctively he thought it might be Bach. As always the scent of incense wafted from the bedroom aft.

He put down his briefcase, peeled off his coat and tie, and in the kitchen mixed a stiff brandy and soda. He drank that down and fixed another, then looked across the main saloon to the passageway aft, bathed in a soft golden glow. She was back there, but she never called for him. She was like a cat, necessary yet independent.

Sipping his drink, he walked back to the bedroom. A yellow scarf was draped over the small table lamp, casting an almost luminescent glow on Toni's naked body.

She was propped up on the big bed, one knee up, her brunette wig lying on the floor, a glass of champagne in her hand. She had just taken a line of coke. He could see it in her eyes and in the parting of her moist lips.

"Hello, Al," she said languorously. "How about a hit?"

"Later. I need a shower."

She grinned broadly. "No. I want you down and dirty tonight." She laughed. "Real dirty."

She reached over and snatched a bottle of clear body lotion from the nightstand and deftly tossed it up to him. "I need a rub."

Tyson's heart was thumping, and a muscle in his gut was jumping. He pulled off his clothes, and when he was nude he got into bed with her, poured some lotion into his hands, and when it was warm he began to massage her body, starting with her neck and shoulders.

Toni tossed her half-filled champagne glass aside and took a marijuana cigarette from a small wooden box on the nightstand. She lit it, took a hit, and held it up for Tyson.

He drew a deep drag of smoke into his lungs, and holding it, began to massage the oil into her breasts, her nipples erect and very warm.

"That's nice," she purred, arching her back a little. She had admitted to him the first night they met that the way to her bed was via her breasts. "Since I was a kid, you just had to touch my tits and I was off to the races."

He took her left breast in his palms, and with the forefingers and thumbs of both hands, stimulated her nipple.

Her body rose off the bed. "Harder," she moaned, and he dug his fingers into her soft flesh.

"God . . . Christ," she cried.

He did the same with her right breast. She took another hit and passed it to him. He was already feeling the effects. The edges of his consciousness were getting fuzzy, and he had to fight down a rising paranoia, the effect of the chemical.

Getting more lotion, he gently massaged her belly as she smoked, finally letting his fingertips brush the inside of her left pelvis. She shuttered. It was another of her erogenous spots.

She passed the joint to him again, and he took another big hit. He felt as if someone had plugged a sixty-cycle line into his central nervous system. He was humming.

Moving lower, he took her toes into his mouth, one at a time, his tongue flicking between them.

"That's good, Al," she said. "Very good."

He massaged oil into the calves of her legs, and her knees, and finally, gently, teasingly into her inner thighs, his fingertips brushing the lips of her vagina from time to time.

Toni shoved him away and rolled over on her back. For a long time he just looked down at her. The diffuse light illuminated the blond peach fuzz along the small of her back. At that moment he thought it was the most beautiful, sensuous sight he'd ever seen.

"Nice," he said softly.

Toni reared up on her hands and knees, her legs spread, and with one hand reached back for him. "Fuck me," she cried breathlessly. "Al, fuck me before I explode!"

She had lotion on her hand, and she masturbated him for a few seconds and then guided him not into her vagina, but into her anus.

He started to recoil, suddenly an overwhelming sense of alienness, of wrongness coming over him, but her sphincter muscle held him in place, pain so sharp it made him cry out. Then he was pumping, suddenly deep inside her, her ass coming back to meet his pelvis, all sense of propriety gone. He grabbed her breasts and pulled, wishing to inflict pain on her as she was inflicting it on him, and she began to scream in pain and pleasure as he came and came and came.

"Now sleep," Toni said softly afterward.

Tyson lay on his back, his head spinning from the effects of the marijuana as well as the drug in the brandy he'd drunk. His paranoia was gone, as was the sexual urgency that had threatened to blow off the back of his head. He felt good, loved, safe. As if he were in a cocoon, nearly ready to be reborn.

"You've had a difficult day, Al," she said as she dialed the combination of his briefcase. The snaps clicked open and she looked at him, but he hadn't heard.

She took the papers out of his briefcase and over to the dresser and began photographing each page.

"Tell me about MOHAWK, Al. I'd really like to know about it," she purred, looking over at him.

His mouth was open and a line of drool rolled down his chin to form a slick pool on the sheet. Not the only pool of body fluid this night.

"MOHAWK, Al," she cooed. "Tell me about it, and then we'll fuck again."

Tyson left at seven, in a hurry because he said he was late, and after Toni had watched him drive out of the marina she padded back into the bedroom, where she rewound the Bach Toccata and Fugue in D Minor and the preludes in E-flat and C. Only an electronics expert would be able to determine that this tape recorder recorded at the same time it played. Everything that had been said in her bedroom last night, while the Bach was playing over and over, was down on the tiny digital tape cassette.

She took a quick shower, and after donning her most demure mouse-blond wig and conservative suit, left the houseboat and drove her gray Volvo station wagon across the river into Washington. She left the car in the parking lot of the National Academy of Sciences and walked across the avenue to the Vietnam Veterans Memorial in Constitution Gardens.

There were a few people searching for names on the black stone. There were almost always some people here, which was one of the reasons they used the place for drops. Toni's legend included a brother who had been killed in Vietnam. She came here every single day she was in town, drop or no drop.

A cold front had come through in the night, and the wind had shifted to the northwest. It would snow soon, and then the temperature would drop. The marina had put bubblers around the boats to prevent ice from forming.

It would be a cold night, she thought. Lonely in a foreign land. Though this place was certainly more civilized than her native Siberia, she still missed home. Family. Friends.

She had to laugh at her maudlin sentiments. If her family or friends back home were told what she did here, they could not possibly understand.

"I'm glad to see that you are happy in your work," a man said at her elbow.

She didn't reply, nor did she even look at him, but as she turned to walk away, she passed the digital cassette and the film cartridge to him.

Within ten minutes she was heading back across the river on the George Mason Bridge, thinking only about the long, hot bath she was going to take before she went back to bed. To sleep, finally.

Vyacheslav Sedov, a nondescript man who always slouched, took great care with his tradecraft this morning. Leaving Constitution Gardens on foot, he walked the half dozen blocks to the Corcoran Gallery of Art, where he had parked his car. If he'd been followed he would have gone inside and hurriedly left by another exit. But this morning, so far as he could tell, he was clean, which was just as well considering what he was carrying.

Still taking no chances, he retrieved his car and drove to the Russian Embassy north of the White House by a very roundabout route, constantly checking his rearview mirror. He did not go in until he was absolutely certain he had not been followed.

In the basement laboratory, he personally saw to the development of the film, and afterward went up to his office, where he transcribed the material on the digital tape, his playback machine automatically muting the music.

It was nearly noon by the time he went upstairs, knocked once on the door of the KGB Washington *Rezident*, and let himself in. Yuri Truskin looked up.

"Have you got it?"

"Yes," Sedov said, approaching Truskin's desk and handing him the file. "It looks good this time. Very good."

"Very well. I'll add it to the other, and send it immediately."

KGB Major Ivan Pavlovich Kiselev had a small but pleasant apartment just off Gor'kiy Street near the Byelorussian Rail Station in Moscow's northeast district. He had a few people over for a late supper and drinks. They were listening to the sometime dissident and poet Yuri Zamyatin read his love poems, which he called *Moscow in the Snow*.

Kiselev headed the Komitet's Department One of the First Chief Directorate, with offices in a big building out on the Circumferential Highway. His department's job was to run all the KGB's "illegals" in the United States and Canada, among them the spies, the deep-cover agents, and even the doubles working within the government or the American or Canadian military-industrial complex. Now that the KGB's domestic activities had been sharply curtailed, the service was spending the primary amount of its money, talent, and energy on spying outside Russia, especially in the West.

He was a fairly small, compactly built man who looked like a gymnast. He was good-looking even by Western standards, his English was perfect, and at the beginning of his career he had worked out of the United Nations in New York and later from the embassy in Washington. He enjoyed his work, and he was very good at it. Never married, Kiselev was considered to be a ladies' man, which irritated some of the older men at the Center, but not enough so that his career had been held back. He believed that most of them secretly admired him for his "exploits" as they were called, and for the fact that he was not afraid to take risks.

At midnight someone knocked at his door. He excused himself to answer it. His number two, Pavl Medvedosky, stood in the corridor, a determined look on his bulldog face.

"Sorry to disturb you so late, sir, but we've gotten an incoming from Washington that needs your attention."

The fact that Medvedosky himself had come here instead of sending a messenger or using the telephone, or simply waiting until morning, was very sobering.

"What is it, Pavl Fedorovich?" Kiselev asked, lowering his voice.

"Source KHAIRULLA, and some other material."

"Wait downstairs, I'll join you in a minute," Kiselev said, and even before Medvedosky had turned to leave, he shut the door and went back into the living room.

Everyone looked up.

"The bad news is that duty calls, and I have to go back to the office. The good news is that there is plenty of food and drink, and I want you all to stay and enjoy yourselves."

"Will you be back tonight?" one of the women asked.

"Probably not until very late."

"I'll wait," she said, and the others laughed good-naturedly. The girl was a Bolshoi dancer, and she would get into trouble for staying out overnight.

"Okay," Kiselev said. He got his coat and hat, made his apologies again, and hurried downstairs, where Medvedosky was waiting for him with a car and driver.

It took nearly a half hour to reach the office, and on the drive out of the city neither man spoke. The need-to-know list on Source KHAIRULLA was fairly small, and the number of people who knew the source's actual name was much smaller.

After they had been identified, they pinned their security badges on their lapels and took an elevator up to the fourth floor. They left their overcoats and hats in Kiselev's outer office and went across the hall to the Department One briefing and conference room.

Medvedosky opened the safe, took out a file of message flimsies, and handed them to Kiselev.

"This was transmitted a few minutes after thirteen hundred Washington time. I happened to be here when they came in, but it wasn't until two hours later that those idiots down in Thirteen got around to notifying me." Department Thirteen was responsible for the First Chief Directorate's communications.

Kiselev sat down and quickly read through the material that their agent in Washington had supplied, and the material in the photographs she had taken of a series of documents on White House stationery. He saw the problem almost immediately, and he looked up.

"Puts us in a difficult spot," Medvedosky said. "But we can't ignore it. If it ever came out, they'd line us up against a Lefortovo wall and we'd get our nine ounces, all right."

"Have you had a chance to find out about this operation MOHAWK of theirs?" Kiselev asked, taking off his jacket and draping it over the back of his chair.

"That'd be Second Chief Directorate, Department One. Lieutenant Colonel Vilkov. A real prick."

Kiselev had to smile at Medvedosky's loyalty. Vilkov's position was less important than his own, but he already had his colonelcy because of his family connections, and because his office was downtown in the Lubyanka.

"Have you got anyone over there who could make some quiet inquiries for us?" Kiselev asked.

"A little bird?" Medvedosky asked, grinning.

"Something like that. But listen to me, it will have to be done quickly, and very discreetly. I don't want any fuckups, for more than one reason."

"Not now," Medvedosky agreed. "Fuck your mother,

we're too close to have it screwed up for us. What about the general, can we ask for his help?"

"No," Kiselev said. "For the moment this has got to stay with us."

"It's a dangerous game."

"Yes, it is, Pavl Fedorovich. Do you want to get out?"

"*Nyet,*" Medvedosky said without hesitation. "But the timing stinks. MOHAWK, what kind of a name is that, I ask you?"

Kiselev shrugged. "We spy, they spy," he said, lighting a cigarette. He held it in the American way, between his first two fingers. "In the meantime almost everything is ready for us in Washington."

"*Almost* everything," Medvedosky said, reflexively lowering his voice. "But what about this American operation? Will it affect us, do you think?"

"I don't know, Pasha. If it leads us to the traitors here in Moscow, then perhaps it will. We'll just have to wait and see."

"In the meantime people could get killed."

"Yes." Kiselev nodded thoughtfully. "Yes, they could."

4

THE SWEENEYS' CAR, A REASONABLY NEW FORD TAURUS, WAS free of listening devices this week. Every day it was electronically swept; and from time to time a bug would be discovered. Sweeney was not considered terribly important by the KGB, but the Finance Ministry had some interest in him, so it was assumed they'd requested the bugs. The embassy technicians would leave the listening device in working order for a few days to tease the opposition, and then they would remove it. A new bug invariably showed up within two or three weeks, though no one had yet discovered how. It was one of the games still being played in Moscow.

"Mind telling me what's bothering you?" Katherine Sweeney asked her husband on the way into the embassy. It was her day for the car.

"What do you mean?" Sweeney asked. They'd not been able to talk in the apartment.

Katherine looked at him and smiled wanly. "If I didn't know any better I'd say you were having a fit of conscience over something."

He laughed. "Remind me again never to play poker with you."

"It's twenty years of marriage that'll do it every time," she said. "Anything we can talk about?"

He concentrated on his driving for a minute or so. Traffic was heavy this morning. Their apartment was in a foreigners' building near the university across town from the embassy, a twenty-minute ride. On extremely cold mornings like this the car never completely warmed up.

"Not yet," Sweeney finally said. It was Larissa Dolya and what he was sending her to do. Like Pool, he found that sort of thing distasteful in the extreme. He figured he had an old-fashioned sense of morals.

Katherine reached over and brushed her gloved fingers across his cheek. "I'm sorry, darling," she said. "I wish there was something I could do to help you. I get frustrated sometimes, seeing you like this."

He managed a smile. "Hell of a way to make a living."

"What living?" she joked. "Pull the plug anytime you want, Ernie, and I'll be behind you one thousand percent."

"I know."

"You'd better."

Anatoli Kaplin had been spending more and more time at his little Gor'kiy Park nest, as he preferred to think of the safe house Sweeney had supplied him. He'd brought over a few of his things: books, extra pillows, a couple of paintings for the walls, and a large Afghan wool throw rug for the bare floor.

Still the place wasn't very much, but it was illegal, which suited his almost little-boy sense of mystery and intrigue; and it was an unknown, which made him feel truly free when he was in residence.

Although he had never been anything but an analyst for the Komitet, he had gone through the service's School One outside of Moscow, and understood the tradecraft that the Surveillance Directorate had elevated to a science. Leaving his real apartment in the fashionable district just off Kalinin Prospekt around ten in the morning, he walked the few blocks to the House of Friendship. It was Saturday, and although the weather was still extremely cold, the streets were busy because it was sunny. Russians hated to be cooped up.

The house, once the residence of a rich industrialist, now was a museum and a favorite meeting place for Russian writers and artists, and even foreigners.

He stayed a full twenty minutes, drinking tea and talking with a couple of gay Americans from California who had come to Moscow and St. Petersburg on a thirty-day sabbatical, they said, to study iconic art.

After giving them his blessings for their endeavor, which seemed to please them immensely, Kaplin wandered down to the Kremlin, where he looked in at a couple of the museums before crossing Red Square to GUM, the big department store where there were definitely more people than goods.

Slipping out a side door, he hurried up to the Metro station on Revolution Square and rode the train to Gor'kiy Park.

At noon, certain that he had not been followed, Kaplin entered the apartment building and trudged upstairs. On the second floor a slightly built blond woman, several packages at her feet, was fumbling with the door lock to the apartment below his. Sweeney had said it was empty.

"Hello, then, little girl, are you a housebreaker?" he asked, startling her.

She looked up, dropping her keys, her eyes wide and her nostrils flared in fright. "Oh," she said, and tears immediately came to her eyes.

"I'm sorry I frightened you," Kaplin immediately apologized. He was bemused. The girl was young, perhaps in her late twenties or early thirties, and was quite pretty. "Do I look like that much of an ogre?"

"I don't know. It's just that I . . ."

"This apartment was empty, did you just move in?"

"Yes," the girl said, relieved. "Yes, I did, just this morning, but I can't get this lock to work, there's no electricity whatsoever in my flat, and there was no sausage in the store. Only bread."

"Ah, but you must be from the country," Kaplin said,

picking up the keys. She stepped aside for him as he tried the lock.

"Petrozavodsk," she said.

The door opened, and Kaplin held out the key for her. "See, it was just stuck a little from disuse. And I'm sure that if you talk to the babushka downstairs, she will turn on your electricity."

She took the key. "Thank you very much . . ."

"Anatoli Kaplin. And you? What are you doing so far from home all alone?" Sweeney had probably sent her to watch over things here. It was a safe bet the KGB wouldn't have sent someone like this.

"I am Larissa Dolya, and I've got a job at GUM, only I fell and hurt my ribs, and besides, there was nothing in my department to sell so they sent me home for a few days, or maybe a week. But I don't know what there is to eat now. And . . ." Tears were streaming down her cheeks.

"All right, all right, cut out the waterworks, little Lara, and I'll read you a poem while you fix us our supper."

"But I have only bread and pickles."

"Perfect," Kaplin said, clapping his big hands together. "You will bring your bread and pickles upstairs to my little nest, where I have sausages and cheese and even some sweet wine."

She looked doubtful.

"What do you say?" he asked. "If you are a good little girl, I will even tell your fortune. As you can plainly see by my hair and my beard, I was raised by Gypsies, and my grandfather as a boy even knew the great Grigori Yefimovich Rasputin. Now, what do you think about that?"

Nancy Perigorde shivered as she got out of her car and used the phone booth at the side of the road. She'd driven almost all the way into Washington before she was convinced that she wasn't being followed.

As always the number she called was answered on the first ring by a man she only knew as Dr. Hamilton. "Hello."

"He's made a breakthrough," she said.

"Did you get in with him?"

"Yes. He used a ten-digit numerical sequence to get past the rose, and then he asked for something called Payment Green Grass, but he was denied access."

"Christ, we're actually inside the KGB's fucking Finance Directorate computer?"

"Yes, sir."

"How long can you continue to screen your entry?"

"From us or them?"

"Us," the man answered after a brief pause.

"I don't know," Nancy said. "A little longer, but not so long." She was being paid a lot of money. On the first of every month an envelope containing five thousand dollars in cash was placed on the front seat of her car while she was at work. It never mattered if her car was locked or unlocked, the envelope always appeared.

But she was getting frightened now. She didn't know how long she could keep it up. She wanted one hundred thousand dollars. So far she'd been paid half that. But ten more months seemed like an impossibly long time.

"Can you stick with it?" Dr. Hamilton asked.

"Yes, for a while. But we're talking about the unauthorized use of a NSA ELINT satellite. If I'm caught I'll go to jail for a very long time."

"You'll be rewarded."

"I don't know . . ."

"Very well rewarded. Do you understand?"

"Yes," she said after a pause. It was starting to snow. All she could think of these days was sun and warmth and the blue water of the Caribbean.

"Tell me what else our little friend in Moscow has learned."

Kelly Pool and his wife, Jeanne, maintained an apartment in the embassy. Just now she was back in the States. She'd gone home after the coup. Sweeney knocked at his door and Pool answered it almost immediately, as if he had been standing there waiting.

"Good of you to drop by," Pool said.

Sweeney had been up here often, but each time he was struck by how much larger the Pools' apartment was than his own, and how well furnished in the American style it was. "I can only stay a few minutes."

"Are you done . . . *with the questions for Kaplin*?" Pool asked, mouthing the last five words silently.

"Just about."

Pool's eyes were narrow. Something was wrong. "Have you had your lunch yet? Would you like a bite to eat?"

"I had a sandwich and soup in the canteen around noon."

"Care for a drink?" Pool asked, nodding toward his study.

"Fine," Sweeney said, following Pool into his small, windowless study. His "thinking closet," as he called it, had actually been a pantry off a large kitchen once upon a time. It was furnished with a small desk and chair, an overstuffed easy chair, a small globe on a stand, and two walls of books. Some of the books had been taken off the shelves and were packed into cardboard boxes. The room was free of microphones.

Pool poured them both a drink. "Forgive the mess," he said.

"What's going on?"

Pool handed him his drink, then picked a message flimsy off his desk and gave that to him. "I've been relieved. As of this moment you are the new Moscow chief of station."

Sweeney was flabbergasted. The message was very short and to the point, relieving Pool immediately as COS, appointing Sweeney as acting COS until further notice, and ordering Pool to return to Langley by "the most expeditious means." The last paragraph dealt with instructions to follow by book cable for Sweeney.

"Your cable should be here later this afternoon. I'd like you to remain in the embassy at least until then." Pool smiled deprecatingly. "I'll be out of here within twenty-four hours if you and Katherine would care to move in."

"Not yet," Sweeney said in a daze. "I don't want to upset

the status quo here. If we can keep them guessing for a little while, it'll help." He shook his head.

"Not totally unexpected under the circumstances."

"I don't understand."

"I was due to be relieved in any event, but my objections to MOHAWK apparently struck a nerve. Adkins called me this morning, just before this came in, and explained everything. Said he had complete confidence in you . . . an opinion which I seconded . . . and that I was needed on the Russian desk."

"You're being transferred to Intelligence?"

"I started out there after college," Pool said. "It'll be like old home week. Not as exciting as Ops, but the work is steady, and Jeanne will like it."

"Shit," Sweeney said after a beat.

"Yeah." Pool motioned Sweeney to the easy chair as he sat down behind his desk. "You're in for a tough haul here, Dick, and that's not sour grapes talking."

"The job has never been easy. But . . . hell, I never wanted it like this."

"Save the sentiment. If there's any pity to be dispensed, give it to yourself, you'll need it from time to time. Adkins will be keeping a very close watch on what you do here."

"Your replacement should be here soon . . ."

"Forget it," Pool said. "You'll be given ninety days either to prove or hang yourself. It's up to you. But at the end of that time your appointment will either become permanent or you'll be ordered home."

"I don't want the job. I've already told Adkins no. Katherine and I are returning home in a year."

"That's a long time, Dick. In the interim you're in the hot seat. You made a big impression in Washington, and they're calling you the pivotal man."

Sweeney just looked at him.

"We're at the turning point here," Pool said. "Your lecture. On the left hand is, or *was,* the cold war, and on the right is, or *will be,* anybody's guess. In the meantime no one has a clue which way this will rebound. You made sense back home, so they're willing to take your lead for the moment. It's going to turn on what happens here."

"MOHAWK."

"Seems like it."

"The project wasn't even my idea."

"Maybe not, but you're the one implementing it."

Sweeney sat back and drank his cognac. It was good.

"More?" Pool asked, rising and getting the bottle.

"I don't think so, Kelly."

Pool poured him a drink anyway and freshened his own. "One piece of advice: Never trust anyone out here."

"Maybe that's what got us into trouble with each other in the first place."

"No. The Russians are different, and don't forget it. They've got eleven hundred years of history, versus our two hundred; they've lived under the rule of czars, we haven't; they've lived under the rule of dictators, we have not; and more recently they lost twenty million people in the war, and we didn't lose a fraction of that. They've not forgotten. They cannot."

"You may be right," Sweeney said.

"Damned right I am, just as I'm right about Clark, the little spy the administration sent out here to make sure we were doing our jobs correctly."

"What did Adkins say about him?"

"Nothing, except that we were to cooperate," Pool said. "But I'd bet anything that Langley had no idea he would show up here." Pool shook his head bitterly. "You've got your hands full, Dick. Watch yourself."

"I would like to meet with Kaplin," Clark said. "This evening if possible."

Sweeney had just come down from Pool's apartment, and was in no mood for any sort of a confrontation. The White House man had been waiting for him in the conference room and had stepped out into the corridor as Sweeney passed.

"I'm sorry, Mr. Clark, but that won't be possible," Sweeney said, entering his office. Clark followed him in.

"Why not?"

"Because the situation here is very delicate. You wouldn't understand."

"I think I would. I worked for the Company."

Sweeney was exasperated, but he held his temper in check. "When was that?"

"Some years ago," Clark replied mildly. Sweeney decided that the man was deceptive.

"In what capacity?"

"I was special assistant to Mr. Tyson during his tenure as deputy director of intelligence."

"Then you can understand why I cannot allow you to approach one of my sources. Especially this one at this time."

"He's special?"

"The entire operation is special, Clark. Otherwise you wouldn't be here snooping around, getting into everyone's way."

"I'll talk with Mr. Pool," Clark said.

"Go home," Sweeney snapped. "Pool can't help you here. He's been relieved. I'm the new COS. This is my station now."

"Then I suggest you call the White House for verification . . ."

"Bullshit. I'll leave the ass kissing and power brokering up to you. You want to see Kaplin, it'll be after my resignation."

"Is that necessary?"

"Yes, it is," Sweeney said. "Now, get the hell out of my office, I've got work to do."

Clark closed the door and came over and sat down. "Let me tell you why I'm here, Mr. Sweeney. Maybe I can change your mind about me and my mission."

For just a brief moment Sweeney entertained the notion of physically throwing Clark out of his office, savoring for just that instant the little thrill of pleasure. But then he went around behind his desk and sat down. "I can give you five minutes."

"It won't take that long," Clark said. "The President read

the MOHAWK report. He and his national security adviser agree that the project is worthwhile but dangerous. Should something go wrong, it would place our government in a bad light, and it would severely damage our relations with the Kremlin and the Russian Parliament. I was sent here to evaluate your progress as well as your chances of success."

"Fair enough. You attended this morning's briefing. You tell me what are our chances of success."

"With Mr. Pool gone and you in charge, your chances have improved."

Sweeney bridled. "I'm not going to listen to that . . ."

"You asked for my opinion, I gave it," Clark said impassively.

"Then why do you want to see Kaplin?"

"He's another link in the chain. Next to yourself, the most important. If he is involved in a KGB disinformation plot, not out of the question, then it would be us walking into a dangerous trap."

"Which is why I've sent Larissa Dolya into the operation."

"Yes," Clark said. "Will you arrange a meeting between me and Kaplin?"

"No," Sweeney said. "You were instructed to come here and evaluate us. I'm sure that you were also instructed not to be intrusive. No one wants you to upset the applecart, which is exactly what you would be risking by meeting with Kaplin. He may already be under suspicion by the KGB, and he may be watched. I've set up a safe house for him, but there's no telling how long that will remain secure. Certainly no time at all if you insert yourself into the situation. No matter how good you are, you're here as an American diplomat. You have no legend."

"You're right, of course," Clark agreed, a faint hint of amusement evident at the corners of his mouth. He got up.

"I'm glad you see it my way," Sweeney said. "When will you be returning to Washington?"

"Not quite yet," Clark said, and he left.

The assassin had begun to think of himself as Vincent Privet from Milwaukee.

"When you are in the field, you must blend completely with the background, by actually *becoming* your cover identity," they'd taught him at School One.

Become a chameleon and survive. Remain a redbreast and die. It was simple, and he was very efficient at it.

He looked up from his menu at the Rive Gauche Restaurant to his attentive waiter and ordered a light salad, a cup of clam chowder, a grilled sole, with extra lemon, and to accompany his meal an excellent imported Riesling.

"Very good, sir," the waiter said. "Would you care for another cocktail first?"

"No, I'll just have my wine now, if you please. Good and cold."

"Of course, sir."

What he was doing out like this was dangerous, but in his estimation, based on experience, necessary. He had easily ditched Radchenko and his driver, and so far as he had been able to determine, no one else in this city seemed in the least bit interested in him. Yet there was a feeling of tension here, just like there was in any world capital.

And just like any other foreign city, Washington had its own ground rules: about traffic, about the police, about restaurants and public buildings, about walking down a street alone at night. There were a thousand little differences from one place to another. So many so that it was impossible to totally blend into a place that wasn't your home. But with a little study enough of the differences could be mastered so that you could become unnoticeable, or nearly so.

Privet had been ordered to Washington to kill someone. Before he actually performed that act, and subsequently made his escape, he wanted to be prepared.

It was homework he was doing here like this. But in the doing there was no reason he couldn't enjoy himself. It was myth that intelligence agents did not enjoy themselves; at least it was myth for this agent.

Charles Gleason was one of the brightest men in the United States. He had two Ph.D.'s, one in political science and the other in economics, though his true love was the philosophy of leadership. Gleason was also an agent for the KGB, and had been since his student days in Boston and Cambridge, and then in Washington, where he had helped work out the political and economic ramifications of SDI.

For the past two years he had headed a special think tank in Reston, Virginia, to which he had lured some of the best minds in the country to work on only two projects: getting the United States out of its increasingly horrible economic jam, and somehow bringing Russia economically into the twentieth century.

"Two cusps of the same issue," he was fond of saying.

At two in the afternoon he drove to a small coffee shop about three miles from his office, where his contact, Donald Hamilton, was waiting for him. He slid into the booth, and when the waitress came, ordered tea with a slice of lemon.

"I was surprised to hear from you, Don. Trouble?"

"I think we're going to have to up our timetable," Hamilton (which was not his real name) said. He was a much larger man than Gleason, and fairer of complexion. "We're getting a few rumbles from our friends."

"Homeward Bound?"

Hamilton nodded. "What do you think, Charlie? Can you pull it off this early?" They'd worked together as agent and handler for more than ten years. The duration of their relationship was nearly unprecedented in this business.

"I'll make a few calls, but I might be able to do it. Anything I should know about . . . these rumbles?"

"Apparently somebody is playing games with the KGB's computer system. Finance."

Gleason shook his head. "A computer hacker in Moscow. Nothing surprises me anymore."

"That's what I'm hearing."

"An amateur?"

"Unknown, Charlie. But it doesn't look like it."

"What's being done about it?"

"Accelerating Homeward Bound."

"Have we got the go?"

"Not yet, but it's coming. It's our job to be ready for it."

Gleason looked out the window at the lightly falling snow. "It's hard to believe, especially now, after everything that's happened."

"Believe it," Hamilton said. "Especially now, as you put it. We don't have any other choice. But I want you to watch your step."

Gleason turned back. "Sure," he said. "You too."

5

THE TALL, THIN WOMAN WAS PRETTY BY RUSSIAN STANDARDS. Her hair had been pushed up into a drab brown babushka and she wore no makeup, but her features were delicate and her skin had a porcelain quality. A glow. A youthful health that belied her twenty-nine years.

She was dressed in a threadbare overcoat with the remnants of what had once been a fake fur collar. The tall white boots on her feet were run-down at the heels. But she carried herself with dignity and class. If she was down on her luck now, she hadn't always been this way. Besides, the entire country was in trouble. Everyone seemed to have plenty of rubles, but there was simply nothing to buy in the stores and markets, and the situation had worsened after the Kremlin coup and the disintegration of the Union.

No one gave Marina Serafimovna Demin a second glance as she entered the Voykovskaya Metro Station at nine in the morning and boarded the first train into the city center.

There weren't many passengers at this hour. Most people were already at work; and market day, when vegetables and other difficult-to-obtain staples came from Finland, was two days away. Then the trains and buses would be crammed with housewives who, no matter the weather, would line up for hours in advance of the market's opening, sometimes arriving on nothing more then the strength of a rumor that butter or cabbage might be available.

Settling gratefully in her seat, and half closing her eyes as if she were really tired, she felt the train lurch out of the station and gather speed. Her heart began to accelerate.

Odessa seemed like long ago, yet this day had come much faster than she'd thought it would. Now that it was finally here, she had to consciously bring herself to remember why she had agreed.

Loyalty? Devotion to duty or country?

You will be my banner, he'd told her. And looking into his eyes that evening, and making love afterward, she believed him. Not only that: She believed *in* him. Perhaps this was for love, then.

But Odessa had been another, warmer place where she'd felt safe and loved for the very first time in her life.

Someone sat down next to her, and Marina looked up, startled. But it was just an old grandmother, who smiled. Marina smiled back, then looked away and returned to her thoughts.

At times, trying to remember what her life had been like in Leningrad as a young girl, and here in Moscow attending the university, some of her memories were confused. Implants and legends, her instructions were called. What she'd actually lived and what she'd learned to remember were merged, melded into something foreign. At times her memories were disorienting and, like now, she sometimes felt a momentary panic that somehow she had lost her own identity. Her mind had failed her.

She opened her eyes and looked at her reflection in the window glass. Her eyes were large and very dark, almost black, with sharply defined eyebrows that nearly met above the bridge of her nose. Her features were tiny, sometimes bony.

Just lately she had lost some weight, so that when she examined herself in the bathroom mirror she could see that her pelvic bones protruded sharply, and her knees were all angles.

Not very attractive, she told herself. But then she was supposed to be a has-been. A once-was. A discard. That, too, was part of her legend. She was to evoke some sympathetic feelings. Americans loved the underdog.

More people had boarded the train, so that when Marina finally got off at the Barrikadnaya Station, the car was half full.

Upstairs she stepped out into the stunning cold and trudged several blocks past the Moscow Planetarium and Zoo to Vosstaniya Square, where she entered the steamy warmth of a small, crowded tearoom. A photograph of Yeltsin was mounted over the serving counter at the back. Government workers came here on their breaks, but so far the photo had not been mutilated.

Marina went straight through the shop into the tiny kitchen, where she picked up the telephone and dialed a number in the city. The old woman who was cooking and the boy who was washing dishes didn't even look up. They were KGB.

The number was answered on the first ring. *"Da,"* a man said.

"I'm ready," Marina replied softly.

"Just a moment," the gruff voice instructed, and the line went dead for several seconds, before he came back. "Yes, all is in readiness."

"Are there any special instructions?"

"None."

"Very good," Marina said. She hung up, and hesitated for a moment or two in the warmth of the kitchen. It would be so nice, she thought, to take off her coat and scarf, order a tea and something to eat, and not go.

But then she smiled wanly, hunched up her coat collar, and left the restaurant, heading on foot over to Tchaikovsky Street just around the corner.

*   *   *

The KGB's Second Chief Directorate, Department One, was charged with the task of subverting foreign diplomats from the United States and Latin America, and denying them any unapproved access to Soviet citizens.

Operating out of offices on the second floor of the Lubyanka Center in downtown Moscow, the department was very ably administered by Lieutenant Colonel Boris Nikolaevich Vilkov, a man with good family connections, and a man who had no understanding whatsoever of such notions as mistake, defeat, error, second chance. He'd managed to keep clear of the coup and had survived the purges afterward.

Officers who worked for Vilkov and who did a good or even outstanding job were ignored. Those who made mistakes were thrown out, their government service careers ended. There was no appeal.

Yevgeni Andreyev and Valentin Grigoriev, Department One surveillance officers, sat in the cold in their parked Moskvich sedan across the street and twenty meters up the block from the U.S. Embassy on Tchaikovsky Street.

"This is a wasted effort," Andreyev, the much smaller and lighter complected of the two, said.

"Tell that to Nikki," Grigoriev replied with a laugh. He was a husky Georgian with thick, dark hair and a swarthy complexion. He was a good field officer, but everyone in the department figured that sooner or later his irreverent attitude would earn him the ax.

"You tell him," Andreyev said nervously.

"Better yet, let's send a bomb out to those First Directorate pricks. It's all their fault."

A spy from the rival directorate had been caught snooping around the Lubyanka, looking for something about an operation that the Americans were supposedly mounting. Something called MOHAWK. There were rumors that the operation might have something to do with a break-in at the Finance Directorate's computer, though no one was saying much of anything. But everyone was on edge.

Colonel Vilkov had sent the First Directorate *pizda* back to his own territory and had tripled their surveillance efforts. Nearly every American of importance in Moscow was being watched like a hawk, a difficult task under the current conditions.

Grigoriev laughed again. "I wouldn't mind if this were summer. I don't like freezing my balls off."

"Better than having them cut off," Andreyev replied.

"True."

Sergeant Pavl Medvedosky was behind the wheel of the dark brown two-door Lada, Major Kiselev in the passenger seat. They cruised down Barrikadnaya Street in the official lane, Medvedosky nervously watching his rearview mirror for overtaking traffic.

"There she is," Kiselev said softly.

Medvedosky took his eyes away from the mirror, spotting Marina Demin just as she disappeared around the corner onto Tchiakovsky Street.

He sped up, shooting across the square and slowing but not stopping for the red light against them.

Around the corner Medvedosky slowed even more. Marina had disappeared. There weren't many pedestrians, so she hadn't melded with the crowd. Nor had there been time enough for her to cross to the other side of the broad street.

"Where is she?"

"There," Kiselev said a moment later as Marina stepped out of a shop doorway and continued down the street. She limped slightly, as if she had hurt a leg or as if her feet were sore.

"What's she doing?" Medvedosky asked.

"Her job. Now drive past her and turn around at the corner."

Medvedosky sped up a little, and neither man looked over at Marina as they passed her, but as they passed the American Embassy a half block farther, Kiselev studied the front entrance and the four Militia officers stationed there.

In the old days the police, backed by the KGB, would have stopped any Russian citizen who had no legitimate business at the embassy. Now they mostly watched, stopping only those Russians who carried suspicious-looking packages. Something that might conceal a bomb or a weapon.

The Militia officers stationed in front of the American Embassy were also trained in spotting persons who were classified "essential to Russia," such as nuclear physicists, military officers, or high-ranking government officials.

But Marina was an unknown. Kiselev expected no trouble. Still, this operation was extremely important. A lot could go wrong, with disastrous results. But if they were able to pull it off, it would be the greatest intelligence coup since Philby and the other four Brits were recruited. And for Kiselev it would mean an express elevator to the top. Family connections, or the lack of them, would mean nothing. Source KHAIRULLA was everything. The mother lode.

On the upper side of the street, Marina caught a brief glimpse of Kiselev in the brown Lada as it passed. Her step faltered, and she turned abruptly to look into the window of a shop selling shoes. The displays were made of plaster of Paris and painted to look like the real thing. It was likely that what shoes they actually had inside were of very poor quality, and in sizes that hardly anyone wore. So close and yet so far, she thought. If they had pulled over, she would have jumped in the backseat and they could have gone somewhere out of the cold. But that had been an irrational hope. She turned her head and looked down the street. The Lada had disappeared in traffic, but she could pick out the Militia officers in front of the American Embassy about seventy meters away. A black limousine came from the opposite direction and turned into the embassy gate. Two of the Militiamen came over, but then stepped back and the limo went in. Marina wondered if her entry would be so easy.

"That was Major Kiselev," Yevgeni Andreyev said, looking away from the rearview mirror.

"Did they see us?" Grigoriev asked, snatching the radio handset from its bracket.

"I don't see how they could have missed us. I don't know what the hell they're doing here like this, but I'll tell you it was no chance pass. I'll bet anything on it."

"Unit two, this is one. Did you see that brown Lada?" Grigoriev radioed. The second surveillance unit was stationed around the corner where they could watch the side and back approaches to the embassy.

"We saw them."

"Did they spot you?"

"I don't know. Maybe. But was it who I think it was? We only got a quick look."

"It's him, but we don't know what he's doing here. Something . . ."

"Here's something, I think," Andreyev interrupted. He grabbed the motorized Hasselblad camera from the backseat and propped it against the steering wheel. He took a rapid sequence of six photographs, adjusted the focus and f-stop, and took six more photographs.

"Stand by, two," Grigoriev said, watching the slender woman in the drab coat coming down the street. There was something about her, something almost un-Russian. Although her movements seemed furtive, even from this distance she didn't seem to have the diffident stance of the average Muscovite.

Reaching the front of the American Embassy, she was stopped by one of the Militia officers.

"Let me see," Grigoriev said, taking the camera from his partner. He had to steady it by leaning forward with his elbows on the dash.

The woman's back was turned to him as he focused on her head and shoulders. The Militia officer had evidently asked to see her papers because she was digging them out of her purse. She handed over her booklet.

Grigoriev adjusted the focus slightly, and the woman turned so that he caught a three-quarters facial shot. He snapped several photographs.

She was a good-looking woman. Certainly not a peasant or a country girl, nor did she look as if she were from Moscow. Maybe Leningrad, Grigoriev thought instinctively. They had more class over there, closer to the West, and with their own history of architecture and the arts. Grigoriev was a professional. He knew when to trust his instincts.

"Do we know her?" Andreyev asked.

"Not offhand," Grigoriev said, taking several more photographs as the Militia officer handed the woman's papers back to her and she entered the embassy.

He lowered the camera.

"That was no coincidence, was it?"

"I don't think so," Grigoriev said. He radioed the other surveillance unit. "Have our friends returned?"

"They're at the end of the block."

Andreyev looked in the rearview mirror. "They're back there. A hundred meters."

"What are they doing?"

"Nothing," the radio blared. "Just sitting there."

"Cameras?"

"Not that I can see."

"When they leave, tail them," Grigoriev radioed, and Andreyev looked sharply at him.

"Are you sure?"

"Yes," Grigoriev radioed. "And I don't give a shit if they spot you. Just find out where they go." He slammed the handset back on its clip.

"That might not be such a good idea, Valentin Gerasimovich," Andreyev said.

"The hell with that," Grigoriev said angrily. "This is our territory, not theirs! Besides, they sent their little weasel to spy on us. It wasn't the other way around."

"What do we do now?"

"Find out just who that skinny little girl is. Who she belongs to." Grigoriev opened the door and got out of the car. "Wait here. I want to ask that Militiaman what sort of papers she showed him."

*   *   *

Marina was shuffled into a room with a half dozen other Russians, all of them with the down-at-the-heel look of the economic dissident. A sign on the frosted glass door read "Visa Applications," in English and Russian.

After two hours, when it was her turn, she stepped up to the counter and leaned a little nearer to the woman clerk on the other side. The woman was older and smelled of sachet. But she was American.

"I want to speak with someone who represents the Central Intelligence Agency," Marina said in Russian.

The clerk grinned. "You've been watching too many episodes of *Spy Smasher*. There's no CIA here."

"For ten years I have been the mistress of a man in the Kremlin. An important man. I wish to defect."

The clerk's thin-lipped smile became rigid, and her pale blue eyes narrowed. "I don't know what you're talking about . . ."

"Listen, you slut," Marina whispered in English. "I'm not leaving this place until I talk with someone from the Company. I'm not fucking around here. My life is in danger. But if you want to keep up the pretense while someone comes down from the third floor, I'd be happy to speak with a consular officer."

"Just a moment," the clerk said, and she turned and left through the door into the back.

"She's been in there long enough," Kiselev said.

"And now Vilkov's pricks know that we're involved," Medvedosky replied, shaking his big, square head. "They might even pick her up."

"She's not traceable."

"Those bastards could sweat something out of her."

Kiselev looked at his partner. Unlike other men he'd worked with, Medvedosky was intelligent, and at times even creative. These days if you wanted to survive in the new KGB, such qualities were necessary; those and a craftiness. All eyes were constantly on you from the outside, while from inside, the deeply buried, but still very much in control, hard-liners had lost little or no power. And they demanded results.

"If we can throw them off, maybe they'll lose interest in Marina," Kiselev said.

"If they follow us."

"They will."

Medvedosky grinned. "Where do you want me to lead them?"

"How about the Kremlin, Pavl Fedorovich? That'll give them something to think about."

"But what are they doing here?"

"They caught our little bird," Kiselev said. "We should have expected this. Now, let's give them something to report to Colonel Vilkov."

Roy Rodgers looked up from Marina's identification booklet and handed it back. They were seated across a plain gray table from each other in a small undecorated office in the consular section of the embassy.

"Now. Ms. Demin, what can we do for you?" Rodgers asked, his Texas accent strong even though he spoke Russian.

"In English," Marina said. "Do you work for the Central Intelligence Agency?"

Rodgers smiled. "That's a hell of a question, darlin'. Of course I'm not CIA, and you're not KGB. Nevertheless you came to us. What do you want?"

The only light in the windowless office came from a single fluorescent tube in the ceiling. It hummed with an irritating buzz.

"I want to go to America. There is someone I know there."

"So does half the world want to go to America."

"I can trade."

"With what?"

Marina leaned forward. "Look, I was the mistress for ten years of a very important guy in the Kremlin."

"Who?"

Marina sat back. "If I tell you this, will you let me speak with someone in charge here?"

"If you want to talk to someone, you talk to me. Simple."

"We're getting nowhere."

"No," Rodgers said. In charge of counterintelligence and surveillance, he had seen this sort of thing before: A supposedly defecting Russian who was really KGB and whose only purpose was to get inside the embassy to identify Company officers. Ten years ago the tactic had been effective. But no one was doing it these days. And this woman's effort was crude. Still, he thought, there was something bothersome about this situation. Something he couldn't quite put his finger on.

Marina unbuttoned her coat and took off her scarf, letting her hair hang free. "What I have to trade is very important to your government. Just being here places me in grave jeopardy." She pointed at the door in a dramatic gesture. "I could be shot the moment I leave."

"Yes, you might be killed," Rodgers said. "But what about your friend in the Kremlin, couldn't he protect you? Couldn't he pull some strings?"

Marina just looked blankly at him.

"Why don't you apply for a visa to Israel? It'd be a way out. You're Jewish, aren't you?"

"No," Marina screeched, jumping up. "Can't you understand my English, you cocksucker?"

"Just then, very well, ma'am," Rodgers replied dryly.

"Well?" she demanded, brushing a strand of hair from her eyes.

Rodgers thought that with a little makeup and some decent clothes, she would be good-looking even by Western standards. She was in the Audrey Hepburn style: thin and graceful.

"Let's start with the name of this friend of yours."

"He's very important."

"Yes?"

"I won't talk to you," she said.

"Fine." Rodgers got to his feet and went to the door.

"Wait," Marina cried, and he turned back to her. "His name is . . . Mukhin. Mikhail Lukich Mukhin. He's an assistant foreign affairs adviser to the President."

Dear God, Rodgers thought, but he kept a poker face. "All right," he said. "Wait here, I'll see what I can do for you."

He stepped out of the office, and the moment the door was closed he raced down the hall to the stairs and took them two at a time to his own office on the third floor, his heart pounding, but not simply from the exercise.

Richard Sweeney was in the small canteen on the fourth floor pouring himself a cup of coffee when the phone rang and Zuckerman picked it up.

"He's here," the diplomatic officer said. He and Roland Clark had been having breakfast together. He hung up. "That was Rodgers," he said to Sweeney. "Wants to see you downstairs on the double."

Sweeney looked up. Clark was watching him. "Where, his office?"

"Right."

"Okay," Sweeney said, and he left, taking the elevator down, his mind a thousand miles away.

6

THEY HAD TO BE CAREFUL NOT TO MAKE TOO MUCH OF A FUSS on the ground floor of the embassy, because half the employees on that floor were Russian nationals. Many, if not all of them, worked for the KGB.

The moment they discovered that Marina Demin had wandered off, Rodgers went to talk to the marine guards just inside the front doors, while Sweeney slipped into the empty office adjacent to the interview room. Opening a closet door with his key, he stepped into the equipment room, rewound the videotape partway, and then played that section back on the monitor.

Marina was seated at the table, her coat open, staring at the door. At first she did nothing. But then she turned, looked directly at the camera as if she'd known that the lens was concealed as a blemish in the wall plaster, got up, and left the office.

Rodgers was right, she was a good-looking woman. But who in the hell was she?

Sweeney rewound the tape completely and took it out of

the machine. Back out in the corridor, Rodgers was just coming from the front. He was shaking his head.

"She just walked out," Rodgers said on the way upstairs. "There was no reason to hold her."

"Anybody notice which way she went? Was she met by a car, or did she leave on foot? What?"

"No one paid any attention."

Sweeney nodded. It was a mistake, and Rodgers knew it, so there was no reason to bring it up. But at the next staff jam session he'd damned well make sure everyone learned their lesson: Loose cannons were *not* to be allowed to roam freely in and out of the embassy. And this woman was definitely a loose cannon.

"How'd she seem, Roy?" Sweeney asked when they got off on the third floor and went down to the office of the chief of station.

"Like she was lying through her teeth," Rodgers answered. "But she was definitely shittin' in her britches. She wasn't KGB, I'd bet on it."

The corridor, like most in the old building, was narrow and dimly lit. The wooden floors creaked loudly, and when it was very cold outside, the entire building snapped and popped, sometimes so violently it sounded as if someone were shooting at them.

Pool had left yesterday and Sweeney had moved into his office earlier this morning. It felt strange being here like this. He figured it was going to take him a few weeks or perhaps even months to get used to it. The temporary promotion was as gratifying as it was upsetting. He wanted out of Moscow, but in the meantime his new office was four times the size of his old one down the hall. He had a large desk that had been handmade in Hong Kong years ago, his own bookcases, built-in file cabinets, a safe, and a large window looking out over the courtyard. Some previous station chief had even brought in an oriental-style rug. It was a little threadbare, but it made the big room pleasant.

"Just go with the flow for the time being," Katherine said when he'd discussed his reservations about the appointment with her. "You've got the option of pulling the plug anytime you want."

"It's a big responsibility."

"Damned right it is, Ernie, and you're up to it. Don't ever forget it."

Sweeney smiled as he gathered her into his arms. He always felt a little extra love for her whenever she was obviously manipulating him, or stroking his ego—which in this case she was. As usual, he needed it.

"Let's take a look at the tape before we call up the MOHAWK committee," Sweeney said, handing the video-cassette to Rodgers, who set up a small monitor.

"What about Clark?"

Sweeney shrugged. "This may or may not change a thing, but I suppose he'll have to be included."

"It'll change things," Rodgers said, and hit the play button.

The taped images on the ten-inch television screen showed Rodgers and the woman entering the interview room. The camera had activated the moment the door opened. The antisurveillance devices were keyed to the fluorescent lights. The buzz, however, was electronically removed from the audio section of the videotape.

The meeting had lasted only a few minutes. When they got to the point where Marina got up and walked out, Rodgers rewound the tape and played it again.

"She gave Mildred a hard time out front," Rodgers said.

Sweeney was staring at the woman's image on the tiny screen. He nodded thoughtfully. "She got her attention." Sweeney looked up. "When's the last time that's happened around here?"

"The war's over, Dick."

"I wonder," Sweeney said. "They're still holding as many strategic nuclear weapons as before. Makes you ask yourself why."

They both turned back to the television monitor. "*All right,*" Rodgers' voice came from the speaker. "*Wait here, I'll see what I can do for you.*"

"So far as I see it, we're faced with two possibilities,"

Rodgers said, switching off the tape. "Either she was Mukhin's mistress, as she said she was, and she wants to defect now, or the KGB has found out about MOHAWK and they've sent her to shake us up."

"If she's telling the truth, we'll have a cross-check on Kaplin's product," Sweeney said, but there was something else bothering him. Something the woman had said in the interview room.

"If not, we're in serious trouble."

Sweeney nodded. "Either way we can't ignore her, Roy."

"I wasn't suggesting that. But unless she comes back, there's not much we can do."

"She'll return," Sweeney said. "You just scared her off. Go back now, to the start of the tape."

Rodgers rewound the tape to the point where he was looking up from her identification booklet.

"*Now, Ms. Demin, what can we do for you?*" Rodgers asked her.

"*In English. Do you work for the Central Intelligence Agency?*"

"*That's a hell of a question, darlin'. Of course I'm not CIA, and you're not KGB. Nevertheless you came to us. What do you want?*"

"*I want to go to America. There is someone I know there.*"

Sweeney sat forward. "There. Play that part back."

Rodgers saw it at once. "Shit," he swore, rewinding the tape. He hit the play button.

"*. . . go to America. There is someone I know there.*"

Rodgers stopped the tape. "I missed it the first time," he said. "What do you suppose she meant?"

"I don't know," Sweeney said, staring at Marina's frozen image on the screen. "But I think we'd better find out."

"I'll call the others."

"Make it a four o'clock meeting," Sweeney said, looking at his watch. It was past ten.

"What about Clark?"

"I'll brief him before lunch," Sweeney said. "And then I think I'll see Kaplin."

"Won't he be at work?"

"He's switched himself to nights."

Rodgers nodded. "Watch yourself. If she's a setup, you could be walking into a trap."

Sweeney smiled. "This entire country is a trap. Has been since the tenth century. The communists didn't change a thing. And the social democrats, or whatever the hell they're calling themselves these days, haven't either. Besides, I'm still not important enough to ring any bells at the Lubyanka. At least I don't think so."

The photo lab technician came upstairs to Department One territory just ahead of Andreyev.

The parent directorate was housed at the Lubyanka downtown. But Department One, which watched Americans and Latin Americans, was headquartered in a five-story building that looked like a warehouse. It was located just a half kilometer from the American Embassy. More than five hundred officers and support staff worked here.

The pimply-faced technician handed the sheaf of prints to Grigoriev, who'd been staring at the big map of Moscow in the operations room.

"Do we have an identification on her?" Grigoriev asked, flipping through the shots he and Andreyev had made.

"Marina Demin, just like you said."

"Where does she work?"

"Unknown. We got her file from the driver's license bureau at the Militia headquarters. There's nothing else yet."

"All right," Grigoriev said, dismissing the man.

Andreyev waited until the technician was gone. "Fuck your mother, you'll never guess where Kiselev and his ass-kissing sergeant went."

"Evidently not back to their office," Grigoriev said. "The Kremlin?"

Andreyev's face fell. "How did you know?"

"It was a mistake that could cost you the entire MOHAWK operation," Roland Clark said.

"You're right, unfortunately, but we're going to do what we can to contain it. In the meantime, if she was telling us the truth, it's my bet she'll be back," Sweeney said. They were meeting in his office.

"You'd have a confirmation of Kaplin's and Mukhin's stories, unless they were involved in some sort of a plot. Kaplin made the first move."

"Yes, he did," Sweeney admitted. "But to date his product has been without flaw."

Clark said nothing.

"In the meantime we wait for her to return."

"When are you going to see him?" Clark asked.

"Kaplin?" Sweeney asked, not really surprised. Although he did not like Clark being here, watching over their shoulders, he'd come to have a grudging respect for the man's obvious intelligence and ability. Clark was nobody's fool, even though by his own admission he was nothing more than a gofer.

Clark nodded.

"This afternoon."

"I'd like to come with you."

"No."

Again Clark nodded. "Tell me about the woman's friend in the States."

"That's the dicey part," Sweeney admitted. "I've queried Langley about her, but we've no record that she ever applied for or was issued a visa to go to the United States."

"Then he or she came here," Clark said. "Perhaps her friend worked here in the embassy. Perhaps for the Company."

The thought was chilling, but certainly possible, and Sweeney admitted as much. "She would have been on someone's encounter sheet in that case. But she hasn't turned up in any of our files yet."

"Yet," Clark said. "You haven't had the time to do a proper records search."

"No."

Clark looked at the blank monitor screen. "What does Rodgers say? Did he believe her?"

"He thought she was frightened."

"That came across on the tape. But what about in person?"

"He thought she was lying, but about what, and for what purpose, he wasn't sure."

"He doesn't want to take her at face value."

"None of us do."

"You could be in trouble with this one," Clark said. "Especially now. If MOHAWK were to blow up in your face, it would put everyone in a tenuous position."

Sweeney studied the other man for a beat or two. Clark seemed perfectly neutral. As if none of this mattered. As if they were discussing the day's weather.

"Is that what you'll tell Tyson?"

"What do you want me to tell him?"

"That we're in the middle of a complex and very difficult operation. That a new wrinkle has developed. And that we'll do our best to contain the situation."

"All right."

"What?"

"You've convinced me, Sweeney," Clark said, rising. "I think you're up to your necks in shit here, but I think you'll manage. You're doing a good job."

Sweeney got up. "When do you return?"

"In a few hours."

Sweeney had to laugh. "You wouldn't have had the time to see Kaplin with me this afternoon in any event."

"No."

They shook hands. "Have a good trip home. And thanks for the vote of confidence. I think I'm going to need it."

"Anything I can do to help from Washington, let me know."

"Will do."

Sweeney hadn't told Clark everything, of course. No mention had been made of Larissa Dolya's almost instanta-

'neous success with Kaplin. So far as Tyson's man knew, that aspect of the operation had not matured yet.

Though in all reality it wouldn't have mattered much if Clark had been advised of her situation, because she'd not produced anything of value yet except getting him to switch the hours he worked at the Lubyanka. No one expected spies to operate during the daytime. It gave Larissa a certain advantage.

It was two in the afternoon by the time Sweeney got over to Gor'kiy Park and walked the few blocks to the apartment. The overcast had deepened, lending a gloomy air to the city and making the cold seem even more intense than it was. Sweeney hated the place.

Kaplin's door was open, and the big Russian was hunched bare-chested over the tin sink, washing his thick hair. When Sweeney knocked on the door frame, the man reared up and spun around, soap and water flying everywhere.

"Sorry I startled you," Sweeney said.

Kaplin's eye went guiltily to the daybed, which had not been made up from the night. A woman's panties lay crumpled on the pillow.

"What are you doing here, Richard?"

Sweeney saw the panties and he felt bad. But Larissa had volunteered. It wasn't on his conscience. Yet it was.

"We need to talk, Anatoli Stepanovich. Something has come up," Sweeney said. He gestured to the panties. "Will she be back?"

"Later."

"What you do on your own time is your own business, so long as nothing jeopardizes our arrangement."

Kaplin laughed disparagingly. "Your threats are hollow. They mean nothing. What do you want with me?"

Larissa was already in strong with him. It was better than they expected. Certainly sooner.

Sweeney shut the apartment door. "Does the name Marina Demin mean anything to you?"

Kaplin thought a moment but then shook his head. "No, I don't think I've ever heard this name. Is she important?"

Sweeney took a couple of photographs they'd made from the videotape and handed them to Kaplin.

The Russian studied them, but when he looked up he shook his head again. "Poor quality, but I would recognize that face if I'd seen it before. She's a looker."

"She claims she was Mikhail Mukhin's mistress for ten years."

Kaplin grinned broadly. "I wouldn't be surprised. You should see his wife. But what does she want now? Has she come to you to sell her little secrets?"

"That's exactly what she's done. I want you to talk to him. Find out if this girl is telling the truth."

"It could be a KGB counterespionage plot. How secure is my file here in Moscow and in Washington?"

"Very."

"My life is on the line."

"We know. And if it ever gets bad, we'll pull you out."

"I don't want that," Kaplin retorted angrily. "I'll find out about this little girl, but we may have another problem to deal with."

"What sort of problem?" Sweeney asked.

"There've been some rumors floating around the Lubyanka the past few days that a wise guy is tampering with one of our computers."

"What do you mean, wise guy?"

"You call them computer hackers. He may be tampering with Finance Directorate records. And this is very big, Richard. The biggest."

"But not so big that everyone in the KGB seems to know about it. Not something I'd suppose they'd advertise."

"It's not that, Richard. Listen to me, I mean really *listen* to me. The Finance Directorate is the sacred cow. Even today, no one knows what goes on over there. No one. The fact that there are rumors means the information must have come from someplace else. Someplace *outside* of the KGB."

"I don't understand."

"It sounds to me, and to everyone else, that the CIA may have someone within the Finance Directorate. A source."

Sweeney was shaking his head.

"You wouldn't tell me in any event, Richard, I know that. But the screws are being tightened on all Americans here in Moscow because of this. So watch yourself."

"Find out more, will you?" Sweeney asked.

Kaplin looked at him for a long second or two, and then slowly nodded. "I'll see," he said. "And I'll find out about this little girl. But be careful, Richard. In Moscow it is very easy for an accident to happen. Even now, even among friends."

As the Aeroflot Ilyushin airliner lifted off from Moscow's Sheremetyevo Airport, Roland Clark felt relieved. During his short stay in Russia he had not admitted to himself that he'd been tense, on edge, but he had been from the moment he'd set foot on Russian soil.

Seldom did anyone or anyplace frighten him, but watching out the window as the countryside disappeared beneath the clouds, he shivered.

Napoleon and Hitler had both felt the Russian cold. It had defeated them. And in the end it might defeat the West, Russian reforms or not.

Clark had developed the feeling—and it was a strong feeling—that we had no business in Russia. None whatsoever.

The Americans had taken the bait; and Marina Demin was so excited, she'd not been able to come down all afternoon, wandering around the city like a tourist.

She'd done exactly as she'd been instructed, and it had worked. The look on the woman's face behind the visa applications counter had been wonderful, as had the expected skepticism of the man who'd interviewed her.

"He'll be a CIA officer, Marinka, there'll be no doubt of that," she'd been assured.

His name was Roy Rodgers. She'd recognized him from the photos she'd studied. He was the officer in charge of the

CIA's counterespionage and surveillance efforts in Moscow. It definitely told her what they thought about her story.

It was wonderful.

Except for one tiny thing that had nagged at the back of her head all day, and bothered her now past six in the evening, as she let herself into her small apartment in Timiryazev Park on Moscow's far northwest side.

Rodgers had had no reaction when she'd made mention that she knew someone in the United States. But he had practically dropped his teeth when she'd told him that she'd been the mistress of Mikhail Mukhin.

What had it meant? she asked herself for the tenth time today. Had they picked the wrong Kremlin official? There was no way that the Americans could get back to Mukhin, according to her instructions. Yet Rodgers had reacted as if he was very familiar with the name. As if Mukhin was working for them.

But that was not possible. Not even now.

"There is so much confusion, so much corruption behind the Kremlin walls now, that it wouldn't surprise me if every second bureaucrat was an American spy," Ivan had told her in Odessa.

She smelled cigarette smoke the instant she opened her apartment door. American cigarettes.

"Ivan?" she called.

"In here, Marinka," Major Kiselev called back. "I've been waiting for you."

It was late again, and although Zimin had managed to get a few hours of sleep, he was still very tired. His parents had been very poor, and as a child he'd developed rickets from malnutrition, which had left him crippled. He'd compensated by being the head of every class he ever took.

Sipping his tea, he carefully watched the new program he'd written scroll down his screen. In concept it was simple, but in actuality it was so complex he'd used another, even more powerful IBM in the Kremlin to help him write it. Now he was ready.

Loading the new program onto a disk, he brought up the Finance Directorate's rose and entered the Tchaikovsky concerto.

WELCOME TO DIRECTORATE ONE FINANCE AC-
CESS
STATE YOUR MENU CHOICE
ALARM SEQUENCE IN PROGRESS

The problem was Deputy Mukhin's information; it was out of date, and Zimin's boss, Deputy Secretary Malakhov, had suddenly developed cold feet about using the man again.

"Is there any other way in?"

"I don't know," Zimin said. "How much leeway are you authorizing me?"

"I don't understand. Forgive an old man who hasn't caught up with the computer age."

"I might be able to inject a virus into the system, which would attack only the alarm sequences. It would be a onetime affair, though. Once the alarms were down, I could get inside and find out what we needed to know and get out."

"But they would know you'd been there."

"They would know that someone had been tampering, but not that it was me, specifically."

"But then they would be on their guard," Malakhov said. "No. You must find another way."

"Very well, Comrade Deputy Secretary, I will work on it."

"Our search may take a long time, once we're in. Keep that in mind. We are looking not merely for one bit of information, but for an entire library."

"I'll keep it in mind," Zimin said.

Zimin entered his next sequence:

PAYMENT GREEN GRASS
FIRST FISCAL QUARTER 1992

The computer responded:

RESTRICTED ACCESS
BETA LEVEL AND ABOVE
IDENTIFICATION PLEASE

Zimin typed:

OPEN RESTRICTED ACCESS FILE
NAME: PIGGYBACK

For a second it seemed as if the computer were hesitating, or as if it were going to ignore his instruction. But then his new file name came up, with a sequence number.

Zimin entered the next stage:

BETA LEVEL AND ABOVE ACCESS WILL BE MAINTAINED
PIGGYBACK WILL BE A PARALLEL ACCESS FILE
PIGGYBACK IDENTIFICATION LIMITED TO ONE USER
USER IDENTIFICATION: THOR

The computer replied:

ENTERED

Zimin punched the send button, which dumped his own parallel identification program into the Finance Directorate's computer. Included was a fail-safe. The instant his program was discovered, and someone began to tamper with it, a virus would be released which would destroy the entire system.

Zimin smiled. It was time to cover his own ass, because from the looks of things, if something were to go wrong, neither Deputy Mukhin nor Deputy Secretary Malakhov would be able to help.

"He's in," Nancy Perigorde said into the phone.
"Are you sure?" Dr. Hamilton asked.

"Yes. And he's brilliant, whoever he is. He came up with his own restricted-access program."

"We need to find out who he is and where he's located."

"Moscow . . ."

"I mean specifically, and very fast. Work on it."

"I don't know if it's possible . . ." Nancy Perigorde said, but Dr. Hamilton had already hung up.

7

CLARK WAS STILL ON MOSCOW TIME AS HE DROVE ACROSS THE Potomac River and up to the White House. He was passed through the west gate and went directly up to the third floor. His body clock was telling him it was four in the morning, while here in Washington it was eight in the evening.

He'd telephoned Tyson at home from Dulles the moment he'd arrived. "I'm back."

"How soon can you be at my office?"

"Half hour."

The regular White House staff had long since left for the evening. Tyson, dressed in slacks and an open-collar shirt and sweater, was alone in his office.

"How was it?" the assistant national security adviser asked directly.

"They're in trouble, but since Pool has left, I think Sweeney will be able to handle it. He has some good people working for him."

"I heard about Pool. What'd you make of it?"

"He's burned out."

Tyson nodded his head thoughtfully. "Would you like a drink?"

"No, sir."

"All right, what do I tell the President, Roland? What are MOHAWK's chances?"

"They have two major problems to overcome. If they can solve both, they'll have a shot. If not, the operation will almost certainly fail. If and when it comes apart, it'll be spectacular."

Tyson's eyes narrowed. "You say Sweeney is up to the task?"

"Yes, sir, but still it could go either way. First he has to stabilize his main contact, Anatoli Kaplin. The Russian is apparently a prima donna. Sweeney's plan for handling him depends on a woman, of Russian extraction but an American. Sweeney has confidence in her."

"Kaplin's a skirt chaser?"

"So I was told."

"What's the second problem?"

Clark took a couple of photographs of Marina Demin from his pocket and handed them to Tyson. They were prints from the videotape and were not very clear.

"This woman showed up at the embassy while I was there, claiming she wanted to defect. She said she had been the mistress of Mikhail Mukhin for ten years."

Tyson looked up from the prints, an oddly intense expression on his face. "One of Kaplin's people?"

"Precisely. If it's true, she would make a good cross-check on what Mukhin gives us. If not, she could be a KGB agent."

Tyson stared at the photographs. "Was she given asylum?"

"Something evidently spooked her, because she walked off."

Tyson nodded. "What else?" he asked, tight-jawed.

"What bothers them the most is that she claimed to have a friend in this country."

Tyson said nothing.

"They're checking on her as best they can. And in the meantime they can only wait until she shows up again."

"If she doesn't?"

"Sweeney didn't say," Clark replied evenly. "I'm sure he doesn't know. But I'm equally certain that he'll figure it out."

"So, MOHAWK is in trouble," Tyson said.

"Fifty-fifty," Clark answered.

"Not a very encouraging report to pass to the President."

"No, sir. Will you want a written report?"

"No," Tyson said. "But keep available. We may want a follow-up."

The number was answered on the first ring by a man speaking very good English. "Yes?"

"Is Uncle Harold back?" Vincent Privet, the Russian assassin, asked.

"What do you want?"

"I must speak with Radchenko," Privet said. He gave the telephone number of the phone booth he was in. "This number is secure. I'll wait two minutes." He hung up, and looked up across the remodeled main concourse of the Union Station on Massachusetts Avenue with pleasure. He'd been told that in America everything was new. That Americans despised tradition. But this belied that instruction.

The telephone rang less than a minute later. Privet answered it. "Yes."

"What do you want?" It was Radchenko.

"The name."

"Not yet."

"The name," Privet said. "Or I will leave in the morning."

"What?" his control officer shouted. "Who do you think you are?"

"You know," Privet said. And he waited.

"You have your orders."

Privet said nothing.

"Why do you wish this information now?"

"If I am to be successful, I will need to do my homework."

"There'll be plenty of time for that later."

"Are you sure?"

There was a silence for a beat. "How do we know that you won't simply go ahead without the word?"

"I don't work that way. Check my record."

Again there was a silence.

"The name," Privet said.

"Albert Tyson. He is the assistant national security adviser to the President."

Even Privet was impressed. Assassinating a man such as Tyson was serious, made even more so by the state of relations between Russia and the United States. But why Tyson, specifically? And when did they want it done? Why the delay? What were they waiting for? There were dozens of questions, the answers to which he was determined to learn before he actually carried out such an assignment. If the word, as Radchenko called it, were ever given.

"What are you going to do?" Radchenko was shouting, but Privet hung up.

He sat in the phone booth for another minute as he contemplated his next moves. The key to any assassination, of course, was making good an escape. He decided he would need more information.

Leaving the Union Station, he retrieved his rental Buick Regal and drove over to the Hyatt Regency on D Street, where from another phone booth he telephoned the White House.

"Connect me with Al Tyson. This is Senator Dave Durenberger," Privet told the operator.

"I'm sorry, Senator, but you just missed Mr. Tyson."

"Is he on his way home?" Privet asked. "The reason I'm asking is that I have that committee report he wanted. He has to have it tonight."

"I would assume he's going home," the operator said.

"Have you got his address handy? I'm not in my office."

"Of course, Senator," the operator said, and after a moment she gave him the address. It was a street in Georgetown, not far from the safe house Radchenko had provided him. It made sense now.

"Thanks," Privet said.

Outside he got back in his car and headed over to Georgetown. School was about to begin.

Toni Wagner poured Tyson a drink and brought it to him in the living room. She'd not been expecting him. Her hair was pinned up, and she was dressed in an old pair of blue jeans and a Harvard sweatshirt. She'd been watching television.

"I was working late. I thought I'd stop by to see you," Tyson said. He was very nervous, and didn't want to sit down, nor did he want to stand. "You don't mind, do you?"

"Don't be silly," Toni said. "But, Jesus, you look like a wreck. What happened?"

Tyson stopped his pacing and looked at her. He shook his head. "I wish I could tell you. God . . . you couldn't even begin to guess."

Toni held up a hand. "I don't want to hear any grubby little political secrets. We agreed from day one that I'd be a shoulder to cry on, but not a sounding board."

"I couldn't tell you anyway," Tyson said.

Toni went into the bedroom and brought out a small, square mirror, a razor blade, a short plastic straw, and a vial of cocaine. "Sit down," she ordered.

Tyson's eyes were glazed. He tossed back his drink, set the glass aside, and then sat down, licking his lips.

Toni tapped out a small pile of powder on the mirror and expertly flattened it, spread it out, and cut it into four lines. She handed the straw to him. At first he was hesitant, but then he bent over and took a line up his right nostril.

"Again," she said.

He took the second line up his left nostril, the drug starting to hammer his brain, his heart palpitating several times.

He didn't often do this with her, although it had been happening more frequently lately. But tonight he needed the release.

"Someone is trying to catch up with me," he said, lying back.

Toni curled up next to him on the couch. He leaned

forward and took a third line. When he sat back again, she began massaging his temples.

"Who?" she purred.

"Someone from a long time ago. She was a friend of Joseph's. Kent State. The name is the same. Maybe this one is her . . . daughter."

"What about her, Al?" Toni asked, her voice low, soothing.

"I don't want to go back," Tyson said. "I don't ever want to go back. They can't make me."

Yakunin was nervous. He drove slowly up Avon Place toward R Street, the traffic very light. Across the broad thoroughfare Montrose Park seemed dark and mysterious to him at this moment.

That fool Radchenko had gotten himself worked up over Privet's call. "I don't know what the sonofabitch is going to do, but I think he means to begin stalking Tyson."

"Isn't that the idea?" Yakunin had asked. He was a large man with a broad chest and thick neck. He towered over the smaller, dapper Radchenko, and yet in the presence of the case officer, Yakunin felt *nekulturny* . . . like a rumpled bed in an ambassador's apartment, out of place.

"Not yet!" Radchenko had shouted. "Too big a risk for a mistake to happen. Truskin wants him back under wraps. Now."

"Well, where is he?"

"There's no answer at the safe house, but that doesn't mean a thing. I'll head over to see if I can catch him there. In the meantime I want you to make a couple of passes by Tyson's house, and if that bastard shows up get him off the street."

"What if he doesn't want to come with me?"

Radchenko was suddenly subdued. "Do whatever it takes, Viktor Valdimirovich. But this has top priority, very top priority, do you understand?"

"No, comrade, I do not." Yakunin had been a Komitet

field officer for enough years to understand when a clarification of orders was necessary for his own survival.

"Tyson is important, Privet is not."

Yakunin waited.

"Under no circumstances is Privet to be allowed to make contact with Tyson . . . any sort of contact. Is that clear?"

"Yes," Yakunin said. "But again I must ask the question, Comrade Radchenko: What if Privet does not want to come with me or stand down? What are my orders?"

"As soon as I check at the safe house, I'll join you there."

"What if you are not in time?"

Radchenko hesitated for a long second. "Then kill him, Viktor, if there is no other choice."

"I suggest you hurry," Yakunin had said, and he'd left the embassy.

He'd taken out his Makarov pistol, levered a round into the firing chamber, and switched the safety off. The gun lay on the seat next to him, and as he stopped at the intersection he reached over and touched it. Assassins were generally not shootout artists. More often than not they were snipers, killing their subjects from great distances. Nonetheless, Privet was a killer, and going up against him made Yakunin extremely wary.

A car came up behind Yakunin and he pulled out onto R Street, turning left and heading the long block up toward Tyson's house, scanning both sides of the street as he drove.

On his first pass on foot, the assassin had spotted the dark blue Toyota van parked across the street and thirty meters down the block from Tyson's imposing three-story house. In his time here in Washington he had noted the license tag series on vehicles coming and going from the White House, FBI headquarters in the J. Edgar Hoover Building, and the Soviet Embassy. The van's plates were of the series the Bureau used.

Which meant what? That the FBI was protecting the acting national security adviser? But the Secret Service did that, which meant it was possible that the Bureau had manned a surveillance operation on Tyson. It meant they suspected him of something.

Privet had parked his car a couple of blocks away on 29th Street and had walked back, a newspaper in his coat pocket and a bag of groceries in his left arm. Out in the open, but inconspicuous.

Five minutes ago he'd taken up position in the dark doorway of a basement apartment in a brownstone two doors from 31st Street, across from which was Tyson's house.

He didn't think that whoever was in the van had spotted him yet. Their attention would be turned toward the national security adviser's house. Sooner or later, however, they would move or they would be relieved. Either that, or Tyson would make a move, and he would be able to determine for certain that the Bureau was watching him.

A light gray Ford sedan passed, heading east on R Street, and Privet hunched back a little farther into the shadows. He knew the car. It was the one Radchenko often used. The same registration tag number.

As the car turned left down 31st, Privet caught a glimpse of the driver. He didn't know who the man was, but he wasn't Radchenko.

It was someone else here from the embassy. Why now this evening, except in response to his telephone call to his control officer? They meant to come here and stop him. They were fools.

It was Privet, Yakunin was sure of it. He'd caught a glimpse of someone in the dark doorway of that brownstone, and as he'd turned the corner he got a brief look at the man's face. There was no mistake.

Turning up Avon Lane and stopping, he waited for a green Datsun to pass and then he backed out onto 31st and headed the way he had come.

The Datsun turned left at the stop sign, and Yakunin, not stopping, turned right.

Privet was still there, in the doorway, as if he'd been waiting in ambush. The crazy *kulak*.

Yakunin pulled over to the curb, grabbed his pistol, and jumped out of the car. He aimed the pistol over the roof, his stomach jumping all over the place, and his legs weak. The bastard was a paid killer. No telling what he was going to do when he realized he was cornered.

"Get in the car and there'll be no trouble," he shouted.

Privet was waving him off.

"Get in the car now, or I have orders to shoot you," Yakunin shouted, this time in Russian.

Privet came out of the doorway, his hands in plain sight. He hadn't drawn his weapon, for which Yakunin was instantly grateful. He didn't want a shootout here with this one.

"FBI," Privet whispered urgently as he crossed the sidewalk. "The van across the street, you stupid bastard."

Yakunin was momentarily confused.

"Put your gun away and get us out of here," Privet ordered as he reached the car and started to open the door.

Yakunin turned in time to see two men getting out of the van, one from the driver's-side door, the other from the rear. They were both armed. Pistols.

FBI? He should have spotted the fucking van when he'd made his pass! But it was too late now! He was a Russian national with diplomatic immunity. But he was armed. The worst that would happen to him would be immediate expulsion from the country. Within ninety days he'd be settling in at his new posting.

"FBI! FBI! Put your weapon down!" one of the agents shouted as he and his partner started across the street in a dead run.

"Don't shoot," Yakunin shouted, turning and raising both hands above his head.

Privet fired two silenced shots from behind him, and one of the agents went down.

"*Stoi!*" Yakunin shouted desperately, realizing too late that Privet would not have diplomatic immunity, and at best he would face a long prison term. His own government would deny him, of course.

The other American cop started firing wildly, one shot catching Yakunin in the left kneecap, knocking him down. But Privet wasn't returning fire. What the fuck was the man doing?

A second shot hit Yakunin in the chest. An instant later he returned the fire, hitting the agent in the head, driving him backward.

Privet came around to the driver's side of the car, and through his daze Yakunin could see that the man had an erection. Impossible to believe. The man was crazy.

"Help me . . ." Yakunin said, when Privet raised his pistol and shot him in the head.

Radchenko had hurried over to R Street as soon as he'd determined that Privet was not at the safe house. Like Yakunin, he was very nervous. There was no telling what the assassin Moscow had sent them would do, especially if he was confronted by Yakunin.

The man was going to have to be contained. "At all costs," Truskin had warned. "Privet at this moment is more important than you or I. Or anyone else here for that matter, except Tyson. Is my meaning clear?"

"Perfectly . . ."

"You, Vsevolod Sergeevich, are expendable. Either fix your error, or I will have someone else do it. Now."

Something was happening on the street, and Radchenko's stomach rose up into his throat as he came around the corner from 31st Street and slammed on his brakes, screeching to a halt.

Privet was standing over what appeared to be Yakunin's body. The headlights of Radchenko's car illuminated the scene like daylight.

But that was impossible.

Two other men were down in the middle of the street, and a car that had come west down R Street had pulled up and the driver was desperately trying to get turned around.

What had happened?

Privet, his pistol still in hand, came over to the car and

Radchenko reared back, his eyes wide. The maniac was going to kill them all.

"Get rid of your car, and meet me at the safe house," Privet said. "Be careful that you are not followed, and call no one."

Before Radchenko could say a word, Privet pocketed his gun, turned, and ambled off into the night, for all appearances a man without a care in the world.

Before he started his car, the assassin rolled down his window and cocked an ear to listen. In the distance he could hear sirens. A lot of them. Soon the area would be crawling with police officers. He hoped that Radchenko had enough presence of mind to get out before it was too late.

Driving away, he wondered how this evening's debacle would ultimately affect his assignment. The Americans would react, of course, and probably very harshly. On the surface it would appear that a shootout between a KGB officer and two agents of the FBI had occurred. But the Bureau's ballistics experts would soon discover that another weapon had been used. That there had been others present. Eyewitnesses might even be able to describe him or Radchenko, though he doubted that a reliable sketch could ever be made. It was dark, and the only motorist who had chanced on the scene had been more intent on making his own escape than on getting a good look at faces.

A protest would be lodged with the Russian ambassador, who would deny any knowledge of the incident at first. Later an apology would be issued. The man had been unhinged by the pressures of his work and by problems at home. Surely Americans would understand. It was the same in this country. A man despondent over his job or family opens fire in a crowded McDonald's, or in a post office or an insurance company. Who can predict or prevent such tragedies?

The greatest tragedy here, besides the terrible waste of good lives, was that the madman happened to be Russian at a time when cooperation between Russia and the United States was at such an important, delicate juncture.

"No, he was *not* a KGB agent. Nor was he on any assignment for the embassy. He had worked alone, and no, we cannot provide any explanation for the presence of the fourth man. A bystander, perhaps, who shot in self-defense. Many of your citizens have guns. In Washington someone is killed with a handgun every day."

The furor would eventually die down, leaving behind what?

His assignment had been to come to the United States to kill Albert Tyson. A Tyson who was evidently under investigation by the FBI.

Something was happening, and he would find out what before he went any further.

In any event there was going to be plenty of time now for contemplation. They'd all have to lie low until the dust settled. For the time being, at least, Tyson was going to be unapproachable.

Roland Clark woke instantly, as he had every morning of his life since he'd served as a combat marine in Vietnam. For him the cold war had started out not so cold, but now it was finally winding down, and he was glad of it.

The bedroom was dark even though the window curtains were open. He glanced over at the clock radio. It was a few minutes before eight; he had slept longer than he wanted to, though Tyson had told him to take the next few days off.

"Just stay available, Roland. The President might want more."

It was an overcast morning and would probably snow again. He didn't mind. As bad as the Washington area ever got, the weather was nothing like Moscow's. He shivered thinking about it. It had been more than the weather, of course. Moscow had struck him as the capital of a bankrupt nation. Like a bankrupt Wall Street stockbroker, there was a possibility the Russians might commit suicide, taking the rest of the world with them. The Kremlin coup may have advanced democracy over there, but in exchange, something had been lost.

He could hear his wife, Ginny, in the kitchen, and the television in the den: odd, he thought. The kids should be in school. He had two boys (actually three right now): Kevin, who was sixteen; Justin, who was thirteen; and their foreign exchange student from Leningrad, Anatoli Vasilevich Smirnov, who was fifteen.

The only time the television was on in the den during the day was when the boys were off from school.

He'd had to get permission from the FBI and the Secret Service before he was allowed to accept a Russian exchange student into his house. But the permission had been given gladly. In fact, at the time, he'd gotten the impression that the Bureau had been overjoyed. "It'll make the Russians understand that our people in government are nothing more than ordinary people," he and Ginny had been told. Which, considering who and what he was, was ludicrous.

He was prejudiced against Russians and communist Chinese. It came from his college days, when he found that he could not accept what the campus protestors were telling him. And his distrust had deepened to hatred during his stint in Nam, only slightly softening in the intervening years.

He and Ginny, who in his estimation was a saint, had discussed it before they had agreed to accept Anatoli into their home for the nine-month school year.

"Are we going to do this so that you can prove to yourself that you can accept anything, even a communist?" Ginny had asked him. "Show that you can take it like a man? Because if that's the case it would be unfair to the child."

"Maybe there's a little of that, but it won't get in the way."

Ginny had looked into his eyes. She was the only person on earth who could completely see through him. She knew everything that he knew (something the Bureau, the Secret Service, and Albert Tyson did not know).

"You haven't changed your mind about things, considering what's been going on over there, have you?"

"Not yet, but I may have to eventually."

"When?" she asked sharply.

"They've been bastards for seventy years. We'll see."

Ginny nodded. She was a slightly built woman with prematurely graying hair. Three years ago she'd lost her left breast to cancer. Her illness had not slowed her down. She was a member of the PTO. She'd been a Boy Scout Council member. She was president of the Lincoln High School Football Boosters Club, and it was she who had first broached the subject of hosting an AFS student, though she'd never dreamed they'd be assigned a Russian.

But Anatoli had fit in well. The boys called him Andy, of course, and sometimes "booze breath," because of his last name. And the girls at school found him fascinating, because he was someone new.

At first he and Clark had been wary of each other. The boy had obviously been briefed by someone. And in the third week the tension in the house had built up to such an extent that Ginny had suggested they throw in the towel.

"This is not working, Roland," she'd said. "Either fix it or let's call AFS. Find Anatoli another family."

That night Roland had sat the boy down and they had talked for a couple of hours about everything, but mostly about politics, about Clark's continuing mistrust of Russians, and about Anatoli's fears of Americans, and especially the CIA.

"We are taught as little children that the CIA watches everything we do," Anatoli said.

"And we were taught that the KGB watched you."

Anatoli had smiled. "Perhaps both are lies now."

"Perhaps," Clark had said. And the ice had been broken. Since then they had avoided discussions about the international scene, and Anatoli had become one of the family . . . almost.

Ginny appeared at the bedroom door. "Breakfast or just coffee, chief?"

"Coffee. Are the boys home?"

She laughed. "It's Saturday. You must still be on Moscow time."

"Don't remind me. What's on the calendar?"

"I'm open for suggestions."

"How about you and I go for a drive in the country?"

"It's going to snow."

"It'll be pretty," Clark said.

Ginny smiled again. She almost always smiled.

"Give me an hour," she said, and she went back into the kitchen.

Clark remained in bed for another minute or two thinking about his Moscow trip for Tyson, glad that he was home. It was a terribly dangerous world out there.

Briefly he wondered about Tyson's reaction to the photographs of the Russian woman who'd tried to defect to them in Moscow. There was something there. Something he couldn't quite put his finger on, except that he would have bet almost anything that Tyson knew the woman, or thought he did.

8

IT WAS A LITTLE AFTER EIGHT IN THE MORNING WHEN YURI Truskin arrived at the Georgetown Russian safe house. The assassin had spent the long night with Radchenko and two nameless henchmen from the embassy. They looked as if they had stepped out of a Doublemint chewing gun ad that Privet had seen on television, except that neither of them smiled or spoke. He'd seen their type before, and he ignored them. They were nothing more than furniture, though he supposed that if he attempted to leave the apartment they would stop him. Or try.

Radchenko let the Russian *Rezident* in. Privet was watching television, which he found fascinating here in the United States. He'd already had his breakfast of tea, toast, herring, and cheese, and he wanted to go to bed. But he'd expected that the local chief of KGB operations would be showing up sooner or later for an explanation. Which was fine, because Privet had a few questions of his own.

Truskin was more Russian-looking than Privet had thought he would be. So far nearly every Russian he'd seen here looked American. They'd been trained to blend in. But not this one, though his clothes were obviously American and expensive.

Truskin stood just within the doorway looking across at Privet as he listened to something Radchenko was saying to him. There was a scowl on his face, but that look was something Privet had long been accustomed to. Not many people had the desire or presence of mind to smile in the company of an assassin.

Radchenko looked over at him, then motioned for his two legmen to get out. When they were gone, Radchenko said something else to the *Rezident,* and then he too left, softly closing the door behind him.

Truskin came the rest of the way into the room. "Turn off the television set," he said.

Privet waited a moment, then got up and turned off the set. When he turned back, Truskin was taking off his overcoat and then his suit coat, his motions deliberate. As if he were stripping for a fight.

When the *Rezident* loosened his tie, he offered Privet a cigarette, which the assassin declined, and lit one for himself.

"I didn't realize that you were losing your hair," he said in Russian.

"They tell me I look ordinary because of it," Privet replied.

Neither of them made a move to sit down. Instead they stood facing each other, like the adversaries they had become. Adversaries, Privet thought, yet necessary allies unless plans had changed.

"Why did you shoot one of our people?" Truskin asked.

"He was unstable. He had just shot an FBI agent to death."

"We would have dealt with him. Had you brought him in, there would have been no link between the deaths of the Bureau agents and our people."

And this one was the *Rezident,* Privet thought. He shook his head. There was an old Russian proverb that said: The Russian is clever, but it comes slowly—all the way from the back of his head.

"Had you thought of the possibility that the second agent, the one I was forced to dispose of, had radioed that his partner was in trouble?"

"No," Truskin admitted. "Nonetheless, had they not been left with a Russian body, it would have further muddied their investigation."

"With a body, a Russian body, they will have something to chew on," Privet said calmly. "Something so big, considering the present relationship between Moscow and Washington, that they will almost certainly have trouble swallowing and digesting it. It will divert their attention."

"Or focus it on us. On you."

"Have you also asked yourself what the FBI was doing on that street last night?"

"Yakunin had evidently been followed."

Privet hadn't known the man's name. He shook his head. "They were almost certainly there to watch the home of Albert Tyson."

Truskin was startled; it showed on his face.

"Watch him, Comrade *Rezident*, not protect him."

"I didn't know."

"No. But I would like to know why the man you have selected for me to kill is under investigation by his own government."

"You're telling me that Al Tyson is a spy for the Russians?" the President said. "My assistant national security adviser?"

"No, Mr. President, I'm not saying that," the director of the FBI said. "He is, however, seeing a woman who almost certainly is an agent for the Soviet government."

"Who is she?"

"The name she is using is Toni Wagner. But we believe that in reality she is Raya Nechiporenko, a very capable KGB field officer who surfaced briefly about four years ago in Paris as a runway model for an internationally famous designer. She was bedding the French minister of defense, but the man killed himself when he learned that he was being investigated, and Ms. Nechiporenko disappeared."

Wilder had been the attorney general of Arkansas when the Justice Department tapped him to become the assistant attorney general for the Criminal Division in Washington. Five years later, in 1985, he'd been appointed deputy director of the Bureau. A few months ago the director had stepped down, and Wilder had been elevated to the job of top cop.

He was a dapper man of fifty-two who always wore three-piece suits, winter or summer, and maintained the diffident manner of a southern gentleman who knew he never had to prove his own worth by patting his own back. With his pale blue eyes and graying hair he looked more like a banker than a policeman. But when Wilder spoke, even presidents listened. He was *never* wrong.

"Why don't you arrest her?" the President asked.

"Then we would learn nothing, sir. Who her KGB contacts are, and if indeed Mr. Tyson is guilty of anything but a sexual indiscretion."

"I hope you realize what you've done for my day," the President said, but before Wilder could comment he continued. "Does Al know that he's under investigation?"

"After last night it is a possibility."

"Go on."

"We've had a surveillance unit watching Mr. Tyson's house . . ."

"Why wasn't I told of this earlier?" the President demanded angrily.

Wilder didn't flinch. "Because I was not certain that Mr. Tyson had done anything illegal, as I have said, Mr. President."

"Are you certain now?"

"No, sir. But now the Russians have become directly involved. Two of our agents were shot and killed last night in front of Mr. Tyson's house. In addition, a KGB field officer by the name of Viktor Ivanovich Yakunin was found at the scene shot to death. My ballistics people tell me that one of my agents was killed by Yakunin's pistol. My other agent, however, and Yakunin himself were shot and killed by another weapon. Eyewitnesses place at least one other person at the scene, although so far we've not been able to get a firm identification."

"Albert Tyson?" the President asked. "Was he the fourth man?"

"No, sir, we do not believe so."

The President thought about what he'd been told for a long few seconds. He and Wilder were alone in the Oval Office. At Wilder's request the tape recorder in the President's desk had been switched off.

"I sincerely hope, Ed, that no one has approached the Russian Embassy with this."

"No, Mr. President. We have performed an autopsy on Yakunin's body, of course, but he is being held at the city morgue as a John Doe. The District Police became involved and they immediately asked for our help because of the presence of our two dead agents, and because of Yakunin's identification."

"Who was the fourth man, Ed?"

"Unknown, Mr. President. But we're now assuming a higher probability to Mr. Tyson's active role as an agent for the Russian government."

"Do you want to question him?"

"Not yet."

"What do you want me to do, Ed? Spell it out. With Bob Harms gone, Al is my chief national security adviser. If he's working for the Russians, it puts us all in an impossible situation."

"I understand, Mr. President. But I can offer you no advice, short of informing you what the Bureau suspects."

The President turned and looked through the bulletproof windows at a very gray morning. It had begun to snow.

"We've got our hands full at the moment. I need the steady hand of a trustworthy national security adviser. A man I always thought Tyson was. You're telling me that at the very least his judgment is suspect. On that basis I'm to make a decision."

"Yes, sir."

"What's the next step, Ed? How soon can you wrap this up and give me a definitive answer?"

"It could be months, even years, although after last night's shooting it's anyone's guess."

The President looked at his FBI director bleakly and shook his head. "Keep me posted, Ed. Day or night, no matter the outcome. And thanks for coming over this morning."

Wilder left for the ride back to the J. Edgar Hoover Building. He'd been in some form of law enforcement all of his life, and over the years he had developed certain instincts. This time his nose was telling him that Tyson was guilty as hell, but that something else was going on. The Russians were up to something. He was going to find out what.

Kaplin looked into the mirror he had mounted over the kitchen sink as Larissa Dolya appeared at the open doorway. "No time now, little one."

"Are you going to work already? It's barely six."

Kaplin laughed. "Already you're nagging like a good Russian wife."

"I just wondered."

"I have to meet my friend again, try to convince him to be truthful with me."

"The one who has that mistress you talked about?" Larissa asked. Kaplin was a gossip. He'd told her about Marina Demin's claim that she'd been Mukhin's mistress for ten years.

Kaplin got his coat and pulled it on. "The dumb bastard says he never rat-finks on a woman. They're too precious, he tells me. And he should know. He has had many of them."

"More than you?" Larissa teased.

"Ah, you have become like a wife," Kaplin said. He stopped a moment, his head cocked as if he were listening to something. "But he's worried about this computer thing. He doesn't want to tell me, and yet he's . . . desperate."

"What?"

"Nothing," Kaplin said. He came across the room, took her in a big bear hug, and roughly slapped her behind.

"Do you want me to wait up for you?" she asked.

"Sure," Kaplin said. "I'll show you just how precious I think you are."

Sweeney met Larissa Dolya in Gor'kiy Park across from the bandstand at seven. A very bad rock-and-roll group was playing something very loud and unintelligible. The park was busy.

"Mukhin thinks women are precious," Larissa said. "He's not the kind to kiss and tell."

"But he didn't deny her story," Sweeney said.

"Apparently not. But Anatoli was going to meet with him again tonight. He's going to try to persuade the man to fess up."

Sweeney thought about that for a moment. Lara had telephoned around six-thirty telling the embassy operator, in Russian, that she had meant to dial the Moscow Library, but had made a mistake. It was their signal that she wanted an immediate meeting.

"What does Kaplin think? Is Mukhin telling the truth? Is he protecting his reputation? Or could he and the girl be plants?"

Lara looked up at him and smiled wryly. "The permutations and combinations are endless, aren't they?"

"You can say that again."

"Anatoli thinks the man is on the level. At least at the mention of Marina Demin's name, Mukhin didn't run off into the night."

No one paid them any attention. They were just within the fringes of the crowd listening to the band.

"It hasn't spooked him?"

"Anatoli or Mukhin?"

"Either."

"Anatoli was worried at first, I think. He wasn't himself after you told him about this girl. But after he talked with

Mukhin he seemed to perk up a bit." Lara wrinkled up her nose. "I think he's concerned, but no longer worried."

Sweeney felt a little better, though there was still a lot that could go wrong. "Has Kaplin mentioned me?"

"Not a word," Larissa said. "Officially I don't even know what he does for a living, although he's told me that his work is silly but just now very necessary. We talk mostly about what I think about the *Rodina*. He's very much in love with Russia. But he thinks his country is still sick, and he'll do anything to help cure her."

"He's a patriot."

Lara nodded. "And you know what that kind is capable of doing."

"What about Mukhin? Any indications that he's been put off?"

"None that Anatoli has mentioned. But like I said, they're meeting again tonight. We'll see in the morning. Oh, and something else has apparently come up that's bothering Kaplin. Something about a computer that Mukhin either is or was involved with."

"He mentioned it the last time we met. Is he going to talk to Mukhin about that as well tonight?"

"I don't know. But he said that Mukhin was desperate."

Sweeney nodded. It was bothersome, but he couldn't put his finger on exactly the right questions to ask. "Find out what you can." Again he fell silent, the raucous music brittle on the cold night air. Maybe he was developing a conscience after all, as Kay had suggested. Maybe like Pool he was becoming a burnout victim. But the business did get in your blood. And it was necessary.

He looked up. "How about you?"

She shrugged. "I'm doing okay. My ex said I was like a cat. No matter how often the rug was pulled out from under me I'd end up on my feet." She smiled. "I'll get out one of these days. In the meantime I'd just as soon continue sticking it to the bastards. There's a lot of catching up to do."

A lot of Larissa's relatives had died in Soviet labor camps. They'd been a family of dissidents. She was like a Jew who had lost family in the Nazi death camps. She had a lot of hate stored up inside which supplied her with an immense amount of physical and mental energy.

Sweeney was back at the embassy before eight. Zuckerman, Rodgers, and the embassy's general counsel, Tony Havlachek, were standing by in the screened room on the fourth floor. Together they constituted the Agency's Product Risk and Evaluation Committee. They were the first line of defense against fraud beyond the actual agent handler, in this case Sweeney himself. It was up to them to make a preliminary determination as to whether their source was lying, and whether continuing contact with him constituted a greater risk than was warranted by the information he was giving them.

With Kaplin they were willing to take almost any risk, his product was potentially so valuable. Still they were cautious. They had to be. There were lives as well as governments at stake.

"To this point it seems as if the woman is on the level," Sweeney said.

"Mukhin confirmed her story?" Rodgers asked. He'd been intrigued by Marina Demin, he'd said, from the moment she'd called him a cocksucker. "If nothing else the girl's got moxie," he told them.

"Not directly, but he didn't deny her, which under the circumstances I would have expected him to do had she been lying."

"What exactly does that mean?" Zuckerman asked, leaning forward. Ever since Clark had come and gone he'd maintained a nearly permanent scowl.

"He apparently told Kaplin that he never told tales out of school. He's in love with his women. All of them."

"What?"

"He's an even bigger ladies' man than Kaplin."

"What next, Dick?" Rodgers asked. "I'd like the green light."

Rodgers wanted to mount an operation to look for Marina Demin. Sweeney had been holding him off.

"Kaplin is supposedly meeting again with Mukhin in an effort to get him to talk about the woman. Hopefully we'll know something tomorrow. In the meantime we're just going to have to hold on."

"What if she comes back in the meantime?" Havlachek asked. He was thinking about the legal ramifications of accepting the woman as a legitimate defector.

"We're not going to let her walk out on us, that's for sure," Rodgers said before Sweeney could speak.

"We'll have to play it by ear, but Roy is correct."

"What about Langley?" Zuckerman asked.

"I'm going to query my boss as soon as we're finished here."

"I mean what's their reaction been to this woman?"

"Pursue as planned with caution. Need more information."

"SOP," Rodgers said. "How is Lara holding up?"

"So far so good," Sweeney said. "But we're going to pull her out as soon as Kaplin is stabilized. Agreed?"

Zuckerman was the last to indicate his agreement. "We'll need to come up with another safeguard."

"We'll think of something, David."

"We'd better."

"In the meantime when do Kaplin and these others begin producing?" Havlachek asked.

"Soon," Sweeney said. "I've asked for a sample of a Defense Council transcript."

Havlachek whistled.

"August fourth?" Rodgers asked, and Sweeney nodded.

"Wait a moment," Zuckerman said. "Why August fourth?"

"Because we happen to know something of what went on at that meeting. But the Russians don't know that we know. It's been saved for a cross-check."

"How did we come up with that?" Zuckerman asked. "I heard nothing about it."

"The information didn't come from us. Someone in

Washington apparently came up with it, when the Russian minister of defense and his staff visited the Pentagon."

The data had become an intelligence benchmark, a rare and precious commodity. It was time now to use it. And spreading that bit of information just now would serve as an additional check for leaks within their own intelligence community.

"Okay, if there are no other questions, gentlemen? Thank you." Sweeney turned to Rodgers, whom he had elevated to temporary assistant chief of station. "Has the video gone out?"

"The acknowledge receipt came when you were out."

"That'll save on explanations when I talk to Adkins," Sweeney said.

"Yeah," Rodgers agreed. "Which will put him up to speed with Clark and his boss."

"We're still calling the shots, Roy."

"I wonder for how much longer?" Rodgers said.

"Probably not much," Zuckerman said at the door. "After all, the Russians are no longer our enemies, or hadn't you heard?"

Sweeney pursed his lips. "We and the Japanese were still smiling at each other when they bombed Pearl Harbor." '

"That's different."

"Is it?" Sweeney asked, and he sincerely wondered. Kay understood. She saw it in him every day. He was frightened.

Deputy Director of Operations Richard Adkins was standing by in Langley for Sweeney's call. It was nine in the morning in Moscow, and one in the afternoon in Washington. Sweeney sat in a secure room in the basement communications center. His telephone call was being encrypted by a National Security Agency KL-31, the signal bounced off a geosynchronous communications satellite above the pole. The crypto machine broke the human voice into two components—voice (which was tonal) and unvoice (which was mostly sibilant)—and transformed them into a digital form, which was in turn mixed with random digital hits generated by a complex circuit that followed the mathematical chain of the Italian Leonardo Fibonacci. The signals were virtually unbreakable by an eavesdropper.

"We have a partial confirmation of the woman's story," Sweeney told his boss.

"That's good, Richard, very good. When do you expect to have it nailed down?"

"Hopefully by tomorrow. But, Dick, there's the chance we won't know for sure until it turns around and bites us in the ass. You saw the tape, I presume."

"Yes, I did."

"Then you caught the woman's statement about knowing someone in the States."

"Yes, we did. But there's absolutely no record of her ever being here, nor can we find anything that would indicate a relationship between her and one of our people in the Soviet Union—or anywhere else, for that matter. What's Mukhin saying?"

"He's not denying her. But he may be playing it coy for some reason. In the meantime I'd like to be ready for her if and when she comes back."

"What have you got in mind?"

"Rodgers wants to go after her."

The encrypted line was silent for several beats. "It'd be helpful if we had background on her. Go ahead."

"Yes, sir. In the meantime Kaplin is working on our test case."

"Good," Adkins said. "The consensus here is that you're doing a damned fine job."

"Thanks, but I still want a replacement. It's time for Kay and me to come home for a while."

"Patience. We're working on it. Meanwhile we have something else for you. One hell of a coincidence, as a matter of fact. Your Mikhail Mukhin is an assistant foreign affairs adviser to the President."

"Yes?"

"Well, watch your step out there, Richard. We've just

learned that our assistant national security adviser is at the very least in bed with a known Russian agent."

"Tyson?"

"One and the same," Adkins said. "Roland Clark's boss, who now knows all there is to know about MOHAWK."

"Except for Larissa's exact role," Sweeney said. The news hit him hard.

"She may be our only advantage until Tyson is cut out of the picture, if he's guilty."

"Is there any doubt?"

"There's always doubt in this business."

"What about the President . . . ?"

"He's not going to do a thing for the moment. Not until the Bureau can come up with the proof."

"Anything we can or should be doing from this end?"

"See if Kaplin has ever heard of a KGB operative named Raya Nechiporenko. I've sent what little we got from the Bureau over to you."

"I'll see what we can do, Dick, but in the meantime you can check on something for me. Kaplin has mentioned something about a computer hacker going after Finance Directorate records. He told Larissa that Mukhin is somehow involved and that the man is desperate. His words."

"Finance is a sensitive area for them," Adkins said. "What else?"

"So sensitive that there wouldn't even be any rumors floating around the Lubyanka unless the information is coming back to the KGB from the outside. Such as a spy . . . one of ours . . . inside the directorate."

"Not us," Adkins said flatly. "I'll put Bob Drury on it, see what we can come up with. In the meantime keep your head down, Richard."

"Will do," Sweeney said.

Marina Demin and her lover, Ivan Kiselev, returned to the city from the major's tiny dacha (actually a two-room shack that had once been used as a hunting cabin) on the Istra River that night a little before midnight. They'd not been able to spend much time there lately because of Marina's assignment and Kiselev's work load. But they both loved the place for what Kiselev called "its splendid isolation."

"They'll be checking your background now," Kiselev said. "Of course they won't get far, but they'll want more."

"What about Mukhin?"

"He's being isolated. Believe me, Marinka, you have nothing to worry about with that one. He knows nothing. Your story is safe."

"Who is watching him?"

"One of our analysts. A good man, I'm told."

Marina had always been a day person. Bright sun and openness were what she craved. These days, however, she relished the darkness of night for what it could hide. Herself included.

"Once I'm inside, assuming I get that far, there won't be any easy way out for me."

"Just concentrate on that much. A step at a time, it's all I'm asking of you."

Marina looked at him. She was in love, but she was deeply frightened. None of this could possibly turn out well.

"I'll be right behind you," Kiselev said. "Look over your shoulder—I promise I will be there."

"When do I pay the embassy a second visit?"

"Monday, I think. I will get word to you."

She'd caught something in his voice. What? Worry? Concern? Even doubt? "What is it, Ivan?"

"What do you mean?"

"Is something the matter?"

"No," Kiselev said, looking her in the eye. "Everything is going exactly according to plan." He smiled and shook his head. "In any event there is nothing for you to worry your head about. Do you think that I would send you into a situation that I knew was dangerous?"

"No," she said after a slight hesitation, but she wondered.

Kiselev glanced at the road and then back at her. "No," he said. "Unless there was no other way, and your assignment was desperately important for the *Rodina*."

"Is it?"

"I can't tell you. I can only say that I love you and that I wish no harm to come to you. Neither does the *Rodina* . . ."

"Don't say that anymore," she whispered, shrinking a little into herself. "Just don't say that again, Ivan. Please."

"As you wish," Kiselev said, his smile so slight as to be unnoticeable.

Tyson was being followed, or at least he thought he was. The problem in his mind, however, was that he didn't know who it was watching him.

After last night's incident on the street practically in front of his house, combined with the photographs Clark had returned with from Moscow, Tyson was convinced that the Russians were after him. But two of the dead men on the street were FBI. The other, according to his source at the Bureau, was a John Doe, possibly drug-related. Since Mayor Barry had fallen, there'd been an ongoing drug investigation into the connection between Washington and St. Thomas in the U.S. Virgin Islands.

Tyson had begun to believe, however, that his source had been lying to him. That the third body gunned down on the street was that of a Russian. And somehow the incident was connected with the photograph of Marina Demin.

The streets downtown were practically deserted this evening, which made what he was trying to do much easier.

He'd told Kit that he had work to do at the office to get ready for his Monday-morning briefing to the President. He drove to the White House, watching his rearview mirror. Twice he was certain he'd spotted a suspicious car behind him, but then it was gone, another in its place.

At his office he told the White House operator that he was working and was not to be disturbed under any circumstances. As soon as he hung up he headed for the door, but the phone rang. He hesitated for just a moment but then went back and picked it up. It was the operator again.

"I almost forgot, Mr. Tyson, there was a message for you."

"Yes?"

"Did Senator Durenberger contact you?"

"No. What did he want?"

"He called about the committee report you wanted. Said he had to get it to you immediately. That was last night. I gave him your home address. That was okay, wasn't it?"

Tyson was shook. "Ah, yes, I remember now. You did just fine."

"Yes, sir. Thank you, sir."

Tyson was having a little trouble catching his breath. He was expecting no committee report from Durenberger.

Outside, he got his car and drove directly to the Watergate, where he parked in a garage and then waited in the shadows for five minutes to see if anyone was coming after him. He and Toni had met here once.

When no one showed up, he went into the bar, had a drink, and then left by the parkway exit that faced the rear of the Lincoln Memorial. He knew he would be able to get a cab here.

So far as he could tell, he had not been followed to this point, yet when the cabbie asked him where he wanted to go, the address nearly died at the back of his throat.

"The Columbia Island Marina, please."

Charles Gleason had not been sleeping well lately, and it showed on his face. For most of his life he had prepared for a day such as the one coming, and although he had done good and valuable work for the Soviet Union, and now Russia, he'd hardly ever dared to believe the day would actually arrive. Now that it was here he was practically falling apart.

He sat in his office looking out his window toward the woods. In summer this was a pleasant spot. In some respects it reminded him of England: the countryside, the long walks, the stimulating discussions with his peers. The challenges.

All of it leading this way.

His secretary buzzed him and he picked up the phone. "The President is coming on the line for you, Dr. Gleason," she said.

9

LARISSA DOLYA HAD LIVED FOR ONLY TWO THINGS IN HER LIFE. The first was hatred for all things Russian—the language, the music, the people, and especially the government. She never ate blinis, caviar made · her physically ill, and borscht reminded her of what drunks did with their dinners after they'd had too much to drink.

The second thing she had lived for was love, or rather the thought that someday it would be okay to love all things Russian—the language, the music, the people, and especially the government.

The first was here, but the second was still a distant dream. "We can't eat ideals," the people of the street were crying, as the Union disintegrated.

Maybe Russians were not ready for freedom, after all. Traditionally, anything they were frightened of, they destroyed.

Waiting in the dark apartment above her own for Anatoli Kaplin to return, her hate-love kept her warm and awake.

* * *

"The question is *not* whether we use him, the question has become: Is he any longer usable?" Lydia Lubiako told Yuri Truskin. They held hands across the table at the Washington Hilton's main cocktail lounge. She was dressed in a large summer hat and bright yellow dress and matching coat, and she stood out like a neon sign.

"There were only four people here in Washington who knew what his assignment was. Yakunin is dead. Radchenko is frightened of him. I don't know the answers to his questions, which leaves . . ."

"Me," the horse-faced sister of the Russian deputy under-secretary said, squeezing Truskin's hand affectionately. She smiled warmly. "You're a fucking incompetent, and if the need-to-know list wasn't so small out of necessity, you would be fired."

Truskin forced a smile for the benefit of the pair of FBI watchdogs they'd picked up on the way over from the Russian Embassy. "If insulting me makes you feel better, then by all means continue. In the meantime we have a big problem here."

"Yes, one of control."

"How does one control an assassin? The man is absolutely fearless, I tell you."

"Not quite true, Yuri Fedorovich. Everyone has a point of weakness. Even Achilles had his."

"Shooting an arrow into this one's heel may not be enough, though he may have to be destroyed as you suggest."

"Oh, no," Lydia said. "Not that." She smiled and squeezed his hand again. "Now, escort me up to our room so that I can lose our friends."

"You mean to see him now, alone?"

"Yes, of course. I'll be two hours at the most. In the meantime you are not to leave the room or answer the door under any circumstances. Afterward we will both behave quite guiltily. Won't we?"

"Yes, of course," Truskin said.

* * *

Radchenko left the safe house when Lydia Lubiako showed up. The look on his face was one of genuine relief. Privet was almost sorry to see the man go; he'd been amusing in his own way with his almost constant anecdotes about life in America—as he called his little stories. But looking up at this woman, dressed in the uniform of a hotel maid, he could clearly see competence, and something else. Something he wasn't quite sure of. A certain self-assurance that seemed to go beyond mere professionalism. She knew something, he decided. She had some piece of information that she would use against him in an effort to assure his cooperation. Which was counterproductive, and almost silly except for the deadliness of his mission. All he wanted was knowledge. What exactly was his assignment, and what exactly were the difficulties in his path?

"Good evening, assassin," Lydia Lubiako said, taking off her drab brown coat and tossing it over a chair. She came the rest of the way into the living room, glanced at the television, and then went into the kitchen, where she poured a glass of wine from one of the bottles Privet had bought.

He watched her movements warily, as if he were an animal being circled but not quite certain yet if he was under attack.

She came back into the room and perched on the arm of the couch, her legs slightly spread so that Privet could see all the way up her skirt. She was a substantial woman, he thought, but not bad-looking.

"You have some questions, comrade, and so do I," Lydia Lubiako began. "Perhaps between us we will be able to come to a mutually satisfactory understanding."

"Have I been assigned to kill Albert Tyson?" Privet asked directly.

"Yes," she answered just as directly, her eyes never leaving his. "But not yet. Not until the word is given."

"Why the delay?"

"I do not know. My orders come from the Center."

"Are you aware that Tyson is under investigation by the FBI?"

"We are now, but so far we have been unable to determine why, although we suspect that his Russian controller may be under suspicion."

"Does that change the nature of my assignment?"

"Possibly, though I do not know. We still await word from Moscow. Will you cooperate with us?"

"I may. But I will not sacrifice my life or my freedom for this kill. Do you understand this?"

Lydia Lubiako nodded.

"Why is Tyson to be killed? He is a very important man. His death will certainly cause repercussions. A scenario could be developed in which I was sacrificed for the greater good of what's left of the *Rodina*."

"I cannot tell you."

"Cannot, or will not?" Privet asked sharply.

"Will not," Lydia Lubiako said evenly.

"I may leave."

"To go where?"

Privet looked at her for several long seconds. "Not home."

"Not anywhere without funds." She quoted a number which identified his Swiss bank account.

"I see," he said.

She quoted a second number which identified his secret account in Brussels. "Shall I continue?"

"Yes," Privet said. "Do."

She smiled. "I think it is not necessary, comrade. You understand my meaning."

"Perfectly," Privet replied, lowering his eyes in defeat. But he had won! She would have quoted his Channel Islands account number, his most important by far, if she'd known it. But she hadn't. Which meant he was free to do as he pleased. He had his way out. At the last moment, then, the decision would be his and his alone whether Tyson lived or died.

It was late, nearly 2:00 A.M., and Valentin Grigoriev was in a foul mood. He and his partner, Yevgeni Andreyev, had lost the woman they'd photographed entering the U.S. Embassy on Friday. Her name was Marina Serafimovna

Demin, she was twenty-nine, she'd been born in Leningrad and had attended Moscow University, where her trail all but stopped.

There was nothing else on her. Nothing in their files, nothing apparently in the files of the other KGB directorates they'd queried, and nothing in Militia files, except a record of a driving license application which listed an address in Lenin Hills. The babushka there vaguely remembered such a young woman, but the girl was long since gone.

Marina Demin's trail dead-ended there. Soon Colonel Vilkov would find out something was amiss and all hell would break loose.

Andreyev, who'd been gone since noon with a team to check the admittance records of every hospital in the city for the past five years, came in, his tie loose, his collar button undone, and a big coffee stain on the front of his shirt.

"I sincerely hoped that you would have had the good sense to go home and get some sleep," he said. "Which would have meant I could go home."

"What did you learn?"

"Our little Marinka is definitely a healthy girl, or else she goes to a voodoo doctor and not a real one. There was nothing."

"There can be no mistake?" Grigoriev demanded.

"None."

"She is here in the city. We saw her with our own eyes, we have photographs of her. And we know that she entered GUM after her visit to the embassy. So there must be a record of her somewhere. Someone must know about this skinny little girl. Someone must!"

It had been Grigoriev's decision not to follow the woman beyond GUM. In fact, he had gotten sloppy with his legwork and had managed to lose her. He wouldn't admit that, however, even to his own partner. Especially not now.

They stood in front of the big map of Moscow in the always busy operations room. A lot of surveillance operations came to a head around this time of night, because Russians loved to party late, and these days most KGB domestic operations were done under cover of darkness. If there were to be indiscretions, they often happened at night, and in the very early hours of the morning.

"Then we must find her, or it will be our necks," Andreyev said. "Nine ounces for sure."

Grigoriev stared at the map, the noises in the big room ebbing and flowing around him like the sounds of surf on a beach. Short of mounting an all-out effort to find her, which would alert everyone in Moscow to the KGB's illegal internal spying, he could not think of a way of salvaging what was rapidly becoming a career-busting situation.

Colonel Vilkov hated failure, but perhaps he admired honesty. "I am sorry to report that I have failed, Comrade Colonel," Grigoriev could hear himself reporting.

He shook his head. In Moscow they ring the bells often, but not for dinner. They'd ring the bells at his funeral, but only to mark the passing of a fool, not a hero.

One of the photo technicians from downstairs shuffled across the operations room and began pinning glossy eight-by-ten photographs on the "number one" board, which these days belonged to Richard Sweeney, who was one of the current suspects as chief of station for CIA activities in the Soviet Union. Pool had been definitely pegged, and there'd been no new incomings, which left Sweeney and his typically aggressive American wife as the new candidates.

The board was the exclusive territory of the current CIA chief. Any stray reports or photographs that were generated on a routine daily basis, anything at all, was pinned up for any department officer to look at. Over the years this system of disseminating information on their number one enemy had produced some amazing results. More than one COS had fallen by the wayside because of connections made here. One of them had been stupid enough to be caught buying icons from the black market. A chance photo had made a connection in the mind of a Department One officer whose brother worked in the Militia Illegal Transfer of Property Division.

Andreyev drifted over to the board and studied the photographs. "Gor'kiy Park," he said. "Sweeney's got himself a good looker."

Grigoriev was only half listening, but something of what Andreyev was saying suddenly registered, and he looked over. "What?"

"Sweeney. Looks as if he might have himself a little girl. But it's probably nothing more than perspective."

Grigoriev joined him at the board as the photo technician finished pinning up the last of a dozen photographs and left. The shots were all date and time stamped. The action they depicted had taken place earlier this evening, in Gor'kiy Park and the area, including Dobryninskiy 1.

The first couple of photographs showed Sweeney entering the park alone. In the next series he was apparently standing next to a slightly built good-looking blonde. But Andreyev was right; they might not have actually been together.

But in the next series the woman was seen leaving the park, Sweeney turned her way.

In the last photograph Sweeney was boarding a bus, while in the distance they could just make out the figure of someone entering a building. The tiny image stood out from the darker background because of the white jacket. The same color jacket the woman who'd stood next to Sweeney in the park had worn. And from the way his head was turned he could have been looking in her direction.

In a proprietary way? His girlfriend? Mistress? Or his contact? A spy, perhaps?

Grigoriev got a magnifying glass from the duty officer's desk and studied the last photograph. It was the same woman, he'd be willing to bet almost anything on it.

"It's her," he said, and his hand shook.

Andreyev was watching him with a blank expression on his face. "Who?"

"The woman with Sweeney."

Andreyev shrugged. "He's not our target . . ."

Grigoriev roughly pulled his partner aside. "We've lost Marina Demin. She's gone. And unless we do something quick, we might just get our Russian insurance." It was a

Stalinist-era euphemism for death: With "Russian insurance" nothing could touch you. You were safe at last.

"But it's not the same woman . . ."

"No, but if we can prove that this is Sweeney's mistress, or better yet, some cheap little spy working for him, maybe the colonel will overlook our one mistake."

Andreyev, understanding, finally brightened. "I would have never thought of it," he exclaimed.

"No," Grigoriev said dryly. "Get your pistol, we're going quail hunting."

"But . . . we have no orders."

Grigoriev took his partner by the arm. "In the new order, Yevgeni Vladimirovich, initiative will be the watchword of the advancing officer."

They stopped by the weapons locker, where they signed for their pistols, then retrieved their car from the parking lot across the street and drove south across the river. Contrary to popular belief in the West (and episodes of *Spy Smasher* on Russian television), KGB officers normally did not go around armed. They carried weapons only on special assignments. In the morning they'd have to write a detailed report as to exactly why they'd checked out their pistols, but by then Grigoriev was confident that he would have something very positive to report. Andreyev, although somewhat worried about how all of this would turn out, was a follower, content to take Grigoriev's lead for the moment.

The temperature had dropped and it was extremely cold; manhole covers all over Moscow were steaming, and smoke from chimneys rose straight up.

They parked a half block from the apartment building in the photographs and sat for ten minutes watching; the engine was running but the heater did little against the bone-numbing cold.

There was little or no traffic in this part of the city at this hour. Gor'kiy Park had closed earlier and everyone had gone home. In the distance they could hear the siren of an ambulance, the sound crisp on the subzero air.

The apartment building was old, prerevolutionary; constructed of yellow brick, it seemed to sag into the street like all the other buildings in the block, though it was the tallest. The only light showing came from a window on the top floor. Grigoriev's eyes were drawn to it, the only apparent life in a dead neighborhood, and he shivered.

"I agree," Andreyev said. "Let's go inside before we freeze to death out here."

A shadow passed behind the curtains, then came back. Grigoriev didn't move.

"What is it?" Andreyev asked.

For several seconds whoever was in the top room remained standing at the window. Probably looking down at the street, at the car, Grigoriev figured. Sweeney's girl? It certainly was possible.

The shadow moved away from the window finally, and after another second or two Grigoriev let out the breath he'd been holding.

"Let's go," he said. "Top floor." He switched off the engine and got out of the car.

Andreyev was right behind him as they entered the building, softly closing the door behind them. The corridor was mostly in darkness, the only light filtering down from somewhere above. But it was reasonably warm and Grigoriev's nose immediately began to run.

He cocked an ear to listen as he took out his handkerchief but there were no sounds. Except for the shadow on the top floor, everyone in the building was apparently asleep.

Dabbing at his nose, he started carefully up the stairs, his step light. At the first landing he and Andreyev stopped again to listen. Still there were no sounds from above, although the light was stronger now.

At the next landing Grigoriev could see up the last flight to the top floor. The apartment door up there was open, the light spilling out and down the stairs. A shadow passed in front of the light and Grigoriev ducked back out of sight as a woman dressed in slacks and a bulky sweater appeared in the doorway.

It was her! The woman in the photographs with Sweeney!

"Anatoli?" Lara called softly. "Are you playing games with me now?"

Who the hell was Anatoli? Grigoriev wondered. Unless it was the name Sweeney used when he was with her. A false identity. Or perhaps it was a code name. His gut was tight. This could be the stroke of luck they needed.

"Anatoli?" Lara called again, less certainly this time.

"*Da,*" Grigoriev grunted, and he started up the stairs.

There was a sudden swift movement in the apartment above, and the light went out, plunging the stairwell into darkness.

"*Stoi!*" Grigoriev shouted, bolting up the stairs, any need for trickery or stealth gone.

Something that sounded like cloth tearing was followed by breaking glass, and a blast of icy air hit him as he reached the top landing and burst into the apartment.

Lara was breaking the rest of the glass out of the window with her elbow, and she started to climb through, when Grigoriev crossed the tiny room in two giant strides and took her by the waist, pulling her back inside.

Lara screeched something and turned on Grigoriev, biting, kicking, and trying to gouge out his eyes with her fingernails.

Andreyev had to help, yet between the two of them it took a full minute to get her subdued, up against the wall, Grigoriev pressing his much greater bulk against her slight body.

"The light," Grigoriev said, and Andreyev switched it on.

Lara's face was screwed up in a grimace, her eyes narrowed, her cheeks and forehead flushed and splotchy. "What is this? Are you rapists?" she cried.

"I am KGB Lieutenant Valentin Grigoriev, and I am placing you under arrest at this time."

"On what charge?" Lara spat the words. "What are you, fools? You'll never get away with it."

Grigoriev had to smile, though his heart was hammering. "First we are rapists and now fools," he said. "But you are a traitor and very soon we will find out all there is to know about this little nest of spies. Who knows, maybe it will turn out to be a love nest as well."

The telephone roused Sweeney out of a deep sleep. He picked it up on the third ring as Kay switched on the light beside the bed.

"Yes?" he mumbled groggily.

"Krasnya." The caller spoke the single Russian word for "red" and then hung up.

Completely awake suddenly—the caller had been Kaplin and the single word meant life-threatening trouble with the network—Sweeney pushed the covers aside and got out of bed.

Kay was wide awake too. She looked up at him. "Who was it, Dick?"

Madman. He mouthed the word for one of the sources he was running. Out loud he said, "I don't know. Sounded like some nut."

She nodded her understanding. "Well, come back to bed, then," she said, getting up.

"I'm going to get something to eat first."

"Hang on, I'll fix it for you."

Together they went into the tiny study, where Kelly Pool had broken the news of his transfer. It was the only room in the apartment at the moment that they knew was clean.

"Is this the big one?" Kay asked.

"It sounded like it," Sweeney said, picking up his secure in-house phone, which connected him with the communications center downstairs. Living in the embassy had certain advantages. "You'd better put on the coffee."

"Right," Kay said, and she left.

The duty officer came on. "Taylor."

"This is Sweeney. I want a flash to Adkins. Message as follows: 'Red light on MOHAWK. Investigating.' As soon as that goes out, get the committee together in the screened room. But I'll want to see Rodgers up here first."

"Yes, sir," a very impressed OD said. He did not know what MOHAWK was, but he understood the flash designator, which could mean anything, up to and including "War is imminent."

In four and a half hours it would be eight in the morning. Grigoriev figured they had that long to get something from their prisoner before Colonel Vilkov and his staff came on duty, and professional interrogators were called in. There would be questions for which Grigoriev had no answers, so he wanted to present Vilkov with something else to think about. Something to help him forget the mistakes they'd made.

They had put her in one of the second-floor interrogation rooms at the Warehouse a half kilometer from the U.S. Embassy. Grigoriev had patted her down before they'd taken her from the apartment, and he was reasonably sure she'd had no weapons. Nothing with which to do them or herself any harm. But before they proceeded too far she would have to be properly searched. It was a task he was looking forward to personally overseeing.

She'd come on tough, but she appeared to be very young, and he'd seen vulnerability in her eyes. Over the next few hours, with Andreyev's help, he would capitalize on this.

No one had said a thing to them when they'd brought her back, though interrogations were rare these days. Just a year ago it had been different; then, at any given time, there were usually a half dozen or more suspects in-house for questioning. It had been routine.

They'd found nothing in the top-floor apartment, not even her clothing. Not the white jacket she'd worn in Gor'kiy Park. But it had only taken them a few minutes to find that she lived downstairs. And another ten minutes to wake up and intimidate the old babushka to learn that the top-floor apartment belonged to a tall, skinny man whose name she could not recall, but that it had been occupied just lately by the Antichrist. The devil incarnate. And she'd actually crossed herself, but wouldn't or couldn't tell them anything else.

Neither description fit Sweeney, so it was someone else.

Another in the nest of spies. A cutout, perhaps. That, too, they would find out tonight.

Grigoriev took off his pistol and holster and gave them to Andreyev. "Take these back to the weapons locker, then sign for a Polaroid camera and a box of film and bring them back here to the interrogation room."

"What are you going to do?"

Grigoriev grinned. "Interrogate our prisoner."

"To begin with I need to know only three things about you, little girl, and you need to know only one thing about me," Grigoriev said to Larissa Dolya.

Andreyev was seated in a metal chair in the corner, the camera in his lap. Larissa, who stood at the barred window, looked over at him nervously, and she licked her lips.

"First me," Grigoriev said. He'd taken off his jacket, and he'd rolled up his shirt sleeves to display his beefy, hairy forearms. He raised his hands out in front to show her. "I am a man who makes mistakes from time to time. Who knows, perhaps tonight I will fuck up and snap your neck. It is possible. It has happened before."

Larissa said nothing, but she watched him warily.

"Now you," he said. "I must know your name, I must know the identity of this Anatoli whom you called for, and I must know the precise nature of your relationship with this man."

Still Lara maintained her silence.

"Yevgeni," Grigoriev said, and Andreyev stood up, cocked the camera's shutter, and aimed it toward Larissa.

"What is this?" she demanded.

"Take off your clothes. We must conduct a proper search for weapons."

"Fuck you," Lara said, and she backed up as Grigoriev walked over to her.

He backhanded her in the face, slamming her head back against the wall. "Take off your clothes."

Andreyev adjusted the camera's focus.

Lara hesitated, and Grigoriev hit her again

"My name is . . ."

Grigoriev hit her. "Too late. First we must search you."

"But you said . . ."

Grigoriev hit her again, blood trickling down her chin. "Take off your clothes."

Her eyes were wide more with fright than hate. Grigoriev raised his right hand as if to hit her, when she stepped aside and suddenly pulled the bulky knit sweater over her head. She was nude, her breasts were very small. Andreyev took a photograph of her, the flash bright in the room, and he took another picture as she undid the top button of her slacks.

Sex would not bother her, but pain would. Grigoriev had her key. Scratch a Russian and you found a peasant. Plain and simple.

10

"WHAT DO WE DO NOW, KELLY?" RICHARD ADKINS ASKED.

Pool, who had a home in the Washington area, had agreed to cut his leave short and come back to Langley for an early debriefing. He and Morris Segal, the CIA's general counsel, sat across from the deputy director of operations.

"I warned that something like this might happen, and now that it has you're going to have to make some very tough decisions. The KGB won't handle her with kid gloves."

Adkins shot a look at Segal and nodded. "We know that, Kelly. What would you recommend at this point?"

"She's an American, but you have to balance that against the fact that Kaplin is a gold seam . . . a platinum seam. Which means he has to be protected."

"I agree," Segal said ponderously. He was a heavy-set man, and when he spoke, his words sounded fat.

"Let him finish, Morris," Adkins interrupted.

"She and Kaplin can tag Sweeney, of course, so the entire Moscow operation could fall apart."

"If they kicked Sweeney out, we'd dismantle their operation here," Segal said. "It's happened before, and by God it'll happen again and they know it."

"We have MOHAWK to consider," Adkins said.

"If she identifies Kaplin, everything will be lost," Pool said. "As much as I hate to say it, in this case we have no other choice but to get Kaplin and the others in the network out immediately. At all costs. Here at least they could give us something."

Segal was shaking his massive head. "Favoring traitors over Americans."

"It's never been pleasant, those decisions," Adkins said. "I'll have to get authorization upstairs."

"Is the General still here?" Pool asked.

"Yes. He wanted to see me as soon as we finished," Adkins said, getting to his feet. "Stick around, would you Kelly?"

"Sure thing," Pool said, following the DDO and Segal to the outer office. "I'll just get a bite to eat."

"Do that," Adkins said. "I won't be long."

Ever since Special Agents John Fay and Terry White had been gunned down in Georgetown, questions had been flying in the Bureau. The need-to-know list on the Tyson investigation was very small, and so far no direct connection had been made linking him to the shootings, but the word had spread that something was up. Something big, maybe even as big as Watergate.

Those who were in the know had convinced themselves that Tyson was guilty as hell. At best he was sleeping with a Russian agent. At worst he was working for them himself. The moment Special Agent Charles Goode and his partner, Tom Parker, had lost the assistant national security adviser in the Watergate, they had driven directly over to the Columbia Island Marina, beating Tyson by a full fifteen minutes. It wasn't exactly SOP, they realized, because in those fifteen minutes Tyson could have gone anywhere, seen almost anyone, but it saved time.

"Actually I wouldn't mind getting a bit of that poon

myself," Parker drawled. He was from Birmingham, Alabama, and still spoke with a thick accent, and still called sex by a whole series of boyish terms, among them "poon," short for "poontang."

"You wouldn't know what to do with it if it was staring you in the face, you dumb bastard," Goode replied. Goode had been born and raised in the Bronx. He'd begun his law enforcement career as a New York City cop. He'd never lost his streetwise toughness.

They were parked in their van behind and above the marina office from where they had a reasonably clear sight line down to the woman's houseboat. It was snowing too hard, however, for them to be able to see much, though they would be able to spot Tyson leaving.

"I say we go in and bust the bastard right now," Parker said. He was watching the houseboat through binoculars. "Catch him with his pants down and he's likely to sing."

"You'd look good in Leavenworth dungarees, now that you mention it."

"For what?" Parker asked, looking up.

"Hassling a presidential adviser."

"The sonofabitch is guilty as hell, Charlie, and you know it."

"That's what we're here for."

"Don't shit me. You and I both know we're here because somebody upstairs is scared to make a move. We're going to have to catch him literally turning over secrets."

"That's right," Goode said. "And if the man is guilty, he'll be caught. In the meantime our job is to trail the sonofabitch, and that's exactly what we'll do. No more, no less."

Parker carried a Smith & Wesson specially built nine-millimeter automatic. Since the shooting in Georgetown he'd been loading custom-made exploding bullets that would blow a man apart. He was itching to use them.

"Are you going to stay here to watch me until it is time?" the assassin asked.

"No," Lydia Lubiako replied. She glanced at her wristwatch. It was eight-thirty already. "In fact, I am late now. But I wanted to make sure that you understood the situation here perfectly."

"I do," Privet said. He understood that Tyson was the object of some sort of plot by the KGB, and that an assassin had been sent to Washington to stand by in case something went wrong. The *primary* mission here, he decided, was not Tyson's death, but Tyson's cooperation with something. But the man was a very high-ranking government official who had the ear of the President. Manipulating him would be exceedingly dangerous. And, he suspected, this operation did not have the sanction of the Kremlin or the Russian Federation.

"I also wanted to make certain that you were comfortable here. That you had everything you needed."

Privet looked at her. During their two or three hours of conversation she had moved back and forth from the kitchen, where she had replenished her wineglass, to various perches around the room. Each time she'd sat down, she'd made sure that Privet got a good look up her skirt. She'd been trying to seduce him all this time, and he smiled inwardly.

He had nothing against sex, though he'd never sought it on a regular basis. His greatest moments of sexual fulfillment came at the time of a kill, but with this one he thought sex might be interesting.

She was one of the new power brokers out of Lubyanka. Sex for her would be a tool with which to control a recalcitrant but necessary man. She'd already demonstrated her need to control him by mentioning his bank accounts. Now she wanted to control his sexual emotions as well.

He had to suppress an outright laugh. What did she expect? That he would fall in love with her?

"I'm happy that you came," he said, going into the kitchen and pouring himself a glass of wine. "More wine?" he called out to her.

"It's not necessary," she said, coming to the doorway. "Would you like to make love to me?"

He smiled and drank his glass of wine straight down, then

put the glass on the counter. "Is that what you meant when you said you wanted to make sure I had everything I needed?"

Lydia Lubiako grinned, her broad *kulak* nostrils flaring. Her hips were wide. Made for bearing children. The salt of the Russian earth. Practically the *Rodina* herself.

"We must keep our important field officers happy," she said.

"And fulfilled?" Privet asked lightly.

She laughed out loud, her laugh surprisingly gentle and girlish. "Yes, that too."

"But I thought you were late."

"There is time," she said, starting to unbutton her maid's uniform. "And this is exciting for me. You're an assassin. Who knows, maybe you will hurt me. I wouldn't be able to cry out, of course, because you would kill me for sure. And perhaps the neighbors would hear something and call the police."

"I might be savage, and lose control," Privet said, playing her game.

She smiled, turning away and looking over her shoulder at him as she walked off.

He followed her into the bedroom, where she was stepping out of the dress. She tossed it aside, pulled the slip over her head, and then undid the clip of her bra, letting it fall away.

Privet took off his shirt so that his chest was bare, as Lydia Lubiako peeled off her pantyhose and then stepped out of her plain white panties. Her skin was white, and marked with red blotches where her bra straps had pressed. Her ass was broad. She stood with her back to him, her legs slightly spread so that he could see a tuft of pubic hair from behind. He didn't feel very much sexual excitement yet.

"Do you want me to turn around?" she asked. She stood next to the bed.

"No," Privet said softly. "Bend over."

"Please don't hurt me," she whispered.

"Bend over, you fucking *kollectiv* whore. You bitch. You fucking *kulak*."

She bent over the bed, supporting herself on her elbows, her legs spread a little wider. Privet was across the room to her in two steps and he slapped her on the ass with every gram of his strength, the noise sharp and loud like a pistol shot.

But she did not cry out.

He hit her again, her sturdy legs nearly buckling under his assault.

"Were you in Afghanistan?" Privet asked.

"Yes," she whimpered.

"Then for sure you fucked camels," he said, and he hit her even harder, the imprints of his blows raising red welts on her skin.

"Have you been to Africa?"

"Yes," she cried softly.

He hit her on the small of her back, just over her left kidney, her muffled cry not faked. He hit her again on the other side, then pushed her down on the bed and rolled her over on her back.

"Whore," he said, and he doubled up his fist and punched her in her left breast. "You let the black men fuck you."

"No," she squealed.

He bent down and slapped her hard across the mouth, then with his fist punched her other breast.

Her eyes were wide, and blood trickled from her mouth as Privet dropped his trousers and underwear and stepped out of them. He had a booming erection now, and he was on the verge of coming. He had thought about his last kill, how it had been.

"Now, suck my dick, bitch, if you want power. Get it from me. Good Russian cum."

As she rose to take him into her mouth she began to smile because she thought she had won. The way to a Russian's heart and soul is through cruelty. The more unbelievable the better. The czars had discovered it, as had Stalin after them. But it was something the peasants always knew. And Lydia Lubiako was a peasant . . . the very core of Russia.

*   *   *

It was just coming up on five in the morning in Moscow, but Grigoriev was no longer tired; in fact, he was humming, fairly bursting with energy and goodwill. He could sense that even Andreyev, seated behind him, could feel it as well. The little girl was on the verge of breaking.

"You see, Lara, I would like to use drugs on you," Grigoriev told Larissa Dolya. "But that requires the presence of a medical doctor. One is not available, so . . . we must use other methods."

"I have told you everything," Larissa said weakly through cracked, swollen lips. Her slender body was a mass of red welts and bruises. But she bruised easily. Hell, a man barely touched her and she turned black and blue.

Her breasts were much too small, in Grigoriev's estimation, and now the nipples had turned inward, as if they'd been amputated, leaving two narrow slits behind. It wasn't such a bad idea, he told himself.

They'd moved to a basement interrogation chamber, which was equipped with only a single metal chair. A caged light illuminated the stark concrete cubicle. The floor sloped toward the rear where a trough led to a drain hole. A length of black hose was connected to a spigot.

Larissa stood in the middle of the small room, no longer trying to cover her breasts or her pubis with her hands. She only wanted to sit down, but the floor was wet and the big one wouldn't allow her to use the chair.

She'd given them her name, but she would only admit that a man named Anatoli was her lover. She told them that she didn't know his last name, nor did she care about it. Nor did she know who exactly he was. Or where he was at the moment.

But they had not asked her about Sweeney. Nor had they even hinted that they might suspect she was an American, and not a Russian citizen. There was still hope, though not much.

"I think that you have told me nothing of importance. Such as Anatoli's last name and where he works. You know these

, and of course, you will tell me. In the end it will
pen." Grigoriev grinned. "Unless of course I make a
mistake and kill you. But I will try not to do that."

"I don't know . . ."

"Yes, you do," Grigoriev said. He nodded for Andreyev,
who came forward to the water spigot.

Larissa looked nervously over at him. "I've told you
everything that I know. I swear it."

"On the Bible?" Grigoriev asked. He picked up the hose,
a few drops of water dribbling from the end. "Who is this
Anatoli? Let's begin with that. His last name, for starters."

"I don't know."

"Over the chair," Grigoriev ordered, stepping forward.

Larissa tried to back away, but he caught her arm and
forced her to the chair.

"Bend over, spread your legs, and hold on tightly. This
will hurt."

Grigoriev twisted her arm so suddenly and so viciously he
nearly dislocated it at the shoulder. She cried out in pain.

"Bend over!"

Slowly she did as she was told, and with the toe of his shoe
Grigoriev spread her legs farther apart. She did have a sweet
little ass, he told himself.

"Why are you doing this?" Larissa asked, when Grigoriev
grabbed her by her narrow waist so that she could not pull
away, jammed the hose eight or ten centimeters up her anus,
and nodded for Andreyev, who twisted the cold water spigot
on full.

Larissa reared up violently as the hose entered her body,
but Grigoriev was far too strong for her. An instant later,
when the stream of icy water slammed up into her bowel, an
inhuman scream was torn from her throat. The muscles in her
legs and along her flanks stood out sharply, and her back
arched so violently she was on the verge of doing herself real
harm.

Andreyev shut off the water, and in one smooth, practiced
motion, Grigoriev yanked the hose from Larissa's body,
released his grip on her, and stepped aside.

She lurched forward with a huge sob, as a stream of water and shit and blood spurted from her anus, and she collapsed in a heap on the floor, her legs jerking spasmodically.

"His name, little girl," Grigoriev cooed, careful not to foul his shoes in the mess.

"Kaplin," Larissa muttered, out of breath. "He is . . . one of . . . you."

Grigoriev clapped his hands in triumph. "Get someone in here to clean her up. And fetch a cup of tea, Yevgeni. We have much ground to cover this morning."

One of us? he wondered. He didn't know where they were going, but he knew they'd won.

Tyson spotted the cab's lights as it came through the gate above the marina office, and he turned away from the window. "My taxi is here."

"I don't like to see you go like this, Albert," Toni Wagner said with concern. She'd been almost withdrawn all evening, and it bothered him.

"Everyone has their demons sometimes," he said, pulling on his coat.

"Maybe we shouldn't see each other for a while."

"Don't say that," Tyson snapped, his stomach lurching. "Christ, don't I have enough trouble as it is?"

"Well, at least not here."

"Where?"

Toni shrugged. "I don't know, I'll think of something." She came over and straightened his coat collar. "In the meantime try to calm down. Get some rest, you know."

"Will you call me?"

"I'll, leave a message for you."

"The usual place?" he asked. In the beginning they had played a little game—a spy game, she'd called it—with chalk marks on a section of the metal fence in front of the White House. She'd given him three telephone numbers to memorize, one of them here at the houseboat, and two others for places he didn't know. One chalk mark meant call the first number. An X meant call the second. And a smiling face meant call number three. He was to use a pay phone.

"Sure," she said. "Where'd you leave your car?"

"The Watergate. Downstairs."

Something passed her eyes, but then was gone. "Do you think your wife has hired detectives to follow you?"

The question startled him. The thought had never entered his mind. But he nodded. "That's possible," he said. "It's probably that."

"Then from the Watergate you've nothing to hide."

He nodded again.

Toni kissed him on the lips, her tongue darting inside his mouth, which never ceased to give him a little thrill. "Go home, Albert. Get some rest."

"That's probably a good idea," he said, his hands running over her ass. "But I'd rather stay."

"I know," she said. "But your cab is here. Go before I lose control."

Grigoriev stared at the photograph of the man with wild hair and even wilder beard, in utter disbelief. Larissa Dolya had described her lover, but he'd thought she was exaggerating. Perhaps the man had worn a disguise. But if anything, she'd downplayed his radical appearance.

"Wait until you read his service summary," Andreyev said behind him.

Grigoriev turned the photograph over. It was stamped on the back, "Personnel Directorate," and identified the man as Anatoli Stepanovich Kaplin, KGB Captain, Analyst, First Chief Directorate, Planning and Analysis.

This was the department within the Chief Directorate that supposedly reviewed past operations to weed out the mistakes so that they would never happen again. In actuality only aging officers or troublemakers too important to fire were sent to that department. And by the looks of Kaplin, he was definitely a troublemaker.

Andreyev had a cousin who worked the overnight desk at

the Lubyanka, which is the only reason he was able to come up with anything from Kaplin's file.

"He's one of their top men," Andreyev said.

"Has he any important family?" Grigoriev asked, thinking ahead. They were on the edge of something very big here, he could almost feel it.

"None," Andreyev said.

"No connections, no mentors, no one in the Kremlin, Yevgeni Vladimirovich?"

"Apparently not, although there is mention made of the Poets Union."

Grigoriev looked at him.

"The man has won awards for his poetry. But on the other hand there are three reprimands in his file. For dissident activities, of all things." Andreyev shook his head, thinking about a KGB officer involved in dissident activities.

"But he was not fired."

"No. As I said, he is considered the department's best analyst. And there's something else."

"Yes?" Grigoriev said patiently. It was seven in the morning already. In an hour Colonel Vilkov and his staff would arrive. He was no longer dreading that.

"Kaplin is a Jew."

Grigoriev's smile broadened and he began to laugh. "That's good . . . very good. Not let's go arrest him and see what the dissident poet has to say for himself."

The address listed in Kaplin's KGB summary file turned out to be a fashionable apartment off Kalinin Prospekt near Arbat Square and the House of Friendship, which everyone in the city knew was practically a den of foreign spies.

They first checked back at the apartment where they'd arrested Larissa Dolya, but Kaplin had not been there all night, though the babushka on the first floor identified him from the photograph.

Across town they parked around the corner from Kaplin's apartment. If the man was indeed a spy, which at this point looked reasonably certain, then he might be taking precautions. Maybe he was watching the street this morning. It was possible he'd found out that Larissa Dolya had been arrested.

They'd checked out their weapons again, and hurrying around the corner, Grigoriev felt beneath his coat for the reassuring bulk of it. They were going to take no chances with this one. Not only did Kaplin look wild, according to his file he was a very large man.

Kaplin's apartment was on the eleventh floor of a nice building, but not one so important it rated security guards. They were able to take the elevator up without having to explain themselves.

Andreyev stood to one side, his pistol drawn, as Grigoriev listened at the door. There were sounds from within. Perhaps a television, and something else, water running?

Andreyev shrugged his shoulders, and Grigoriev shook his head. Kaplin was evidently at home, and just as evidently he was not expecting trouble. Or he was very good, and was offering them a business-as-usual front.

Grigoriev knocked at the door, neither harshly nor timidly, but with just the right hint of authority, he thought. These things were important, especially if trouble was expected.

The door suddenly opened as Grigoriev was about to knock a second time, and filling the opening was an apparition with a huge beard that dripped water down the man's hairy— almost furry—chest. He was an animal. A bear. A gorilla. Not a human being.

"Well?" Kaplin boomed after several beats.

"Anatoli Stepanovich Kaplin?" Grigoriev asked, finding his voice.

Kaplin peered at Grigoriev, then leaned forward and looked at Andreyev standing with his pistol pointed up at the ceiling.

"Is this a robbery, or is that one hunting light bulbs?" Kaplin demanded, and he threw his head back and laughed out loud, all the way from deep within his gut.

"Are you Anatoli Kaplin?" Grigoriev repeated. This was going to be harder than he had thought it would be.

"Of course I am," Kaplin roared. "What do you want, you little pissant?"

"You are under arrest."

"By who?"

"I am Lieutenant Valentin Grigoriev, KGB . . ."

"Do you know who I am?" Kaplin shouted even louder.

"Yes," Grigoriev said. "I believe that you are a traitor . . ."

But it was a mistake. He'd not been positive enough, and Kaplin poked a finger roughly into his chest.

"You *believe* that I am a traitor? You little fucker! And you come here to try to arrest me?"

"If you will just get dressed and come with us."

"What if I don't? Are you going to shoot me right here?"

Grigoriev's knees were a little weak. But, shit, the girl had positively identified him, and so had the babushka at the Gor'kiy Park apartment building.

"We merely want to question you."

"Fuck you," Kaplin swore, and he started to step back and swing the door closed, when Andreyev stepped around the corner, pointed his pistol directly at Kaplin's face, and cocked the hammer.

"I've not qualified with this pistol in nearly a year, and I'm very nervous now," Andreyev squeaked.

It was just the right thing to say, because all the color left Kaplin's face, and he seemed to deflate in front of them.

"All right, you don't have to shoot."

Tyson pulled into his driveway and parked at the back of the house. As acting national security adviser to the President he rated a limousine and driver. But he only made use of that privilege when he was moving around the city in an official capacity.

He'd heard the criticism around Washington that he was the President's only "blue collar" adviser, but such comments didn't bother him; he took them as a compliment. He'd always had a "sense of the people," as he called his outlook.

Sitting in the dark car, listening to the engine tick as it

cooled down, and watching the snowflakes immediately begin to build on the windshield, he tried to reason out what was happening to him.

He had not been followed from Toni's. He was reasonably certain of that. And her suggestion that perhaps Kit had hired a private detective to watch him was making more sense the longer he thought about it.

It wasn't like her, but then these were extraordinary times, more so for her if she believed that her husband was being unfaithful to her.

In a way he wished it were that simple.

He was brought back to the shooting practically on his front doorstep yesterday. Coincidence? Not likely. But what did it mean? Russians here shooting it out with the FBI, or drug runners, as he was being told, cornered just here?

The problem was, of course, there was no one to talk to about all this. Not Toni. Not Kit. No friends, male or female. No advisers.

At this moment he sincerely wished that Joseph were here. That somehow they could all be back at Kent State in the halcyon days . . . at peace only in the sense that he knew where he was going, because the riots had already begun before he'd graduated. Joseph would know how to advise him. Joseph would know exactly what he should do.

And her. Little Marinka. He'd only slept with her a few times, but it had been such an experience that he'd carried the vivid memories with him his entire life. In fact, many of the sexual techniques—the caresses, the moves, the timing—that he used in his lovemaking with Kit had originated in Marinka's bed.

He sat forward slowly, burying his face in his hands, and he began to cry. Softly, without noise. He was frightened deeply, way into his soul, for the very first time in his life. He did not know what to do. He did not know where to turn. Nor did he know how it could be possible to extract himself from the mess he was in. Even worse, he had no idea how he could continue on his present course.

He could not go back, he could not go forward, and he could not remain where he was.

Also for the first time in his life, Tyson began to seriously think about the benefits of suicide.

Traffic in downtown Moscow was in full swing by the time Grigoriev climbed in the backseat with Kaplin, and Andreyev pulled away from the curb. Kaplin seemed immediately surprised at the direction they were taking and he turned to look out the rear window.

"Where are you taking me?" he demanded. "Not the Lubyanka."

"No," Grigoriev said. "Do you wish to go there, or Lefortovo? We are taking you to the Warehouse."

Kaplin looked at him. "You're Department One pricks, then." In the past, the department was the one most Soviet citizens had any contact with. It was hated.

"That's right. You have a problem with this?" Grigoriev asked, matching the larger man's disdain.

"You know that I am an officer of the State Security organ. I am very big . . ."

"Oh, yes, we know all about . . . your size," Grigoriev said, pleased with his little play on words. Larissa had told them a great deal about Kaplin's lovemaking. It had sparked an idea about how he could bring the man around quickly.

"I hold the rank of captain. My directorate chief will be very much interested in what has happened to me."

"Yes, I'm sure he will be. I expect that at your trial he will provide the court with much amusing testimony about your dissident activities."

"Maybe the Poets Union will read from his works," Andreyev said from the front seat, and Grigoriev chuckled.

The car turned off Vorovsky Street, and Andreyev parked behind the five-story Warehouse. Grigoriev got out first and held the door for Kaplin. Andreyev jumped out and led the way into the building and downstairs to the interrogation section.

"Just in here," Andreyev said, opening the door to one of

the large interrogation rooms, this one furnished with a steel table and a couple of chairs.

It was a quarter before eight. In fifteen minutes Colonel Vilkov would be here demanding an explanation. Grigoriev crossed his fingers behind his back.

"Oh, Tasha, I'm so sorry," Larissa Dolya cried out, and Kaplin reared back almost as if he'd been shot.

Andreyev stepped aside, and Grigoriev nudged Kaplin the rest of the way into the room.

"Have a seat, will you?" Grigoriev said pleasantly.

Larissa was seated at the table. Her face was animated with fear and sadness. And something else, Grigoriev thought, watching her closely. Was she trying to pass her lover a message? It was possible.

They had dressed her in cotton pants and a long-sleeved cotton shirt. Most of her bruises could not be seen.

Kaplin sat down across the table from her, and folded his hands calmly in front of him. He cocked his head. "Well, you're a pretty little thing, but I don't think we've met, though your face is very familiar."

"But I told them everything . . . about us," Larissa said.

There it was! Grigoriev was certain of it. She'd paused between *everything* and *about us*. She'd confessed to everything *about them*. What was it she had not told them about?

"We have plenty of time. We'll learn it all, believe me," Grigoriev said.

"I don't know what you're talking about," Kaplin said. "But unless you mean to shoot me, as you threatened to do at my apartment, then I will leave."

"If need be, we will shoot you, Anatoli Stepanovich . . . pardon me. Tasha. So I would suggest your heartfelt cooperation, and with luck we will be finished in time for you and Lara to have lunch together."

"What do I stand accused of?" Kaplin asked after a beat.

"Why, treason, of course," Grigoriev said.

"Bullshit!"

"No? Let me tell you that I have established a link between you and this little whore. She was waiting for you in your little Gor'kiy Park love nest. She even called your name. The grandmother identified your picture."

Kaplin lowered his eyes. "So I couldn't keep my pecker in my pants. So what? Even in Moscow that is not against the law."

"Even in Moscow?" Grigoriev asked sharply. But he didn't wait for an answer. "And we have established a link between your pecker bait and Richard Sweeney, the chief of station for American Central Intelligence Agency activities in Moscow. They were practically holding hands in Gor'kiy Park last night."

That got a reaction. Kaplin's lips pursed behind his bushy beard, and Larissa went pale.

"Do you deny that?" Grigoriev shouted.

"It's a lie, all of it is a lie," Larissa cried.

"What, that you fucked Comrade KGB Analyst Kaplin?"

"That I know this American," she retorted with surprising vigor, considering what she had already gone through this morning.

"We'll see," Grigoriev said. "I'll be back, and we'll see."

Outside in the corridor, Andreyev practically tripped over his own grin. "They're not going to get out of this one so easy."

"No," Grigoriev agreed. "Wait here, I'll go up and talk to the colonel."

"About what?" Andreyev asked, puzzled.

"About how far we may go with these two."

Lieutenant Colonel Boris Vilkov was a cruel-looking man, with a long, lean, aristocratic face and a broad scar that rose from high on his left cheekbone to split his eyebrow and disappear into his hairline. He'd been wounded in Afghanistan when the aircraft he'd been aboard had been shot down by a rebel hand-launched rocket. He called the mark his "dueling scar." Anyone who got to know him understood that such an explanation could easily have been as true as the Afghanistan story. Vilkov was a fighter, always had been. He gave no quarter, nor did he expect any. When the need arose, he could become extraordinarily savage.

He listened in silence to Grigoriev's report, his secretary seated to the side, taking notes.

"I felt that under the circumstances, Comrade Colonel, I would need authorization to continue my interrogation of the suspects."

"Under what circumstances?" Vilkov asked, his voice as soft as a light wind across a wheat field, and all the more menacing because of it.

"Anatoli Kaplin is a fellow KGB officer."

"Unless you are a traitor, he is no *fellow*. Do not concern yourself with his rank or status. Here that is of no importance."

"Yes, sir."

"Will you require the assistance of a medical doctor?"

"Only to stand by. I will not use drugs, at least not initially. I believe I have the key to breaking these suspects quickly, and without the risk of ruining their minds. I will, however, require the assistance of one or two additional officers."

"Draw what and who you need, Lieutenant. And you may use whatever means you deem necessary."

"Yes, Comrade Colonel," Grigoriev said. He saluted and turned to leave, when Vilkov called softly to him.

"Results."

Grigoriev's breath caught in his throat. "Yes, sir."

"And Lieutenant?"

"Sir?"

"You may drop your investigation of Marina Demin. I do not believe she is of any importance."

A Department One doctor and two field officers who'd just come on duty crowded into the interrogation room with Grigoriev and Andreyev.

Kaplin and Larissa looked up warily as they trooped in, but neither of them said a word, nor had they spoken while Grigoriev had been reporting to Vilkov.

Andreyev and the two field officers took up position behind and on either side of Kaplin.

"Take off your clothes, please," Grigoriev told Larissa. "The doctor would like to examine you."

Larissa glanced at Kaplin, who had stiffened slightly, but she said nothing as she got to her feet and pulled off her shirt.

Her body was bruised, already black and blue in some places, and her nipples were still inverted. A black, angry look had come over Kaplin's face, but he maintained his stony silence.

She slipped out of her pants and laid them over the chair. One of the field officers actually licked his lips. "Battered merchandise, but a nice piece anyway," he said in Kaplin's ear.

Kaplin did not respond.

The doctor listened to Larissa's heart and then her lungs. Pulling on a rubber glove, he turned her around, had her bend over, and did a brief, reasonably gentle rectal examination. His explorations obviously caused her pain. She cried out, and when the doctor removed his finger from her anus, the glove was bloody.

Still Kaplin said nothing.

The doctor took off the glove, tossed it in the wastepaper can, and donned another. "Squat," he told Larissa, and she complied, spreading her legs slightly, tears filling her eyes as the doctor did a quick vaginal exploration. When he withdrew his gloved fingers, they too came away bloody.

Removing that glove and throwing it away, he gently palpated Larissa's abdomen, again causing her to wince in pain.

When he finished, he turned away from her. "Some internal injuries as we suspected, but nothing life-threatening yet, though there is a risk of rupturing the bowel if you continue. Attendant risk of infection." He looked over at Larissa, who stood obediently next to her chair. "There may be some fairly extensive damage to her womb. Could mean she'd never have children. I'd have to do a more thorough pelvic first. But on the face of it, I'd recommend a hysterectomy when you're finished here. Just to be on the safe side."

It was monstrous. Even Grigoriev felt it for just an instant. But this was treason. She should have thought of the consequences before she'd started down that path. His own son, who was a homosexual, had AIDS. It was a cruel world. A man became bitter.

Grigoriev nodded. "Thank you, Comrade Doctor. If she is alive when we finish here, we will consider such corrective surgery."

"Why do you do this?" Kaplin asked after the doctor had left.

"Do you wish us to stop?"

Kaplin looked bleakly at him for a moment, then glanced at Larissa. "I have nothing to say."

"No?" Grigoriev said. "I didn't think so. You are a cocksman. A ladies' man. A real stud, as they say."

Kaplin said nothing.

"I want to know what little secrets you have passed to Larissa for relay to Sweeney. Basically a very simple question, which I will make even simpler. I will need only a yes or a no. Have you made such an arrangement with the Americans? Are you spying for the Americans? Have you passed secrets?"

Kaplin stared at Larissa.

"Very well, let's get a look at your manhood," Grigoriev said. "Take off your clothes."

"Fuck you," Kaplin said.

Andreyev calmly took out his pistol, cocked the hammer, and placed the muzzle against the back of Kaplin's head. "Nine ounces here for you. If you want it."

After a moment Kaplin got to his feet and began taking off his clothes. Larissa's tears were gone, but she breathed shallowly through her mouth as she watched.

When he was nude, Grigoriev whistled. "You are a hairy bastard. But you can tell you're a Jew boy. That is, if you look close. Not much of a stud after all."

One of the field officers shoved the table and chairs aside, and moved Larissa into a corner.

"On your back, on the floor, legs spread," Grigoriev said crisply.

Kaplin started to protest, when the two field officers grabbed his arms, and Andreyev jammed his pistol into the man's face.

Slowly, and with much venom in his eyes, Kaplin complied. Andreyev straddled him and sat down on his chest, pressing the pistol into the man's forehead.

The two field officers each took a leg, holding Kaplin firmly in place.

"Why do you do this?" Kaplin asked. "Does it give you pleasure, you little man?"

"Yes, it does," Grigoriev said, stepping between Kaplin's legs. The man's scrotum lay loosely on the concrete floor. Grigoriev reached out carefully with his right foot, catching Kaplin's testicles between the thick sole of his shoe and the floor.

Kaplin tried to pull away, but Andreyev and the field officers were ready for him, and Grigoriev began to step down, slowly increasing the pressure.

At first Kaplin tried to struggle away, but then a muffled, gargling sound escaped from his throat.

Grigoriev began to lean into it.

"Nooo!" Kaplin screamed.

Larissa turned away, her hands to her face.

Grigoriev increased the pressure, Kaplin's testicles flattening against the concrete.

Kaplin screamed again, the horrible sound totally unrecognizable as a word, or even as human.

Grigoriev increased the pressure, twisting the toe of his shoe as he bore down.

"You will cooperate with me," he said through clenched teeth. "You will."

11

"HE'LL BE ALL RIGHT," LYDIA LUBIAKO TOLD YURI TRUSKIN on the way back to the embassy. She'd returned to the hotel unobserved, and after she'd changed into her street clothes, they'd left together. They had picked up their FBI tail the moment they stepped outside. "How did he seem? Will he cooperate with us?"

"We talked about his two bank accounts."

"There could be others," Truskin said. "With a man like that you can never be certain. Radchenko is terrified of him, you know."

"Yes, I do know. But I don't think our friend will be wandering off. No. I think there is plenty of interest on his part."

"I'm happy for that much at least," Truskin said. "But I'll tell you that I will be relieved when this business is finished. Independent operations make me nervous. When they fall apart there is no safety net. You're on your own." He looked over at Lydia Lubiako. "And the fall would be a very long one. Everything in Moscow is changing. Too fast."

Lydia said nothing more the rest of the way back to the embassy, and inside, before she went to her quarters, Truskin stopped her.

"What happened to you over there?"

She smiled. "I'm just fine," she said.

"No," Truskin said. "I meant that you look happy."

She laughed. "Everything will be fine."

Nothing was going fine for Richard Sweeney. In fact, he was having one of the worst days of his life. It was after ten in the evening, and yet the day did not want to seem to end. One disaster had piled on top of another with no relief in sight. Kaplin had called with his emergency message, which, Rodgers had confirmed, concerned Larissa Dolya. She had disappeared. Presumably the KGB had picked her up; no other explanation sat right. Under almost any other circumstances she would have made contact with them, or at the least with Kaplin. And now Kaplin was gone. One of Rodgers' people had seen him leaving his building under the obvious escort of two men. Their car had been parked around the block, its license plates of a known KGB series, which clinched it in Sweeney's mind. Larissa had been arrested. She had been broken. She had named Kaplin. And Kaplin had been arrested. All in one bloody day!

"We must assume that she named you as well," Rodgers told him.

They were in the screened room. Sweeney passed him the message that had come in from Langley. "Adkins agrees. I'm to stay put until the situation stabilizes. Which hamstrings me."

Rodgers quickly read the message. "The general doesn't have to be at every battlefield as long as he knows the lay of the land and the situation."

"And has good troops, which I do," Sweeney said. "In the meantime our network is going down the drain before it hardly got a chance to get started. We're going to have to get word to those people somehow. And get them out if need be."

Rodgers nodded thoughtfully. "There's nothing we can do for Kaplin, but what about Larissa?"

"If we claim her as one of our own, she's lost. At the very least they'd dredge up one of her long-lost cousins or something and she'd collapse."

"Which has already happened," Rodgers gently reminded him.

"No, you don't understand, Roy, what it means to be a Russian . . . even a displaced Russian, or a second-generation Russian. Hell, there are still Russian Jews alive in Israel who escaped Stalin's pogroms and who pine for the *Rodina* to this day. For every ounce of hate Larissa Dolya has for Russia, she has an equal if not greater amount of love."

"Then what do we do?" Rodgers asked.

"The best we can," Sweeney said gently. "But you must understand that it may already be too late for her."

"But we've got to try."

"We'll try," Sweeney said. "We owe her, and the others, at least that much."

At forty, Grigoriev was a senior lieutenant, but only a lieutenant, a rank at which he would probably remain until his retirement too many dreary years ahead to think about. Unless he pulled off his own coup, which seemed less and less likely the further they got with this case. Kaplin lay at this hour unconscious in the Lefortovo Prison Hospital across town, and Larissa Dolya had dropped into a nearly catatonic state after witnessing the pain Kaplin had been subjected to.

The colonel had asked for results. So far all Grigoriev could offer him were the battered bodies of two people. Spies, to be sure, but useless at least for the moment.

The doctor had mentioned something about Kaplin's heart condition, which had been written in black and white in the man's service summary. But they had missed it. And they had nearly killed him.

The woman was bleeding internally, though so far her injuries were not life-threatening. But after a more thorough examination this afternoon, the doctor had told them that if they continued, or if they tried to use drugs on her at this time, she would be lost. Her mind would go blank, she would become a vegetable. Better to shoot her than have to support her for thirty years or more.

All they had, then, was the link between Kaplin and Larissa, and the tenuous link between her and Richard Sweeney. Tenuous because they had not firmly established that the two of them had actually met in Gor'kiy Park.

They damned well were meeting. She had passed some bit of information to the American. Something vital, but something brief.

A warning? Then why hadn't she run? Why had she waited for the KGB to show up? And why had Kaplin waited at his apartment? Why hadn't he disappeared?

That answer was simple, Grigoriev told himself on reflection. Because neither of them had known that Larissa had been linked by the KGB to Sweeney. Now they did, of course, which meant what?

Trying to make the connections, trying to run the thread out to its logical conclusion, was not easy because there were too many possibilities, some of them innocent, to be one hundred percent certain of any path.

But Grigoriev, like many intelligence officers before him, had a nose for the business. There definitely was a connection between Sweeney and Kaplin. But he did not believe it stopped there. No, for a man of Sweeney's stature (they did not promote idiots to chiefs of station, no matter the propaganda to the contrary) Kaplin would have been only one of many. Who knew how deeply into the Komitet the Americans had penetrated?

Of course it brought him back again to the girl. She was an unknown quantity, and that bothered him deeply. Kaplin was a KGB analyst. But why had Sweeney recruited Larissa Dolya? She was a nothing.

Then he had that as well. Kaplin was a ladies' man. A stud. A true cocksman. So Larissa was nothing more than bait. She was a whore whose price was probably something other than money. It left an interesting question as to exactly how she had been recruited.

Then Sweeney. There were others in his stable, no doubt. He was the ringmaster of a network of so far unknown persons.

Sweeney was his only target.

Sweeney would become the object of his investigations from this point on.

His wife, Lipa, came to the kitchen door, and he looked up from his glass of vodka. "Yevgeni is here to see you," she said softly.

Grigoriev smiled through his haze. "There's enough here. Tell him to come in."

"You don't understand. There has been a call. You must get dressed and go back. It is General Nedosorov."

Andreyev was waiting in the car for him. His hair was slicked back with pomade and he was freshly shaved. Grigoriev felt like an old bed sheet next to him.

"Colonel Vilkov himself called," Andreyev said.

"Lipa said it was the general." Nedosorov was the deputy in charge of the Second Chief Directorate.

"It is. He is waiting for us, along with Major Kiselev."

"That First Directorate bastard?" Grigoriev shouted so suddenly he practically swallowed his words. Kiselev was Colonel Vilkov's rival. It was he who'd sent the little pissant sergeant to spy on them.

"That's what he said. It has to be because of Kaplin. For all we know the fucker has died."

It was the most forceful Grigoriev had ever seen his partner, and he sat back morosely in his seat. It was only a matter of time now until the ax fell. And fall it would, he had little doubt of it.

Results, Colonel Vilkov had told him. The bottom line, as the Americans called it, had come to Russia.

A big Chaika limousine was parked at the rear of the Warehouse. Andreyev parked in the shadows well away from it, and they went upstairs to the operations room, where Colonel Vilkov's secretary had put out the word that they were to report immediately to General Nedosorov. It was late, but everyone looked crisp. It all served to deepen Grigoriev's sour mood.

The general's primary office was downtown at the Lubyanka, but in addition he maintained a secondary office here at the Warehouse. For all Grigoriev knew, the man had offices in dozens of spots around Moscow.

He and Andreyev got off the elevator on the fifth floor, where they were patted down by a couple of pricks from the general's staff before they were shown into a palatial office which looked out across the city toward the U.S. Embassy on Tchaikovsky Street. From here, Grigoriev had the fleeting thought, a man could make grand decisions.

The general was dressed in floppy old iron-gray trousers and a paint-spattered, disreputable sweater. Across the desk from him, Colonel Vilkov in uniform was seated next to Major Kiselev, also in uniform. Both of them looked as if they had just stepped out of an Army recruiting film.

"No need to formally report," General Nedosorov said genially. "Tell me what conclusions you have drawn from your excellent interrogation of the two prisoners."

Grigoriev could hardly believe his ears. But then the general was merely putting them at ease. Give the idiots enough rope and they're likely to hang themselves. It had never been easy living in Russia. It wasn't any easier these days, especially not for a KGB officer.

"Comrade General, I believe that Richard Sweeney, whom we believe to be the CIA's new chief of station, has established a network of spies, among them Anatoli Kaplin. There are, I believe, others."

"What about the girl?"

"Kaplin is a ladies' man. I believe that Larissa Dolya works for Sweeney in the capacity of a . . . honey trap. She is a prostitute."

"We no longer have to worry about either of them, from what I understand."

"No, sir," Grigoriev said. It was the understatement of the year.

"And Sweeney has been isolated?"

"He and his wife remain within their embassy, which means, of course, that the Americans know we have broken their network."

"It is called MOHAWK," Kiselev said.

"What?" Grigoriev asked, confused. The bastard had interrupted the general. But the general didn't seem to mind. Nor did Colonel Vilkov. This was just a First Directorate major.

"This is most confidential, Lieutenant," General Nedosorov said. "Apparently the intelligence comes from a well-placed source in the United States, isn't that correct, Major?"

"Yes, sir, though I am not at liberty to make such a disclosure . . ."

The general held up his hand to stop Kiselev. "That's not necessary. What we're after here are the results. Cooperation between the directorates. These days we must stand together. I'm sure that General Ryazanov agrees."

"Wholeheartedly, Comrade General. But we have a conflict just now that will have to be resolved. Sweeney is part of an operation that we have been working to put in place for months. He must not be interfered with for the moment."

"Along with this woman," Colonel Vilkov said. "Marina Demin."

"Yes, she is the one," Kiselev said. He turned to Grigoriev. "I understand that it was you and your partner who watched her enter the American Embassy the other day, and that since then you've been trying to run her to ground."

Grigoriev looked to his colonel.

"Yes, we discussed her," Colonel Vilkov said. "I told Lieutenant Grigoriev just yesterday to drop his investigation of her. I thought she was of no importance. I couldn't have been further from the truth."

"It's just as well, Comrade Colonel. And we appreciate your cooperation."

"Yes," General Nedosorov said genially. "And of course we shall expect the *quid pro quo*."

"Naturally," Major Kiselev said. "Unfortunately at this

moment there isn't much else I can help you with, sir. MOHAWK is an American operation being run by Sweeney. From what our sources have gathered so far, the network consists of three or more well-placed individuals within our service, as well as at least one highly placed man in the Kremlin, and another man or men who are attempting to break into the KGB computer system."

General Nedosorov was taken aback. "Tremendous," he said. "Then the rumors we've been hearing . . . there may be some truth to them."

"Yes, sir. Our sources are working on gathering further information, but as I said, that line of investigation may interfere with our own delicate operation."

"But you will do what you can for us."

"Yes, naturally," Kiselev said.

The general turned back to Grigoriev. "Then your task is clear," he said. "You have two sources. Kaplin and the girl. From them you will have to make your investigation."

Marina Demin took the nine o'clock Metro train out of the Voykovskaya Station. The platform had been jammed and the train itself was packed to capacity, so that she had to stand all the way to the Barrikadnaya Station, where she got off. She trudged slowly across the platform and took the escalator up to street level.

It was extremely cold, and a wind had come up, biting in its Siberian intensity. Marina shivered as she pulled up the collar of her threadbare coat and hurried up toward Tchaikovsky Street past the Moscow Planetarium and Zoo. Traffic was heavy. Mondays the world over had the same quality, a frantic busyness after, likely as not, a drunken weekend.

Around the corner the wind finally was at her back for the last block, which made the going easier. Yet she couldn't shake the feeling that she was a condemned woman walking to the gallows.

"You will be my banner," Ivan had promised her. And she was, and intended going ahead with her mission. But it was difficult, even for love's sake.

The usual crowd of onlookers mixed with Militia was outside the U.S. Embassy. Marina approached cautiously, expecting to be stopped again to show her papers, but one of the Militiamen just glanced at her, then looked away as she passed and entered the building.

Had there been a hint of recognition? Or was her imagination working overtime again? Ivan had promised that help would come, sometimes in little, unexpected ways. Was this his doing?

Inside she went into the visa applications office, which was, as before, filled with people, and took a number before she sat down on one of the benches and undid her coat so that some warmth would seep into her bones.

Once again she thought of Odessa and the summer breezes. She wondered if she would ever have times like that again.

Roy Rodgers came down the third-floor corridor in a rush and burst into Sweeney's office. He was all out of breath.

"She's here," he said. "She came back."

Sweeney looked up, startled. "Marina Demin?"

"Mildred just called. It's her, all right. She's down in Visas."

"All right, I want the building secured. I don't want her walking away again. Go down and get her. Bring her up to the screened room."

"Is that wise, Dick?" Rodgers asked.

"Hell, they had the blueprints to the place before we did. I'll meet you there."

At the door Rodgers looked back. "A coincidence?" he asked.

"Makes you wonder, doesn't it, after MOHAWK blew up in our faces."

12

THE SNOW HAD STOPPED OVERNIGHT, BUT THICK CLOUDS WERE again building from a system out in the Atlantic. Forecasters were predicting that by afternoon the entire Washington area would be under a snow emergency, with accumulations of six to eight inches possible. The city would shut down in that case.

The automatic garage door of a pretty Rosemary Hills ranch started up, and FBI agent Jim Schaeffer noted the time in his log as 7:27 A.M.

His partner, Michael Wood, seated next to him in the back of the surveillance van parked down the block, was studying the house through a pair of binoculars. Because of the one-way window glass the image was not good.

"Looks like Ginny Clark . . . and the boys," Wood said.

"Roland?"

"Negative. They're taking the Wagoneer."

When the Jeep station wagon was warmed up, Ginny Clark pulled out of the garage, the automatic door came down, and she drove off.

Someone in the house picked up a telephone and dialed a seven-digit number. Georgetown exchange. It was 7:31 A.M. The connection was made and on the third ring it was answered by a man.

"Yes?"

"It's me," Roland Clark said. Both agents recognized his voice. "Do you want me to come in this morning?"

"I don't think so. Are you going to be available all day?"

"You can always reach me on my beeper, sir," Clark said.

"Very well. I don't anticipate anything, but don't go far."

"Yes, sir. Have a good day."

"You too," the man said, and the connection was broken.

Schaeffer, who was nearest to the monitor speaker, looked up. Wood started to say something, but Schaeffer held him off. A moment later Clark hung up his phone.

"Sonofabitch," Wood said. "He might have heard the load on the line."

"Not from us," Schaeffer said. "But that was Tyson. His phone is tapped too. Between them. Clark might have heard something. He's a sharp bastard."

"What do you want to bet he gets out of there within the next ten minutes?" Wood asked.

"No bet," Schaeffer said.

At 7:40 A.M. the Clarks' automatic garage door opened, and Clark got in his Chevy Beretta and left. Schaeffer radioed their chase units. "This is twenty-seven. Cochise is on the move. South on Ross."

"Roger, two-seven."

Toni Wagner, dressed in a sharply tailored charcoal-gray coat with fur trim, and tall, soft-leather boots, left her houseboat a few minutes before eight and climbed into her gray Volvo station wagon.

As she waited for the engine to warm up, she adjusted the rearview mirror so that she could touch up her makeup. At the same time, she was searching the line of boats on either side of hers. If the FBI was watching her, it would be logical for them to station a surveillance unit on one of the boats. But she could see nothing out of the ordinary. Nothing suspicious.

But she was being followed. She was almost one hundred percent convinced of it. "An officer of lesser caliber would fold under such conditions," her new control officer had told her. "Only you can say when you want to get out. We will be standing by for you."

She'd not met him, she'd only talked to him by phone. She liked his voice.

She left the marina, driving across the river on the Arlington Memorial Bridge, and parking as usual at the National Academy of Sciences.

Twice on the way into Washington she'd thought she'd spotted a tail, a light gray Toyota van, a man in a blue jacket driving. But by the time she turned down Constitution Avenue the van was gone.

She walked across the busy avenue to the Vietnam Veterans Memorial, where she headed immediately to the name "Thomas Wagner" inscribed in the black stone. A man wearing a dark brown overcoat and brown hat stood looking up at a name near the top row. He glanced at Toni and smiled. She smiled back, tears forming in her eyes.

She always thought when she came here that no matter whose war it had been, these were the names of a lot of good, decent young boys who might otherwise have grown up to be writers or painters, teachers or scientists. Afghanistan had been stupid too. All wars were stupid.

She pulled off her leather gloves and stuffed them in her coat pocket as she stepped closer and reached out with her right hand. Her fingertips brushed Wagner's name. He was an orphan from Boise, Idaho, whose only known relative, a sister, had disappeared when he was twelve. Research had done a fine job. The legend wasn't airtight, but it was close.

After a couple of minutes Toni stepped back and pulled the gloves out of her pocket, dropping a small white envelope, which contained a videocassette and audiotape cassette, into the snow. She hid the action with her body so that no one could possibly see it, and then turned and walked back to her car.

FBI Agents Charles Goode and Tom Parker were on duty again in Georgetown. This time they were parked in their Toyota van on 29th Street, two full blocks from Tyson's house. The Toyotas were the latest FBI joke. No one would believe that a U.S. government agency would buy Japanese. Especially not these days. It wasn't much of a subterfuge, but it was hoped that it helped lower their profile.

"This is nineteen," their radio blared. "Geronimo is on the loose. East on R Street."

Geronimo was the code name for Albert Tyson.

"Roger, nineteen," Goode radioed as Parker eased out into traffic on R Street.

"I didn't think you got up this early, sweetheart," Marty Ryan quipped as Toni Wagner came down the third-floor corridor to her tiny office, where she worked part-time for the Internal Revenue Service's Public Information Division. Her section was in the IRS Building on 12th and Constitution. Her job was to copyedit IRS news releases and bulletins (something she found ludicrous—a Russian correcting the English grammar and spelling of Americans). She'd contracted to work twenty hours a week. *Any* twenty hours she wanted, which gave her a lot of leeway.

"The President asked for me," she retorted.

Ryan's nose crinkled. He never knew when she was joking. He was a senior copywriter.

"He asked me to straighten out your latest batch of bulletins before the entire Eastern Seaboard rises up in a tax revolt."

He grinned. "You must have had a hell of a weekend."

Passing him, she patted him on the cheek and smiled demurely. "You'll never know, Marty."

Kit Tyson, driving a Mercedes 560SL, pulled out of the driveway behind her house in Georgetown and drove off. On

Monday mornings she worked at a halfway house for drug addicts in the city. She usually had lunch in town with a friend and was rarely back home before three in the afternoon.

"Move in," Sandy Senarighi told his driver, and Len Harding pulled away from the curb and headed up the street to the Tyson driveway.

Senarighi was a team leader for the Bureau's Special Investigations Division. He was one of the best second-story men, bar none. The van that he, Harding, and his other three team members rode in was marked "Empire Plumbing and Heating," which was a legitimate Washington-area company run by the FBI.

Harding pulled up behind the Tysons' home and the team members made entry into the house at 8:19 A.M., easily opening the Yale Dreadnought locks and bypassing the sophisticated electronic alarm systems.

This was Washington, agreed. But it made one wonder what Tyson had to hide, he'd buttoned up so tight.

"Look sharp, people," Senarighi said, moving to the stair hall at the front of the house. "We have less than three hours to finish this job. We *will* be gone by eleven hundred hours. David, you and Susanne take the upstairs. Nelson, you go with Len on this floor. If there's time we'll split the basement and attic. Watch for secondaries. And with respect, people. This is America . . . even gentlemen are innocent till proved guilty."

This got a chuckle, but then the team split up and went efficiently and quietly to work.

Senarighi remained for a moment or two longer in the stair hall, soaking up the atmosphere of the house: the smell, the feel, the vibes, as his fifteen-year-old daughter called such things. Clean, orderly, not rich, but certainly not poor or even middle-class. A hundred thousand a year for a number of years now. Maybe more if there were silly games somewhere to be uncovered. Though men of Tyson's ilk, if the man was a traitor after all, usually didn't betray their countries for money. It usually turned out to be more complicated than that.

Turning, he went into the living room and took a quick peek up the fireplace. There was nothing obvious at first glance.

Following the hall, he went back into the kitchen and looked in the refrigerator and poked around the cabinets, his rubber gloves leaving no prints.

Not surprisingly, the Tysons were heavily into fresh vegetables and fruits, but their freezer was also well stocked with fish and meats. Good cuts. A couple of huge lobster tails which had to have set them back thirty or forty bucks each.

Senarighi made thirty-eight five a year. And even in Alexandria, with only a wife and one child, he sometimes wondered how the hell he would make ends meet.

Moving again down the corridor, he stepped into the study. Nelson and Harding had started here first. You always began with the hottest prospects.

Harding's camera clicked and he looked up. "I didn't know he had a daughter at Kent State."

"You didn't do your homework," Senarighi said, stepping over to the desk. He picked up the letters Harding had just photographed. One was from Tyson's daughter, and the other, a partially written letter, was his reply.

Poignant, Senarighi thought. But significant? Probably not. The zealots could read anything they wanted between the lines. Senarighi was a realist.

He handed the letters back to Harding, who would replace them in the exact position he'd found them.

"Any telltales yet?"

"None," Harding said.

Telltales were little pieces of fuzz or hair or anything that when disturbed would indicate that someone had been here. Indicate that the man of the house had something to hide.

Senarighi wasn't disappointed that such things had not turned up yet. He was never disappointed by facts, only by traitors.

Back out in the corridor he went upstairs. Susanne was in

the master bathroom when he came around the corner. She was carefully placing a pair of men's jockey shorts into a clear plastic bag.

"What is it?" he asked.

She took the shorts back out of the bag and spread them open. There was a black smudge at the bottom of the front slit. It looked like grease.

"Black lipstick," Susanne said. She was a short, plain woman of thirty-seven who'd never been married and probably never would be. She loved her work too much.

"The wife?"

"Not unless she hides it," Susanne said. "I'm betting Ms. Wagner."

"We'll see," Senarighi said.

Senarighi had lunch at his desk: the liverwurst sandwich with radishes that his wife had packed him, along with the carrot sticks, celery, and orange that his daughter had added. He'd rather have had a plate of spaghetti, but then he wasn't even tasting his lunch.

Tyson was not going to be easy. Of course no one had thought he would be. If he was a traitor he would probably be a professional (considering his position) much like Kim Philby so many years ago. He would leave nothing incriminating to be found. Of course if he were innocent, there'd be nothing outwardly incriminating. So how to tell the difference?

Step by step, Senarighi sifted through what little they'd come up with, matching each with the room it had been found in.

They'd found a number of letters between father and daughter, and a much lesser number between mother and daughter. Albert Tyson loved his daughter, and she him, there was little doubt of that.

I guess I can sort of feel how you must have felt then. Sort of sad and scared and angry all at once, the daughter had written to her father.

I clearly remember those days in the sixties and seventies, and yes, they were "awesomely rad" and yes, I was sad and scared and angry all at once, the father had replied.

But I was also young, and so sure that I could make a difference in the world that I was not intimidated by anything or any person. My voice would count . . .

Didn't make him a traitor.

The laboratory would undoubtedly identify the grease mark on Tyson's underwear as lipstick. Probably from Toni Wagner's mouth (a thought Senarighi would rather not have pursued). But they knew he was having an affair with her.

Still didn't make him a traitor, except for the fact that the woman was probably a Russian. But then she had targeted him. And if he had turned, if he was telling her his country's secrets when they were in bed together, it made him an unwitting traitor. It would be another Profumo scandal, something not needed on these shores in the wake of Watergate or the Iran-contra deal.

So far as Senarighi knew, the Bureau's efforts to bug the woman's houseboat (what sort of a person lived on a boat in this climate?) had failed miserably. Within days of installation the equipment malfunctioned. It had happened three times.

She never telephoned Tyson or anyone significant from her home phone, and although she worked downtown, the bugs planted in her office had produced absolutely nothing.

She had first come to the Bureau's attention when the IRS had requested a routine background check (which it did for all its employees). She claimed that her brother was Thomas Wagner, who'd been listed as missing in action in Vietnam. According to military records, Wagner was probably a deserter who might have defected to Hanoi. A British journalist had apparently spotted the American in 1987.

At the time, she had been cleared for employment, but on a closer look, it was believed that Ms. Wagner was really a Russian woman named Nechiporenko, a KGB agent who'd worked in Paris. There were no fingerprints to match from Paris, but photographs showed a striking similarity, as did the woman's methods of operation.

In Paris the government official she'd targeted had committed suicide when he'd found out that he was under investigation.

After the episode in front of Tyson's house the other night, the man might be suspicious. There'd been reports from the field that he was beginning to act oddly. Perhaps he suspected that he was being followed. But was he contemplating suicide?

It was one of the things Senarighi's team had looked for but not found. But not everyone who placed a gun to his head first advertised his intention.

Today had been a bust so far, Senarighi had to admit. It was something he didn't admit often, but when it happened he redoubled his efforts. If there was something there, he would find it.

"It's a gross misuse of a valuable resource," Yuri Truskin told the group assembled in the *referentura*.

"A *potential* resource," Lydia Lubiako corrected. "Which is the sole object of this entire exercise. Or at least it has been to my understanding, unless something has changed. Something we haven't been told about?"

"The FBI has become involved, probably because of the man's connection with Raya. She is under suspicion. It is insanity to continue using her."

"An interesting choice of words, considering the latest information she has supplied us," Vladimir Baturin said languidly. He was the new liaison between the KGB and the Soviet ambassador.

"It will be the ambassador who will have to pick up the pieces, if any, when the situation disintegrates," Truskin replied sharply.

"That is our concern," Baturin said. He leaned forward, his well-manicured hands on the table in front of him. "We need the information that this source can provide us. Now more than ever before. If this operation fails, it could very well be our last."

"Save the melodrama . . ."

"There are certain aspects that you do not know. Perhaps it is time for you to return to Moscow."

"Are you threatening me?" Truskin demanded, his voice rising. KGB activities *always* enjoyed an autonomy from the diplomats, although since August even that had changed.

"In any event we have Comrade Privalov to fall back on if the need arises," Lydia Lubiako said.

"I would never authorize such a drastic measure," Truskin said.

"It's not up to you."

"It would be unfortunate if news of this operation were to leak, especially to the West, because someone in Moscow could not keep his mouth shut. Someone unauthorized to share not only in the product but in the day-to-day operational planning. Such things have happened before."

"Don't threaten me," Baturin shouted.

"With care, Vladimir Nikolaievich," Lydia Lubiako said, her right forefinger touching the side of her nose. "As you say, we need the information now more than ever before. It is up to the KGB to provide such information. Please, allow us to do our jobs."

Kiselev was just about to leave for the day when the runner came up from communications with the incoming that had to be personally signed for. It was just past eight in the evening, and Medvedosky had already gone home.

Breaking the seal, Kiselev opened the folder. The top sheet was stamped: "Most Secret, Source KHAIRULLA."

He quickly scanned the contents of the message, including the on-site agent's evaluations. As he read, he made notes only in the margins of the message, not on separate pieces of paper.

There was nothing new on MOHAWK, but what was included was just as important, even more important now that the Second Chief Directorate had at least one of the MOHAWK sources in custody.

It was time to take the next step. Here in Moscow his

players were in place. And now in Washington Tyson had been taken to the first plateau.

Kiselev picked up the telephone and dialed the twenty-four-hour number of General Aleksandr Ryazanov, the deputy of the First Chief Directorate and number two behind KGB Chairman Novikov.

"The only thing that we can prove Tyson guilty of is indiscretion, Mr. Director," Senarighi told Ed Wilder. "We found nothing conclusive at his home."

"Except for a pair of his underwear with lipstick stains."

"Yes, sir," Senarighi said uncomfortably. "But his wife may own such lipstick. It's unusual for a man, if he is having an affair, to dump the evidence in a place where his wife is bound to find it."

"Maybe," Wilder said. "Could be that he didn't notice the stain, or it could be that his wife doesn't do the laundry. Maybe the maid does, and she doesn't care."

Senarighi nodded. "We need a mike and camera aboard that houseboat. Short of that, I'd like to search the place."

"If she's who we think she is, you probably wouldn't get away with it. She'd find out and bolt."

Senarighi was very uncomfortable. Whenever his professional abilities were questioned, he got upset. "My people are up to the challenge. Just give us the word, Mr. Director."

"Not now," Wilder said. "But it may come to that. We may run out of choices."

"Yes, sir. We'll be standing by." Senarighi left the director's office and went back downstairs to his own.

Len Harding was waiting for him. "Well?"

"Who's the best underwater man in the Bureau?" Senarighi asked, taking off his jacket as he went around behind his desk.

"John Niven. San Diego," Harding replied without hesitation.

"Know him?"

"He's my brother-in-law."

Senarighi had to grin. "I guess I haven't been doing *my*

homework. I want you to get him on the phone. See if he can get himself and his equipment out here."

"Have we got the green light?"

"Not yet," Senarighi said. "But we will, and when it comes I want to be ready."

Kiselev was dressed in uniform. He approached General Ryazanov's desk, slammed his boot heels together, and saluted crisply. "Major Ivan Kiselev reporting, sir."

Ryazanov, a young man, barely five years older than Kiselev, returned the salute. It was ten in the evening, and he did not look happy, only alert.

"Report," he said, without allowing Kiselev to stand down.

"Source KHAIRULLA is ready to go into the pre-implementation stage."

The general's right eyebrow rose. "Your people are in place?"

"Yes, and nearly everything is within optimum limits."

"Nearly?"

"The shooting in Washington over the weekend was connected to this operation. Privalev made a move outside the scenario which our Washington *Rezident* interpreted as hostile, so he sent one of his own people into the field to intercept the man before it was too late. Two FBI officers were shot and killed, as was one of our officers."

"What is Washington Station doing in response?"

"Since the FBI has made no accusations yet, nothing. It may be passed as a street crime."

"Chairman Novikov made mention of the incident this morning."

"Yes, sir."

"I told him it was an accident, but that in no way will it jeopardize our normal North American operations. Chairman Novikov asked for my personal guarantee. I gave it to him."

"You have mine," Kiselev said.

"Yes," the general replied, and the temperature in his large office seemed to drop ten degrees. "What else?"

The general meant what else in the negative. "Tyson may have come under suspicion by the FBI. The shooting took place very near his Georgetown residence. Privalev feels that the FBI was on site on a surveillance operation involving him."

"Routine?"

"Not known, but I doubt it. His interim control officer has probably come under suspicion. In this case it may mean nothing more than that the Bureau suspects him of an indiscretion that is quite common in the States."

"That, added to the weekend shooting spree, will give them direction, Major. The Americans are not stupid."

"On the contrary. But there is no proof. If we remain silent, which our people in Washington are doing, and if we take care with our handling of Tyson, which is also happening, the crisis will pass. It has happened this way before. In other places."

"Yes, and always our agent was uncovered."

"Usually not until we had gotten our money's worth."

Ryazanov said nothing.

"This is an important operation. I have put myself and my staff on the line. This may be the most important operation to the RODINA in more than forty-five years. The stakes may be less well defined, but they are higher than before."

"The cold war has not been re-instituted, Major." General Ryazanov was playing devil's advocate.

"No, sir. But in the interim we are engaged in an invisible war with the West. Make no mistake, Comrade General, the West means to bury us with its technology, with its consumer goods, with its factories and unions, with its interstate highway system and flashy automobiles, television commercials and department stores. This war will be much subtler than the shooting wars or the cold war. We're not strictly after territory now. *Lebensraum*. We're after self-defense first. And secondly we are after hearts and souls."

"Is that what you believe, Major?" General Ryazanov asked. It was hard for Kiselev to tell if the man was patronizing him or not.

"Yes, sir. But even if that were not the case, or if what I have to say is nothing more than the ramblings of a naive man, the United States is our enemy. That will never change. That *can* never change. The gulf between us is simply too vast."

"If you are wrong?"

Kiselev thought about that for a moment. "Then history will judge me, Comrade General. Because I will be dead and gone for a long time before our conflict has been settled."

The general looked away for a long moment, a gesture uncharacteristic of him. When he turned back, his expression was bleak. "At ease, Major," he said.

Kiselev broadened his stance and placed his hands behind his back. He did not slouch, however. This was unknown territory.

"Now, tell me what is happening in Washington. You say that we are ready to proceed?"

"Tyson has been talking about the old days. About Marinka and about Joseph. It's a sign that he is looking back, and worrying if his past will catch up with him."

"Another Paris? Will he kill himself?"

"There are no indications to this point," Kiselev said. "And Raya would know. She feels she is closer to him now than his wife is."

"A dangerous assumption, but go on."

"She told him not to come back to the houseboat. He agreed to go back to their original system, which, as long as they are both careful, should give them a little breathing room."

"He suspects the FBI is after him?"

"Maybe not. He hasn't given any indication yet."

"The man is an assistant adviser to the President of the United States on security matters. Surely he cannot be that naive."

"You would be surprised, Comrade General," Kiselev said, thinking about other Americans who'd held power, among them President Carter, who held prayer meetings at

Camp David. The world had been laughing at him and he hadn't known it.

"Perhaps you're right," the general acceded. "But if the FBI suspects him, would they not have gone to the President?"

Kiselev had simply not thought of that possibility. He nodded as he desperately tried to work it out in his head. "Tyson would be isolated, in that case," he said slowly. "Any new developments would certainly be withheld from him. But it would mean a new national security adviser would have to be appointed. Harms is still ill. So, unless or until that happens, the President will have to stick with Tyson. In any event, if the FBI was certain of its evidence, he would have been arrested by now."

"Maybe they are hoping for more."

"Pardon me, sir, but what more could there be beyond a national security adviser to the President of the United States?"

"Russia."

Kiselev started to speak, but then he thought better of it, realizing what the general meant. Relationships between Russia and the United States had changed for the better since the Kremlin coup. Something like this, however, if it got out, would put them back years, almost guaranteeing that any kind of trade agreement with the West would be impossible. The truth was that Russia was fractured. No longer was there a clearly defined line of control between the Kremlin and the Lubyanka, at least not in the eyes of Westerners.

"I want the situation resolved, Major. At the earliest possible date. There are factors here that even you don't understand."

"Of course, Comrade General," Kiselev said. He came to attention again and saluted.

The general returned his salute, and Kiselev turned and headed to the door.

"What about MOHAWK?" the general asked. "Anything new?"

"No, sir," Kiselev said, turning back.

"Nedosorov is pestering me. Seems as if his people are at a dead end."

"Perhaps we could send some of ours over to help out."

Ryazanov smiled for the first time. "I suggested that, but he declined."

"Yes, sir. The moment anything new comes in, I'll pass it along."

"So long as it does not jeopardize our operation," General Ryazanov cautioned, and Kiselev knew exactly what he meant. "Any further word on Tinker?" It was the code name they were using for the computer hacker.

"He's here in Moscow, and he actually got into the program. But then he got cold feet and backed out."

Ryazanov thought about that for a moment. "It could be that he's working for someone and had to wait for instructions."

"That's what we thought, Comrade General. Fortunately we learned about this soon enough to sidestep him. For the moment."

The general nodded. "He's clever. How long can your people hold out in Washington?"

"There is some question about that, but I think they can hold out long enough for Homeward Bound to be put into place. Then it won't matter."

"No," the general said.

When Kiselev was gone, the general called a Moscow number on his secure telephone. It was answered on the second ring by an old man, whose voice was as dry as autumn grass.

"We're moving forward as planned, Comrade Minister," General Ryazanov said.

"That fool Novikov still has no idea what is about to happen?"

"None."

"I presume there are no problems?"

"None that we cannot handle, comrade. Let me assure you . . ."

"Save the empty words, General. This time we must have results. Time is running out for all of us . . . including you."

"I understand, Comrade Minister."

The old man chuckled. "I hope you do, Comrade General."

Dr. Thomas Heller stood alone on the frozen shore of Lake Mendota, the buildings of the University of Wisconsin rising on the bluffs behind him. He was a tall, gangling man who looked more like a modern dancer, or a starving artist, than the mathematician he was. His face was thin, almost ascetic, and his violet eyes were dreamy and faraway. The girls used to say he looked "haunting." It drove them mad. And still, each semester there was at least one young woman in his class who did everything within her power to get him into her bed. Most of them did not succeed.

He'd been here fifteen years now. Married twelve of those to his wife, Elizabeth, who held a doctorate in biophysics. Together they presented the picture of stolid academia. Both of them had tenure, and it was expected that they would eventually graduate, as their students did. For them it would be to professorships emeritus and emerita.

In the past few years, however, Tom Heller had begun to sink into depression. Slowly at first but just lately with increasing speed, he began to not care about anything: his students, his teaching, his wife, least of all his future.

He was fifty-seven. Liz said he was summing up. "You're going through your midlife crisis a little later than everyone else, that's all."

A lone figure had come down from the Edgewater Hotel and started up the beach. The sky was overcast and the light flat, so it was impossible to tell even if it was a man or a woman.

Liz was right, of course, but for reasons completely different than she thought. It seemed to him that everything he'd worked for all of his life was disintegrating before his eyes. All of his goals had disappeared into thin air. His principles had been proved false. His idols proved worthless. His real career a dead end.

The figure on the beach was much closer, and Tom Heller could see that it was a man, dressed in snow boots and a bright blue ski jacket. The man waved.

This had been a cold winter so far, and today the wind was raw. But Tom Heller had come down here for the solitude. The one place in Madison where he could be alone to think. He did not want to be disturbed now. But as the man got closer, there was something about him that got Heller's attention. Some air, some . . . professionalism. Something not midwestern.

"I spotted you down here all alone," the man said, smiling. He stuck out his hand.

"I don't think we've met," Tom Heller said, shaking the man's hand.

"Oh, you wouldn't remember, but we met briefly a number of years ago. Out East."

A spasm clutched at Heller's gut. "Yes?"

"At Kent State. And now, Joseph, we need your help again. Something has come up."

13

"I'M HERE WITH A PERSONAL REQUEST," KISELEV SAID, pocketing his KGB identification booklet. "I don't know what else to do." He'd arrived first thing in the morning at the Militia's Office of Missing Persons in the City Soviet Building downtown. Legends began small, and in order for them to remain airtight through their useful life, all the details had to be right. The clock had begun as of yesterday, the moment Marinka had walked back into the American Embassy and asked for asylum.

"If you'll just come around the counter, I'm sure my captain will want to speak with you," the young woman clerk said.

The only comfort Marinka had was knowing that her track was being watched and covered. Her past would not betray her. Nor would the *Rodina*.

Kiselev followed the woman across the squad room with its dozen or so desks. She knocked once at a door and then opened it.

"Captain, there is a KGB major here to speak with you," she said.

Kiselev brushed past her as a small, rat-faced man in Militia uniform rose from behind his desk. He looked flustered, and Kiselev immediately wondered what cookie jar his hand had been in.

"This is unofficial, Captain Fomenko," Kiselev said, reading the man's name off his desk plaque.

The clerk withdrew, leaving them alone.

"What can Militia do for State Security this morning, Major?"

"A friend of mine is missing," Kiselev said, taking out Marina's photograph and handing it across. "Her name is Marina Demin. We have been . . ."

The photograph showed Marina in a bikini on a beach in Odessa. The captain looked appreciatively at it. "You have been close."

"Exactly. When I came back from work last night, she was gone. No note, no trace of her whatsoever. Naturally I do not want to use my own people to track her. We have other work to do."

"Yes, I see," Captain Fomenko said, tearing his eyes away from the photograph and looking up. "Did you have a fight with her? Was she unhappy?"

Kiselev's eyes narrowed.

"I'm sorry to be so indelicate, Major, but in cases such as these . . . well, one must ask the questions."

"I understand," Kiselev said. "No, we were very happy. It's not that. You see, I think she was kidnapped."

"Kidnapped?"

"Yes. By the Americans. She was not only my friend, she had been the . . . mistress of a man of some importance in the . . . Kremlin."

All the air went out of Captain Fomenko and he sat down. "Fuck your mother," he said softly.

"We must find her, and we mustn't make too much noise about it," Kiselev said. "Do you understand?"

The captain looked up unhappily. "Yes, Major, I understand. All too well."

Medvedosky was waiting impatiently in the ready room when Kiselev finally arrived at the First Directorate's vast headquarters on the Circumferential Highway outside of Moscow. No one, he said, had told him anything.

"Everything is in place," Kiselev said on the way back to his office.

"Have you sent the 'go' signal?"

"Not yet. But we'll do it this morning. It's a little before one in the morning in Washington, which will give them the rest of the night to implement."

"What did the general say last night about Tinker?" Medvedosky asked when they were inside and out of earshot of anyone else on the staff.

"He's behind us, but he is becoming impatient. This must be resolved within the next few days."

"If Tyson holds together that long. It's becoming a real problem. Have you given that much thought?"

Kiselev unlocked his security file cabinet, withdrew a folder, and from it took a message flimsy, which he handed to his number two.

Medvedosky quickly scanned the lengthy message, then read it again slowly. When he was done he looked up. "It was convenient that he was in Chicago just now, and could get up to Wisconsin."

"Maybe not so convenient," Kiselev said, taking the message flimsy back and refiling it. "I've given this a lot of thought. Everything has to be just right."

"It's like a game of chess."

Kiselev had to smile. Medvedosky's loyalty knew no bounds. The man was always good for the right comment at just the right time.

"Maybe not so complicated."

"But more important."

Kiselev looked at him. "For you and me, definitely. And for the *Rodina* . . . one would hope."

Medvedosky was breathless. Like a hunting dog at the edge of a promising country field.

"Send it," Kiselev said softly. "Implement Homeward Bound. And as soon as that's off, I want you to go over to my apartment and pick up my things. They're in a leather bag just outside the door."

"We'll be here for a while?"

"A few days, hopefully. For the duration."

Medvedosky nodded. "My bag is in my car. I figured it would be today or tomorrow at the latest."

Yuri Truskin had been expecting the "implement" message as well. It was two in the morning when it came in. A runner came to his apartment within the embassy and he got dressed immediately and went downstairs to his office, where he translated the already-twice-encrypted order.

"Implement Homeward Bound."

Simple, Truskin thought, holding a match to the flimsy, except that now heads could get cut off. And almost certainly there would be trouble of one variety or another. He hoped that no further blood would be shed, however.

He was not a philosophical man, but the enormity of what he was about to do—or at least take part in doing—gave him pause. Whom to trust? In the words of his favorite movie character, the King, as played by Yul Brynner in *The King and I*, it was ". . . a puzzlement!"

The Americans were not the aggressors, but neither was his country any longer. Yet the gulf between them was so vast as to be nearly unbreachable. Maybe it would take time. Of course in the meanwhile the Americans were closing in on a viable Star Wars defense system; their military triad of ground-, air-, and submarine-based missiles, all nuclear, was still intact; and every four years there was an election in this country for a new president and vice president. Which meant a new cabinet. New advisers. New attitudes.

He thought for a moment about his wife, Serafima, whom he'd sent back to Moscow two months ago. They'd never been able to have children, much to his mother's disappointment. These days, however, he wondered if it wasn't for the best, after all. What kind of a world was this, where you didn't know who your enemies were? Nor did you know who was still your friend.

The *Rodina* stood fractured and alone now. Dangerous. Very dangerous.

Downstairs, in the embassy's communications room, Truskin made a telephone call on a new piece of equipment the Technical Directorate was calling a "masking modulator."

The Americans had developed the technology with which the telephone number of the caller could be instantly determined electronically. Some telephone companies were offering the equipment to their customers so that they would be able to know who was telephoning them before they answered the call. All the law enforcement agencies had picked up on the technology, of course. The days when it took minutes to trace a call were gone.

Japanese technicians had invented a countermeasure, which the Russians had stolen, by which the outgoing telephone signal was somehow modulated in a fashion designed to fool the electronic tracing equipment. The only foolproof method of tracing a number was still actually eyeballing the telephone switching equipment.

When Truskin placed his call from the embassy communications center telephone, tracing equipment placed it as originating from a house in Bethesda.

The call was answered on the first ring by Raya Nechiporenko. "Yes?" she said.

"Oh, I'm sorry," Truskin said in a British accent. "This is the second bloody time I've dialed the wrong number tonight." He hung up.

"Frankly, we need some help," Sandy Senarighi told the CIA officer in the man's office at Langley. "But at this point my request is unofficial."

"Officially I can't guarantee a thing," the officer, Roger Geiger, said. He was an assistant to Chris Roberts, the deputy director of intelligence. "But what have you got?"

"Someone on the White House staff is having an affair with a woman here in Washington who goes by the name of Toni Wagner. Just now she works for the IRS. Public Information Division."

"Not so uncommon. There's a but?"

"A big one. We believe that the woman's real name is Raya Nechiporenko."

"KGB?"

"Probably. Some weeks ago the Agency told us, through official channels, that the woman had probably last operated in Paris."

"I see," Geiger said. "This White House staffer. High up?"

"Unfortunately yes."

"And you are conducting an investigation of him to see if he is working with this Russian woman. You think we may have a spy in the White House?"

"Maybe nothing so dramatic, but anything's possible."

"Yes, isn't it?" Geiger said. "So arrest her, and watch what he does. If the Russians throw him a lifeline, if they try to contact him, or he tries to contact them, nail the bastard."

"It's not as easy as that," Senarighi said, a little uncomfortable now. Perhaps it wasn't such a good idea coming here like this.

"That high?"

Senarighi nodded. "There are some other factors to consider as well . . ."

"Holy shit," Geiger interrupted. "Georgetown. The shooting over the weekend. Was that drug runner a Russian by any chance?"

Senarighi was very unhappy now, but he nodded.

"And your White House man is . . ."

"Yes," Senarighi said, sitting forward. "I would like to know who Raya Nechiporenko's control officer is. Her Moscow boss."

Geiger's eyes narrowed. "And?"

"I have a feeling that something else is going on. I want to

know from your people in Moscow if her control officer is up
to something."

Roland Clark pulled over at a telephone booth on Massachusetts Avenue, and called an old friend of his who was one
of the seniors at the Department of Motor Vehicles.

"I need a small favor, but I need you to keep your mouth
shut about it, Tommy. No matter what."

Tom Rothman was a little hesitant. "What do you need,
Rollie?"

"Your promise first that this won't go any further."

"All right."

"I need a trace on a license plate. Federal."

"What's up, someone having you followed?"

"I think so."

"I see," Rothman said after another hesitation, and Clark
gave him the license plate number of the gray Toyota van that
had been following him for several days now. "Just a sec,"
Rothman said.

Traffic was heavy despite all the snow that had fallen in the
past thirty-six hours. Some back avenues were still impass-
able.

"Are you in some kind of trouble?" Rothman asked a half
minute later.

"No, but something is happening. I'm trying to get to the
bottom of it. Who belongs to those plates? The Bureau?"

"Their Counter Espionage Division," Rothman said. "Talk
to me, Rollie."

"Later," Clark said, and he hung up.

Half the offices in the Executive Office Building west of
the White House were empty because of the weather. Clark
got a cup of coffee from a machine in the basement and went
up to his own office.

The White House lawn was snow-covered, as was the
White House roof. He could see from his window where
someone had cleared the snow off the communications and

satellite antennae up there, and he could see where the snow had been shoveled in a path from the roof door.

Clark locked his office door, took his telephone off the hook, and powered up his computer. Using the proper code sequences and passwords, he gained access into the Secret Service's background investigation files on every member of the White House staff. From the janitors and cooks, all the way to the assistant national security adviser:

TYSON, ALBERT FENRIGHT
UNIVERSITY—KENT STATE

The heavy snowfall had slowed Raya Nechiporenko down, so that she didn't know if she would make her rendezvous at telephone number two . . . the number she'd been instructed to go to at noon by Truskin's call. He'd said it was the second wrong number he'd dialed that night. The second *bloody* time. It was the emergency signal.

The main highways out in the countryside were in much better condition than the streets within the city, so when she'd finally gotten across the river, clear of Washington, she began to make reasonably good time.

Phone number one was at her houseboat, and number three was at the Watergate apartment of an airline stewardess. Number two had been reserved for trouble. It was a safe house out in the country off U.S. Highways 50 and 29 in the hills southwest of Fairfax. The approaches to the property in every direction were clear for more than a kilometer. The nearest neighbor was farther than that. And they rented the place from a former CIA officer. The spot was perfect as a refuge.

She'd been followed from her houseboat back into the city, but the last she'd seen of her tail—a yellow Toyota van—it was stuck in a snowdrift just off Dupont Circle. She was certain she'd not picked up another tail.

The driveway up to the house had been plowed since the snow had stopped, probably sometime this morning. Then it had been sanded and salted. She could see the tire tracks heading away from the house. She parked under the carport on the west side of the long, two-story ranch, and back out in the driveway she looked down the hill the way she had come.

She could see Fairfax in the distance, and the highway that ran east to Alexandria. Normal traffic. Next, she scanned the sky in all directions. Off to the northwest she could see a jet airliner coming into Dulles for a landing, but there was nothing else in sight. No helicopters approaching, no light surveillance aircraft. Yet she was jumpy.

She let herself in the front door, stamped the snow off her boots, and walked into the living room as she opened her coat. A fire crackled in the fireplace, and she pulled up short, her heart skipping a beat.

She'd missed the smoke coming from the chimney!

After slipping off her boots, she took her .32 automatic from her purse, levered a round into the firing chamber, and switched off the safety catch.

The only sound in the house was the crackling of the fire. She'd been a fool!

Letting her coat fall to the floor, she padded back out into the stair hall, where she again cocked an ear.

Something? A noise in the kitchen?

Silently she crossed the corridor into the dining room and then around the long table to the open door that led into the kitchen.

A very tall man with longish blond hair, broad shoulders, and narrow hips was opening a bottle of wine at the counter. He was dressed in a thick turtleneck sweater and baggy corduroy trousers. He wore no shoes or boots, only thick woolen socks.

"Do you prefer white wine or red?" he asked in English, his accent midwestern or perhaps Californian.

"Who the hell are you? What are you doing here?" Raya asked.

The man turned around with a grin, and Raya decided that he was quite handsome. "I'm Igor Mikhailovich Lubiako, your control officer. Didn't you recognize my voice?"

Raya was stunned. She had not recognized his voice until just then.

"But my friends call me Misha. Please," he said, holding up a glass of white wine. "White or red?"

"White," she said, lowering her pistol and easing the hammer down. "No phone call?"

"No," he said, coming across and handing her the glass of wine. His eyes were pale blue and deep. "We thought you would need a break before you got started."

"Homeward Bound?"

He nodded. "The message came last night. How do you feel?"

"Now that it's finally come, or the fact that I've met you face-to-face?"

Lubiako laughed out loud. "Both."

"Relieved," she said after a pause. "On both counts."

"Has it been bad for you?" he asked. His voice was confidential, understanding, sensitive. Even sensuous, Raya thought.

"He may destroy himself because of me."

Lubiako nodded in his intelligent way. "It is the risk we're going to have to take. Are you up to it again . . . I mean so soon after Paris?"

He reached out and touched her hand. It felt as if she'd received an electric shock, and her knees weakened. She couldn't say a thing. There was Russia in his eyes, in his manner, in his voltage. She began to cry with relief.

"I understand," he cooed. "Believe me, I do."

"Al Tyson is guilty of nothing more than a sexual indiscretion, is that the bottom line, Ed?" the President asked.

"So far as we have been able to determine, that's the extent of it," Ed Wilder said. "Of course we're still in the evidentiary stage . . ."

"What evidence? Specifically what have you found?"

Wilder sighed. "Nothing, Mr. President. Nothing directly, other than the woman."

"No evidence that Al knows his . . . mistress *may* be a Russian?"

"None."

"What are your recommendations? What's your next step?"

"We will continue to watch him."

"For how long?"

"Until he's *proved* innocent or guilty," Wilder said assertively. "I don't think we have the luxury of benefit of doubt in this case."

"What else? That can't go on forever."

"At some point I want to take Mr. Tyson into our confidence. I'd like to tell him who and what we suspect Ms. Wagner of being, and ask for his help to uncover whatever else it is she's doing."

"Sonofabitch," the President swore, but not at Wilder. "When would you expect to talk to him?"

"Soon."

"But you don't recommend I fire him."

"I can't make that recommendation, Mr. President."

"No," the President said. "Not until you have the proof."

"That's right . . ."

"What do you think? What's your gut feeling?"

"Something is going on," Wilder said without hesitation. "But I'm not sure yet what it is."

The President nodded glumly. "Thanks for dropping by, Ed. Keep me posted, please."

"Yes, Mr. President," Wilder said, and he got up and left.

A moment later, Ray Geller, the President's appointments secretary, came in and started to tell him about his next appointment.

"I know, Ray," the President said, holding him off. "Just give me a couple of minutes. In the meantime ask Al Tyson to step in."

"Yes, sir," Geller said, and within sixty seconds Tyson knocked once and entered.

"Good morning, Mr. President. I'm not quite finished with

the afternoon summary, but I can bring you up to date, if . . ."

"Sit down, Al. I've only got a minute or two before John Riemer and that crowd come in."

"They're waiting outside," Tyson said. Riemer was the Speaker of the House, and a vociferous opponent of the present administration.

"How is Bob Harms doing? Have you talked to him in the past few days?"

"Last week. He's getting better, but it's likely to be a while yet. Are you missing him?"

The President managed to smile. "I've always valued his counsel. That's not to say you're doing a bad job, on the contrary. It's just that Bob and I . . . we go back a long way together."

"I understand, Mr. President," Tyson said, but it was clear from the expression on his face that he did not.

"Is everything all right for you at home?"

Tyson was rocked. "Sir?"

"I don't want the same thing happening to you that happened to Bob. His heart attack."

"I'm fine. Is it something . . ."

"No, no." The President waved him off. "You're doing fine. At least the media haven't blasted you yet. Though that'll come."

"I'm sure it will."

There was a small, awkward silence.

"I just wanted to make sure you were holding up okay, Al," the President said.

"Yes, sir."

"If there's anything, anything at all, you want to discuss with me, don't hesitate," the President said, looking up at his national security adviser. "I need one hundred percent of your best efforts and loyalties. I can't afford to have anything less."

"I understand, Mr. President," Tyson said. "And you have mine. You've always had mine."

"Good," the President said. "Send Riemer and his head-hunters in now."

Tyson smiled thinly. "Yes, sir."

"He was running scared," Roy Geiger told his boss, Deputy Director of Intelligence Chris Roberts. They were gathered in the sixth-floor office of the deputy director of operations, Richard Adkins.

"Who the hell is he?" Adkins asked.

"He's a break-and-enter expert. I looked up his file. One of the best in the business."

"What about Raya Nechiporenko?"

"There was a Bureau query about her a couple of weeks ago," Roberts answered. "She was involved in Paris with a government official who killed himself when his own people got wind that something was up."

"We're sure she's the same one?" Adkins asked.

Roberts shrugged. "Hell, Chris, there's no way of calling that one for sure short of a DNA match. We didn't even get prints from the French."

Adkins opened a file folder in front of him. "If she's Nechiporenko, then her boss is a major in the First Chief Directorate by the name of Ivan Kiselev. Sharp, from what we know. He's definitely on his way up, even under the present circumstances over there."

"What's he been up to lately?" the DDI asked.

"I don't know. Moscow Station has got its hands full at the moment, but I'll query Sweeney, maybe he knows something. But in the meantime what about Al Tyson? He definitely the target?"

"According to Senarighi," Geiger said. "He was way outside his charter, coming to us, and he knows it. But he's afraid that their investigation will peter out for lack of evidence."

"Let me find out what Moscow has to add," Adkins said. "In the meantime keep this quiet. But if the Bureau returns in any fashion, with any request, let me know immediately.

We'd better open a file on this one, just to be on the safe side."

After Roberts and Geiger were gone, Adkins stepped across the corridor to the office of his assistant deputy director of operations, Bob Drury. The man had the build and square face of Aldo Ray.

"Anything yet on that computer hacker in Moscow?" Adkins asked.

"It's not one of our operations."

"I didn't think so. Check with NSA, see if it's their baby."

"Will do," Drury said.

The driver deposited Zimin at the rear of the big dacha well outside Moscow. Again it was too late. Past midnight, and waiting in the cold, Zimin felt sorry for himself. He'd become like a bat, or a mole—a creature that never saw the light of day. He yearned for summer.

Deputy Secretary Malakhov came out the back and led Zimin away from the house and the car. "They know that you've gained access to the computer."

Someone had put a jolt of electricity to his body. "My name, they know who I am?"

"Not that, not yet. But they know that someone is tampering with the Finance Directorate's computer. They're calling you Tinker, and at first they thought you might be an American, CIA, now they're not so sure."

"But how could they know? My parallel program is undetectable."

"Apparently the information comes from an outside source."

"I don't know what you mean."

"Someone outside of the KGB is giving them information," Malakhov said, careful to keep his voice low enough so that it would not carry.

"But you promised that there would be no leaks from your office!"

"And there are none. We think that this information is being supplied to the KGB by someone in the United States."

"Impossible . . ." Zimin said, but he stopped himself. "We're using ordinary telephone lines. The American National Security Agency might be capable of monitoring those lines. But that's incredible. It would mean . . ."

"That we have managed to place a spy in NSA. Interesting, and dangerous."

"I'll dismantle the operation."

"No!" Malakhov said sharply. "We only have a little way to go now. We need that information, Valentin. It's very important. Maybe even so important that the future of the *Rodina* could depend on it."

"Politics."

"Yes, but politics provides the butter as well as the guns. Think about it."

14

THE LUXURIOUS SURROUNDINGS OF THE WATERGATE HOTEL served to deepen Thomas Heller's depression. He checked in as Joseph Courtney, and was shown to his room on the fifth floor overlooking the river. A basket of fruit and a bottle of champagne on ice were waiting for him.

Capitalism had won, in the end. Or it appeared to be doing so. Eastern Europe was in shambles, and so was the Soviet Union, what was left of it.

In the sixties and seventies, Heller (which was his real name) had been a young idealist. The Vietnam War was merely an indication of the West's immorality. The burning of Detroit and Milwaukee by dead-ended blacks was another symptom of a decaying system. (Hadn't the Berlin Wall been erected to keep the cancer from spreading to the innocent East Berliners?)

He had truly and honestly believed that despite some problems, communism as practiced in the Soviet Union was the only hope for the future of mankind. The disparity between the rich and poor was growing in the West.

Civilization could not survive if such vast inequities were allowed to exist, indeed, to flourish.

Striking a blow, however small and however late, would bring him some measure of personal relief. In the meantime he would simply have to put up with the outward trappings of capitalism's success.

Someone knocked at his door. He thought it was the bellman, who may have forgotten something. But opening the door, he came face-to-face with an incredibly beautiful woman.

"Hello, Joseph," she said, holding out her hand. "My name is Toni Wagner, and I'm your Washington contact. How was your trip?"

For several beats he was dumbstruck. She was expensively dressed, her hair was perfect, and her makeup directly out of some fashion magazine. She was the opposite of everything he'd ever found enticing in a woman. Yet he could not deny the almost overwhelming feeling that came over him of wanting her.

"May I come in?" she asked, smiling.

"Yes, sorry," he said, stepping aside.

She brushed past him, her scent wafting into his nose. "We're going to have to move fast," she said. She pulled the bedcovers back, rumpled up the pillow, and then went into the bathroom, where she took out his razor, toothbrush, and a few other things and laid them on the counter. Next she opened the bath soap, ran some water in the tub, and mussed up several towels. She pulled some toilet paper from the roll, flushed it down the toilet, and splashed some water on the counter and the mirror above it.

"Leave everything and come with me," she said, emerging from the bathroom.

"Where are we going?"

"I have an apartment here in the Watergate. I've got to start your briefing immediately. We have a lot of ground to cover."

"Where is the woman at this moment?" FBI Special Agent John Niven asked Senarighi. The two of them, along with

Niven's brother-in-law Len Harding, had driven directly from Dulles to Boundary Road across the lagoon from the Columbia Island Marina. They stood within the trees twenty feet up from the river's edge.

"At work downtown," Senarighi answered. "I checked just before we picked you up at the airport."

Niven was a fairly short, stocky, almost muscle-bound man with a broad face and thick but pleasant features. He looked like a diminutive Arnold Schwarzenegger.

"How long will she be gone?" he asked.

"Unknown. But probably another couple of hours. Say, until two or two-thirty."

Niven lowered the powerful binoculars he'd been using. "Not enough time for us to set it up this afternoon, but I could go over there tonight, after dark."

Senarighi shivered involuntarily. The thought of climbing into the frigid water of the river, and then submerging in the darkness . . . it was like someone had walked over his grave.

"We don't have the authorization yet."

Niven shot a glance at his brother-in-law. "My supervisor in San Diego is bound to start asking questions before too long."

"I'll take care of that," Senarighi said. "I want you to concentrate on this job."

"Piece of cake."

"You won't be going on while she's aboard. In the first place there's no telling what detection equipment she has going for herself over there."

"Or what protection devices," Niven said. "If the boat is set to blow up, it won't be with her aboard. We don't want to spook her, nor do we want to harm her. Could scare the enemy off."

Senarighi had to smile. It was gallows humor. "Something like that."

Niven raised the binoculars again and continued to study the lagoon, the line of docks in the marina, and the houseboat. From here they could read the name on the transom. She was the *Raggedy Ann* out of Dover, Delaware, and belonged to a rental agency here in the city. Toni Wagner had signed a three-year lease nine months ago. She'd planned on sticking around for a while. There'd never been any trouble with her, and she always paid her rent on time. The rental agent had been unable to recall anything else about her, except that he'd thought she was good-looking.

Nor had discreet inquiries among her co-workers produced anything useful to their investigation. Of course the Agency had been careful about what questions they'd asked and how they'd posed them. It was hinted that Ms. Wagner was being considered for promotion to another, more sensitive division of the IRS. The questions were routine, and were not to be discussed among themselves, and certainly not with Ms. Wagner.

"All you want is a bug on the hull?" Niven asked.

"Whatever it takes," Senarighi said. "I want to be able to hear everything that goes on inside."

"Three bugs," Niven said. "One in the middle, and one at each end. We'll have to run a wire back here. You'll need to post a surveillance unit somewhere nearby. Should be no problem, unless the she checks out this side of the lagoon. Or has someone else do it for her." Again Niven lowered the binoculars and looked at Senarighi. "I would if I were a spy in a foreign country. Wouldn't you?"

"Maybe. But I don't think she operates along those lines. Her specialties are cocktail lounges and bedrooms."

"Right," Niven said. "I've seen everything I need to see. How soon before we get our authorization?"

"I don't know," Senarighi said. They started back to their van. "It depends on a number of factors. But it won't be long. I can guarantee that this case is going to break one way or the other pretty soon."

"Who's she entertaining over there?"

"You wouldn't want to know," Harding said. "You're lucky you don't know."

"That bad?" Niven asked.

"Worse," Senarighi replied.

*   *   *

Toni Wagner (she always thought of herself by her current work name when she was in the field) hunched up her fur collar against the biting wind as she hurried down Pennsylvania Avenue. Most of the streets and sidewalks in the city had finally been cleared of snow, but the sky was deeply overcast and more snow was threatening.

Misha had been a very pleasant surprise. He was a real man: gentle, kind, understanding, handsome. A Russian in the truest sense of what that word meant to her. Joseph, on the other hand, had been a disappointment. When Ivan Kiselev first began her briefings on this mission, Joseph was described to her as a legend. "A Renaissance man of the late American sixties." A frontline soldier for whom there'd never been retreat. Now he was nothing more than a lonely, frustrated, frightened little man not sure of anything. Practically useless, except for this one last assignment.

The White House was on her left, through the tall iron fence and up the long, snow-covered lawn. She did not hate America or Americans. Nor did she hate the American government or its military. But like any "modern Russians," she was slightly intimidated by the raw freedom that was part of the new order, and wary of any nation that had the bombs and planes and submarines to annihilate the world ten times over.

Elect a madman to the White House, she thought, and the unthinkable might happen. Look at how close it had come during the Cuban missile standoff, or again over the hostages in Iran, and more recently the Grenada, Panama, and Iraq-Kuwait crises. America had proved that it would fight. There was no doubt of that in anyone's mind.

But would America use the ultimate weapons if she felt threatened enough?

It was Toni's job to find that out. That's all they wanted to know. That one bit of information. Intent, in the end, was what it was about. "Given the means, do they have the intent to kill us now that we're so vulnerable?"

She was certain that she had not been followed from the

Watergate to where she'd parked her car at the Hay-Adams Hotel. She'd come the rest of the way on foot.

At the corner up from the Executive Office Building west of the White House, Toni took a piece of chalk from her pocket, and stopping as if to look through the iron fence, she chalked a smiley face on the second vertical post from the end. It was the signal for Tyson to telephone her at number three—Watergate. Soon.

A moment later she turned, and crossed the street with a break in traffic. She headed up past the Blair House and turned right on H Street back to her car, still certain that she had not picked up a tail.

This time she was driving a dark blue Chevrolet Caprice, which she kept in the garage at the Watergate. It took her fifteen minutes to make it back, taking a roundabout route to make doubly sure she wasn't being followed. But so far as she knew, her FBI tail was still at the IRS parking lot off Constitution Avenue watching her Volvo.

Joseph was pacing the living room when she entered the apartment. "Well?" he asked.

"Any telephone calls?"

"None," he said, a note of exasperation in his voice. "Did you make contact?"

"He'll be calling."

"What if he doesn't recognize me? What if he calls a cop, for Christ's sake?"

"Don't worry," Toni said. "You'll be going back to Wisconsin in a day or two with our gratitude. Everything will be fine, believe me."

After taking off her coat and boots, she telephoned the American Automobile Association and asked them to pick up her Volvo from where it was parked. "It didn't want to start. Maybe the fuel line is frozen."

"It'll be at least an hour, maybe longer."

"That's okay, I'm in no hurry. I'll call first thing in the morning to pick it up." Toni gave the dispatcher her membership number and then hung up.

Joseph was looking at her, a bemused expression on his face. "Triple A, for Christ's sake?"

Toni smiled and was headed toward the kitchen when the telephone rang. She stopped and turned back. It rang again.

"Him?" Joseph asked.

"Maybe," she said. She went back to the phone and picked it up on the third ring. "Hello."

"I just saw it," Tyson said. He sounded out of breath.

"How are you?"

"I don't know. It seems like everything is coming apart at the seams. When can I see you?"

"Where are you calling from?"

"A phone booth on Pennsylvania."

"I don't think we should see each other tonight."

He started to protest, but she held him off.

"Listen to me, Al, not tonight. If it's your wife having you followed, coming to me could be dangerous."

"What then?"

"Take her out to dinner tonight. Someplace nice. Someplace public so that the world will see what a good husband you are."

"Toni . . . ?" Tyson said, obviously hurt by her sarcasm.

"Get hold of yourself. I'll be here. I'm not going anywhere. Take your wife out. The Rive Gauche would be nice. Make it eight o'clock."

"What?" Tyson sputtered. "What the hell are you saying to me?"

"Eight o'clock, Al. The Rive Gauche. We'll talk later."

"I think that this has come just in the nick of time," Kit Tyson said as her husband held the car door for her.

"What do you mean?" he asked. "Have I been that bad lately? Or are you getting tired of your own cooking?"

"Both," she said, grinning.

"I'll bet," he replied, closing the car door and going around to the driver's side. He'd decided not to use the chauffeured limo tonight. It was hard enough keeping himself together in front of his wife, let alone a driver who was a Secret Service agent. He felt as if he were walking on a lightly crusted pit of quicksand. Everywhere he looked was danger. If he broke through, he'd be irrevocably lost. There would be no coming back. Yet he could not see his future. He had no idea where all of this was leading, except that the President himself now knew or suspected something is wrong.

"I'm glad we're having dinner alone," Kit said as he started the car.

"Me too."

"I didn't want to share you with anyone tonight. As it is lately, we hardly see each other, you've been gone so much."

"I know," he said, looking at her. He felt so goddamned guilty. "Trouble is, it's not going to get much better very soon. Leastways not until Bob Harms is able to come back."

"How's he doing?"

"Not well."

"I see," Kit sighed. She reached out and touched his cheek. "But you are making a difference, darling. The rest of us can see it, even if you can't."

"Thanks for the vote of confidence."

"I meant it."

"I know," Tyson said glumly. He started the car and backed out of the garage.

"Here they come," Charles Goode said. He and his partner, Tom Parker, had been alerted that the Tysons would be on the move tonight, after the unit monitoring their phone had picked up Tyson's call for reservations at the Rive Gauche.

"We could've stayed home," Parker said. "Jeez, they're just going out to dinner. Five'll get you ten, they return home by ten or ten-thirty."

"You may be right, but this is a break in his routine. He's got a girlfriend and suddenly he takes his wife out to dinner?"

"Guilty conscience. Happens all the time. With some guys it's flowers, with others it's dinner."

*   *   *

The valet parked their car for them, and inside they were given an excellent table near the far corner of the room where they could see and be seen. In Washington the national security adviser and his wife commanded respect. The man had the ear of the President.

This evening, as was often the case, the restaurant was nearly full to capacity, but the acoustics were such that the sounds of conversations were little more than a muted hum. The Rive Gauche was a restful, if expensive, place to have a meal.

The maître d' fawned over them, helping with their napkins and making certain that their place settings were in perfect order. He introduced their waiter as Ricky and their wine steward as Dominick, and promised that if they had the slightest question about absolutely anything he would be instantly at their service.

"Enjoy your evening, Mr. Tyson, Mrs. Tyson," he said, and he left.

Tyson ordered a martini for himself and a glass of white wine for Kit, and as their waiter left, his glance strayed across the room to a man seated alone at a small table along the wall. There was something oddly familiar about the man. Something from the past.

"Beam me up, Scotty," Kit said.

Tyson turned to her. "What?"

"Wherever you are, that's where I'd like to be," she said.

He smiled a little too quickly. "Sorry." He forced himself to calm down. When they'd first come in, he'd looked for Toni, but she wasn't here. Maybe, he thought, she'd meant exactly what she told him. Simply to take his wife out to dinner.

"By the way, Debbie called this afternoon," Kit said.

"I still haven't finished that letter."

"She didn't mention it. But she thinks she might be able to come home this weekend. That is, if we're not going to be too busy."

"She can come home anytime she wants to."

"She wants to see you, I think. She didn't say it in so many words, but she's been having a hard time in the Foreign Affairs Club."

"Defending me?" Tyson asked, giving his wife his full attention.

Kit nodded. "I expect so. You're apparently not very popular at Kent State these days."

He had to smile. "The old adage: You work like hell to get your man elected or appointed to government, but once he's no longer a candidate, once he's actually in office, he becomes a crook."

"That, and you have the audacity to be a Republican."

"They'll get over it in another ten years or so."

"It's a tough world," Kit said.

"You can't imagine how tough," Tyson replied absently. His eye had strayed again to the lone man across the room. Christ, he knew the man!

"Yes, I can," Kit was saying. "I've been seeing it on your face lately. But how about it?"

"How about what?" he asked, again turning back to her.

"Debbie. Coming home this weekend."

Tyson shook his head. "Probably a bad idea if she wants to spend some time with me. The rest of this week, the weekend, and probably the next few weeks are shot."

"Okay, Al," Kit said softly. "I understand."

"I told you we should've stayed home," Parker complained to his partner. He and Goode were seated at the bar. They could see Tyson's reflection in the mirror behind the liquor bottles.

"He's spotted someone he knows across the room," Goode said.

Parker put his drink down, slipped off the barstool, and went into the dining room. He stopped uncertainly until a waiter looked up and came over to him.

"Sir?"

"The men's room?"

"Back through the bar, sir," the waiter said.

"Thanks," Parker mumbled, and he went back to his stool. "Not her," he told Goode.

"It could have been anyone, then."

"Yeah," Parker said. "But it would have made Reilly and Mote happy. As of six they still hadn't caught up with her."

Tyson tried to concentrate on Kit and on their meal, but he was continually drawn back to the man across the room. He wasn't at all sure, after a while, that he really did know the man, but the face, the build, the gestures, were all so damned familiar he couldn't let it go.

They'd begun with a half dozen oysters Rockefeller each, followed by an outstanding Caesar salad and a wonderful lobster bisque, switching wines on the steward's recommendation with each course.

Their Dungeness crab, flown in fresh from Puget Sound, was being presented to them when the man across the way signed his credit card slip to pay the bill. He looked up at that moment, and his eyes met Tyson's. For a second his stare lingered, but then he shook his head as if to tell himself that he was mistaken, and turned back to his waiter, who was saying something.

He did know the man! He was sure of it now. It was Joseph from Kent State. Older, of course, his face a little less gaunt perhaps. But definitely the same man. Tyson had sat across from him for hours on end, listening to his mesmerizing logic, looking into his eyes, studying his face. Here is a man who *knows!* Here is a man who has *seen!*

"Just fine," Tyson said, looking up at their waiter.

The man's eyebrows knit. "Sir?"

"The crab. It looks just fine. Thank you."

The waiter had been disjointing the big, complicated crab for them. But he put down his utensils and served it whole to them both. "Enjoy," he said, and he withdrew.

"Speaking for myself, I could have used some help," Kit said, bemused.

"Sorry," Tyson said, realizing what he'd done. "Do you want me to call him back?"

Kit smiled. "No. I guess I'm game." She turned her attention back to her plate.

Tyson sneaked another glance over at Joseph's table, but the man was gone. Disappeared into thin air. But that was impossible. Then Tyson looked up, and he was five feet away. My God, it was him!

"Al?" Tom Heller called. "Al Tyson, is it really you?"

"I don't . . ." Tyson stammered, but Joseph grinned and stuck out his hand.

"It is you. Good Lord, I didn't think I'd get to see you like this. Kent State. Been a long time."

Tyson half rose and shook the man's hand. His heart was thumping so hard in his chest that it was almost painful.

"You must be Mrs. Tyson," Heller was saying. "I'm Joseph Courtney. Your husband and I were students one semester at Kent State." He laughed. "It was a heck of a semester, so maybe he didn't tell you about it."

"He's mentioned Kent State once or twice," Kit said, shaking the man's hand. "In fact, our daughter is a student there."

"Ah, I see. It was a good school then, and it still is, from what I hear." He turned back to Tyson. "I mean, look at the talent it's produced." He shook his head again. "My God, those were the days. Diogenes the Dog, remember that?"

It was Toni's doing. But how in Christ's name had she known? And where had she dug him up? But more important, what was he doing here now?

"Would you care to join us, Mr. Courtney?" Kit asked.

"As much as I'd love to, I can't, dammit. I've got a late plane to catch at Dulles, and I'm going to have to hustle." He was digging in his coat pocket, and he pulled out a business card and stuck it in Tyson's lapel pocket. "Give me a call one of these days. I'd really like to talk."

"It's been a long time," Tyson mumbled.

"Boy, has it ever," Heller said. "Take care, now." He turned and left.

"Follow that sonofabitch," Goode told Parker as the man who had just made contact with Tyson headed for the door.

"I'll radio control and have them send a unit over," Parker said, slipping off his barstool.

"Tell them to move it. Tyson looks shook. No telling how long he'll stick around here."

"Right," Parker said, nonchalantly leaving the bar. Outside, he was just in time to see the man climb into a blue Chevy Caprice, a woman who looked like Toni Wagner behind the wheel.

"Shit," he swore, sprinting for his van parked down the block.

As the Caprice passed he tried to get the tag, but the light over the plate was out and he couldn't make the numbers.

The Chevy made a left against the light on Wisconsin Avenue, and by the time Parker got to the van, got it started, and headed around the corner, it was gone.

Racing north, he got on the radio. "Control, this is seventeen. We need help at the Rive Gauche. Charlie is on foot tagging Geronimo."

"Roger, copy, seventeen. Help is on the way. What's your status?"

"Am in pursuit of Hiawatha, driving a dark blue Chevrolet Caprice. License unknown. White male passenger, six feet two, slight build, graying, thick hair, dressed in a gray tweed sports coat, dark blue trousers."

"Say name of passenger."

"Unknown. But he made a pass to Geronimo in the restaurant."

"Roger, understand. Stick with them."

"Right," Parker said, hanging up the mike.

He hauled the van right on P Street, and a few blocks later left again on 30th, back toward the Tysons' house on the off chance they were headed there. But when he passed the house a minute later, there was no sign of the Chevy, and he knew that he'd lost them.

He got back on the radio. "Heads up, control, I lost them. Subjects may be headed back to Hiawatha's abode. Copy?"

"Roger."

*   *   *

It was getting late, and still they had not come up with the right photograph. Parker had worked with a sketch artist to re-create a reasonable likeness, though he had not noticed the man in the restaurant until he'd approached Tyson. Parker had not gotten a decent look at the man's face until outside, and then only for an instant. But it was something.

Using a half dozen general parameters of description, such as the shape of the face, the nose, the hair, the build, a computer selected photographs of known or suspected Russian agents or sympathizers from Bureau files.

To this point Parker had looked at more than five hundred photographs, some of them fairly close. In each near miss, however, backup files proved it was impossible that the subject in question could be in Washington. In one case the man was dead, in a couple of others he was in prison, and in one he was under surveillance in Berlin, and a quick phone call confirmed that as of six this evening (Washington time) he was still in Germany.

Parker had identified the blue Chevrolet as a late-model Caprice, but nothing had come of that from the Division of Motor Vehicles. Neither Toni Wagner nor any other Russian or known Russian sympathizer was the registered owner of such a car.

"Makes you wonder just how far their anti-American sentiment runs," Senarighi had quipped. "What's wrong with a Chevy?"

Senarighi and Len Harding had been called in because their team was heading up the Tyson surveillance. Natalie Reilly and Bill Mote were there because they had lost Toni Wagner, and still had not located her. And Allen Young, the chief of the Bureau's Special Investigations Division, had cut a dinner party short to sit in on the ID attempt. They were meeting in one of the small downstairs auditoriums adjacent to a computerized records terminal area.

"Are you sure the woman at the wheel was Toni Wagner?" Senarighi asked.

"Reasonably," Parker said. "But I wouldn't bet my life on it."

The next series of photographs came up, but the man looked nothing like the one Parker had seen.

"Next," he said.

"It could have been her," Natalie Reilly said. She'd been an FBI agent for three years. She was short, a little on the hefty side, and at times seemed hard as nails. She'd been a Tampa policewoman. "Triple A picked up her car around six-thirty. Said they got a call from her earlier in the afternoon."

"So she knows we're watching," Parker said, not looking away from the screen. "Next."

"Maybe not. Maybe she's staying with a friend."

"Hell, Natalie, for all we know she's spotted us and bailed out," Parker called over his shoulder.

"Not with Tyson as her prize."

"What good's a prize if the opposition knows you're after it?

"Hold that picture," Parker said, and he turned around. "She's been in bed with the man now for a while. We have to assume that some damage has already been done. So maybe they're going to cut their losses and run."

"Maybe Paris was no accident, have you thought of that?" Allen Young asked from where he was seated above and behind them all.

"I don't think so, sir," Natalie Reilly said, turning. "Paris was an accident."

"Then why target Tyson?" Young continued. "Have any of you thought of that?"

"He's young . . ." Natalie Reilly started to say, but Senarighi cut her off.

"Now listen, that's a good question. Why pick on Tyson, who is after all only the *acting* national security adviser? Why not Harms?"

"Harms is solid," Parker said.

"Maybe there's something out of Tyson's past," Senarighi said. "Maybe he was a bad boy last year, or the year before.

Some little indiscretion when he was a kid. He served in Vietnam, maybe he screwed up over there."

"Maybe he was approached at an early date," Young prompted. "Maybe Mr. Tyson has been a sleeper for a lot of years. Maybe they've decided that he's become too important these days to leave idle."

"Begging your pardon, sir, but why reactivate him now?" Natalie Reilly asked.

"Have you noticed any lessening of action from the Russians since the coup?"

"The opposite."

"Right. They're in the spying business in as big a way, if not bigger than they've ever been."

"Us too?" Senarighi asked irreverently.

"One would certainly hope so," Young said. "The questions for us are clear. Is Al Tyson a spy for the Russians? Where is Toni Wagner? Who is this mystery man and what did he pass to Tyson? I suggest we get on with it."

─────── 15 ───────

THE DINNER PARTY WAS ONE OF MANY THAT SEASON HOSTED BY Washington's leading socialite, Gloria Newgate. Sooner or later everybody who was anybody was invited to one of her parties, which usually lasted until one or two in the morning.

A *Washington Post* columnist had once quipped that perhaps more actual government work was done at her parties than in the various offices around the city.

Allen Young returned a little after eleven and pulled FBI Director Ed Wilder and the Bureau's general counsel, Ernest Reid, aside, and briefed them on the identification session he'd just attended.

"She'll have to be arrested sooner or later," Young said. "After all this I'd hate to see her walk off."

"Technically she's violated no law, dammit," Reid said. "Unless you can prove that she is indeed Raya Nechiporenko, in which case we can arrest her for a passport violation."

Wilder looked to Young for a reply.

"I'd be willing to risk a false-arrest suit. I'm convinced she is not who she claims to be. Once we book her and run a formal identification check, we'll know."

"That should already have been done."

"No clear prints on the Wagner woman from Idaho, or from this one here. We'd have to use dental records. And the real Toni Wagner has an appendix scar."

"Do you want to arrest her at this time, Allen?" Wilder asked.

"I would like the authorization to step up our surveillance of Tyson, and if he's contacted again by her, assuming she surfaces, I would like to arrest her."

"On what charge?" Reid asked.

"Espionage."

Wilder was nodding. "I'll have to go to the President with this. But I agree with you, Allen. In the meantime put your people on alert."

"Yes, sir. Thank you." Young made his apologies again to the hostess and left.

Surveillance of the Tyson house was now being accomplished around the clock entirely by electronic means. Three high-resolution, low-light television cameras were mounted, one on the roof of a building across 31st Street, one on a streetlight pole, and one in a tree across R Street in Montrose Park near Lovers Lane Walkway. Unless you knew exactly what you were looking for, you wouldn't see them.

All three telephone lines to the house, including the direct line to the White House, were tapped, as was the facsimile line into Tyson's study.

When Senarighi and his crew had entered the house, they had left behind enough ultrasensitive bugs to pick up conversations, even whispered conversations, in any room of the house. Filters and computer enhancing devices could subtract any kind of noise up to and including electronic white noise from those conversations. Short of some very extreme measures, it would be nearly impossible for anyone within the Tyson household to mask their voices.

The monitoring equipment and team were set up in the

basement of the Dumbarton Oaks Research Library less than two hundred meters to the northwest.

Tyson was at home, and Goode and Parker, unable to come down, drove over to the private library, where they parked behind the big, ornate building.

The night was dark, the trees in Montrose and Dumbarton Oaks parks heavily laden with snow. There was no traffic in Georgetown at this hour, and in fact, it seemed as if the entire city were holding its collective breath, waiting for something sinister to happen.

"What's going on over there?" Goode asked one of the technicians.

"Collecting a little overtime, Charlie?" he asked.

"I want to nail the bastard, then I'm going on vacation," Goode said. "Bermuda, maybe." He took the headphones and listened to the pickups inside the house, while he watched the three monitors showing the outside.

"They're sleeping," the senior technician said.

Rhythmical sounds, such as the refrigerator motor, the furnace blower, and even the grandfather clock in the living room, were being automatically filtered out. There were almost no other sounds from within the house. Perhaps the rustle of blankets or sheets, Goode thought. Nothing else.

"Anything?" Parker asked.

Goode looked up, shook his head, and then took off the headphones. "Nothing."

"You two might as well go home," one of the technicians said.

"Good idea," Parker said. "Charlie?"

"Call us if anything comes up, will you?" Goode asked.

"You bet," the senior technician said. "Now get out of here. You guys look like hell."

Vincent Privet's short time in America was coming to an end. He could feel it by the way Radchenko treated him. The man hardly dared to look him in the eye. And when your watchdog began to get that nervous, it was a sure sign that something was in the wind.

That, combined with Lydia Lubiako's simply incredible behavior, and appetites, was enough to convince him to begin his preparations.

This time he would use a suppressed .22-caliber handgun. An automatic with a twenty-one-shot magazine, the highly accurate weapon had been designed and built for him by the KGB's Technical Services Directorate. It was a lovely, well-crafted weapon that in the right hands could be extremely deadly over fairly long ranges.

Radchenko watched nervously as Privet brought the gun out of its case and began disassembling it, carefully inspecting and cleaning each piece.

"What are you doing that for?" Radchenko asked.

Privet looked up and smiled gently. "I'm getting ready to go to work."

Marina Demin was bunking with one of the female consular officers in a section of the embassy where the Russian housekeeping and maintenance staff were never allowed to go. No one had come breaking down the door looking for her, or demanding her release yet, but Sweeney wanted to keep her isolated until the situation had a chance to stabilize.

Besides, too many odd things had been piling up on them over the past days for them to take any chances.

Kaplin and Larissa Dolya were definitely out of circulation. Rodgers had managed to get word to the others on Kaplin's MOHAWK list, but so far as they were able to tell, the message had had no effect. No one had run for the hills, nor had anyone asked for asylum.

It was strange, Sweeney thought more than once, but it seemed like the calm before the storm, before the very large and devastating storm.

"A fucking hurricane," Rodgers said. "All we know for sure is that the Moscow Militia is looking for her, but that doesn't tell us much. Could be and likely is a KGB-prompted investigation."

"But they're being very low-key about it," Sweeney said. "What does that suggest?"

"That no one gives a damn about her."

"Or that she's telling the truth, and they don't want to make a major case out of it lest they embarrass a top government official."

"Sorry, Dick, but I think you've got a preconceived notion about this girl. You should put her and Kay together for an afternoon. We'd soon get our answers."

"We can't simply turn her back out on the street," Sweeney said. "Admittedly we don't care about the bedroom antics of Mukhin or any other Russian leader. But she's giving us some good insights into the man. Cross-references for the network."

"For a network that no longer exists. Let's face it, MOHAWK is a dead duck."

"Then we're going to have to change our targets, because the problem still exists. Once the dust has settled, we'll have to start over again."

"Right, and in the meantime what about our little Russian guest who is willing to tell us everything we don't want to know about the goings-on in the Kremlin, but nothing about her supposed pal in America . . . if he exists?"

"She's frightened."

"Goddamned right she's frightened, Dick. I'd be frightened in the same situation. What she thought was her ticket out of Russia turns out to be worthless. So now she'll tell us anything we want to hear."

"But she hasn't."

"Give her time to invent her story," Rodgers said cynically.

"You're probably right. But in the meantime, until she opens up she stays here."

"Fine," Rodgers said. "How far do you want me to take this query from Adkins?"

"About Major Kiselev's activities these days?"

Rodgers nodded. "He seems anxious."

"What have we got so far?"

"Nothing. Kiselev still works for One, but if he's been up to anything lately, we haven't gotten wind of it."

"Send a reply to that effect, and then see what else you can dig up. Maybe Adkins will tell us what he's got in mind so that we can get a little more specific with our investigation."

"That was an FBI agent outside the restaurant, wasn't it?" Tom Heller asked Toni Wagner. They were back at the Watergate apartment.

"Most likely, but you handled yourself well. You didn't panic, that's the important thing."

"What was he doing there? Waiting for me?" Heller was frightened. In the old days there was always Moscow. He wasn't so sure of that now.

"No, they're watching Tyson."

"They suspect him?"

Toni nodded. "But you're safe. Even if they got a good look at you, which in the darkness and under the circumstances I don't think happened, they won't be able to identify you. You've got no record. No arrests. No military service. Nothing."

"But what about the note I passed him? Marina Demin is dead. She can't want to see him. I don't understand."

"Neither do I, Joseph. I just follow my orders like you."

"Are you trying to turn Tyson, make him a mole for the Center? Like Kim Philby and the others?"

Toni grinned. "You've been watching too many spy movies."

"Goddammit, talk to me. Tell me what's happening."

"No," Toni said point-blank.

"But my life is on the line too."

"You're going back to Wisconsin in the morning. Your work here for us is finished. You did a good job, as usual. Don't screw it up now."

"But it's been so many years out there," Heller pleaded. "Christ, I never knew what was going on. I never knew if you'd call me again. Or if I was just forgotten. It gets lonely, goddammit. Don't you people understand? It's not like the old days."

"No, it's not like the old days," Toni said gently. "But I'm sure that after what you've done for us this time, Center will be calling on you again. Very soon."

Heller nodded. "I understand," he said. He managed a slight smile. "You should have seen the look on his face when he finally recognized me. I thought he was going to have a heart attack."

"Do you remember him from the old days at college?"

"Yes. He was always shooting his mouth off about how he wanted to save the world from itself, while screwing his way across campus."

"Who was Marina Demin?"

"My wife," Heller said.

Toni was rocked. She hadn't known.

Heller read something of that from the expression on her face. "His biggest infatuation of all was with her."

"What happened to her?"

"She went back to Moscow." Heller turned away. He felt ashamed that the ache was still so strong in his heart. It had happened many years ago.

"Did you ever hear from her? You said she was dead."

"She was killed in a car accident in Leningrad, or so I was told."

"And that's it? That's all you ever heard?"

Heller looked bleakly at Toni. "That's it," he said, his throat constricting. Christ. Christ.

"It makes me sick at heart," the President said. "I'm going to have to begin isolating him. But if I bring someone else in to fill his shoes before Bob Harms is able to return, the media is going to raise hell."

"Yes, Mr. President," Wilder said. It was a couple of minutes before eight. The President had agreed to see him first thing in the morning. As on the previous two times when they'd discussed Tyson, they met alone. It had been the President's suggestion.

"Then go ahead," the President said. "Step up your surveillance efforts, and if the woman surfaces, and she makes or attempts to make contact with him . . . arrest her."

"We'll do our best to keep it low-key."

"Yes, do that," the President said.

Back in the J. Edgar Hoover Building, Wilder called Allen Young up to his office. "He gave us the nod to go ahead with Tyson. Are your people in place?"

"As of last night," Young replied. "Starting now we not only intercept his phone calls, but we'll get his mail at home and at the White House. His driver will be one of ours, his secretary will get sick, replaced by one of ours, and we'll begin watching his friends and staffers."

Wilder nodded his satisfaction, if not his pleasure. Tyson was a patriot. He'd served in the CIA as its deputy director of intelligence, and in the National Security Agency as its assistant director. Those were two of the most sensitive posts in the entire world. Had he been selling us short all this time, the results would have been devastating. But the opposite had happened, hadn't it? The cold war was over. The Berlin Wall had come down. Freedom had returned to eastern Europe. And the democratization of the old Soviet Union had begun.

"What about the woman?" Young was asking.

"If she tries to make contact with Tyson, arrest her."

"Yes, sir."

Wilder leaned forward. "With care, Allen. And I do mean, with care."

Toni Wagner watched as Joseph got into a cab for the airport, and she felt a twinge of sadness for him. He had been displaced by an entirely new generation, and he was aware of it, but there was nothing he could do. The man would crack sooner or later, and Toni decided she would have to put that in her report when this operation was over.

Dressed in a sensible tweed suit, with a nice hat over a dark wig and a burgundy leather coat and matching boots, she got the Caprice out of the garage and headed immediately across the river on the Key Bridge into Rosslyn, where she picked up Interstate 66 west. She was taking a chance driving this car. The Bureau man outside the Rive Gauche last night had certainly made it, though not the license plate. But she would switch cars at the Fairfax safe house. Although the Bureau was undoubtedly looking for this car, they certainly wouldn't post roadblocks.

Now that Homeward Bound had begun, she felt a sense of anticipation for her next assignment, whatever it might be, though in between she was going to have a nice long visit with her family in Yakutsk. Afterward she was going to have an even longer sojourn with Misha, if he was free and he would have her.

Driving through the overcast, gloomy morning, she suspected that she was falling in love with her control officer, something she had never thought would happen to her.

Nonetheless she was glad of it.

Goode and Parker were back on the street by eight in the morning. It would snow again soon. Already it was being called Washington's worst winter.

They were parked around the corner on Avon Place. Two other units were in the neighborhood, and two more were stopped along the usual route Tyson took to work. In addition they had a tracer on his limousine, the driver was one of theirs, and one radio channel had been left open to monitor conversations inside the limo.

"Geronimo units, subject is on the move." Their communications radio came to life.

Goode snatched the microphone. "Control, seventeen, we'll go first. Look sharp, people. Any deviations, let the rest of us know."

Three minutes later the long black Cadillac limousine passed on R Street and turned south two blocks later on 29th. It was Tyson's usual route.

So far so good, Goode thought.

Tyson was desperately trying to shake out of the daze that had come over him. He hadn't slept at all last night, but he'd been afraid to get out of bed, or even move around too much, less Kit wake up and ask what was wrong. He was coming apart, and he knew it.

I guess I can sort of feel how you must have felt then. Sort of sad and scared and angry all at once.

He could not answer his daughter. How could he?

The front side of the business card Joseph had stuffed in his pocket was blank. But on the other side he'd written a note: *I'm coming from Moscow. I want to see you.*

Impossible. His head swam at the thought of it. What is happening? he wanted to scream.

The note was signed "Marinka."

Marina Demin.

"I must get back into the city to keep up appearances," Lubiako said. "But Joseph is gone, and you are ready for the next phase?"

"Yes, but the Chevrolet was spotted last night, so I will have to take another car."

Lubiako had been rinsing out his tea things in the kitchen sink, and he looked up. "The Bureau? Did they spot you?"

"It's possible, but it was dark and we were moving fast."

"Where did this happen?"

"Outside the restaurant."

"They were there watching Tyson, which means they also spotted Joseph."

"True, but they will have no way in which to identify him," Toni said. "He's completely clean."

Lubiako came over and looked into her eyes as he took her hands. "Nobody is completely clean. Not Joseph. Not you. Not me. If they catch us we will go to jail."

"Not for long. There will be a trade and we will soon be back in Moscow."

Lubiako smiled. "Do not be so sure, Raya. Times have changed."

"They won't abandon us."

"Look at Joseph," Lubiako said, and it was the first time she'd heard any bitterness in his voice.

"Did you know him?"

"Only of him," Lubiako said. He smiled again. "Even if we were sent back to Moscow, we'd probably end up unemployed. So take care."

Something else dawned on her. "You don't want to go home."

"Not yet," Lubiako said. "I just got here."

"But when this operation is over . . ."

"If we're successful, I'll stay, eventually taking Yuri's place as *Rezident,* and you will return home the hero."

"Somehow that no longer seems so attractive as it once did," Toni mumbled half to herself.

Lubiako brushed a kiss on her cheek, but the gesture was a hollow one. He didn't seem so understanding or kind now as he had at first.

Lubiako left first, and Toni watched from the living room window until his car had disappeared down the long hill toward the highway. In a way she felt a sense of betrayal, and yet she knew that she was being silly. Stupid, actually. This was not a sentimental business they were in. It was deadly serious. Entire peoples had been lost for lack of intelligence information.

It was also an honorable business, she told herself. Paris had shaken her more than she wanted to admit. She did not want the same thing happening here.

She was going to have to baby-sit him now, very carefully paying attention to his needs through the remainder of this phase and into the next, which hopefully would be the last.

She did not want to think what might happen beyond that point if something were to go wrong.

Rousing herself, she got her coat and hat, but before she went out, she took the .32-caliber automatic pistol from her purse and laid it on the kitchen counter.

The car, the last available to her, was a gunmetal-gray Nissan Sentra with less than five hundred miles on the odometer. This one was registered in her work name and was barely two weeks old. She'd bought it at a dealership up in

Rockville, across the river, and she did not think that the FBI had picked up on it yet.

She took Highway 50 down to Interstate 395, through Alexandria, and then the Rochambeau Bridge past the Jefferson Memorial into the city.

Washington, in Toni's mind, and in the minds of a lot of other Russians she knew, was like imperial Rome. A city filled with statuary, monuments, and columns that was the seat of an empire that hopefully was dying, too, because it had rotted within. There was as much major crime here as there was in cities such as Shanghai and Calcutta—maybe even more. There were graft, greed, corruption, and lies everywhere.

America, she'd been told before she'd ever been here, is a country of great lies. "Everyone lies to everyone else. Advertisers in magazines and on the television lie to their customers, husbands lie to their wives"—well, maybe Russian men sometimes did the same thing—"even presidents lie to their people."

She wanted to go someplace warm after this, she decided. Warm and sunny. Not dark and cold like here . . . or home.

Most of the surveillance units watching Tyson had stood down once he arrived at the White House. He would be watched from within. The moment he made a move word would go out.

Other units were watching Mrs. Tyson, Roland Clark, and individuals within the assistant national security adviser's circle of friends, co-workers, and acquaintances. But the main focus of their investigation now was on Tyson himself, and on Raya Nechiporenko, who still had not materialized.

Charles Goode was running purely on adrenaline. He had been putting in a lot of hours over the past days, and he hadn't been sleeping worth a damn when he did go home.

Parker wasn't in any better shape. Wherever his partner went, so did he.

They were driving east on Pennsylvania Avenue past the Blair House when Goode spotted Raya Nechiporenko on foot coming through Lafayette Park. He had to do a double take, his brain automatically rejecting the idea that she would show up here and now. But it was definitely her.

"Sonofabitch, it's her," Goode shouted. He grabbed the radio handset.

"What?" Parker said, but then he too spotted her.

"All units this frequency, this is seventeen, eastbound on Pennsylvania just across from the White House. We've spotted Hiawatha. Repeat, Hiawatha has surfaced. On foot, wearing a wine-red coat and boots, fur hat."

"Roger, seventeen, control. Hiawatha units, did you copy that?"

Goode replaced the handset and turned the radio volume down as Parker made a U-turn just across from East Executive Avenue.

The woman had already crossed the street and was walking very close to the tall iron fence a few meters from West Avenue.

The smiley face was still there on the fence where she'd put it. Tyson had only made the one call, however. The note Joseph had passed him in the restaurant had shaken him—at least that's what they had planned for. "The man won't know what's happening," Major Kiselev had promised. "You'll be hitting him three times: once when you tell him not to come to you for a while, a second time when Joseph shows up, and the third with the note."

But no one had told her that Marina Demin was Joseph's wife, come back to life. If indeed Joseph had been telling the truth. This was a nation of lies, after all.

"It will be time to hit him again. It is a psychological battle we'll be waging. We cannot afford to let up so that he can catch his breath."

Toni had already taken off her gloves. The fingers of her left hand curled around the chalk in her coat pocket and she took it out.

Parker slowed down about sixty feet behind the woman, pulling over nearly to the curb so that traffic would not back up behind them. Someone might blow a horn and the woman would turn around.

"She just took something out of her pocket," Goode said, sitting forward and peering intently out the windshield.

"I can't quite make it out . . ." Parker said, cutting himself off in midsentence. "Wait . . . wait. She just did something."

"It's a piece of chalk," Goode said excitedly. "The bitch just made a mark on the fucking fence. Let's get her, Tom."

"For what?" Parker demanded. "Defacing government property?"

"It's a fucking signal to Tyson, goddammit!" Goode exploded. "It's as plain as the fucking nose on my face!"

"But there's been no contact, man."

"I don't give a shit! I say we pick her up now! Right now!" Goode knew that he wasn't thinking right, but he didn't care. They had her cold, and he wasn't going to let this opportunity pass. He hated traitors, but he figured he hated Russians even worse. Old animosities died hardest.

Pocketing the piece of chalk, Toni continued to the corner across the street from the Blair House and turned abruptly away from the fence. The second smiley face would shake him up. He would not be able to hide from it.

Call me, Al. Now. Immediately. I need you. It was what she was telling him with the second mark. He would read the significance of it.

She would be back at the Watergate long before he spotted the flag. It would give her plenty of time to make herself something to eat, have a long, hot soak in the tub, and then perhaps a glass of wine. When he called she would be ready for him. He would be up, jumpy, frightened. She would be calm, relaxed, happy to see him. In his state he would tell her anything she wanted to know.

Across the street a Toyota van had pulled up at the curb and two men were getting out.

She stopped short. They had FBI stamped all over them.

They were looking directly across at her. One of them tried to cross, but there was too much traffic.

How had they traced her here? It was impossible. She would have bet anything that she hadn't picked up a tail in the last twenty-four hours.

Then she had it. Tyson. They had stepped up their surveillance of him. Drastically increased their efforts. She should have anticipated such a possibility.

She turned and headed down West Executive Avenue, outwardly calm, but inwardly frightened. This wasn't going to turn out so good. But at least she had left the goddamned pistol at the safe house.

Where the hell was the bitch going? Goode had expected her to bolt when she spotted them, but not that way. It was too . . . incriminating for her. Was she actually trying to run to Tyson, her lover? Jumped-up Jesus, was she that stupid?

Toni resisted the almost overpowering urge to look over her shoulder. She knew damned well the two had crossed Pennsylvania Avenue and were coming after her.

Misha, she thought. *I hope you are watching this. I hope you are seeing what is happening so that you can get word to Tyson.*

Else all their work would have been in vain.

She got about thirty meters when she heard them behind her. She tensed. A moment later someone grabbed her arm and spun her around.

"Raya Nechiporenko, you are under arrest," Goode said breathlessly. He seemed very angry. His partner stood back and to one side, his right hand in his jacket pocket. He seemed nervous but very competent.

"What?" Toni shouted, pulling out of his grasp and stepping back. "Who the fuck do you think you are? What is this?" How the hell had they come up with her real name? This was worse than she had thought it would be.

Goode pulled out his badge and awkwardly clipped it to the

lapel of his jacket. "I'm Charles Goode, Federal Bureau of Investigation. You're under arrest on suspicion of espionage against the United States."

Another Toyota van had come from Pennsylvania Avenue and pulled up behind the two Bureau agents. One man got out, and the other was talking on the radio, the microphone to his lips.

Toni laughed out loud. "You've got to be fuckin' kidding, you asshole! What the fuck is this, Russia? You the fucking KGB?"

A flicker of uncertainty crossed Goode's features, but then he pulled a set of handcuffs from his pocket.

Toni took another step backward.

Parker pulled out his pistol. A second later the agent who'd gotten out of the Toyota van pulled out his pistol.

Toni threw down her purse and raised both of her hands above her head. "Okay, okay, guys. Time out, all right? Jesus Christ, you want me, you got me. Just don't fuckin' shoot, they'd never believe it back in Idaho."

16

"She has disappeared, and we can only assume that the FBI arrested her," Igor Lubiako told the others in the *referentura*.

The table was silent. No one had expected this, at least not yet. She'd been so careful with her tradecraft. Everyone who'd worked with her gave her the highest marks. Paris had not been her fault. No one had pointed a finger her way.

"Then we must also make the assumption that Homeward Bound has been totally compromised. Is that what you are saying, Misha?" Lydia Lubiako asked.

"Not necessarily."

"What, then?" Truskin demanded sharply. "Moscow will have to be told something. And soon."

"Yes, I agree. But her arrest may not spell the end of the mission. Her legend was designed to withstand more than a casual scrutiny."

"They'll give her that much at least," Lydia Lubiako interjected.

"Physically she is near enough a match to what the real

Toni Wagner probably turned out to be to fool them. And there are no fingerprints. It was one of the first items our people out West checked on. Unless the real Toni Wagner surfaces, which is not likely—the woman has been gone for more than fifteen years—or unless Raya is broken, the mission is still viable."

"They'll break her," Lydia persisted.

"How, with torture?" her brother asked. "Here in America? It's not very likely, is it?"

"Then drugs," Lydia Lubiako said.

"There'd be no reason for it. Her only crime is sleeping with the assistant national security affairs adviser. Whatever they might suspect can only be that—a suspicion. Their attempts to place surveillance equipment in her houseboat have failed three times and they have not tried again."

"Which in itself tells us something," Lydia Lubiako argued. "The FBI has to be suspicious of her on those grounds alone."

"Not necessarily so. Our technical people tell me that in each case an analysis of the FBI's equipment will show product failure, not tampering."

"Can they be so sure?"

Lubiako shrugged. "One would hope so."

"I urged caution, you may recall," Truskin said.

"It's too late for that," Lubiako replied. "And too early for recriminations."

"Why did they arrest her, can you tell us that?" the ambassador's liaison, Vladimir Baturin, asked.

"That's the question, but I have no concrete answer," Lubiako admitted. "At least not yet. But I wouldn't be surprised if they got nervous and jumped the gun. She'd sent Joseph back to Wisconsin, and she'd come out to see me. From the Fairfax house she was returning to town to place a second mark on the fence. Afterward she was going to wait at the Watergate for his call."

"Somebody spotted her leaving the mark?" Truskin asked.

Lubiako shrugged.

"If that's so, then she's going to have a difficult time explaining herself."

"Again, not necessarily so, Yuri," Lubiako said. "Her mark was a smiley face, of the variety the Americans love to draw on nearly everything. Remember, she is presenting herself as the eccentric sister of a Vietnam MIA. But Tyson's surveillance team probably spotted her, and got nervous. Such things have happened before."

"How do we know that she has been arrested?" Baturin asked. "Or have I missed something?"

Lubiako shook his head. "You've missed nothing, comrade. As I said in the beginning, we can only assume she was picked up. She was to have returned to the Watergate apartment, but she did not. Nor has she appeared at any of her other usual places: the houseboat, Fairfax, her work, or . . . here."

"We're watching all of those places?" Baturin asked.

"Some of them electronically, others physically, yes. Which brings me to a final point. Tyson spotted the mark, and as of noon, has already telephoned twice."

Lydia Lubiako sat forward very fast, her eyes gleaming. "He doesn't know yet that she's been arrested?"

"No," Lubiako said. Intelligence evidently ran in the family. "Which is another reason to believe the mission may still succeed."

Toni Wagner felt pretty good under the circumstances, although the room she was in seemed warm by American standards. A thin line of sweat had formed on her upper lip, and she was panting a little, as if she had just run up a flight of stairs.

"How are you?" the man asked her across the table. He was speaking Russian. His complexion was gray and pockmarked. As a young man he'd probably had acne. "Are you being treated okay?"

She was an American, and she wasn't supposed to understand Russian.

"You have rights, you know."

What he was saying was reasonable. She nodded, and managed a slight, conspiratorial smile.

"Of course you do. Would you like me to call a defense lawyer for you, Raya?"

He should not have used her real name. But she did not need an attorney. She shook her head.

"Well, you will be able to walk out of here just as soon as you answer a few questions for us."

Fuck your mother, there it was, she thought. The catch. "I don't know what you're talking about," she said in English. "But I want to leave. Now. I don't have to answer any of your fucking questions."

"How about that?" Sandy Senarighi said from the adjacent room where they could see the woman and her interrogator, Leonard Mamedov, via closed-circuit television.

"We had her the moment she drank her water," Bureau psychiatrist Dr. Carlo Varelis said. "It was laced with thiothixene, which is a powerful antipsychotic. It has relaxed her without making her suspicious."

"We're going way out on a limb here," Allen Young said.

"Yes, sir," Senarighi answered, not taking his eyes off the monitor. "She should not have been picked up until she made actual contact with Mr. Tyson." He turned to his boss. "But pardon me, sir. If we let her walk out of here now, the entire investigation will fall apart on us. She'll run for home, and we'll be left holding . . . nothing."

"Twenty-four hours and there'll be no trace of this drug, or of the thiopental sodium I'll employ."

"She will remember this."

"In a vague sense, yes," the doctor said. "She will remember that she was arrested, of course, and that she was questioned. But none of the details will be clear to her. A little suggestion or two will alter her memory in a subtle way, so that if she were to be released, the Bureau would be in the clear."

Even Senarighi had to look sharply at the doctor, as did Young. This was America. They both were uncomfortable.

"She will not cooperate with us any other way?" Young asked, turning to Senarighi.

"No, sir. I'm afraid we *are* out on a limb with this one. But considering the stakes . . ."

"I don't like it," Young said.

"No, sir. Neither do I. No other choice."

After a moment, Young nodded, the movement of his head barely perceptible. Then he got up and left the room.

"The President wants to keep this as low-key as possible, which is why I am here," Ed Wilder said.

Secretary of Defense Francis Lipton looked across his desk at the Bureau director, and hid his dislike behind a mask of interest. In the seventies, when he had quit the House to run for the Senate from his home state of California, Hoover had had him investigated. The FBI had somehow found out that he'd been a John Bircher for a brief period one fall. He'd been a kid, and he'd wanted to find out what the organization was really all about. Once he was in, however, and realized what he'd gotten himself involved with, he'd immediately quit. But Hoover had been convinced that he was a radical. Lipton had not trusted a Bureau director since. They all had too much power, so far as he was concerned.

"What can I do for the Bureau, Ed?"

"I need some information."

"On what or whom?"

"Army records from the Vietnam era for someone who served on Westmoreland's staff."

Lipton's eyes narrowed slightly. "You cannot, or you would not, prefer to go through normal channels?"

"It's Al Tyson," Wilder said.

"I see," Lipton replied after a beat. He sat forward and buzzed his secretary. "Get the President on the phone, please. Tell him I have Ed Wilder in my office."

"Yes, Mr. Secretary," the woman said.

"We would like to keep our exposure as minimum as possible. There are other factors."

"Have you spoken with the general, or with Doug Gelderman?" "The General" was Robert Vaughan, the director of the CIA. And Gelderman was chief of the National Security Agency.

"Not yet," Wilder admitted.

"What is he suspected of?" Lipton asked evenly.

Wilder met his gaze without reaction. "Since you'll be speaking with the President, ask him."

Lipton's secretary buzzed. It was the President. He came on a second later.

"Good afternoon, Mr. President. I'm here with Ed Wilder. He's brought me some rather disturbing news about Al Tyson."

"Nothing has been proved yet, Francis," the President said. "But I want you to cooperate with the Bureau."

"I see," Lipton said heavily. It felt as if someone were pressing on his chest. He'd gone fishing in the Rockies with Tyson last year. "Then there is the possibility he's done something."

"Yes," the President said. "Is there anything else?"

"No, Mr. President. I merely wanted to verify."

"I understand," the President said.

Lipton hung up. "Exactly what is it you need, Ed?"

"Tyson's service record. The *complete* record."

National Security Agency Director Douglas Gelderman at fifty-eight was the picture of the high-powered CEO of some major international corporation. (In fact, he had held that position with IBM for a number of years before accepting his current job from Reagan.) He wore a dark, pin-striped suit, with vest and gold chain and fob. His hair was thinning and gray at the sides. He wore gold wire-rimmed glasses, and the shine on his wing tips and the buff on his manicured nails were impeccable at all times. His manner and bearing and thinking were precise. The job demanded it. From its eleven-acre headquarters compound at Fort Meade, Maryland, NSA monitored communications around the entire world. Military, diplomatic, and commercial traffic sent by radio, telex, teletype, and microwave were listened to and recorded. Satellite communications and telephone calls were eavesdropped around the clock. If a Kremlin minister of armaments in Siberia wanted to speak with someone in Moscow, chances are his telephone call would be picked up and monitored by NSA computers. Communications between ships at sea . . . ships of any nation . . . were monitored. And electronic code machines, and code-breaking machines, were devised and put to use by NSA. Now the agency even monitored and decoded the electronic emissions and control signals of machines talking to machines, such as telemetry data between satellites and ground stations.

Fran Lipton had called a half hour earlier, and Gelderman sat at his desk rapidly scanning NSA's own file on Al Tyson. The man's record was spotlessly clean. He had served as deputy director of the Agency for two years. Gelderman's predecessor, Dr. Mark Hammond, had written a glowing evaluation of Tyson's performance.

"Selfless devotion to duty . . . he's brought to his office imagination, insight, and compassion . . . a rare intelligence not limited in any way . . . a true patriot . . . a good American."

All the key words and phrases were there. No reservations, not a single *however* or *but*. Tyson had done an outstanding job for the NSA and was well respected for it.

Gelderman looked up from his reading. All that remained was politics, he thought. Someone was out to scalp Tyson. In Washington it never mattered if you were guilty or innocent. If an accusation was made, and made strongly enough, you were out.

He'd never thought Ed Wilder had such an ax to grind, but then again one could never tell.

Gelderman got his secretary. "Call the General, tell him I'd like to talk to him this afternoon."

"There or here, sir?"

"There. And if Ed Wilder calls, tell him I'll see him tomorrow. Advise the General to do the same."

"Yes, sir."

Whatever they were trying to do to Al Tyson would have

to be nipped in the bud. A good man such as Tyson simply could not be ruined that way. It would be a terrible waste. No matter what the President had somehow been convinced of, this could not be allowed.

"It looks as if your people jumped the gun arresting her like that," Wilder told Allen Young. "No clear link has been established between her and the Russians. Nor have we established that Tyson believes she's anything other than she says she is."

"We have established that the chalk marks on the White House fence were made by her. The same chalk was in her coat pocket and traces of it were found on the fingers of her left hand."

"So she's a graffiti artist," Wilder said sharply. Both Gelderman and Vaughan were gone for the day. He suspected that Lipton had called and warned them off. Tyson was a favorite son at both agencies. They would want to protect their own. And Lipton himself had been friends with Tyson for a number of years. On top of that the secretary of defense had no love for the FBI. Hoover may have been correct, investigating the man's past, but he had gone about it the wrong way. But that was then and this was now. He debated calling the President on it, but in the end decided to wait until tomorrow to see both men.

"Tyson left the White House twice to make telephone calls. He used a different phone booth each time."

"Did we get the number he called? Part of a number? Something?"

"No," Young said.

"Then it's still circumstantial until we get a mismatch on her physical description."

Young looked suddenly uncomfortable. "The woman we arrested does have an appendix scar, and her dental records more or less match the records we obtained in Idaho."

Wilder just looked at the man.

"There are a couple of anomalies, but we're going on the

assumption that she had dental work done elsewhere since those records were current."

Wilder thought back to the days when he was the top cop in Arkansas. He had the governor to answer to, of course. But ultimately he had to satisfy the will of the people. He'd been called everything from inflexible and hard-nosed to idealistic and even naive for his belief that the law was of and for the people.

He'd always thought that the man who sat in this office was the watchdog of this principle applied nationwide. Now that he was that man, he found that his ideals were a little blurred around the edges.

Young, realizing that something was wrong, stopped talking.

"Are you telling me that this woman voluntarily showed you her appendix scar? That she voluntarily opened her mouth so that you could compare her dental records? I hope you're telling me that, Allen."

"No, sir." Young sighed and passed a hand across his eyes. "She was given a glass of water to which a light dose of an antipsychotic drug was added. It relaxed her, took her normal reflex of flight-or-fight away from her, or at least diminished it."

Wilder said nothing.

"We used a Russian-speaking interrogator who questioned her in Russian. Although she did not respond in that language, she made indications, very clear indications, that she understood what was being said to her."

"Where is she now?"

"Downstairs, resting."

"Resting from what, or for what, Allen?"

"Varelis has given her some thiopental sodium. He wants her condition stabilized before we continue."

Wilder thought back again to Little Rock. His father had gone bankrupt and had shot himself to death. "Ambition can kill the best in us," the old man had preached. In the end it had destroyed the father, as it was about to destroy the son. Washington was a different arena than Little Rock.

"Do you understand what you've done?" Wilder asked, careful to keep his voice even.

"Yes. If she's innocent, if she really is Toni Wagner from Idaho, then we're in trouble. But we've gone too far now to back off." Young leaned forward. "That woman downstairs is Russian, I'd bet my life's salary on it."

Wilder looked at him. "You just might have to."

As she had done almost daily since Odessa, Marina Demin examined herself in front of a mirror, checking the almost nonexistent paunch of her belly, checking the few moles on her flanks and back, and fingering her small breasts for signs of lumps. There were none.

There were times, such as these, during which she barely knew who she was, or what motivated her. Ivan said she was driven by hate. Sometimes that was true. But just as often as not, she felt that she was driven by fear . . . mostly fear of the unknown toward which she was being propelled head-long.

Again she tried to sort out her memories in an effort to pick out the legitimate recollections from the implants that had been given to her. A difficult task, made even more difficult by the fact that her childhood had been so confusing, so lonely.

"There are three reasons you will do this thing, Marinka," Ivan had pointed out. "The first is for me. Because you love me, and it is what I wish you to do. The second is for the *Rodina*. You have your life, you have been nurtured. There is a debt to be repaid. But finally you will do this thing for yourself. The only question you must ask is about your motivation: Is it curiosity or revenge? Only you can answer that. But one of those reasons may end up killing you, so be very careful."

She could leave now, she told herself as she turned away from the mirror. She pulled a knit dress over her head and then slipped into a pair of sandals that tied around her ankles. In the bathroom she ran a brush through her dark hair.

If she put up a big enough fuss, the Americans would

release her. Sweeney was fascinated by her, she'd seen it in his eyes. He would intervene on her behalf and the front door of the embassy would be opened.

Then what?

She went into the living room. Her American watchdog, Donna Eklund, was doing something in the tiny kitchen. Marina picked up the telephone and got the embassy operator.

"Connect me with the Sweeney residence, please," she said in English. She glanced at the clock on the end table. It was just ten in the evening.

Donna Eklund, a thin black woman, came to the doorway. "Hey, what are you doing?"

Marina looked at her just as a woman she assumed was Sweeney's wife answered the phone.

"Mrs. Sweeney, this is Marina Demin. I would like to speak to your husband tonight if I may. Perhaps I can come to your apartment?"

"Of course you may, but just a sec," Katherine Sweeney said.

Sweeney was on the line a moment later. "Marina?"

"Yes. I would like to talk to you."

"Fine, let me speak with Donna. I'll have her bring you over."

The Sweeneys' apartment was large and very pleasantly furnished, but it was nothing less than Marina Demin had expected for the CIA's chief of Moscow Station. His wife, however, did come as a surprise. She wasn't empty-headed, nor did she appear to be one of the soap opera stars. She was good-looking in a solid, though Western, way. And she seemed to be very shrewd, even intelligent.

"Nice dress," she said when Marina came in and perched on the edge of a chair in the study, the only secure room in the apartment.

The knit dress was a little small, and she wore no underwear. The outfit was supposed to have been sexy. But Marina felt cheap now. She folded her hands on her bare knees. "Thank you," she said. "But I didn't bring very many clothes with me."

Sweeney brought her a glass of wine. It was French and much too sour, but Marina sipped it. Katherine Sweeney, smiling, was watching her like a hawk.

"Are you all right?" Sweeney asked.

"I'm frightened," Marina said, which was the truth. "There's something I haven't told you. Something . . . the real reason I came."

Katherine exchanged a look with her husband. "Should I leave?"

"No," Marina said, sitting forward. If need be, she would play to the woman. "I . . . this is very difficult for me, speaking with a . . . man."

Sweeney hesitated a moment, obviously not wanting to involve his wife.

Marina lowered her eyes. "I understand if you want to talk to me alone. Maybe tomorrow would be better."

"Now is fine," Sweeney said. "There is some skepticism downstairs. The Militia is looking for you. Our legal advisers say that we should release you."

"I don't want to go," Marina blurted, her nostrils flared.

"It's believed that you are lying. That you'll tell us anything; that you'll make up stories just to gain a U.S. visa."

"It's true I would like to go to the United States, but not for those reasons."

"What reasons?"

"You know," she said. "Economic. Things are not so good here in Moscow. Or anywhere else in what's left of my country."

"Then why?" Sweeney asked. "What is it you haven't told us?"

Again Marina lowered her eyes. "It is the truth, what I told you about Mikhail Mukhin. I did sleep with him for ten years."

"You must have been very young when you started," Katherine Sweeney said.

"Yes. I wasn't even nineteen. He saw me at the Kirov in Leningrad. I was in the corps de ballet, and he took me away, promising me Moscow."

Katherine Sweeney was still reserved.

"I attended Moscow University for a while, but never danced with the Bolshoi. After a while there never seemed to be the time. We spent a lot of weekends on the Istra River at his dacha. Once he took me to Helsinki, but we had to return the next morning, so I didn't get to see very much."

"Not such a bad life, considering the circumstances," Katherine Sweeney suggested.

"Before then I was in a state school, since I was five."

"Your parents?"

"My mother was killed in an automobile accident in Leningrad. I barely remember her, except that she was very beautiful. She wanted me to be a ballerina. It was what she always wanted."

Katherine Sweeney had softened a little. "What about your father?"

Marina ignored the question. "I wasn't very good, though. It's why I didn't go on. But I was given my chance. The state school promised me that. Just as I was allowed to go to the university."

"What happened?" Katherine Sweeney asked. "What are you doing here? Why do you want to go to the United States? It may not be what you think it is."

Sweeney was watching his wife, but he didn't seem inclined to interrupt her. At least not for the moment.

"While I was with Mikhail I found out something. I wasn't supposed to know about it, but I overheard a conversation one year ago. Then eight months ago I found a file and then a teletype message." Marina stopped. "At first I didn't know what to think. Perhaps they meant for me to hear and see those things, but there was no reason for it."

"For what? What things?"

"I have been gone from Mikhail for several months now. At first the KGB watched me. But then they lost interest. I am just a little nobody. It's always been the same, you know.

Now it is no different. But I had to wait to come here. They would have stopped me before."

"Go on," Katherine prompted.

"Mikhail was working with the KGB, so I knew it was important. It was those One bastards."

Sweeney sat up. "First Chief Directorate?" he asked. "What do you know about the KGB?"

"There were always KGB hanging around out on the Istra."

"Anyone in particular?" Sweeney asked.

"Ivan Kiselev. Mikhail had a lot of respect for him, even though he's only a major."

Sweeney's eyes narrowed. "Was this KGB major the one whose conversation you overheard?"

Marina nodded. "There is a plot to bring down a high-ranking government official in Washington. Someone who works in the White House."

Katherine Sweeney was impressed, but her husband's expression had become unreadable.

"I don't know all the details but I know that it is happening now, or very soon. They said before spring they would have succeeded."

"In so many words they said this?"

Marina shook her head. "No. They were always vague. They would say something and then go to a different subject. But always they talked about 'Homeward Bound.'"

"What does that mean?"

"It was a code name, I think, for the operation."

"To bring down a top White House official?" Sweeney asked.

"Yes."

"Who?"

"I don't know," Marina said. "But he is a very important man."

Sweeney looked at her for a long time. "How were they going to accomplish this?"

"I don't know."

"Then your story is worthless."

"But I can help," Marina cried. "If you will let me. If you will bring me to the United States."

"Help with what? How?"

"My father is involved. I can identify him for you."

"You're telling me that your father is a KGB agent stationed in Washington?"

"No," Marina answered, lowering her eyes again. "My father is an American. My mother worked in the United States in the sixties."

"For whom?" Sweeney asked.

"KGB."

"Then your father is a spy for the Russians?"

"No. It's the reason my mother returned to Leningrad. He wasn't very good. So they dropped him."

"A lot of information for a five-year-old to digest and then remember," Katherine Sweeney commented dryly.

Marina flared up. "I was a very bright girl. My mother spent most of her time with me before her death. I remember the stories."

"How do you know your father is involved in this plot?"

"Because Ivan Kiselev and Mikhail talked about him. His name is Joseph, and he is a teacher at the University of Wisconsin."

"There are a lot of Josephs in the States," Sweeney said.

"Kiselev said it was ironic that Mikhail was screwing his daughter, and that he'd better ease me out."

Sweeney and his wife said nothing.

"I've got nothing now," Marina said. "Not even my dignity. Let me help you before it is too late."

"Why?" Katherine asked. "You are betraying your country."

"The *Rodina* has done nothing for me. And they don't care about my father. He is nothing. Maybe I can save him. I know what he looks like. I will identify him for you, and the plot will be stopped."

"Are you ready?" Dr. Hamilton asked.

Charles Gleason had stopped at a self-service gas station to fill up the tank of his Thunderbird. He looked up. The other man was filling his car on the opposite side of the island. No one else was in earshot.

He nodded. "Is it time?"

"Homeward Bound. Just got the word."

"I'm ready," Gleason said.

17

DARKNESS WAS EVERYWHERE. ANATOLI KAPLIN COULD SEE absolutely nothing, though his eyes were open. At first he thought he might still be sleeping, but when he moved, the pain shot up from between his legs to his armpits and he groaned. He could hear the sound, which meant he was neither asleep nor deaf. It was something.

After a moment he raised his right hand in front of his face, but still he could not see a thing. It was just dark. He didn't think he was blind, though he didn't know why he believed that.

He was dressed in a light cotton shirt, but no trousers. A thin blanket covered his nakedness but provided only a scant warmth against the dank cold of this place.

It was a cell, he supposed. In Lefortovo Prison. Once in this place you didn't get out so easily. Even these days. He'd never signed the order to send a man here, but he knew enough about the place to cause him despair. Hopelessness hovered around him like a suffocating fog.

He didn't know how much longer he could hold out before he betrayed the others to whom he had promised salvation.

At no time in history were a nation's wrongs corrected merely by the voice of the people. Always it took force of one form or another. Revolution was more frequent than decisive elections. Assassinations, riots, demonstrations, and marches were what governments understood. Witness the results of the August coup.

In this new revolution Russia needed an ally—the United States—and so he had decided to spy. And he had convinced the others to go along with him. It was their effort to force even more change on the Kremlin. To guarantee the democratization of the old Union. To force the issue of human rights. To push even harder for the free economy that they'd been promised.

"We're becoming traitors out of impatience?" Boyarov had asked once. "Is this what you're telling me, of all people?" Boyarov was the executive secretary of the KGB's School One.

"If there is no movement soon, Vitali Konstantinovich, the entire country will fall. You know I don't trust Yeltsin."

"Back to the old ways."

"Perhaps. Perhaps only anarchy."

"Which would be worse," Boyarov said.

There was someone or something in the darkness to Kaplin's left. He turned his head that way, a little less frightened now.

"Anatoli," a man's voice whispered.

Sweeney had spent a restless night. He'd gotten up twice to go to the bathroom, and the third time he'd gone into his study, where he spent an hour and a half working on a lengthy query to Langley about Marina Demin. Included in his message were sections of the girl's answers to his questions last night. He'd lifted her words directly off the tape recording he'd made.

If she were to be believed, and he was still debating that with himself, then Operation Homeward Bound, which the

Russians had launched against someone in the White House, was of monumental importance, because that someone was Albert Tyson, acting national security adviser to the President.

He would have caught flak from Adkins had he put the message on the wire immediately. The Russians were not able to read their traffic, they were reasonably certain about that, but they kept a very close watch on the volume of traffic sent, especially the length of messages and the times at which they were sent.

A long message such as the one he'd composed advising Langley about Marina Demin (such messages were called book cables), sent in the middle of the night, would have rung alarm bells all over the Lubyanka. Someone, such as Major Kiselev, might put it together with Marina's disappearance and realize that their operation might have been compromised.

And that was another bothersome detail: the coincidence of Major Kiselev's name coming from two directions within such a short period. The old adage "Where there is smoke there is fire" applied here. In this business, where there was coincidence there usually were machinations, maneuverings, someone's hand pushing the right buttons.

The word *contrived* had come into Sweeney's head while he was listening to Marina on tape. Her story had seemed artificial, as if someone had scripted it for her.

There were holes in her story too. Such as: If she'd been in the Kirov's corps de ballet, why hadn't the Bolshoi here in Moscow accepted her? And why had she merely gone to school at Moscow University while she was a high-ranking Kremlin official's mistress?

But then it was those holes and other little inconsistencies in her story that tended to sway him toward believing her. No one could tell their life story without making glaring errors, forgetting important details while remembering (often incorrectly) other worthless bits.

And if she'd been scripted and rehearsed, wouldn't she have promised more? Wouldn't she have promised to identify the actual target of this KGB plot? The White House official they were supposedly trying to bring down? As it was, he figured he was going to have a tough time convincing Langley to go along with her. The biggest problem would be getting her out of the country . . . no easy task even in this age of openness and freedom.

Getting her out would entail some risks that could jeopardize valuable resources, even lives. And such risks were not taken lightly by Langley, nor did they authorize such operations very often.

Katherine knocked on the study door and came in. It was 8:00 A.M., and she'd been up for some time. She was already dressed.

"How goes the battle?" she asked. She gave him the cup of coffee she'd brought in and then closed the door.

"Thanks," Sweeney said. "I couldn't sleep."

Katherine sat on the corner of the desk. "Did you finish the book cable?"

Sweeney nodded and sat back, cradling the cup in both hands. "I still don't know what to make of her story."

"It was a tearjerker. She's quite the young woman, isn't she?"

This sarcasm was unlike Katherine, and Sweeney looked closely at his wife. "Problem?"

"If she's telling the truth or not, she's got the hots for you, Ernie."

"Come on."

"Come on, nothing. If she can advance her cause by sleeping with you, she will. And she believes it will, and so she'll try. Count on it."

"Still leaves me with the problem of believing her or not."

"Do you think Langley will?"

"I don't know," Sweeney said. "If they do we'll have to get her out of the country and back to Washington."

"Don't you do it," Katherine said.

"What?"

"If Adkins gives you the okay to bring her out, let Roy baby-sit her. Don't you do it."

"I may not have the choice. I am the COS here."

"Then resign, goddammit!" Katherine flared. "I told you that I'd back you one hundred percent."

"Easy, babe," Sweeney said, putting down his coffee and getting up. He came around the desk and took her into his arms.

"I mean it, Ernie. Goddammit, listen to me."

"Listen to what? A warning that the former mistress of a Russian government official will try to seduce me? Flattering, but it doesn't say much for my abilities to resist."

"You're a man. And like all men you think through your crotch sometimes. Besides, there's more to that little girl and her story than meets the eye."

"What do you mean?"

"I don't know. Just call it woman's intuition. But she's trouble, and I don't want anything to happen to us."

"Christ . . ." Sweeney started to pull away, but she held on to him.

"No, Ernie, I mean it. This is only a job. We've got our house back home. The Chesapeake. Sailing. Hiking. Picnics. We could even get some horses. Will you listen to me?"

"I'm listening," he said gently. "Nothing will happen, I promise you. But on this one you're going to have to trust my judgment. You're right, it's only a job, but it's my job and I know what I'm doing."

"You stubborn bastard."

Sweeney grinned. "This could be our ticket home. In which case you'll get your wish about the house sooner than you thought. Unless, of course, you don't stop calling me names."

Eight time zones to the west it was a few minutes past one in the morning in Washington. Tyson, also unable to sleep, had gotten up and gone downstairs to his study, where he sat behind his desk in the darkness.

By the dim light filtering in from outside, he'd poured a stiff measure of Scotch and taken most of it down in one swallow.

He'd tried all day to contact Toni, but there'd been no answer at the number. Later in the afternoon he'd tried the other two numbers, thinking he had made a mistake remembering which one he was supposed to call. But there was no answer at those, either.

She wanted to talk to him. Urgently. There were *two* chalk marks on the fence. So where was she?

He was so alone that at times he could actually feel his sanity slipping away from him. First Joseph showing up here. Then the message from Marinka. And now Toni's disappearance.

His world was falling apart. There could be no happy end to this. He could see no way out.

Finishing his drink, he opened the top left desk drawer. Even in the dim light he could see the dull glint of metal. It was a .38 Smith & Wesson Police Special. An ordinary pistol that he'd bought a few years ago for protection against burglars. It was loaded.

"Al?" Kit called from the stair hall.

Tyson looked up, his heart skipping a beat. "In here," he said after a moment, and he closed the drawer.

A KGB guard pushed Kaplin in a wheelchair into the Lefortovo Prison infirmary. Gray light from an overcast morning came through the tall windows.

"In there," the stern-faced nurse told the guard. "Bed seven, on the right."

The guard pushed Kaplin into a sixteen-bed ward that appeared to be just for women. "You have ten minutes," the young man said, leaving Kaplin at the foot of one of the beds. He turned and left.

A nurse at the far end of the long, narrow room was doing something to one of the patients. She looked up at Kaplin, but said nothing, and went back to her work.

Kaplin wheeled himself to the head of the bed, and suddenly he realized that it was Larissa lying there, her blond hair spilling onto the pillow. She appeared to be sleeping. Her eyes were fluttering slightly, and her lips were moving as if she were dreaming. Her eyes were blackened, and the left side of her jaw was swollen. But at least she was here in the hospital. They were taking care of her. He suspected that if she'd been placed in one of the cold, damp cells, she would have developed pneunomia and died. She'd seemed fragile to him from the start.

They'd brought him here like this in the hope that he and Larissa would talk, incriminating themselves by what they said. It was crude, and not very effective. In fact, he decided, seeing her again was stiffening his resolve not to give in to the bastards.

He'd been staring out the window, which looked onto a small courtyard that in summer might be a pleasant place to sit in the sun, when he felt Larissa's eyes on him. He turned back to her. She'd awakened.

"Good morning," Kaplin said. "How do you feel?"

"Physically I feel terrible, but they said they were releasing me as soon as I'm fit to leave."

Kaplin smiled. "There, you see, little girl. Although it might be dangerous sleeping with a man such as me, it's not illegal or fatal."

"How about you?" she asked, her voice small. "How are you holding up?"

"I've been better. But once those shits realize that I'm innocent and let me go, I'm going to rip them apart. Especially that sonofabitch Grigoriev."

Larissa reached out a hand from beneath the covers and Kaplin took it in his big paws. Her skin felt warm.

"What did they do to you?" he asked.

"The hysterectomy. They said I was bleeding too much. There was no other choice."

Kaplin's grip tightened on her hand. "I'm sorry."

"I didn't think it would turn out this way when I . . ."

Kaplin squeezed her hand so sharply that she stopped in midsentence and nearly cried out. He gave her a warning look. For a moment she seemed confused, but then understanding dawned in her eyes.

"I know," he said soothingly. "But perhaps you will adopt

children. One way or another you will have the family you wished for."

"A big family," she said, smiling.

"An immense family. Twelve children, maybe more."

The young KGB guard came back. "It is time," he said impassively.

"Get away from me, you shit," Kaplin bellowed. "My ten minutes are not up."

The guard pulled Kaplin in the wheelchair away from the bed and pushed him toward the door.

"Well, anyway, when I get out of here I'll see you back at the apartment," he called to her. "We'll have something to eat and drink."

The irritating buzz of the fluorescent lights in the U.S. Embassy's screened room was in actuality the product of a white-noise generator that was one of the electronic means to nullify Russian eavesdropping efforts. So far as the CIA knew, their countersurveillance methods were effective.

More difficult to guard against, however, were human eavesdroppers. Spies. Doubles. Moles. The fact that Marina Demin would be speaking to them in this room made the Product Risk and Evaluation Committee Sweeney had gathered nervous.

"I can't think of a more ingenious way in which to penetrate our security," Tony Havlachek, the embassy's general counsel, commented.

"Once we let her in here, Dick, we can't release her," Rodgers warned. "She'll have to be completely isolated, even if she is smuggled out of the country and brought back to the States."

"At the very least she'd name us," Havlachek said. "It'd be a hell of a start for their Department Two people."

It was approaching 10:00 A.M. Sweeney had listened to the debate for nearly a half hour since he'd passed the proposed book cable around for them to read.

He could have sent the message on his own recognizance, but in light of some embarrassing incidents worldwide with chiefs of station who'd jumped the gun, or had been sucked in by the opposition, a new policy had been formulated. SOP now was for the PR&E Committee to review any and all operations. The only exception was an extreme emergency where time was so critical the committee could not be convened. That decision was the chief of station's.

In this instance, although the business with Marina Demin was of extreme importance, they were not so constrained by time. And they had other matters to consider this morning as well, among them the demise of MOHAWK, the arrest of Kaplin and Larissa (still no one had devised any real plan for helping her), and the total lack of response from the others in the network to their signals for help.

"Before we get started with discussion of this book cable of yours, what about Larissa Dolya?" David Zuckerman, the liaison between the CIA and the ambassador, asked.

"I was about to bring up the subject," Sweeney said. "Langley has denied our request to offer a trade."

"It's not going to help our recruiting efforts," Rodgers said.

"It's felt that because she is, at least in the eyes of the Russian government, still a Russian citizen, they would not release her *quid pro quo*. We would have to give them much more."

"How much more?" Zuckerman asked bitterly.

"All of MOHAWK."

"Hell, they've probably already got that," Rodgers said. "So we'd be giving them nothing."

"Confirmation."

"Then we're back to square one," Rodgers continued. "What do we do about her?"

"Exactly what we've been doing, Roy," Sweeney said. "We continue to watch Lefortovo until she's released. If and when that happens, we snatch her and hustle her across the border."

"The same thing you're proposing to do with Marina Demin if Langley gives us the okay," Rodgers said. "Not so easy. Certainly we couldn't use the same route twice."

"No—" Sweeney said, but Havlachek interrupted.

"Aren't we getting ahead of ourselves here?" he said. "The book cable hasn't been sent yet."

"That's a decision we will make this morning," Sweeney said. "You've all read it. You've listened to the tape I made last night. Now it's your call. Do you want to talk to her before I send it?"

"I think we'd better," Havlachek said, looking at the others around the table. "Hell, I don't think we have any choice, considering what she's telling us. I mean, my God, if it's true about this Homeward Bound of theirs, it has to be stopped. At all costs."

"I agree, I guess," Zuckerman said.

Rodgers nodded after a minute.

Sweeney phoned next door. "Send her in, would you, Donna?"

"Yes, sir."

Kay had rounded up some clothes for Marina. She was dressed in a decent wool skirt and sweater, nylons, and suede pumps. She'd brushed her hair, but she wore no makeup. Sweeney decided she looked a lot less dangerous this morning than she had last night.

There was an empty chair at the end of the table. Sweeney motioned toward it. "Please have a seat, Miss Demin, there are a few questions we'd like to ask you."

Marina was nervous. She sat down and clasped her hands in front of her on the table.

"There is no need for you to know anyone's name here, but everyone has listened to the tape recording I made of our conversation last night."

Marina flinched.

"You're perfectly safe in the embassy, and I promise you that the tape won't go any further."

She laughed uneasily. "It is not so dangerous for me as it is for you."

"That's what we'd like to find out this morning, Miss Demin," Havlachek said.

She looked at the lawyer. "Yes, and what is the exact

purpose of this meeting?" She glanced at Sweeney. "I told everything to Mr. Sweeney last night."

"We'd like to find out if you are telling the truth," Havlachek said.

"I am," she snapped. "What reason would there be for me to lie? Can you tell me this? I am giving up my country. Do you think I will ever be able to come back here?"

"The Militia are looking for you," Rodgers said.

"Those idiots couldn't find anything."

"But they're not looking very hard. Maybe not hard enough. One would think that the Kremlin would have asked for help from the KGB, considering the apparently close ties that Mikhail Mukhin has with Major Kiselev."

"I don't know. They did not take me into their confidence when I was tossed out onto the trash heap. It wasn't so nice. And I didn't stop to ask questions, either."

"But we must," Rodgers said. "Considering the gravity of what you've said."

"What do you lose if I am lying?" she asked. "A trip to the States? Or perhaps I am a spy and when I get back I will tell them about this room, and I will pick your faces from photographs."

"It's possible," Rodgers agreed.

"What do you gain if I am telling the truth about Homeward Bound? Think of that."

There was silence in the room, except for the buzz of the light fixtures.

"You say your father is a teacher in Wisconsin. How do you know this?" Havlachek asked.

"My mother told me."

"That was at least twenty-four years ago. He might not still be there."

"He's there," Marina said. "Or in academia somewhere. We will be able to find him."

"How will you recognize him?" Havlachek asked.

"When I was little I had three photographs of him. I used to study them at night after I had gone to bed. I will know him when I see him."

"Then what?"

"Then you will stop him. You will make him tell you who their target is."

"But you said that your father no longer works for the KGB," Rodgers said.

"He never worked for them. Only my mother did, and he really didn't know."

"But they were married . . ."

"No," Marina said.

"No, what?" Rodgers asked.

"They were not married. At least I don't think they were. That part is confusing for me."

Havlachek sat forward. "Let me get this straight, Miss Demin," he said. "Your father doesn't work for the KGB, but they are going to use him to bring down this White House official."

"That's right."

"How?"

"I don't know that part, except that it has something to do with confronting him with his past."

Sweeney looked up. This was something new. "What do you mean by that? Confronting him with his past? Are you saying that this White House official worked for the KGB sometime in the past?"

"I don't think so. But it was something they felt would be strong enough to turn him."

"Turn him into a spy, for Russia?" Sweeney asked.

"Yes. Major Kiselev believes he can do it. I heard him boasting that once Homeward Bound was in place, he would be the most important spy in the history of the business."

"You can say that again," Rodgers mumbled.

The book cable that had come from Moscow was nothing short of stunning in CIA Director Vaughan's estimation. He'd called Defense Secretary Lipton and NSA Director Gelderman to Langley for a breakfast meeting. He'd also called in the Company's general counsel, Morris Segal.

It was just eight in the morning. The four of them were alone in the director's private dining room on the seventh floor. The servers had withdrawn.

"I've briefed Morris on the situation, and I've asked him to sit in with us this morning because of the obvious legal ramifications of what we may do . . . or not do," Vaughan began.

"You've had some news overnight?" Gelderman asked.

"Yes," Vaughan answered. "When I share it with you, I think you'll agree that it tends to verify what we're all thinking. Namely that Al Tyson is innocent of the charges Wilder is trying to prove against him. And in fact, he has become the target of a Russian plot to bring him down."

"Extraordinary," Lipton said. "But are you telling us that you suspect Wilder is somehow involved with them?"

"No," Vaughan dismissed the suggestion. "Wilder might be politically motivated . . . something we're going to have to be careful to watch for . . . but I don't believe he's working for the Russians."

"Wittingly or unwittingly," Segal interjected.

"But he believes that Al is guilty because of his association with this woman," Gelderman said with some distaste obvious in his voice. "Of all things for the man to do, having a mistress isn't one of them."

"Therein lies the grain of truth which Wilder is following. The woman who identifies herself as Toni Wagner, an American, may in fact be a Russian spy by the name of Raya Nechiporenko."

"Are we sure of this, General?" Gelderman asked.

"No, but if she is a Russian spy, then her control officer in Moscow is a man by the name of Ivan Kiselev. He's a major in the KGB's First Chief Directorate. A first-class officer, I'm told."

"There is a significance to this information?" Lipton asked. "What are you driving at?"

"In just a moment, Fran," Vaughan said. "First tell me about Tyson's Army records. You sent them along to Wilder?"

"Of course. His past is clean. He was a model officer. Westmoreland gave him the highest marks. He went so far as to make a note to Tyson's jacket that if there was anything in his power that he could do to keep Tyson with him, or at the very least in the Army, he wouldn't hesitate to do it."

Vaughan nodded, turning to Gelderman. "Doug?"

"Same as NSA. Mark Hammond gave him top marks. Not a blemish in his record."

"The same here with us," Vaughan said. "Which on the surface does strike me as being a little odd. There's hardly a man alive who doesn't have a little black mark against him somewhere. A disagreement with a boss. A personality clash. A lapse of judgment."

"You forget," Lipton said. "By the time Al got to you and the NSA he was already well blooded. He'd served his youth . . . with its exuberances and mistakes . . . under Westmoreland in the war. I'm sure he made his share of screwups over there, but . . . You know about that mess. No one was lily-white."

"And the President has confidence in him," Gelderman said.

Vaughan hesitated for a moment or two, thinking how ironic it would be if Tyson were actually working for the Russians. The ramifications of such a thing were enormous. It would set back U.S.-Russian relations beyond repair for a long time to come. But if Tyson were indeed working for the Russians, then their supposed Operation Homeward Bound (in itself a curious operational name) and Marina Demin's story would be elaborate ruses to get the CIA to believe that Tyson was innocent. In that subtle manner the Russians would be legitimizing their mole while on the surface apparently trying to bring him down.

But that kind of thinking led to insanity. Was the man a double? Seeming to work for us when in reality he worked for the Russians? Or was he a triple, seemingly to the Russians working for them while in reality working for us?

If that were the case, someone in this country would have to be giving him instructions. Who?

"What I'm about to show you is classified Top Secret," Vaughan said. "It all stays in this room."

"The President . . ." Lipton began.

"Will be told when the time is appropriate," Vaughan said sharply.

After a moment Lipton nodded, and then so did Gelderman. Vaughan took copies of Sweeney's book cable from a folder beside him and passed them across the table.

"This came from my chief of Moscow Station early this morning. So far we've made no recommendations, though Dick Adkins wants Sweeney to escort the woman here."

"What woman?" Gelderman asked.

"Read Sweeney's cable," Vaughan said.

It took them nearly ten minutes to read the lengthy message. Gelderman read it twice. They both looked up, troubled expressions on their faces.

"If they get hold of this on the Hill, the Russian aid package will go down the drain," Lipton said. "They're not supposed to be doing this kind of thing these days."

"But they do, Fran," Vaughan said. "And so do we. But quietly. No one on the Hill will find out about this."

"What, then?" the defense secretary asked. He was a man who'd always believed in frontal attacks. "Call Novikov on your hot line . . . and don't tell me the line to the KGB chairman doesn't exist . . . and inform him that we know what he's up to, and that it must stop."

"No," Vaughan said. "In so doing we would have to acknowledge too many of our own resources. It would be disastrous."

"No more disastrous than bringing Tyson down."

"Maybe. But there's another way. A way in which we can have our cake and eat it too."

"How?"

"We protect Tyson, of course, without ever letting the Russians know we're doing it."

"Or Wilder," Gelderman put in quietly.

Vaughan looked at him. "Unfortunately, I must agree

with you, Doug, even though it'll probably make him look bad."

"He'll be all right," Gelderman said. "We won't let it go *that* far."

"No," Vaughan said. "But Tyson must not be brought down."

"No," Gelderman said.

"Agreed," Lipton added.

"Let me get this straight," Ed Wilder said. "Even under the influence of thiopental sodium you've gotten nothing out of her?"

"Not as much as we'd hoped, no, sir," Allen Young said. "Dr. Varelis suggests we use more powerful drugs . . ."

"No," Wilder said.

"I've already vetoed the suggestion," Young said. "But without direct testimony from her, we have no proof. Or not enough to hold up in court."

"Let's begin with her birth records in Idaho. Footprints?"

"Smudged."

"Medical records? Blood type."

"Same blood type, but of course the hospital where her appendix was taken out kept no blood or tissue samples from which a DNA cross-match could have been made. The dentist doesn't remember the Wagner woman that well. The photographs we showed him were inconclusive in his mind."

"No relatives?"

"None," Young said. "Except for the brother who is a Vietnam MIA. For a time he was suspected of being a deserter. There was a report, unconfirmed, that he'd been seen in Hanoi."

"Driving record?"

"No fingerprints. But everything on the sheet matches."

"Passport?"

"None applied for under that name that matches her photograph or description."

"What about the CIA? Anything from their files on Raya Nechiporenko that would tie her to Toni Wagner?"

"We've heard nothing from them," Young said.

"No one we could bring from Paris who might recognize her?"

"The request has been made through channels, but so far we've heard nothing."

Wilder sat back in his chair and steepled his fingers. "What have we got on the plus side?"

"Not much, sir. But what we've come up with is interesting, and incriminating."

"Besides the chalk mark."

"Washington PD picked up an abandoned vehicle, a Nissan Sentra near the Hay-Adams Hotel. Turns out it was registered to Toni Wagner. Means she had two cars, the Nissan hidden until now."

"How did she explain that?"

"Kept it at a friend's, though she wouldn't explain why," Young said. "We searched her houseboat and came up with a thirty-five-millimeter camera, and a dozen rolls of very fast film. Black and white. Something ordinary people don't often use. We also found a few grams of high-quality cocaine, a couple of ounces of good marijuana, and a cigarette rolling machine and papers."

Wilder said nothing, his lips compressed to a thin line.

"Senarighi discovered that the cassette tape player in her bedroom had been modified to record on one track of the tape while the other was playing."

"That's not unusual, is it? Professional musicians use that sort of thing. Dubbing."

"She's not a musician so far as we know."

"What else?"

"She understands Russian. She won't speak it, but when spoken to in Russian she gives the correct responses. In English."

"Have we asked her point-blank about her relationship with Tyson?"

"She says they are lovers."

"Has she been asked if she is a spy, or if she's spying on Tyson?"

"Yes. She says that it's rubbish, that he tried to tell her 'his grubby little secrets,' as she calls them, but she didn't want to hear them."

"Then she's innocent," Wilder said.

"Or her conditioning is deep. Varelis seems to think her answers come too easily."

Wilder turned and looked out his window. The morning was gray. It looked like still more snow. "We may have to release her," he said.

"Sir . . . ?"

"But first I want another bug put on her houseboat. Senarighi had an idea. And set up an all-out surveillance of her. I want to know every single thing she does, every single moment of every single day and night."

"Yes, sir," Young said with the first enthusiasm he'd shown all morning.

18

"THERE'S AL TYSON. LET'S ASK HIM TO JOIN US. MAYBE HE can help clarify the President's position," Wilder said

He was having lunch in the Executive Office Building dining room with Dr. Howard Bayer, special consultant to the President for narcotics and dangerous drugs. Wilder had set up the meeting ostensibly to discuss the President's views on using the military to back up DEA efforts, especially off the coast of South America. In reality he had come here in the hope of running into Tyson.

Dr. Bayer seemed a little uncomfortable. He was in his late sixties, with thin white hair and a pink complexion that was mottled now.

"Anything wrong, Howard?"

"Perhaps we should leave Al Tyson out of this."

"Why? He is the national security adviser. At least until Harms returns."

Dr. Bayer shrugged. "Maybe not for long. There've been hints that he might be on his way out. Harms may never come back, and word is that the President might ask his old friend

Charlie Gleason to come over from Reston. He'd be the smartest man in that job since Kissinger."

"Is that all you've heard?"

"Look, as odd as it may sound coming from a person such as myself, I don't want to get involved in political infighting, if you catch my meaning."

"I don't," Wilder said, studying the older man's eyes. Dr. Bayer was withholding something.

"May I be frank?"

"Please."

"Whatever trouble there is between you and Al Tyson I don't want to become a part of it."

Wilder nodded. "Where did you hear something like that, Howard?"

Dr. Bayer said nothing.

"Let *me* be frank. Have you spoken recently, by chance, with Fran Lipton, Doug Gelderman, or General Vaughan?"

Dr. Bayer reacted. It was clear Wilder's question had hit the mark.

"Let me tell you something. I have no problem, political or otherwise, with Al."

"Okay," Dr. Bayer said after a moment. He looked across the crowded dining room to where Tyson had taken a seat by himself. A waiter was taking his order. "But I have to run along now. My afternoon is shot, and unless I get at it immediately I'll be swamped."

Wilder said nothing as Dr. Bayer put down his napkin and got up.

"If you want to pursue this thing about a joint DEA-military operation, you can come to my office, or I'll come to yours—with or without Al."

"Fine, Howard," Wilder said. "I'll do that soon."

Dr. Bayer turned to go, but Wilder stopped him.

"Howard, on the way out, ask Al to join me, would you?"

Dr. Bayer's eyes narrowed, but he nodded, and crossed the room. Tyson looked up as Dr. Bayer reached him and said something, and then glanced over to Wilder, who waved. Tyson said a few words, and then Dr. Bayer left.

A second or two later Tyson beckoned his waiter over, told the man something, and then got up and came over.

"Dr. Bayer had to leave suddenly, and I hate to eat alone," Wilder said, half rising and shaking Tyson's hand.

"I don't usually mind, except on a day like this. I'm absolutely swamped."

"Exactly Dr. Bayer's words. But you have time for a quick bite. Besides, there's something I'd like to talk to you about."

Something flashed in Tyson's eyes, but then was gone. "All right," he said, sitting down.

The waiter came over, cleared Dr. Bayer's lunch things away, and laid a fresh setting. When he was gone Tyson sipped his drink.

"Any word on Bob Harms' condition?" Wilder asked.

Tyson shook his head. "He'll probably not be back. The President will be making an announcement soon."

"I'm sorry for Bob's sake, but are congratulations in order?"

"I don't know," Tyson replied tightly. He was obviously nervous. In fact, it looked as if he'd not been sleeping well lately. He finished his drink.

"Is everything all right?" Wilder asked.

"Look, I've got to get back to my office. Perhaps we can talk another time. Call me."

"Actually I wanted to talk to you today. I was hoping I'd bump into you like this."

Tyson said nothing.

Wilder looked directly into Tyson's eyes. "This is going to be a little embarrassing, Al. I'm sorry, but I don't know any other way to do it, which is why I'm glad you're here like this away from the White House."

"What is it?" Tyson asked, finding his voice. He sounded shaky.

"We arrested a woman yesterday, and after talking to her we've come up with a number of questions."

"I see," Tyson answered, seemingly girding himself for whatever was to come. "What is she being charged with?"

"Possession of narcotics. Cocaine. Pot. Practically the whole gamut."

Tyson glanced toward the exit where Dr. Bayer had gone. "What does this have to do with me?"

"Well, that's the embarrassing part," Wilder said, not averting his eyes. Tyson was sweating. "Actually I was hoping to get some help from you. Apparently you and she . . . know each other."

"I see."

"Her name is Toni Wagner."

Tyson flinched.

"We've been following her for some weeks now, and . . . Well, you were seen on at least two occasions entering her houseboat parked at . . . some marina on the river."

"The Columbia Island Marina," Tyson said softly.

"Then you do know her."

"Yes."

"I really dislike asking you this, you know," Wilder said. "But exactly what has your relationship been with Miss Wagner?"

Tyson lowered his eyes. "She and I are . . . lovers."

"I see," Wilder said. "How long has this been going on?"

"A few months."

"Have you ever done drugs with her?"

Tyson looked up, his teeth practically bared. "No."

"Were you aware that she possessed drugs?"

"No."

Wilder nodded and sat back. "What do you know about her background?"

"Not very much," Tyson said miserably. "She's originally from out West somewhere, Montana or Idaho. She has a brother who is an MIA in Vietnam. And she does contract work for the IRS."

Wilder held his silence for a second or two, his eyes locked with Tyson's. "Anything else you can tell me? Anything at all that might help our investigation?"

"No," Tyson said after an equally long silence. "And for obvious reasons I'd not like this to go public."

"I'll do my best, Al," Wilder said. "But of course I can't guarantee a thing. You know how it is. Depends where our investigation leads us." Wilder smiled. "Listen, if you happen to think of something else that might help us, anything, anything at all, give me a call day or night."

"I'll do that," Tyson said.

Tyson's legs felt like rubber. He could sense Wilder's eyes on his back all the way across the dining room and out the door. He had to resist the urge to look over his shoulder, and the even stronger urge to run. There was simply nowhere for him to go.

Outside, he debated going home, or simply driving off so that he could have the time to think. But if they'd been watching Toni, and were still investigating . . . whatever it was they were investigating . . . they might be watching him. He would have to act normal, no matter the cost, until he could figure this out.

Back in his White House office, Tyson instructed his secretary that he was not to be disturbed for the next half hour. He sat behind his desk looking out his windows at the gray, featureless, overcast sky, his heart racing.

The President had asked him if everything was all right at home. And now Ed Wilder had confronted him with the FBI's knowledge of his infidelity. Did it mean that Wilder had spoken to the President?

Christ, how far was this going to go?

Turning back to his desk, he unlocked the center drawer and from beneath a stack of papers took out the card with Marinka's message that Joseph had passed to him. Tearing it into little pieces, he went into his bathroom and flushed it down the toilet, making sure every piece was gone.

He was going to have to be very careful with his movements now. If Marinka was actually coming here to Washington, and if the FBI was watching him, he was going to have to calm down and get smart. It was his only salvation, short of death.

* * *

"We're talking two full days by car," Rodgers said. He and Sweeney, along with Bill Seagren, the embassy's chief of physical security, were hunched over a road map of European Russia. Seagren had been included because of his specialized training. The CIA had taught him not only how to protect against physical infiltration, but to make what were called "exfiltration" plans. Getting out of buildings, cities, even countries.

He was a well-built man with broad shoulders, narrow hips, and very sharp eyes that seemed as if they would be as good as a high-flying hunting bird's eyes.

"Four hundred fifty miles on the Intourist route to St. Petersburg," Rodgers continued. "And another hundred twenty to the border with Finland beyond Torfyanovka."

"Which means you and the lady are going to have to spend a night in a hotel along the way," Seagren said. Despite his position as head of embassy security, he was a diffident man.

"Housekeeping will set that up for us," Sweeney said without looking up. "The Intourist permits and reservations will be legitimate."

"You won't be able to return," Rodgers said.

"No," Sweeney replied. "Two has got me nailed solid in any event, so my effectiveness is all but diluted here." He looked up. "Soon as I'm clear, Kay can begin making preparations for getting out. They wouldn't dare try holding her."

"As long as she's out before you reach Washington, I agree," Seagren said. "And, sir, you can count on her being out of here before then."

"Providing Langley gives you the green light," Rodgers cautioned.

"It'll come. In the meantime we need to address five areas of concern. Identification papers for both of us. A change in our appearances. A car. A legitimate reason for the trip. And of course the Intourist permits and reservations."

"Your identification papers will be no problem, of course," Rodgers said. "Jonesy is standing by. He promises he can have both sets ready a few hours after he's given the necessary data and photographs. And as far as Intourist goes, our resource is still in place, and even more hungry these days than usual."

"You'd better be thinking about the weather, this time of the year, Mr. Sweeney," Seagren put in.

"Check downstairs for a satellite update," Sweeney said. "It'd be a good idea to keep on top of the weather starting now."

"Will do," Seagren said, pleased that he'd remembered the detail.

"Appearances and reason for the trip," Rodgers mused. "So far as I've seen, her English is much better than your Russian."

"Agreed."

"So you'll travel as Americans or as Brits."

"Americans. I don't want to step on any toes if this blows up on us."

"All right, Americans. Embassy personnel?"

"Intourist would wonder why you're not taking the train if it's merely a trip to Helsinki," Seagren said. "Or Aeroflot if it's a trip to St. Petersburg, or Pan Am if it's a trip home."

"Then we're tourists," Sweeney said.

"Intourist will check the entry visas," Rodgers said.

"Those can be forged."

"They'll check the hotels," Seagren argued. "You're tourists. How long have you been in country, and while here where did you stay? You'd have left a track."

"Leaves us two choices," Sweeney said. "Either we go all the way with forgeries, skipping Intourist altogether. Or we go all the way with our Intourist source."

"There's a third choice," Rodgers said. "We try another path out. By air from St. Petersburg."

"Or from Tallinn," Seagren said, stabbing a blunt finger on the seaport. Using the dividers, he quickly stepped off the distance along the Intourist route between St. Petersburg and the border and then the Estonian city. "Two hundred miles."

Sweeney studied the map. "We wouldn't have to use

Intourist at all. We'd go with forgeries. So long as the weather holds we'll sleep in the car. Carry extra fuel."

There was no clear precedent for this sort of thing. It had been years since the CIA had actually smuggled anyone out of the country.

"Helsinki Station can arrange for airline tickets," Seagren said.

"No," Sweeney interjected. "The KGB still maintains its presence down there. Get Helsinki to arrange for a boat to smuggle us out. I don't want to attract any unnecessary attention."

"Right," Seagren said.

"We'll go as American tourists en route on the first leg between Moscow and St. Petersburg. Then we'll switch papers and continue across the border to Tallinn, where we'll pick up the boat for the trip across the gulf . . . what, forty miles to Helsinki?"

"Forty-five," Seagren said.

"Once there we'll fly home."

"What about Larissa?" Rodgers asked.

"If she's released, and released soon enough, and if you haven't heard differently from me, bring her down the same path."

"Sorry, Mr. Sweeney, but who're we talking about?" Seagren asked.

"She's one of our agents. KGB arrested her and is holding her at Lefortovo. But we don't think they have enough evidence to hold her indefinitely."

"We hope," Rodgers commented.

"*If* she's released, we'll get her out of the country as well."

"I can do it," Seagren said. "I'm due to rotate in a few months in any event."

Sweeney and Rodgers exchanged glances. "All right," Sweeney said.

The chances that they'd actually make it to Tallinn were very good. But there was the risk that they would be caught and returned to Moscow, in which case Sweeney would almost certainly be expelled from the country, and Marina would probably be shot for treason. The Moscow vengeance squads were still ruthless.

But then the stakes this time were very high. Worth the risks.

It was shortly after ten in the evening, Moscow time, when the messenger came from communications with the twixt from Langley for the COS.

Sweeney signed for the message without a word passing between him and the runner, and took it into his study. Katherine was in the shower.

```
Z171851ZJAN
TOP SECRET
FM: HQ OPS
TO: COS MOSCOW
A. APPROVAL GIVEN FOR YOUR REQUEST
   Z150107ZJAN.
B. SUGGEST YOU EXPEDITE SOONEST.
C. SUBMIT OPERATIONAL PLANS SOONEST.
D. NOTHING ON COMPUTER BREAK-IN. DRURY
   INVESTIGATING.
GOOD LUCK, DICK SENDS.
XX
EOM
171852ZJAN
BREAKBREAK
```

Except for the personal line attached at the end of the message by Dick Adkins, there was no hint of Langley's interest or lack of it. But then, Sweeney thought, if they had not been very interested, they would not have responded so quickly. Nor would they have given him carte blanche to "expedite soonest."

The one thing in the message that did strike him as odd, however, was Drury's personal involvement with the computer thing. Adkins had to be taking it seriously.

His next hurdle here, though, was going to be Katherine.

*   *   *

Bill Seagren had played football for Florida State in the mid-seventies. He'd come out of an extremely poor school district in West Virginia, and he'd picked the Florida school because he'd been offered the most amount of money and benefits under the table.

He'd developed into a first-class quarterback during his four years. He'd gotten his degree, with a lot of tutoring, in police science and criminology. And he had developed an abiding taste for the good things in life. Things that only money could buy.

Even more important, in some respects, Seagren had made a lot of "good old boy" contacts at Florida State that a few years after he'd graduated resulted in a job offer from the CIA. Which he took. And which, once he was in place, brought him up against the meager salary range of a government service employee.

He'd gone out around noon to have lunch at the newly reopened restaurant in the Metropole Hotel, and he returned there around eleven in the evening, leaving his overcoat with the babushka in the checkroom.

Instead of going right, into the barroom, he went straight back, and certain that he had not been observed, took a service elevator to the seventh floor.

The corridor was deserted. The floor maid was not in her alcove and would be gone for at least an hour. Walking to the end of the hall, Seagren knocked once on the door to 720.

Ivan Kiselev, his jacket off, his tie loose and collar button undone, opened the door and smiled. "Ah, just in time." He stepped aside to let Seagren in and then checked the corridor before he closed and locked the door.

The room was large and well furnished by Russian standards. Kiselev had laid out a quart of Jack Daniel's, glasses and ice, and a couple bottles of Evian.

"I expected your signal sooner than this," Kiselev scolded, but gently.

"The situation is pretty fluid over there." Seagren went to

the liquor and poured a stiff drink, cutting it only slightly with the mineral water.

"But now you have something for me?"

Seagren nodded. He took a long drink of the whiskey. It tasted damned good just now. "If I knew what the hell you were trying to do, I might be able to give you more help."

"It's not necessary," Kiselev said.

Seagren had been recruited six years ago in Mexico City where he was stationed at the embassy there. He'd gotten into some financial trouble at the racetrack, and his landlord was threatening to evict him from his luxury condominium downtown across from the Palace of Fine Arts.

A sharp KGB officer stepped in and offered to help out, as a friend. It took Seagren less than twenty-four hours to decide to accept the help, and he'd been hooked ever since.

Kiselev had become his control officer here in Moscow a year ago, taking over from a Two man. In twelve months Kiselev had funneled fifty thousand dollars in cash to Seagren here in Moscow, and an additional one hundred twenty thousand to a Swiss account. As long as the money continued to flow, Seagren was a spy without reservations or second thoughts.

"Well, he's taken the bait, and as soon as Langley gives him the okay he means to take the girl to Washington."

"Will Washington agree to his request?"

"Presumably. He's counting on it. We worked out his exit route . . ."

"I don't care about those details now."

"What if something goes wrong?" Seagren asked.

"Then we will deal with it. In the meantime I want to know what Sweeney thinks."

"As I said, he's taken the bait. He's convinced. In fact, I think he's moony over her."

"I don't understand."

"I think he's attracted to her. Sexually, I mean."

"I was under the impression that he has a very good marriage," Kiselev said, hardly believing this extra piece of good news.

"That sometimes doesn't matter with American men."

"Could you be mistaken?" Kiselev asked.

"Hell yes," Seagren replied sharply. "I don't know what the hell I'm looking for. I'm operating in the dark. Christ, don't you people trust me after all this time?"

Kiselev just looked at him in amazement. Trust?

"For instance, is it true about this mole in the White House, or is it just so much horseshit?"

"Does Sweeney have any doubts about the girl or her story?" Kiselev asked.

"Plenty, they all do. But her story is so compelling that they're all slavering at the bit."

"Anyone advising him against it?"

"Rodgers isn't so keen."

"Who'll take over for Sweeney once he's gone? He won't be able to return here, he does know that."

"He knows," Seagren said. "Rodgers will probably take over in the interim, but Langley will be sending out someone new."

"We'll have to work on that when the time comes."

"I might not be here."

This was a surprise. "You're not due to leave for several months."

"There's another problem. You people are holding a woman named Larissa Dolya in Lefortovo. She's one of us. If and when she's released, they want me to take her out of the country the same way we're going to pull Marina Demin out."

"I don't think I know the name," Kiselev said.

"I don't have all the details yet. But it's something called MOHAWK," Seagren said. "Evidently she was a part of it. I'm trying to find out what it's all about, but I haven't got very far yet."

"Larissa Dolya?"

"Right. She's one of us . . . them."

"Where's Seagren?" Sweeney asked Rodgers. "We've got the green light from Adkins."

"There's no answer at his apartment. I've sent a runner for him. When do you want to leave?"

"Soon as possible. Tomorrow afternoon if we can swing it. Gives us the correct window for leaving by sea from Tallinn. So far as I can figure, we'd get out of there under cover of darkness."

"You'd better get some sleep," Rodgers said. "Jonesy has everything he needs. He'll be finished later this morning."

"Car?"

"When Bill gets back I'll know better," Rodgers said. "I'm going to miss you around here."

"Bullshit. You just don't want to admit the job of COS stinks. And it's been dumped in your lap."

Rodgers grinned. "That too," he said.

It was late afternoon when Lydia Lubiako showed up at the KGB's Georgetown safe house to relieve an increasingly shaky Radchenko.

"All he does is watch television," Radchenko nervously told Lydia at the door. "Twenty-four hours a day."

"When does he sleep?"

Radchenko shook his head. "Never. The sooner this is over, the better I'll feel. Fuck your mother, but I'm not sleeping either."

"Go to the embassy, you're done here," Lydia said.

"Gladly. What time do you want me back?"

"You're done here, Vsevolod Sergeevich. Your part in this operation is over."

Radchenko paled. "It's happening now?"

"Soon. Now go back to the embassy, have some supper and something to drink, and get some sleep. You look terrible."

Radchenko turned and left the apartment without a further word, and Lydia Lubiako went the rest of the way into the living room. Privet was lounging on the couch, a glass of tea at his elbow, *Wheel of Fortune* playing on the television. He looked up.

"It's time for you to go to work, comrade," she told him.

"I am to kill him now?" Privet asked calmly.

"No. But you are to do your homework now. If and when the word comes, it will happen very fast. There may be no time for preparations."

"I understand. Is the FBI still watching him?"

"Yes, even more closely now, which of course makes your job more difficult."

"What about the girl? His control officer?"

"She has been arrested."

"I see," Privet said. "Before I begin, then, I will need to know everything, absolutely everything."

"I agree," Lydia Lubiako said, taking off her coat and unbuttoning her blouse. "It's why I am here."

•

"Raya Nechiporenko has been arrested?" General Ryazanov asked Kiselev, who stood at attention.

"That is the Washington *Rezident*'s best guess, but there is no concrete proof as yet."

"How does this affect Homeward Bound?"

"Not so seriously at this point that we must call it off," Kiselev said. "In any event our safeguards are in place and fully operational."

"These are extreme measures, Major."

"Yes, Comrade General. But the reward, I believe, is worth the risk."

"I hope you are correct."

As soon as Kiselev was out the door, the general called his Moscow contact. The old man answered.

"The time is now, Comrade Minister, unless you wish to stop the operation."

"It must not be stopped, General."

"There may be trouble . . ."

"Don't you understand that this is our last chance?" the old man said from the Kremlin. "If we fail, nothing will matter, the Union will be completely a thing of the past, with no hope for salvage. But if we succeed . . ." The minister let his words trail off.

"Yes, Comrade Minister," General Ryazanov said. "If we succeed, then the Union will be ours, just like the old days."

Robert Vaughan had been director of the Central Intelligence Agency for seven years. In the beginning the job had fit him like a glove. He'd been a four-star Army general, and he knew how to give as well as take orders. These days his control at Langley was even tighter.

Unlike many of his predecessors, he provided more than broad-stroke directions for the Agency. He did not rely solely on his deputy director or on the men who controlled the four major divisions of the Company (Operations, Intelligence, Science and Technology, and Management and Services) to manage the day-to-day activities at Langley and around the world. He knew what was going on twenty-four hours a day. And he controlled this vast amount of information; it did not control him.

His private helicopter touched down within the presidential compound at Camp David, some sixty miles north of Washington in Maryland's Catoctin Mountain Park. A marine lieutenant escorted him off the pad and down a broad path through the trees to the main lodge. The forest here was loaded with snow, and the air was sharp and clean-smelling.

A big fire was burning on the hearth at the end of the great room. The President was speaking with a half dozen of his advisers.

"Good afternoon, Robert," he said. "Leave your coat on, we'll go for a walk if you don't mind."

"Not at all, Mr. President," Vaughan said.

The President got his parka, and outside they headed down one of the many paths that crisscrossed the compound. "I haven't been out all day," he said.

"Plenty of time for golf when you retire," Vaughan commented.

The President laughed. "That was Ike's game. I'll stick with fishing. Tell me about Al Tyson."

Vaughan was startled. He'd always cautioned himself and others never to underestimate a president. No matter who or what they were beforehand, once they moved into the White House the job changed them. They draw strength from the office. Immeasurable strength.

"Actually it was one of the things I wanted to discuss."

"Ed Wilder is upset. He thinks that you and Doug Gelderman and maybe Fran Lipton have formed a cabal to block him. You know, of course, that the Bureau is investigating Al because of his apparent relationship with a woman who may be an agent for the KGB."

"I wouldn't call it a cabal, Mr. President."

"What, then?" the President demanded. One of the Secret Service agents ahead of them glanced back.

"Something has come up that points in another direction," Vaughan said.

"Don't pussyfoot around, General. It's not like you, and I have neither the time nor the patience."

They stopped. "I've received word from my people in Moscow that there may be a plot afoot to bring Tyson down, accuse him of being a spy."

"Why?" the President asked, his eyes narrowed.

"I don't know. Perhaps because they believe he will succeed Bob Harms, and that he will do too good a job for you. I can't answer that. But, Mr. President, if Ed Wilder is allowed to bring Tyson down, then the Russians will have succeeded without firing a shot. Conversely, if Wilder is told what's afoot, and the Bureau backs off in its investigation, the move could jeopardize our own investigation."

The President looked at him. "Let me get this straight. You're telling me that you think Al Tyson is innocent?"

"Yes, I do."

"And you think that you may be able to expose a Russian operation to remove him from my staff?"

"Yes, Mr. President."

"But that Ed Wilder must be kept in the dark."

"For the moment, yes, sir."

After a moment the President shook his head. "Maybe you're right, General. Maybe I should take up golf."

19

ZIMIN WAS ALONE, AS HE HAD BEEN FOR MOST OF HIS LIFE. He'd sent the others away earlier this morning, telling them that they had done a fine job, but that their orders had been changed. What they had accomplished here was classified Most Secret, so no one was to talk about any aspect of their work.

They were good people, Zimin thought. Devoted. Dedicated. Loyal, to a degree. Loyal to the future but definitely not the past. They were the young, new Russians, who'd not grown up with the living fear of the *Rodina*'s near defeat at the Nazis' hands.

But Zimin remembered. His tiny town south of Leningrad had first been occupied, and then when the Nazis had retreated, it had been leveled.

He brought up the Finance Directorate's rose and dumped in the Tchaikovsky concerto:

WELCOME TO DIRECTORATE ONE FINANCE ACCESS

STATE YOUR MENU CHOICE
ALARM SEQUENCE IN PROGRESS

Zimin entered:

PAYMENT GREEN GRASS
ALL FISCAL QUARTERS TO DATE FOR 1990, 1991,
1992

The computer responded:

RESTRICTED ACCESS
BETA LEVEL AND ABOVE
IDENTIFICATION PLEASE

Zimin typed:

PIGGYBACK ACCESS

The computer replied:

IDENTIFICATION PLEASE

Zimin typed:

THOR

A few minutes later the screen filled and the printer began
to chatter.

PROJECT GREEN GRASS
FISCAL A 90
UNIT 1001 INTOURIST

Nancy Perigorde blanked out her screen and hesitated for
a full thirty seconds trying to calm herself. There was no time
for her to leave work, even if she could without raising

suspicions, because this was too important. It was exactly what they'd been waiting for. A chance to nail the bastard.

She was reasonably certain that her telephone wasn't being monitored, so she got an outside line and called Dr. Hamilton's blind number that was answered day or night by a machine. "Only to be used in an extreme emergency," he'd told her at the beginning.

"He's back in," she said when the connection had been made. "My time zero-six-zero-seven. Looks like he's hit the jackpot and will be in for the duration."

"Miss Perigorde," someone said over her shoulder.

She looked up, breaking the connection and hanging up her phone. It was Tom Stone, her immediate supervisor.

"Sorry," she said. "That was my sister. She's ill. I was worried about her."

"I see," Stone said. He stared at her for a long second, then walked off.

Katherine refused to come downstairs, preferring, she said, to see her husband off in the privacy of their own apartment. It was nearly four in the afternoon and they stood holding each other in the tiny study.

"It's happening too quickly, Ernie," she said. "I don't like it. Everything about it . . . stinks."

"You're thinking through your ovaries again, kid," Sweeney said gently. "This is part of the job."

"Then get out," she protested halfheartedly. Most of the fight had gone out of her.

"When the dust settles, we'll see. No matter what, we're getting out of Moscow early. You'll be in Washington yourself in a couple of days. One wish come true."

"I don't know what I would do without you," she said, looking up into his eyes.

He smiled warmly. "A problem you're not going to have to deal with."

"It'll be dangerous, won't it?"

"More so for her than for me. They could shoot her. But they'd simply kick me out of the country."

"I didn't mean just that," she said softly. But then she kissed him fiercely before she let go and stepped back. "The sooner you get out of here, the sooner I'll see you in Washington."

"Don't worry," Sweeney said.

"Don't be a fool, of course I'm going to worry myself sick. Just go."

"Housekeeping will help you pack up."

"They're coming up first thing in the morning. Go."

Sweeney nodded, brushed a kiss on her cheek, and went downstairs, where Rodgers, Seagren, and Marina were waiting for him in an office adjacent to the rear exit out to the parking area.

"Are we set to go?" he asked.

"Yes, sir," Seagren said. "I'll take you out in the back of the van so no one will see you leaving. Your Intourist car is parked near Dinamo Stadium with easy access to the highway. Gives me the room to make sure we're dragging no tail behind us."

Sweeney had pulled on a black wig, and Rodgers adjusted it for him. Marina had already been made up to look like a blonde, with garish lipstick. What Russians thought every American woman looked like. Rodgers handed him a pair of glasses with neutral lenses.

"The car is a Zhiguli, which will be very easy on gas, but probably tough on your kidneys," Seagren said. "Extra fuel in the trunk, luggage and food in the backseat, and registration papers and maps in the glove box."

"What about Helsinki?"

"They're ready for you," Rodgers said. "The fishing vessel *Suolahti* will be in port selling her catch Saturday night. She'll have to depart as soon as she unloads, which only gives you a few hours' leeway. If you miss the boat, the captain will immediately head southwest to Paldiski. It's off the beaten path, the town is isolated."

"How far?"

"Twenty miles."

"It gives you better than twenty-eight hours to make it," Rodgers said. "Should be plenty of time."

Sweeney nodded.

"We'll be standing by here in case you run into trouble."

"I want Katherine out as soon as possible."

"We're trying for Sunday morning."

"Good," Sweeney said. He and Rodgers shook hands.

"Good luck, Dick."

"You too."

"You ready?" Sweeney asked Marina. She nodded, though it was clear she was very nervous. He couldn't blame her.

Rodgers went first to make certain that no one was in the corridor, and that for the moment the parking area was deserted as well.

"Come," he called softly.

Seagren went out first, climbing behind the wheel of a Dodge van. Marina and Sweeney followed, getting in back.

The embassy had three of the vans, and the fact that they had no windows in the back, and smoked glass in the rear, drove the Russians nuts. But there was nothing they could do about it, because they operated several similar vans out of their embassy in Washington.

"Ready back there?" Seagren asked.

"Ready," Sweeney said, looking into Marina's eyes. She reached out and took his hand.

"Please, just until we're clear," she said.

Out front Seagren showed his embassy identification and the Militia waved him on. Moments later they had merged with traffic on Tchaikovsky Street and headed out of the city to the northwest.

"Clear," Seagren called.

"Good," Sweeney said, but Marina didn't release his hand.

Bob Drury left Adkins' office a couple of minutes before eight in the morning, a troubled look on his heavily jowled, deeply lined face as he headed down to a third-floor conference room. He'd stopped by for a last word or two with his boss in the hope that he might be able to do some good. It was his opinion that the Company was heading for an embarrassment, if not a disaster.

"You understand the problem?" Adkins had asked. "Clearly?"

"Yes, I do. But it doesn't mean I have to like it. What we're setting up here could be construed as illegal."

"Morris Segal will sit in on your sessions."

"I'm not worried about myself, Dick. I'm concerned about the integrity of the Agency."

"So am I," Adkins replied coolly. "But in this instance we cannot trust the FBI to act in the best interests of the country."

"Crap," Drury said. His staff called him the bulldog, not only because of his square-jawed face but because of his attitude. In his case his bite *was* as bad as his bark.

"You don't want the job, I'll give it to someone else," Adkins said just as sharply. "But the fact of the matter is we're talking about a game of politics into which the Russians have cleverly inserted themselves. The FBI is Ed Wilder, and for some reason Wilder is convinced that Tyson is a Russian spy."

"Maybe he is."

Adkins shook his head. "This comes from the top, Bob."

"Are you talking about the General?"

"Higher."

Drury just looked at the man for a second or two. Then he shook his head. "We're outside our charter."

"Just until this Russian operation comes to a head, then we turn it over to the Bureau. *That* word *did* come from the General."

Still Drury had hesitated.

"I need you, Bob. All the way. One hundred percent."

Drury had nodded his assent and gotten out of there.

Stepping off the elevator, he went across the corridor and let himself into the small, comfortably furnished conference room. Segal and the others were already seated around the table, so he flipped the red switch, locking the door and activating the built-in countersurveillance measures.

"Sorry I'm late," he said, going to the head of the table.

"Just got here myself," Segal said.

The three others around the table were Chuck Nichols, from the Company's Technical Services section; Laurie McLaughlin, a tall, willowy electronics expert from the National Security Agency; and Major Louis Doucette, in mufti, from the Army's Intelligence Division. Each of them had been handpicked by someone upstairs, possibly even by the General himself. Each came with the highest recommendation from his or her chief. And each had been extensively briefed *after* they had accepted the assignment. Presumably there were no second thoughts among them.

"I'm Bob Drury, and we have a lot of catching up to do before we're at speed with the opposition. Any questions, gripes, or suggestions, let's get them on the table and out of the way right now."

"Since there's no name for this operation, may I suggest we name our team?" Laurie McLaughlin asked. But before Drury could respond, she went on. "We're the Anti-Defamation League."

Nichols chuckled, and Drury had to smile. His daddy used to say that some days you got the bear, and other days the bear got you. He had no idea which kind of a day this would be, but he'd survived both.

It was a perfect day for a walk, Privet decided as he strolled along R Street past Montrose Park. He did not carry his pistol with him this time. Now he was merely doing his background work, no reason to take the risk of walking around armed. He had a valid District of Columbia permit to carry a gun, but not a silenced weapon.

He would spend the next few days investigating three neighborhoods. First here in Georgetown in the vicinity of Tyson's home. Second along Pennsylvania Avenue, the White House, and the Executive Office Building. And third the Columbia Island Marina.

He was curious about the woman. She'd been arrested by the FBI, and yet the KGB was going ahead with the scheme—Homeward Bound, it was called—to either convert Tyson or kill him before he could testify.

There were several glaring holes in the story he was being told. Holes he intended filling before he came to the moment of truth.

Darkness came very early. Even so, driving northwest toward Leningrad, they could see that the countryside was flat and mostly barren.

The weather would hold, Sweeney had been assured by meteorology, but that was of little comfort now that they were out in the open and exposed not only to the weather but to any Militiaman or KGB officer who happened to cross their path. Russia was still a nation in which travel was looked upon with suspicion.

On the plus side, they'd encountered almost no traffic whatsoever once they were about fifty miles outside of Moscow. And for the past hour they'd not even seen another light, as from a distant farmhouse or a high-flying airliner, not even the glow on the horizon of a distant city or town. The old Soviet Union was a dark country.

The Zhiguli, which was copied from the Fiat, was a small, underpowered, and cheaply built car. But the one Seagren had supplied them, complete with Intourist registration plates and papers, was new and still in reasonably good condition. The heater worked well, something unusual for a Russian-built automobile, and as far as Sweeney could figure, they were getting very good gas mileage, so that it would be absolutely no problem for them to make it all the way to Tallinn without stopping at a gas station (even if they could find one).

"I'm very tired," Marina said.

Sweeney glanced over at her. He'd just checked his watch. It was a little past midnight, and he figured they had gone more than two hundred miles since clearing Moscow around seven. The Zhiguli's odometer was broken.

"We'll find a spot to pull over," he said. "But I'll have to turn the engine off. It'll be cold."

"I'm a Russian. I'm used to it."

Sweeney looked at the road, then glanced back at her again. "Are you okay?"

She looked at him. "No. But I haven't changed my mind, if that's what you mean."

"I didn't . . ."

"I would rather be somewhere warm. Lying on a beach, perhaps, with my clothes off and the sun beating down on me. I dream of that almost every night. And I dream that a man will come to me, and we will be happy together."

Sweeney didn't know what to say. This time her words did not seem so contrived.

"Do you think that will ever happen to me, Mr. Sweeney?"

"I don't know. But I hope so."

"Yes. Thank you for your honesty. I hope so too. I sincerely hope so."

"We've got the bastard," Medvedosky said, bursting into the office out of breath. He'd raced up five flights of stairs from communications.

Kiselev, who was perched on the corner of his desk, looking out the window, turned around. "Tinker?"

"It just came off the Washington link. He's in the computer and it looks as if he's going to be in for a while."

"What have we got?" Kiselev asked.

"A phone number. It's a building on Volkhonka Street. We can make it in twenty minutes, if we hustle."

They hurried back downstairs, checked out with security, got their car from the parking lot, and in three minutes flat were heading into the city.

Zimin was looking out the window down at the street, the feeling that someone or something was closing in on him growing stronger by the minute.

Turning, he went back to his computer terminal, through which the reams of data were coming in from the Finance Directorate, and thought for a moment.

He sat down and pulled up a second telephone line, this one directly to the computer system serving Deputy Secretary Malakhov's office. He entered a series of passwords, gaining easy entry, and then he initiated a new program:

PROJECT GREEN GRASS DUMP
ACCESS: FOR YOUR EYES ONLY MALAKHOV

When the program was established, he shunted the incoming Finance Directorate data across, so that now even if this system were destroyed, the Finance Directorate's Green Grass records would continue to be dumped.

The only lights in the entire building shone from a fifth-floor window.

"Maybe we should have called for backup units," Medvedosky said as they got out of the car.

Kiselev shook his head. "This has to be kept contained, Pasha. You know why. You know what's at stake."

"Are we going to kill him, or them . . . or whoever?"

Kiselev had taken out his pistol, levered a round into the firing chamber, and switched the safety off. He nodded. "No other choice."

Medvedosky pulled out his Makarov, and together they took the stairs up to the fifth-floor corridor, where they listened at the door. They could clearly hear the high-pitched whining sounds of a computer printer.

He and Kiselev exchanged glances, and then Kiselev tried the door. It was locked.

Together they backed up and charged the door with their shoulders, once, twice, and a third time. The lock gave and the door frame splintered.

Kiselev got the impression of an odd-looking man with a great shock of red hair seated at a computer terminal, meters of printout spewing from the printer, when he and Medvedosky both opened fire, hitting the man at least seven times in the head, torso, and legs.

20

LEAVING RUSSIA AND ENTERING ESTONIA WAS LIKE STEPPING from one world into another. They crossed the border at Kingisepp, barely 140 miles from Tallinn, around four Saturday afternoon, and the difference became apparent in the expression on the border policemen's faces.

"Welcome, welcome to Estonia," the red-faced customs officer boomed in English when he found out Sweeney and Marina were Americans. They traveled now under passports that identified them as Jeremy and Janice Copeland from Philadelphia.

"Thank you, it's good to be here," Sweeney said.

A second policeman sauntered over and smiled in at them. "Are you having a fine trip?"

"Yes, and we're looking forward to visiting your capital city."

"Tallinn, yes. Very old, very fine, lots of Finns come to visit us always."

Behind them, the Russian border policemen they'd just passed stood on the road watching them. They had not seemed very happy. It was as if they'd not wanted to give up a car and two Americans so easily.

Marina, too, had seemed agitated all morning, becoming more nervous the nearer they came to the border. She'd not slept very well last night, and he put her agitation down to a combination of wariness and fear of the unknown. Crossing this border took her from the *Rodina*. And she was traveling on false documents with a CIA agent. He felt sorry for her.

"Anything to declare?"

"No," Sweeney said. "Just the rest of our lunch. We had a little picnic."

"Ah, picnic," the Estonian said, laughing. "In the winter in Russia. Something to tell your friends at home."

The policeman handed back their papers and stepped back to let them drive on.

Sweeney half expected them to thumb their noses at the Russians. But they didn't. And then they were busy with a truck that lumbered up to the crossing.

"The hard part is over with," Sweeney said when they had gone a couple of miles. The only town of any size between here and Tallinn was Narva, about twenty miles away. He figured they could stop there for dinner. They would come into Tallinn under cover of darkness.

Marina mumbled something.

"What'd you say?" Sweeney asked, glancing over at her. She looked pale.

"I said the hard part is *never* over. It just gets worse."

"You'll be all right in the States. You'll be taken care of."

She looked at him, a defiant expression suddenly in her eyes. "What, you do this all the time? Smuggle girls to America?"

"No," Sweeney said. "This is the first for me."

"Well, you're doing fine. Now I am hungry."

"We'll stop in Narva."

The gray, overcast days were starting to get to Senarighi. He stood in the shadows in Toni Wagner's living room aboard the houseboat, looking out the window across the lagoon.

Raising a pair of binoculars to his eyes, he studied the opposite shoreline three hundred yards away for any sign of the wire snaking out of the water. But he couldn't find it even though he knew where to look.

His mood had begun to deepen the moment they picked up the woman and began questioning her. It was a question of her civil rights, he'd told Harding. Or lack of them.

The word had filtered down that she was going to be released for lack of evidence, especially considering the fact that her dental records and other points of identification matched the Idaho Toni Wagner's.

"Two of our people were gunned down, Sandy," Young said. "We can't let that slide. We won't let it slide."

"Yes, sir."

"The shooting had something to do with Tyson, and Tyson is involved . . . he even admits it . . . with Toni Wagner. Ergo, we keep an eye on her." No one was calling her Raya Nechiporenko now, except on written reports. It was depressing.

"At the very least we've got her on the drug charges," he'd said to Young.

"Yes, we have that to fall back on. That is, if you screw up."

"Won't happen," Senarighi said.

He lowered the binoculars as Len Harding came from the back bedroom. He carried a walkie-talkie.

"Levels check at the stern," he spoke into the radio.

"Are you midships?" a tiny speaker squawked.

"Roger."

"Level good. Try forward."

"Roger," Harding radioed. "Be done in just a sec," he said to Senarighi, and he went forward, talking aloud as he walked.

They were not going to release the woman until sometime on Monday. First, Dr. Varelis wanted to make sure that her mental condition was stabilized. The drugs she had been given were disorienting. She could possibly do herself real harm if her mind had not been cleared first. There were cases, the doctor had told them, in which a person on misprescribed antipsychotic drugs had walked in front of a moving bus or car in the belief that the vehicle would stop before they were struck.

Second, the plan was to carefully monitor Tyson's behavior during the time she was being held. It was added pressure. It was even possible that he would crack.

It was another aspect of this investigation that was beginning to bother Senarighi, spying on his own government officials. But, as Young had pointed out, they had spied on Nixon and he'd been a hell of a lot more important than an acting national security adviser.

Narva was a good-sized town of more than sixty thousand people built on the banks of the Narva River. Like Tallinn, it was an ancient city complete with castles and a fortress that Sweeney seemed to remember learning somewhere had been built in the fifteenth century by Czar Ivan III.

They drove through the city and on the western outskirts found a small restaurant just off the highway. Inside, the bar and dining area were busy. They were given a small table in the back near the kitchen. Their obvious foreignness caused heads to turn their way, and a lull in the conversation. But after a few seconds, when they'd ordered their drinks and something to eat, the place went back to normal. At least it seemed to.

Marina sat facing the room, her lips slightly pursed. "There is one man sitting near the front door who seems very interested in us."

Sweeney started to turn, but she stopped him.

"No, he is looking at us now. I think he may be a policeman."

"Estonian?"

Marina shrugged. "Russian, I think."

Sweeney had brought a pistol, but it was hidden in the trunk of the car. He'd not wanted to take any chances coming across the border with it on his person.

Their waitress, a buxom old woman with very bad teeth,

came back with their wine. "Your meal will be just a minute. Enjoy the wine."

"Pardon, but that man by the door keeps staring at us," Marina said.

The waitress didn't turn around. She knew exactly who Marina was talking about. "That one is Russian. KGB. Are you in trouble?"

Sweeney started to say no, but Marina interrupted him, her voice urgent.

"Yes! The bastards want to take me back and put me in jail. But I am not going. They will have to kill me."

The old woman glanced nervously at Sweeney.

"I'm trying to help her," he said. "I didn't think they had followed us here. Can we leave the back way?"

The babushka turned back to Marina. "Where are you going, little one?"

"Tallinn," Marina told her without hesitation. "There is a boat which will take us to Helsinki."

Sweeney groaned inwardly. He could see everything falling apart on them. It wouldn't take much to get that information out of the woman.

"You are in danger because of this?" Marina asked.

The woman laughed. "Those snot-nosed little boys won't try anything here. We have our own laws now."

"He just got up," Marina said, rearing back.

Sweeney threw a few coins on the table and he and Marina got to their feet as the old woman called out something and hurried across the dining room.

Entering the steamy warmth of the kitchen, Sweeney got the impression of a sudden commotion behind him, but then they stepped out the back door and rushed around to their car parked in front.

Marina watched out the rear for any signs that they were being pursued until they were several kilometers down the highway, out into the countryside, and then she turned back.

"There is no one back there," she said breathlessly.

Sweeney looked closely at her. Perhaps Kay had been correct when she'd warned that there was more to Marina

Demin than met the eye. She had done well in the restaurant, no one was following them.

Too good?

Major Louis Doucette knew that he was being watched when he pulled up in front of the Tyson house in Georgetown. He'd spotted one well-hidden television camera in the park across the street. He figured there would be others. In addition, Tyson's house (and probably his office) would be bugged, his phones would be tapped, and there would be teams of legmen on the street every time he made a move.

Playing this kind of a game bothered Doucette. Pitting one government agency against another did not sit right with him. Yet the American way was checks and balances. That and the principle that a man was innocent until proved guilty. The way the Bureau was posturing, however, Tyson was guilty in their minds. That wasn't right either.

Pulling his hat low over his eyes, and hunching up his coat collar, Doucette got out of his car, and keeping his face turned away from the camera across the street, without making it obvious he was doing so, hurried up the walk and rang the doorbell.

It wasn't noon yet, and it had begun to snow. The forecast was for another three or four inches. Washington would close down again. Doucette was from Minnesota. Every time the nation's capital city closed because of a little snow he had to chuckle. Hell, the Range cities got more snow than that in the spring, sometimes as late as May, and nothing shut down.

Kit Tyson, wearing a Kent State sweatshirt and matching warmup pants, came to the door. She smiled uncertainly when Doucette showed her his Army identification card.

"I have a dispatch from the President for Mr. Tyson. Is he at home, ma'am?"

"Yes, he is. Come in, please."

"No, ma'am. I'll wait right here."

Kit nodded and went back into the house. A few moments later Tyson came to the door. He, too, was wearing a Kent

State sweatshirt and matching warmup trousers. Something was troubling the man, it was obvious in his eyes.

"You have something for me?" Tyson asked.

"Yes, sir," Doucette said, taking a thin, buff-colored envelope from his pocket and handing it to the man. It was marked "For your eyes only. Assistant National Security Adviser Albert F. Tyson." "You are to discuss this with no one, and destroy the contents as soon as you have read them. Is this understood, sir?"

Tyson looked up from the envelope and nodded. "Yes, I understand."

"Very good, sir. Have a good day." Doucette turned, and keeping his head low so that very little of his face would show up on camera, hurried back to his car and drove off.

The message had been Bob Drury's idea. "We're going to play fair with everyone, and that includes Tyson," Drury had told them. "We're going to let him know exactly what we're doing, and why we're doing it."

Well, Tyson knew everything now. Or he would as soon as he read what was in that envelope.

"Yours was possibly the shortest tenure of any chief of station in the history of the Agency," Kelley Pool told Sweeney at Dulles Airport. They shook hands. Marina held back, obviously moved that she was on U.S. soil, and that they'd had absolutely no trouble coming through passport control or customs.

"What about Kay?"

"She's on her way out," Pool said. "Should be here tonight. I've got a car outside."

"No trouble?"

"None," Pool said, eyeing Marina. "How about you? Helsinki said you came out clean so far as they knew."

Sweeney nodded. "The Estonians are laid-back for the moment, though there could have been an incident in Narva. I'll fill you in later."

"Welcome to the United States," Pool said to Marina.

She smiled slightly and nodded. "I am very tired. Will I be able to get some sleep soon?"

"Yes, of course," Pool said, and he led them out to where he'd left his Ford Taurus station wagon. It looked as if it would snow at any moment. Still, Washington was considerably warmer than Moscow. Or even Tallinn.

Sweeney put their two bags in the back with Marina and got in front with Pool. "As soon as she's settled in I want to see Adkins."

"He's waiting for you at home," Pool said, pulling away and merging with traffic. "We've set up a safe house for her at Walter Reed Hospital."

Marina leaned forward suddenly. "I am not sick. I don't need a psychiatrist."

Pool looked at her in the rearview mirror. "Not that kind of a hospital," he said. "Anyway we're putting you in a house. Not bad actually. Belonged to a colonel on staff who was reassigned two days ago."

Marina was still skeptical. It was obvious from the expression on her face. In Russia the practice of placing dissidents in mental institutions had still not completely died out. It was in the national consciousness.

"Listen, Miss Demin, we mean you no harm," Pool said. "We've gone through a good deal of trouble to get you here, so we're not going to let anything happen."

"I'm too important now," she said, sitting back.

"Yes."

"But what about afterward? No one has said anything about that."

"That'll be up to you," Sweeney said, looking back over the seat.

"What do you mean?"

"This is a free country," he said. "When this business is finished, you will be free to go where you would like."

"But how will I live?"

"We'll take care of it, believe me."

She looked out the window at the passing countryside as

the first snowflakes began to fall from a leaden sky, and she shivered.

The house was a small, two-story brick Colonial on a tree-lined street well away from the main sections of the installation. Railroad tracks ran north behind the property, and when they got out of the car, they could hear the hum of traffic on Interstate 495 not far to the north.

It was only 12:30 P.M., but the day had turned dark with the increasing snow.

Pool parked the car in the driveway and came in with them to introduce Marina to Jim O'Toole, a big, red-faced Irishman from the Company's Technical Services Division who'd act as watchdog, and Mrs. Dorothy Connors, who looked grandmotherly, but who held black belts in karate and judo. She, too, was from Technical Services and would act as baby-sitter.

"I'm told you had a long, difficult trip, my dear. You must be dead on your feet and absolutely famished," Mrs. Connors said sympathetically.

Marina had to smile despite herself. "I would like a bath too."

"Oh, yes, of course, of course," the older woman clucked. She turned to Pool and Sweeney. "Now, if you gentlemen will leave us women to get on with it?"

"Just a minute," Sweeney said, and he took Marina into the dining room, which was in semidarkness. "I've got to go. But I'll try to get back later this afternoon or evening if possible."

"Your wife is due to arrive."

"Yes, I know. At the latest I'll be back in the morning. We'll start your debriefing then."

"When will I be allowed to travel to Wisconsin to see my father?"

"We'll have to find out if he's there first. Believe me, no one is dragging their heels. This will happen very fast."

"And then?"

"It depends on you," Sweeney said. "Your future is going

to hinge on what you do and how you act. We didn't bring
you here for vacation."

"I know," she said. She leaned forward and kissed him
lightly on the cheek. "Thank you, Richard, for believing in
me. I know it has been difficult. But you will see, everything
will turn out for the best."

"I hope so," Sweeney said. "For all of our sakes."

Two Technical Services men were stationed at the bottom
of Dick Adkins' driveway, parked in their car. Pool started to
lower his window as he turned off the street, but they waved
him on. They both looked deadly serious.

"When did Adkins start with the security people?"
Sweeney asked on the way up the narrow, tree-lined driveway.

"Few days ago," Pool said, glancing at him. "Things have
started to get a little flaky here, Richard. But I'll let Dick fill
you in."

The Chevy Chase Country Club was just off to their left,
and through the trees Sweeney caught glimpses of a fairway,
crisscrossed now with tracks made by cross-country skiers.
The rural flavor here made him homesick for his house on the
Chesapeake. Soon, he told himself. Very soon.

They parked in front and let themselves in. No one was
around, though Sweeney got the distinct impression that they
were being watched. It was the first time he'd ever been on
edge in his own country.

"Leave our coats here," Pool said in the stair hall, and
when they'd laid them on the bench, they went back to
Adkins' study overlooking the swimming pool and snow-
covered garden, beyond which was the tennis court. The
house was very large, and lovely. Adkins complained from
time to time that he was in debt up to his ears for the place,
but said that it was well worth it.

Adkins was just pouring a drink when they came in. Morris
Segal sat on the couch, and Bob Drury, Adkins' assistant,
was perched on the opposite arm of it. Sweeney knew him,
but not well.

Adkins looked up. "Ah, here they are at last," he said. He put down the drink he'd poured for Drury and shook Sweeney's hand. "No trouble getting out?"

Sweeney related the incident at the restaurant in Narva. "Other than that, the crossing went smoothly. Seagren set it up, and Helsinki did a good job."

"Glad to hear it. What about the girl, is she settling in?"

"She's at the safe house, but she's frightened."

"Don't blame her," Adkins said. "Care for a drink?"

"Brandy. A little water."

Adkins gave Drury his drink, then poured drinks for Sweeney and Pool. When they were settled, Adkins began, with no preamble.

"Is she telling the truth, Richard?"

"I don't know for sure. But I think so. If it was some kind of a plot, she would have given us more. As it is, she's only promising us that she'll be able to identify her father, who has something to do with it."

"The White House official they're trying to unseat is Al Tyson, and this girl of yours may be only one element of their plan."

Morris Segal sat forward ponderously. "What did you promise Miss Demin?"

"Asylum if she wants it," Sweeney replied. "Is there a problem with that?"

"There may be, but I'll take care of it," Segal said.

"This is a First Directorate operation, I'm assuming," Sweeney said.

"Right. Major Ivan Kiselev, the one Miss Demin mentioned, and as it turns out, probably the agent handler for a woman by the name of Raya Nechiporenko. She's here in the States posing as a U.S. citizen. She's Tyson's mistress."

"Shit," Sweeney said.

"Yeah," Adkins said. "But believe me, Richard, it's even worse than that." He turned to Drury. "Bob, fill him in from your side."

"The FBI has been investigating Tyson for some time now. We don't know for sure exactly how long they've been at it, or exactly how they came to it, but they've established that Tyson has a mistress and that she is probably a Russian KGB agent. But they've put two and two together differently than we have. The Bureau is apparently convinced that Tyson is a spy working for the Russians."

Sweeney sat back and exchanged glances with Adkins. But he directed his question to Drury. "What evidence do they have to support that conclusion? Not just a simple indiscretion?"

"I don't know," Drury said with a straight face. "But two of their people were shot to death outside Tyson's house a few days ago. At least one of them was killed by a KGB officer who worked out of their embassy. He himself was shot to death by a fourth, as yet unknown, party."

"The Russians are apologizing all over the place," Adkins said. "They're not admitting that their man was KGB, of course, but they are claiming that he was unhinged. That he went berserk for whatever reason. And they're offering to pay any compensation that we ask."

"Kelly said things were getting flaky here. He wasn't exaggerating."

"No," Adkins said.

"What if Tyson really is a spy working for the Russians, and his mistress is his control officer?" Sweeney asked.

"What about Miss Demin's story?" Drury asked.

"Maybe we're talking about two different White House officials. Tyson the spy and someone else . . . Bob Harms the object of the second plot." Sweeney sat forward, warming to this new thesis. "Harms may recover and return as national security adviser, replacing Tyson. If Harms is brought down, would Tyson take over his job permanently?"

"It's possible," Segal said.

"Maybe the FBI is right."

Adkins was shaking his head. "Clever idea, Richard, but there's too much weight to the evidence on the other side. Like Tyson's performance in the Army, then in the National Security Agency, and here, of course. The man was as good as gold. He continues to be."

"In any event," Segal interjected, "if the Bureau had enough evidence against Al Tyson, they would have arrested him by now. At the very least the President would have fired him."

"Which he has not," Adkins said. "The General has discussed it with him."

"We're back to a Russian plot to bring him down," Sweeney said. "One that so far has the FBI convinced."

"Right," Adkins said.

"What do we do about it?"

"Miss Demin may be the key," the DDO said. "She'll bring down the plotters for us, starting with her father and whoever his control officer is. Five'll get you ten, it's Ivan Kiselev's baby all the way."

"It's jet lag, my dear," Mrs. Connors told Marina Demin. "Happens to everyone. Goodness, you've just scooted across eight time zones to get here. It'll take your body a day or so to adjust."

"You're probably right," Marina said at the kitchen table. "I can hardly keep my eyes open."

"I know, I know," the older woman cooed. "Time to get you off to bed. If you sleep all afternoon and all night, you'll be ready for whatever they're going to throw at you tomorrow."

"I don't know. I'm afraid I'll have nightmares."

"Bosh. Nothing to worry about. I'll give you a sleeping tablet that'll knock you out for at least eighteen hours. You'll see."

Marina had taken a long, hot bath and, dressed only in a robe and slippers, had come downstairs, where Mrs. Connors had fixed her a big brunch of eggs, pancakes, fried potatoes, bacon, sausages, toast, muffins, tea, and juice.

Back upstairs, Marina changed into a long flannel nightgown and took the two sleeping tablets the older woman offered to her with water.

"I'll check in on you from time to time, dear," Mrs. Connors said at the door as Marina crawled into the big bed.

"Thanks," she mumbled, and she closed her eyes the moment her head hit the pillow.

"Good night," Mrs. Connors called softly, and she switched off the light and left, closing the door behind her.

A few moments later, Marina opened her eyes, then threw back the covers and got up. She spit the sleeping tablets into her hand and padded across the room to the bathroom, where she tossed them in the toilet. They would dissolve in a minute or so. For the moment she did not want to risk flushing, alerting them downstairs that she was still awake.

She opened the corridor door a crack and peered out. The only light came from downstairs, and she could hear a radio or television playing, and possibly the old babushka talking on the telephone. She could only hear one side of the conversation.

After closing the door, she hurried across to the window that looked out across the backyard to the railroad tracks, and beyond, to the superhighway a block away.

The window opened easily, and leaning out, she could see that it was only a little more than three meters to the ground. An easy jump.

Closing the window, she located her clothes and then went back to bed, this time to sleep, but not for eighteen hours. Only until night came.

Privet stood beside his car, the hood up as if he were having engine trouble, looking down toward the Boundary Channel. The Columbia Island Marina was on the opposite shore, barely two hundred meters from where he stood.

On this side of the channel, up behind a copse of trees so that it would be hidden from the marina, was a Toyota van.

From inside the car Privet took out a pair of binoculars and studied the van for a moment. The registration plate was of a series that he recognized as one the FBI used. Evidently the Bureau was watching the woman's houseboat even more closely now than it had before. She'd been arrested, though. This meant they were expecting Tyson to show up.

For a moment or two, Privet considered this place as a

possible spot from which to assassinate Tyson. Of course he'd need to acquire a high-powered rifle and scope from somewhere, but it wouldn't be too much trouble. Illegal guns, explosives, false papers, even such things as hand-held ground-to-air missiles, were fairly easy to come by almost anywhere in the world. Providing, of course, you had the money. There seemed almost to be a universal brotherhood of such people. Once you were attuned to their methods, and the kinds of places they frequented, it was easy to connect with them.

But then another thought crossed Privet's mind. They might be waiting for Tyson to show up here, but it was also possible that the FBI would be releasing the woman for lack of evidence. Lydia Lubiako had assured him that the woman's legend was as airtight as they came.

He shrugged. Anything was possible. Though on reflection this place might not be so good for the shot. He would get closer. Probably near Tyson's home, or hopefully someplace remote if the man could be enticed out of his house.

Closing the hood and climbing back into his car, Privet began to work on that new idea as he headed back down to Arlington, where he would pick up Interstate 295 across the river. He wanted to get up to the Baltimore-Washington Airport, purchase his tickets to Montreal, and be back at the safe house before dinnertime, when Lydia had said she would be returning.

Adkins sat in the backseat of his limousine, already lost in thought by the time the big car reached the end of the driveway from his house and started down to Gallaudet College just north of the Union Square Station.

A previous DCI had maintained a home on the school's grounds, and now so did Vaughan. (It had something to do with a family connection somewhere, although a few Agency wags maintained the director lived there because the college was a school for the deaf. What they couldn't hear, couldn't come back to haunt them.)

Adkins was troubled, as he knew most of his subordinates

were, over this business with Tyson. The last time one
government agency had been pitted against another was
during the fall of Nixon. That had nearly torn the entire
country apart.

This now might not be as bad on the surface, but its effects
in some ways would be even more devastating. This time the
consequences could become international if it got out that the
Russians were actually trying to bring down a national
security adviser.

Adkins shivered. The consequences would be even more
dire if it turned out that Tyson was in actuality a Russian spy.

He passed a hand across his eyes. Lord in heaven,
the permutations and combinations . . . the reverbera-
tions . . . the sheer seismic damage would be so vast as to
be nearly incalculable.

The specter of another protracted cold war with all of its
attendant risks of nuclear war was raising its ugly head.

For the first time in his long government service career,
Adkins felt as if he were in over his head. It was time for the
General to make the decisions. To give them the direction
they so badly needed. There was a lot at stake just on the
surface. No telling how much more was hidden.

It depended upon what Tyson's next moves would be now
that he knew that the FBI suspected him, and what the agency
suspected him of.

It depended upon what the Russians' next moves might be
and if Marina Demin's help might stop them.

And it depended upon what the FBI was going to do. And
that was the most bothersome aspect of this case.

Adkins wondered what they'd do if the Bureau had
evidence they weren't telling anybody about. Something
conclusive that would prove beyond a shadow of a doubt that
Tyson was working for the Russians.

Yuri Truskin arrived in the *referentura* just ahead of Lydia
and Igor Lubiako. They were both in the embassy, though
Lydia had said she was going out within the hour.

"She's here," Truskin said as soon as the door was closed and the antisurveillance measures were up to speed.

"The cable has come?" Lydia asked.

"Yes," Truskin replied. "The woman is here, and we can expect her to make contact at any moment."

Lydia and Igor Lubiako exchanged glances. "Too bad about Raya," Lydia said.

"Yes, isn't it?" he replied.

It had been Young's idea to station a pair of agents at Dulles Airport and other mass-transit terminals in the Washington area. The duty officer in operations called up a few minutes before five in the afternoon.

"Maybe it's something," the man said. "But Stu Garde turned up an interesting pair at Dulles this morning just before noon. Flight from Helsinki. One of the passengers was Dick Sweeney, CIA. He was escorting a woman. Stu swore she was Russian. Said she had the look."

"What else?" Young asked, wondering how it fit.

"They were met by a white male, identification unknown, but presumably CIA."

"Were they followed?"

"No."

"Let's see if we can find them. As soon as possible."

"Yes, sir."

At 7:00 P.M. Mrs. Connors looked in on Marina, who was "out like a light," as she told O'Toole downstairs a minute later.

The moment the door was closed, Marina tossed back the covers, got out of bed, and got dressed in her slacks, sweater, and boots.

She'd timed the woman's visits, which had come every two hours. Unless she made a mistake getting out, she had that long to get clear.

She pulled on her coat, opened the window, and crawled out. Holding on with one hand, she reached up and pulled the window almost all the way closed, and then dropped the three-plus meters to the snow-covered ground.

The landing was much softer than she had thought it would be, and within fifteen minutes she had made it across the railroad tracks and down to the interstate, where she easily hitched a ride back into the city.

21

THE BEDROOM WAS DARK, BUT PRIVET COULD MAKE OUT LYDIA Lubiako's form on the bed, and he could smell her musky odor.

Russians, unlike Americans, paid no particular attention to masking their body smells. It bothered some Westerners. Although Privet had spent much of his adult life living in the West and posing as a Westerner, he found Lydia's odors exciting.

It was the same with his victims. The fear smell, sharply sour before the kill, and the death smell, rich and earthy as they fell, did something inside his head. A switch was turned on that gave him a tremendous rush.

He came closer to the bed to see her better. Her body was marked with red blotches and welts. She lay on her back, her flattened breasts black and blue, the huge nipples still erect from their lovemaking . . . if what they had done could be called that.

"Come now, hold me for a little while before I must go," she said softly.

Privet lay down beside her and took her into his arms as a mother might do with a small child. She sighed deeply, her legs entwined with his.

"You have been busy preparing yourself?" she asked after a minute or so.

"Yes, I am just about ready. Do you have any further word for me about the FBI's investigation of Tyson, or of Raya Nechiporenko?"

"There has been no sign of her since Friday. We're convinced that she has been arrested."

"But you said her legend was very good."

"Yes, and so is her conditioning. It's felt that she will be released very soon."

"I see," Privet said. "What about the investigation of Tyson?"

"We must be very careful now. We cannot get too close to him for fear that our people will be spotted."

"I understand this. But have your people found out anything new?"

"No," Lydia said. "But something else has come up. Something we talked about earlier."

"The girl from Moscow is here?"

"Yes, she arrived this noon. It's expected that she will make contact soon."

Privet pulled back so that he could look down into Lydia's soft brown eyes. "Has she surfaced yet?"

"No. But she will very soon. I thought you should know. It will affect what happens next."

"Yes, indeed," Privet said, digesting this news. "Oh, yes, indeed."

Marina Demin telephoned her contact number from a telephone booth at a truck stop off Interstate 95 in Alexandria. It was 9:00 P.M., and snowing very heavily.

The trucker she'd hitched a ride with had wanted her to continue down the coast with him, he said, all the way to Jacksonville. "Nice and warm this time of the year, darlin'."

She'd almost been tempted, but then had laughed at

herself, given the trucker a kiss on the cheek, and gotten off here.

The number was answered on the first ring by a man with a pleasant voice. "Yes."

"Hello, is Uncle Harold back?" Marina asked.

"Yes, he is. Where are you?"

"At a truck stop in Alexandria," she said, explaining exactly where she was calling from.

"What identification have you got?"

"American passport, driving license, credit cards."

"Throw the passport away, keep everything else."

"Yes, all right. Where am I to go?" she asked.

"Tell me how you got away this evening. How much time do you have before they begin looking for you?"

She told him everything. "They'll have missed me by now. I need to get indoors."

"Yes, of course. This is what you must do. Take a cab to the Columbia Island Marina. If the driver doesn't know where that is, tell him it is in Lady Bird Johnson Park, at the Fourteenth Street Bridge end. Do you have that?"

"Yes."

"There is a houseboat in slip 17A. You are to stay there."

"Will somebody be there?"

"No."

"How will I get in?"

"There is a key on a ledge behind the light to the left of the door."

"Who owns the boat?"

"Never mind."

"The CIA will be coming after me. They're going to be very desperate after what they've already been told. And Sweeney is very capable."

"That is none of your concern at this point," her contact said.

"What if they find me and I am arrested? What do I tell them?"

"Exactly what you have been trained to tell them. Demand to see your father. They will show you photographs."

"But they'll ask why I ran."

"Tell them that you were frightened. That you were trying to find your father on your own."

"What about the boat? How do I explain my presence there?"

"You don't."

For a moment Marina wasn't certain that she'd heard correctly. "What?"

"You needed a place to hide, you wound up at the marina, and you broke into that particular boat."

"That's ridiculous!"

"Nonetheless, that will be your story. You are to make no further contact with this number. Do you understand?"

"No," Marina shouted, but the line went dead.

"When can we go home, Ernie?" Kay asked her husband. They were just sitting down to dinner in their hotel room at the Washington Hyatt.

"Now that she's in place, probably just a few days. Her debriefing starts in the morning. Adkins is getting the team together."

"Why not this afternoon if she's so important?" Kay studied her husband's eyes.

"She was tired and needed the rest. It was a long trip, Katie, even though it went without a hitch."

Kay nodded, but said nothing.

"Do you want to talk about it?" Sweeney asked.

"About what?"

"Whatever is irritating you. We're home, but you're not exactly jumping with joy. What's up?"

"We're not home yet," she answered, when someone knocked at their door. Kay's eyes held her husband's. "Promise me something, Ernie?"

Whoever it was knocked again.

"What?"

"That you'll keep your head. That you won't forget I'm in the wings waiting for you?"

"Not a chance," Sweeney said, squeezing her hand. He smiled.

The knock came louder, more insistent this time, and Sweeney looked through the peephole. It was Bob Drury. Sweeney opened the door for him.

"Sorry to barge in like this, Richard, but we've got a problem," Drury said softly but urgently.

"What's happened?"

"Your bird has flown the coop."

"Shit," Sweeney swore, his gut knotting. "I'll meet you in the lobby in five minutes."

"Do that," Drury said.

"And Bob. Get someone over here to keep an eye on my wife."

Drury nodded. "Already been done. Five minutes."

"Right," Sweeney said.

Kay had not moved from the table. She held a wineglass. Just then she looked very beautiful, and very vulnerable. Sweeney felt an instant of absolute terror that he was going to lose her, but the moment passed.

"I have to go to work," he said, getting his jacket from where Kay had hung it in the closet.

"Adkins decided to start the debriefing tonight instead of waiting until morning?"

"No," Sweeney said. "She's bolted."

Kay's eyes widened slightly. "Be careful," she said softly.

"Will do," Sweeney said. He went over and kissed her on the cheek, then left, taking the elevator down to the lobby, where Drury was waiting for him.

"The housekeeper said she'd given the girl two sleeping tablets earlier in the day, and as of seven there were no problems," Drury said on the way out to his car.

"When did they miss her?"

"A minute or two after nine. Evidently she got dressed and jumped from a second-story window. They followed her footprints out to the interstate, and then nothing."

"No calls from the house?"

"None. But she knew what she was doing. This was a goddamned setup."

"What about the Soviet Embassy?"

"We've been watching it around the clock for the past forty-eight hours."

"And Tyson?"

"Him too. Of course the Bureau has its teams out and about as well."

"Christ, what a mess," Sweeney said as Drury pulled out of the hotel driveway and headed across town.

"We've got a command post at NASA headquarters on C Street. Technical Services set it up so that we'd be closer to the action."

"Yeah," Sweeney said. "And when someone on the Hill or some bright *Washington Post* hotshot finds out what we're doing, it'll provide at least some distance from Langley."

"That too," Drury admitted. "But don't blame yourself. Under the circumstances any of us would have done the same thing, bringing her out of Russia. It was Housekeeping's ball, and they dropped it."

"What are we doing to find her?" Sweeney asked. It was snowing very hard now, and the windshield wipers were having a hard time keeping up with it. If the snow continued, Washington would not have a Monday morning. There would be many closings. The city would all but stop functioning.

"We're going on the assumption that she has something to do with Tyson. So we're watching all of his haunts."

"Right along with the Bureau."

"They're there, all right. Haven't missed a spot."

"What else?"

"We've got people on every known or suspected KGB office in the Washington area. We've got damned near half the Company on it."

"How's security?"

"Good. No one really knows what's up."

"District Police?"

"Adkins doesn't want them involved. It would open up too many cans of worms."

"I agree," Sweeney said tiredly.

Drury glanced at him. "We're doing everything we can, Richard. She'll surface sooner or later."

Another thought struck Sweeney. "How about Wisconsin? She claims her father is a teacher at the university in Madison."

"We sent two people out about twenty minutes ago. Air National Guard transport jet. They'll be in place by midnight. We've checked all the airlines, but so far there's been no sign of her, so even if she is heading west, our people will get there first."

Again Sweeney sighed.

"Maybe she's on her way back home," Drury suggested. "Housekeeping said she seemed depressed."

"Not that. She hates it there. She won't go back."

"Unless she's KGB."

Sweeney looked sharply at him. "Anything's possible," he said. "But let's just wait and see, okay?"

"Right," Drury said, and he drove the rest of the way over in silence.

Technical Services had taken over a section of the basement in the NASA headquarters building that had been used for records storage. Portable lights had been set up, and technicians were busy running cables from a half dozen antennae and communications dishes on the roof to equipment set up along one wall. A huge map of the Washington area had been set up along another wall, and on the third was a big blackboard. Already a series of notations had been made indicating which teams were watching which locations.

At least two dozen people were involved in the effort here, among them a short, dark-haired man whom Sweeney pegged as military even though he was dressed in civilian clothes. Drury introduced him.

"Major Louis Doucette, Richard Sweeney."

The two men shook hands. "Army Intelligence?" Sweeney asked.

"Yes, sir. I'm part of the Anti-Defamation League."

Drury grinned. "We put together a joint team between us,

the Department of Defense, and the National Security Agency to find out what was going on with Tyson."

"He worked for all three," Sweeney said, amazed at what he was hearing. It was as bad as the Watergate days. Perhaps worse.

"Current thinking is that it may be a political fight between the Bureau and Tyson."

"Right," Sweeney said.

"At any rate, sir, our efforts seem to have paid off," Doucette said.

"How's that?" Drury asked.

"The Demin woman has shown up. And you'll never guess where."

"When and where?" Drury demanded, forgetting about Sweeney for the moment.

"Just a few minutes ago," he said. He looked Sweeney directly in the eye. "At Toni Wagner's houseboat. Or should I say at Raya Nechiporenko's houseboat. She knew where the key was located."

"She's there now?" Sweeney asked. "Alone?"

Doucette nodded. "The Bureau sat up and took notice. Besides their team out front, they're running what I'd guess is a wire monitor on the boat. They've got a surveillance van posted across the channel, just off Boundary Road."

The implications were stunning. Sweeney was momentarily speechless.

"The plot thickens," Drury said, obviously still trying to digest what they'd just been told.

"I'll go down there and pick her up," Sweeney said, knowing even as the words left his lips that it wasn't possible.

"Not a chance," Drury said, looking up. "The Bureau would be all over you, and therefore us."

"You're right," Sweeney said. "But at this point there's no reason to suspect that the Bureau knows anything about her. She's an unknown who has shown up."

"Therefore probably a Russian spy," Doucette said.

"But no proof," Sweeney argued.

"Unless we barge in," Drury said.

"So we let her stay put and watch to see what happens next."

"What about a phone tap?" Drury asked Doucette.

"Laurie's working on it."

"Laurie McLaughlin," Drury explained. "NSA."

Another thought suddenly struck Sweeney. "I can't just walk in there and pull her out, but we can't leave her there either."

"Why not?" Drury asked.

"Either she'll do what she was sent here to do, or the Bureau will pick her up. We can't allow either to happen."

"What have you got in mind?"

"A lot," Sweeney said.

Despite the heavy snowfall and extremely limited visibility, Adkins sent a helicopter for Sweeney and Drury. The 206 Jet Ranger touched down in the snowy triangle formed by Maryland Avenue and Fourth Street behind the NASA building in a tremendous roar, blowing snow completely obliterating visibility until the rotors slowed down.

The two of them hurried from a back exit and clambered aboard. The copilot slammed the hatch closed and scrambled up into his seat, and they took off with a sickening lurch, the wind slewing them sharply to the left, until the pilot regained control.

They climbed rapidly, their track curving toward the south, the copilot on the radio, the pilot concentrating on his controls and instruments. Outside the windshield was nothing but a blank gray.

Sweeney thought there were a lot better ways to die than this, but there wasn't much he could do about it at the moment.

Once they were leveled off, Drury plugged into the ship's intercom and had a quick conference with the pilot. When he was finished he leaned over to Sweeney.

"We'll be at the Farm in about an hour," he shouted. "Unfortunately the weather isn't much better down there than it is here."

The Farm was the CIA's clandestine training base at Camp Peary just outside of Williamsburg, Virginia, on the York River. Adkins had tentatively agreed to Sweeney's plan, and would meet them down there. In the meantime a strike team was being assembled.

"What you're suggesting is extreme, Richard," Adkins had said on the telephone from his home.

"We're talking about the assistant national security adviser to the President. If he is the object of a plot to bring him down, or if he is actually working for them, we must respond."

"Worth the risk."

The ends justify the means, Sweeney thought but didn't say. "No one is to get hurt."

"Under no circumstances. God, I don't even want to think about it."

"At the first hint, and I do mean hint, that it's going bad, I'll pull the plug. Agreed?"

"Of course," Adkins said.

"And we'll do this in the daylight, so there'll be less chance of something going wrong."

"I'll see you at the Farm," Adkins said.

"Yes, sir."

They touched down in the lee of one of the hangars, and the helicopter was trundled inside before Sweeney and Drury got out. They were directed by a young trainee in battle fatigues through a door at the rear of the cavernous building. The Jet Ranger they had come down on was the twin of another on the far side. It was Adkins'.

The DDO was waiting for them with two people, one of whom Sweeney recognized as Floyd Hess, the best field instructor at the Farm. The other was a short, stocky, but pleasant-looking woman dressed, like the trainee outside, in battle fatigues.

They'd been studying a big map of the Washington area spread out on a table. Adkins had just arrived, but they hadn't had much of a head start.

"This will have to be a soft operation, Mr. Sweeney," Hess said, shaking hands. "If you think differently, let me know and I'll have to drop out."

"Wouldn't have it any other way, Floyd," Sweeney said. A soft operation meant no violence. He turned to the woman.

"Sarah Yesler. I'm one of Floyd's students."

"Pleased to meet you," Sweeney said, shaking her hand.

"Sarah will be my co-leader on this operation. I have complete confidence in her."

"Good enough," Sweeney said, looking down at the map. "I assume the problem has been outlined for you already?"

"They've been on the phone with Major Doucette, so they understand for the most part what we're up against," Adkins said.

Sweeney was glad that the DDO had come down in person. Between him and Drury, they lent credence to what was being planned.

"There'll be six of us," Hess said. "And unless we get real unlucky, none of the Bureau people on the scene will recognize anybody."

"All right, we have plenty of time to work this out, so I don't want to rush anything," Sweeney said. "Clear?"

Hess and Sarah Yesler nodded. Adkins had stepped aside and was saying something to Drury. Sweeney ignored them.

"We'll go in as soon as it's light enough to see clearly what's going on."

"I have a question for you," Hess interrupted. "This Russian woman, Marina Demin. Is she armed, and if so has she been trained?"

"Unknown on both questions. But I think we'd better assume the worst. If she is a Russian plant, she very well could be capable of defending herself and willing to do it."

"What about this other Russian, the woman being identified as Raya Nechiporenko? It's my understanding that she's being held by the Bureau. Any chance of her being released and returning to the houseboat?"

Sweeney shook his head. "Again, unknown, Floyd. But if

she's inserted into the equation, I think we would be smart to assume that she'll be armed and very dangerous."

Hess nodded, and glanced at Sarah Yesler.

"What's your tentative plan?" Sweeney asked.

"One," Hess said, stabbing a finger at the shoreline across the channel from the houseboat. "Tony Wilkes and Jim Reinert will show up at the Bureau's surveillance post and immobilize it."

"How?"

"They'll carry FBI identification, which will get them close enough to use an Escalomine aerosol. It's a Russian product that'll put them to sleep instantly. Keep them out for a couple of hours."

"Side effects?" Sweeney asked, already knowing where Hess was taking it.

"It'll leave them with one hell of a headache. But more important, it leaves a yellow tinge to their eyes which will be easily recognizable."

"The Russians will get the blame," Sweeney said.

"Yes, sir. Sort of poetic justice."

"Go on."

"Two," Hess said, pointing to the area behind the Columbia Island Marina office. "If the area is clear of onlookers, which we assume it will be if this weather keeps up, Bo Little and I will make the same approach to the unit the Bureau has posted on this side."

"If the area isn't clear?"

"We wait. Nobody is going to get hurt."

"All right."

"When this unit is secured, we give the green light to Sarah and her partner, Judy Tietz. They'll go in and pull the girl out of the houseboat."

"If she resists?"

Hess looked up. "We'll use the minimum force necessary to ensure her cooperation."

"And afterward?"

"We'll bring her down here, where we can keep a better eye on her."

"Okay," Sweeney said, glancing at his watch. It was nearing midnight. "Let's go over it again, this time slowly."

Everyone had been caught flat-footed by the arrival of the woman at the houseboat. Senarighi and some of his people had spent the night going over the few photographs they'd managed to take of her, but as of seven in the morning, when an upset Allen Young showed up at the Bureau, they'd come up with nothing.

"Nobody has any idea who the hell she is, or where she came from?" Young shouted.

"The cabbie picked her up at a truck stop in Alexandria just off I-95 at 9:27 P.M.," Senarighi said. "He took her directly to the marina and left. No one at the truck stop remembers seeing her."

"No identification?"

"Nothing yet."

"What about the audio from the houseboat?"

"She fixed herself something to eat and drink, but she did not turn on the radio or television or stereo, nor did she make any telephone calls. She went to bed around two this morning, and as of six-thirty she was apparently still asleep."

Young said nothing.

"We can go in and pick her up. Find out who she is," Senarighi suggested.

"She's done nothing wrong. What about Tyson, any movement?"

"Nothing so far."

Again Young lapsed into silence. He and Senarighi were meeting in his office. The snow had slowed down, and at least the main roads in and around the city had been partially cleared.

"I've already spoken with Director Wilder about this," Young said at length.

"Yes, sir?"

"If we can't say that this new girl is a Russian . . ."

"We cannot, sir."

"No," Young said. "Then we'll release the Wagner woman and see what happens."

Senarighi grinned, suddenly feeling better than he had all night. Whoever the hell the new one was might come out when Toni Wagner returned to her houseboat. The idea was great.

"When do you want to do it?"

"Is she ready to leave?"

"Yes, sir," Senarighi said. "Do you want me to take her home?"

"No," Young said. "Have her car brought around. I'll send for her and apologize on the Bureau's behalf. We'll even provide her with the procedures packet for bringing a complaint against us."

Senarighi chuckled. "I wouldn't mind seeing that happen, sir. Not this time."

"As a matter of fact, neither would I, Sandy. But I don't think it's going to happen that way."

"No, sir. I guess I don't either."

It was 8:17 A.M. when the two Jet Ranger helicopters landed behind the Pentagon. Seven people disembarked and, hunched low, raced across the parking lot to a line of four cars, all registered to nonexistent people.

Wilkes and Reinert, who would take the Bureau unit across the river from the houseboat, went in one car; Hess and Little, who would take the Bureau surveillance unit in the marina, went in another; Sarah Yesler and Judy Tietz, who would go in and take Marina Demin, used the third; and Drury, who would provide the on-site political muscle should anything go wrong, took the fourth.

They would be in continuous radio contact on a scrambled frequency, and Drury would remain in a transit-authority parking lot about two minutes from the marina.

Sarah and Judy were the only ones who carried weapons. It had been Adkins' decision at the last moment. "There's no telling what's going to happen in there," he said. "I'm not going to have my people shot up."

Adkins was returning to Langley, where he would offer further political backup should the need arise. And Sweeney had remained at the Farm, where he would take charge when Marina was brought down.

The snow had tapered off in the early-morning hours, but it was starting up again, this time even harder than yesterday and last night. So far, however, from what they'd been able to see from the air, most main roads were still passable.

"This is going to go nice and easy this morning." Hess briefed them all one last time. "A friendly points a gun at you, the operation is done. Give the gentleman your name and nothing else. In due course we'll come by to collect you . . . unharmed."

"What about the woman?" Sarah Yesler asked for the sixth time. Everyone wanted to make rock certain of their position.

"Use your own judgment. That's what you're being paid for," Hess said. "No one is to be killed here, but the stakes are high."

"We're working outside of our charter," Drury put in unnecessarily. "If you're busted, there'll be hell to pay."

"But not as much hell to pay if someone were to get hurt."

"Of course not," Drury agreed. "Just do your jobs as best as you know how, and everything will turn out."

"Your words are a comfort," Hess said half under his breath. "All right, unless there are further questions, let's do it, people."

On the drive back across the river to her houseboat, Toni Wagner didn't bother taking any precautions. The Bureau knew all about her, or thought they did, so her effectiveness here was finished.

The bastards had used drugs on her, something American agencies were not supposed to do, but instinctively she felt that they had not probed deeply enough to see beyond her legend and the programming that secured it in her head. Which meant the best they had were suspicions. It was the reason they had released her: lack of evidence. But they would be watching her very closely now to see what she did next.

As long as Tyson stayed away for the next twenty-four hours, she would be able to make her preparations to get out. Mexico City first, then Athens, where she had an old friend. It would be a place to hole up for a few months until the dust settled.

Eventually, of course, she would return home to see her family, and then report for retraining and a new assignment.

Her two regrets were for the failed assignment here, and for what could have been—but would not be—with her control officer.

She would be debriefed of course, and as she drove she tried to go over in her head what had happened to her since Friday. But many of her memories were fuzzy around the edges. She knew, of course, that she'd been questioned, but she felt little or no anxiety about the experience. Nor, she found, did she really care what she'd told them. "Rely on your conditioning," her trainers had told her, over and over again. "Your conditioning will be your safety net if you let it. Relax, accept the questions, and answer your interrogators automatically, without conscious thought. You are Toni Wagner, no one else."

But old habits died hard, and coming into the marina, she automatically scanned the parked cars, her eyes straying past and then going back to a Toyota van she'd seen before.

At least one man was inside. It was a surveillance unit. FBI. Nothing less than she'd expected.

Well, let the bastards watch, she told herself, parking next to a snowdrift up from her boat. By this time tomorrow she would be out of the country, and they could go fuck themselves.

Wearily Toni trudged through the snow, out onto the dock, and boarded her houseboat, where she stopped short. Someone had been here. The footprints in the snow were mostly covered on the dock, but on the houseboat's deck, which was partially protected from the wind, they were still visible.

Reaching above the light on the left, she searched for the key, but it was gone.

The FBI was here. It had to be them. Tyson had his own key, as did her control officer (though he'd never been here to her knowledge), her landlord, and of course the marina manager.

They had probably been here and gone, searching the place while she was being held. The sons of bitches. In this country you were supposed to have rights against search and seizure. Wasn't that one of the messages they'd been touting the world over since the war?

Girding herself for a confrontation in case someone from the Bureau was still here, she let herself in just as a good-looking young woman, dressed in blue jeans and a sweatshirt, her feet bare, appeared at the bedroom doorway, her mouth open in surprise.

Natalie Reilly got on the radio the moment Toni Wagner showed up at the marina. "Hiawatha has arrived." Her partner, Bill Mote, was in the front seat of the van.

"I'm a couple minutes behind her," Senarighi responded. "Eleven, keep your ears open."

"Will do," John Niven radioed. He and Len Harding were stationed across the channel with the audio monitoring equipment.

"Anything yet?"

"Movement, but no one has said a thing."

"Ten?" Senarighi asked.

"She's inside, but nothing has happened yet."

"Hold on, I'll be right with you."

"Is this your boat?" Marina Demin asked uncertainly. It was clear that she was extremely nervous.

"Who are you?" Toni demanded. "And what are you doing here?"

"I'm . . . my name is Janice Copeland, and I was cold."

"What the hell are you talking about? Who are you?"

"There are some men after me. They want to kill me, I

think. But I have to reach my father first . . . in Wisconsin. His name is . . . Joseph."

Toni was rocked back on her heels. The woman sounded American, and looked American, but she had to be Russian. Either that or she was a sleeper. What was Ivan trying to do to her? Now, of all times, with the FBI parked on her doorstep. Were they all fools in Moscow?

Marina started to speak again, but Toni shook her head and went into the kitchen, where she got a pencil and a pad of paper from the counter.

"*Who sent you here?*" she wrote in Russian. She held it up so that Marina could see it. The woman's eyes widened even more.

Marina took the pad and pencil from Toni and wrote, "*Maj. Kiselev. Is this place bugged?*"

Toni nodded and wrote, "*FBI is outside watching. I was arrested. Must leave here today. Operation is over.*"

It was Marina's turn to shake her head. She wrote, angrily, "*Nyet! Nyet! The document must be delivered!*"

Some instinct had drawn Privet to the Columbia Island Marina, rather than back to Tyson's house in Georgetown. Lydia Lubiako had been certain enough about Raya Nechiporenko's legend and training to believe that she would be released soon. And the new field operative from Moscow was supposed to be making contact soon.

But contact with whom? And where?

Everything revolved around Tyson.

Raya Nechiporenko was his mistress. Perhaps the new operative would come here.

He had left his car just off the parkway and was watching the marina through binoculars when he saw a maroon Chevrolet pull up beside the FBI's Toyota van, and two men, wearing FBI caps and jackets, get out.

Hess, holding up an FBI shield with his left hand, while his right held the aerosol canister in his jacket pocket, approached the Toyota van. Little was going around to the other side.

A man behind the wheel cranked down the window, a quizzical look on his face. "What the hell are you guys doing here? Or did Sandy send you?"

"Sandy," Hess said. "Where's your partner?"

"Huh?" the FBI agent asked.

"What is it, Bill?" Natalie Reilly asked as she leaned across the back of the front seat.

Hess took out the aerosol canister and sprayed the gas into the van from a distance of less than two feet.

Bill Mote's eyes got large, and he started to reach for his pistol, when he slumped forward, his head bumping on the door frame.

Natalie Reilly reared back, but an instant later she, too, fell unconscious.

Hess pulled out his walkie-talkie. "Clear one," he radioed.

Little waited five seconds for the gas to clear, then got into the van and manhandled Motes' unconscious form into the back with the woman's. They did not want a chance passerby to look into the van and see the driver unconscious at the wheel.

"Two, clear," Tony Wilkes radioed from across the channel. The two FBI agents manning the surveillance van in the trees had been neutralized.

"Three, come," Hess radioed.

"Roger," Sarah Yesler replied.

Hess and Little closed up the van, went back to their car, and drove back up behind the marina so that they could get out in a hurry or provide backup for Sarah and Judy if need be.

No one was around, so far. The marina office was still closed, probably because of the weather. Conditions were perfect for the grab. But Hess did not feel particularly good about what he had done, was still doing. The look on those FBI agents' faces had been anything but comical. Hess had seen abject terror in the man's eyes. He had thought he was dying.

"Christ," Hess mumbled. The Bureau was going to be mad as hell, and no one could blame them.

Sarah Yesler, driving the green Ford station wagon, entered the marina, spotting Hess and Little waiting just within the gate, above the office. She waved as she passed, and drove directly down to the docks, making a U-turn so that the car was parked nose-out.

She and Judy Tietz checked the loads in their .32-caliber automatics, which they holstered beneath their FBI jackets at the small of their backs.

They looked at each other, nodded after a moment, and got out of the car in unison.

Nothing or no one moved in the marina, and so far as they could tell from a distance of twenty yards, no one was aboard the houseboat.

Sarah approached first, Judy fifteen feet behind her. As soon as she reached the dock she could see that someone had been here this morning. Footprints clearly led through the snow and aboard.

Judy spotted it too, and when Sarah glanced back over her shoulder, the other woman nodded her acknowledgment.

Neither of them was very comfortable with this assignment, but unlike the other two teams, they were not dealing with FBI agents. They would be facing one, and possibly two, Russian KGB agents. Possibly well trained, and possibly armed.

Sarah had a hollow feeling in the pit of her stomach as she withdrew her weapon, switched the safety catch to the off position, and stepped aboard the boat.

She moved to one side of the door as Judy came aboard and took up a position on the other side.

Again they exchanged a glance, nodded, and then Sarah knocked on the door.

At first there was no answer, so Sarah knocked again, this time louder.

Even though it was cold, and her hands were bare, her palms were sweaty.

She was about to knock a third time when the door opened a crack. For a split second Sarah wondered if this was a trap and someone inside was pointing a gun at them, but then she rammed her shoulder into the door, shoving it all the way open and pushing Marina Demin violently to the floor.

"Freeze, freeze, FBI," Sarah shouted, leaping into the room.

She swept her pistol left to right as she sidestepped quickly away from the door.

Only the one woman lay on the floor, a horrified expression on her white face.

Judy Tietz came in a second later, taking up position on the other side of the room, nearer to the kitchen in front.

"What do you want?" Marina Demin cried.

"Get up, you're coming with us," Sarah said, when another woman called to them from the corridor that led aft.

"I'm coming out now, but if you shoot me this boat will explode."

Sarah switched her aim to the corridor. The Wagner woman? The one they'd tentatively identified as Raya Nechiporenko? The Bureau was supposed to be holding her.

"I'm holding the triggering device. If my finger slips off the button, fifty kilos of Semtex will blow."

Semtex was the Polish-made plastique explosive. It was more powerful than C-4. Fifty kilos would take out half the marina.

"Come ahead," Sarah said after a moment's hesitation. "No one wants to harm you."

"That's what you think," Toni said, coming around the corner. She was holding a small device that looked like a television remote-control unit. "Now, close the door, it's getting cold in here."

22

TONI WAGNER DIDN'T KNOW IF SHE WAS STILL SUFFERING FROM the effects of the drugs she'd been given. But she knew enough to understand that the two women facing her were very probably not FBI. She'd watched from her bedroom window as the two men had immobilized the pair in the Toyota van and then driven off. These two had driven up moments later. If they were not FBI, chances were they were not District of Columbia cops either. There was no reason for them to come here like this. She'd broken no local laws. Which left what? CIA?

"Lay your pistols on the floor and step back away from them," she said.

Marina had picked herself off the floor and moved back.

"I don't think you mean to kill us all," the shorter, stockier of the two said.

"It's up to you," Toni said evenly. She moved over to a window and carefully pulled back the edge of the curtain. Nothing moved in the parking lot. She turned back and raised the triggering device. "I'm running out of patience, and somehow I don't think the situation outside is going to remain stable for very long."

Sarah and Judy exchanged glances, then they both safetied their weapons and carefully laid them on the floor. They straightened up and moved back a couple of paces.

"Pick up their weapons and bring them here," Toni told Marina.

She did as she was instructed. Toni took one of the guns.

"Do you know how to use one of these?" she asked.

Marina nodded after a moment.

"Good," Toni said. She laid the triggering device aside. "Now, who the hell are you?" she asked the two women.

"FBI . . ." Sarah started to answer, but Toni cut her off.

"I saw your friends neutralize the Bureau agents in the Toyota. You're not cops. What, then, CIA?"

Sarah laughed. "I don't know what you're talking about, but if I was CIA I wouldn't be here."

Toni switched the pistol's safety catch to the off position, cocked the hammer, and aimed the gun directly at Sarah's head. "If you believed I would blow us all up, you can believe that I won't hesitate to shoot you dead right now."

"All right, all right," Sarah said. "You're right, we do work for the Agency. And so far you've done nothing serious here. At worst you will be kicked out of the country, or possibly exchanged with one of our people in Moscow."

"What the hell are you talking about?"

"We know that you are Raya Nechiporenko and that you work for the KGB."

"What?"

"We know that you are here in this country to either spy on or destroy Albert Tyson. We know all of this."

"And you want to help me?" Toni asked, almost laughing.

"As strange as that may seem, yes," Sarah replied.

Toni could see Marina Demin out of the corner of her eye. What the hell was Ivan thinking about, sending her here like this? He hadn't said anything about her. She didn't fit anywhere in the plan. So what was happening? What was expected of her?

One thing was sure, she would have to get out of here as soon as possible. She needed to make contact with her control officer. She had to know what was expected of her.

Senarighi drove through the gate into the marina and spotted the two men in the maroon Chevrolet but thought nothing of it for the moment.

The first inkling he had that something was wrong came as he rounded the corner of the marina office building and saw the green Ford station wagon parked nose-out in front of the houseboat. The car's engine was running and no one was behind the wheel.

Senarighi pulled up beside the Toyota and got out, butterflies playing in his gut. "Bill?" he called, opening the van's front door, but the word died in his throat.

Bill Mote and Natalie Reilly were both down, and for the moment Senarighi had no idea how badly off they were, or even if they were still alive.

He snatched the microphone. "Unit control, this is team leader. Hiawatha unit ten is down. Repeat, both agents, Hiawatha unit ten, are down. Agent needs immediate assistance."

"Roger, copy," the communications officer at headquarters relayed. "Help is coming. Say exact nature of your situation, team leader."

"Both unit ten agents are immobile in the back of their unit. I don't know their exact condition yet. There is a Ford station wagon, green, registration, Maryland seven-nine-seven, Delta, Ohio, Romeo, parked with its engine running in front of subject's houseboat." Senarighi leaned out the door of the van and looked back the way he had come, but from here the area of the gate was blocked by the marina office building. "A second vehicle on scene may also be involved. I make it a late-model maroon Chevrolet Cavalier, registration unknown, two or more persons inside."

"Roger. Watch yourself, team leader, help is less than five minutes away."

"Roger," Senarighi said, and he crawled into the back,

where he checked Bill Mote's pulse at the side of his neck, and then Natalie Reilly's. Both were on the slow side of normal. They both seemed to be breathing properly, though slower than normal. It was almost as if they were sleeping.

He raised Mote's left eyelid. The iris was narrow, but the white of his eye had a yellowish cast to it. He checked Natalie Reilly's, and it was the same with her.

It came to Senarighi all at once. Victim apparently asleep, no symptoms other than a yellowish cast to the eyes. The Russian aerosol Escalomine. He'd been briefed three months ago.

"Goddamn," he said to himself, pulling out his gun and crawling back out of the van. "Goddammit to hell."

Keeping a wary eye on the station wagon, he hurried on foot around the marina office building.

Bo Little raced back up the hill and clambered into the car. "Get us the hell out of here! Now!"

Hess slammed the Chevy into gear and, spinning tires on the snowy driveway, fishtailed through the gate.

Little was watching out the rear window as Senarighi came around the marina office in a dead run. Spotting the departing vehicle, he pulled up short and dropped into a shooter's stance.

"Christ, he's going to fire!" Little shouted. "Get down!"

They both scrunched down in the seat as two bullets crashed through the rear window, the first deflecting upward through the roof over the rearview mirror and the second crashing through the windshield.

By then they had reached the parkway, and Hess hauled the car into the eastbound lanes, flooring the accelerator.

Cautiously, Little rose up and looked back. "Clear," he said.

"We've got to ditch this car," Hess said, sitting up. "Get on the radio and try to raise Sarah. Tell her what's coming her way. Then call Tony and Jim and tell them to get clear. And then raise Drury."

"Three, you copy?" Little spoke into the walkie-talkie.

Hess lowered his window and tossed out the aerosol canister of Escalomine.

"Three, you copy?" Little radioed again.

They crossed the channel bridge and headed down the south ramp on Interstate 395. There was very little traffic despite the fact that it was Monday morning. It was the snow.

"No answer," Little said.

"Tell her what's coming down anyway, then warn the others."

"Listen, Sarah, we had to bug out. There is an armed Bureau agent heading your way. Presumably he's called for backup. Stabilize your situation if you can, and sit tight. We'll get to you."

Little waited a moment or two, but when there was no response, he called the unit across the channel. "Two, get out of there."

"We're rolling. We copied your previous."

"Any trouble on your side?"

"Negative."

"Unit one, this is papa," Drury radioed.

"Roger, papa," Little responded.

"Ditch your car. I'll pick you up northbound en route to our rendezvous point."

Little looked at Hess, who nodded. "Will do," he radioed. "But three is stuck back there."

"I copied your transmissions, one. Ditch your car! Do it, mister!"

Again Little and Hess exchanged glances. Sarah and Judy were in trouble, not only with the Bureau, but something had apparently gone wrong aboard the houseboat. Otherwise they would have responded by radio. This had been a bad operation from the beginning: Americans against Americans. Yet, as it had been explained to him, they were backed into a corner. There was no other way out.

"No one is going to get hurt," Sweeney had promised them. It had sounded okay, but now Little wasn't so sure.

Boundary Road branched left over Highway 110 toward the Pentagon. Hess had been watching in his rearview mirror.

Just before the turn, he pulled the car off the road, switched off the engine, and tossed the keys out into the snow.

A big truck lumbered past, and a half minute later Drury pulled up in his gray Thunderbird long enough for Hess and Little to clamber in, and then took off.

"What the hell happened over there?" Drury demanded. "The Bureau shoot you up?"

"He came out of nowhere, Bob," Hess said. "We had to bug out."

"You guys all right?"

"We are, but Sarah and Judy are cornered, Mr. Drury," Little said.

"They're professionals, the situation will stabilize," Drury said. "At any rate it's in Adkins' lap now."

"He meant inside the houseboat, sir," Hess said. "You heard our transmissions."

"They didn't respond?"

"Not a word. Which means they might have walked into a trap down there. Either Marina Demin had help, or she's a hell of a lot better than Mr. Sweeney led us to believe."

"Christ," Drury groaned. "Where the hell is this going to end?"

"I don't know," Hess said. "But we can't leave those girls to work it out on their own."

"Well, we're not going to go back over there and shoot it out with the Bureau."

"I'm not suggesting that."

"What, then, Floyd?" Drury asked coolly.

"I say we blow the whistle on the operation. Call the Bureau and tell them what's going down, and have them help get Sarah and Judy out of there."

"I'll pass your suggestion along to Adkins," Drury said.

They could see the two helicopters warming up across the snow-covered field. Wilkes and Reinert were already there, and scrambling aboard one of the machines.

"So will I," Hess said.

"Look here, mister . . ." Drury said, but Hess cut him off.

"I don't give a shit what happens, Bob, we are not going to turn our backs on them just to save someone's ass in the White House."

Sweeney was sitting in the communications center at the Farm waiting for word from Drury that they'd gotten Marina Demin safely out of the houseboat and were back in the air. The waiting was driving him crazy. And the coffee he'd drunk and the cigarettes he'd smoked through the night had given him a bad case of heartburn.

The OD, Peter Thompson, looked up and shook his head. He was startlingly blond and massively built. He'd been transferred from Technical Services for a tour here.

Sweeney sighed disgustedly and started to get up for another cup of coffee, when one of the communications specialists waved a hand. "Here it comes," he said.

Sweeney quickly put on the headset as Drury came on. "Homebase, this is papa. We're a bust. We're heading to the barn."

Something clutched at Sweeney's gut. "What the hell happened, Bob?" he radioed.

"Give us fifteen minutes," Drury said. "Papa out."

Toni Wagner had opened one of the windows facing the marina the moment she heard the shots, and saw the Bureau agent racing back from behind the office.

"Help us! Help us!" she screamed.

The Bureau agent pulled up short, then darted behind the Toyota van.

"There's two of them! They have guns and explosives!" Toni shouted. Then she closed the window and turned back to the others. The walkie-talkie transmissions had given her an idea.

Special Agent Jules Joslow and his partner arrived five minutes later, just ahead of a half dozen other agents who'd been dispatched on Allen Young's orders.

Parking their car on the east side of the marina office, they hurried on foot to where Senarighi was crouched behind the Toyota van, his pistol still drawn.

"What have we got, Sandy?" Joslow asked, studying the approaches to the houseboat.

"I'm not sure yet, but it looks as if we've got a hostage situation developing down there," Senarighi said. He looked back the way Joslow had come. "I hope the doctor is on the way. I don't know about Bill or Natalie. They're still out."

"He's on his way. So is Young. What the hell happened here?"

Senarighi quickly filled the two agents in on what he'd stumbled onto, and how he had reacted, ending with the shouts for help from the houseboat. "I know it's going to sound odd, but I'm sure the woman who called for help was Toni Wagner."

"The Russian?"

"Who the hell knows?" Senarighi said. "I sure don't."

"Then who the hell is in there with her and the other broad?" Joslow asked.

Allen Young and the doctor arrived at the same time as a pair of ambulances and at least ten Bureau agents. The marina operator, a former Navy supply officer, showed up just behind them, and when he was told what was needed, he pointed out the slips of the other four live-aboards. Agents were immediately sent down to get the people out of the way. A second unit, including an ambulance and a doctor, was dispatched to see about Harding and Niven across the channel. For the moment the District Police had not gotten involved, but that would change very soon and everyone knew it. In the meantime Young was adamant about resolving the situation as quickly as possible.

"That car in front of the houseboat is not listed on any hot sheet, and what's more, the registration number does not exist," Young told Senarighi. "What about the other car?"

"I didn't get a tag number," Senarighi said. "But it's probably another fake."

"My guess is that they're Russians," Joslow said.

"Then who the hell is Toni Wagner?" Young shot back.

"Maybe Toni Wagner is who she claims to be," Joslow suggested.

"Bullshit, Jules," Senarighi swore. "She understands the language. I was there during her interrogation. I saw the look in her eye and heard the answers."

"I speak French, doesn't make me a Frog."

The doctor stuck his head out the open door of the ambulance and called Young over. The ambulance was parked on the east side of the office, out of range should anything develop on or around the houseboat. "Bill Mote is awake," the doctor said. "But he's going to have one hell of a head for the next couple of days."

"Escalomine?" Young asked.

"I'll say yes, but I'll know for sure once we do a blood workup."

Senarighi came over and he and Young climbed aboard the ambulance. Mote was awake, but Natalie Reilly was still out, an oxygen mask on her pale face.

"There were two of them, wearing FBI jackets and baseball caps," Mote said, his voice thick in his throat. "One of them even held up his fucking shield."

"Did you get a good look at them?" Young asked.

"Yes, sir, a real good look," Mote said. It was obvious that he was in a lot of pain. He described both men in detail. "I rolled down my window and Natalie came forward at the same time the first one sprayed something in my face. No smell, no burning sensation. Just nothing."

"Listen to me, Bill," Young said. "You told us the first one . . . the only one of them to say anything . . . spoke in English."

"Yes, sir."

"Think about this. Was he an American? Is there any possibility he was Russian?"

"Not a chance in hell, sir," Mote said. "I'd bet almost anything that the son of a bitch was an American. But who?"

Sarah Yesler and Judy Tietz lay facedown on the carpeted floor of the houseboat's saloon, their hands clasped behind their heads at the backs of their necks.

On the assumption that the Bureau and possibly the CIA as well had placed bugs here, Toni had whispered her hurried instructions into Marina Demin's ear. She had to repeat herself twice before she got through to the younger woman exactly what was at stake, and what had to be done.

Marina agreed, reluctantly. At this point she knew that she had no other choice. Kiselev may not have envisioned this situation, but by ordering her to run from the CIA once she got to this country, and to come to this houseboat, he must have known something of what would likely happen.

All this, she told herself, was ordained in a broad sense. There was nothing for her now but to play it out, although she had the feeling that she would be killed.

Toni looked deeply into her eyes, and after a second, Marina nodded.

Toni went back to the window and carefully pulled back an edge of the curtain so that she could look outside. There were a lot of people out there now. Hopefully all of them were professionals. If one of them was nervous, and too quick on the trigger, she could end up dead.

Letting the curtain fall back, she again glanced at Marina, then went to the door and slipped the lock.

"No," she shouted.

Marina fired a single shot into the floor, and an instant later Toni yanked open the door and, screaming for help, leaped outside, jumped down onto the dock, and raced for the line of FBI agents thirty meters away.

Sarah Yesler reared up when the gun was fired, and she was in time to see Toni Wagner disappearing outside. She started to get to her knees, when she looked over her shoulder, and her heart skipped a beat.

Marina Demin, her face extremely white, her hands shaking badly, had the automatic, its hammer cocked, aimed directly at Sarah's head.

"Don't . . ." Sarah sputtered, but Marina violently shook her head and motioned for the CIA agent to be silent.

Sarah complied, and slowly she lay back down on the floor, locking her hands behind her head.

Marina went carefully to the door and pulled it closed. She snapped the lock, then leaned back against the wall, the gun trained loosely on the two women.

From outside she could still hear Toni screaming something. She couldn't make out the exact words, but the screams sounded realistically hysterical to her. Somehow that was no comfort.

"Just hold on," Raya had told her. "It's your part. It's what you must do. The CIA will come rescue you. They won't leave you here."

Toni Wagner ran headlong into the arms of two FBI agents, who hustled her practically off her feet behind one of the Bureau's vans. She counted at least a dozen armed men crouching behind other vans and cars, and several boats up on chocks.

Senarighi and Young raced down from the ambulance on the other side of the office.

"I should have fucking known," Toni said.. "What the hell is it with you people? Hoover's dead, or weren't you told?"

"What's going on down there?" Young asked her.

"What are you talking about, you bastard? This is your show. You tell me."

"I don't have time to play games with you, Miss Wagner," Young said harshly. "I'm going to do everything within my power to prevent injury here. Now, I want your cooperation."

He was running scared, she could see it in his eyes. And it was just as clear from his tone of voice, and his attitude and bearing, that he didn't know what was going on. It's exactly what she'd hoped for. If there was a crack, she meant to slip through it.

She nodded finally.

"All right," he said. "What about those two men down there? What's the exact situation?"

"What two men?"

The two who barged in on you . . ." Young said. "Wait. You tell us exactly what's going on."

Toni shifted her gaze from Young to Senarighi (who was the only one who looked skeptical) and back. "All I know is that when I got home, a woman was waiting for me. She said her name was Janice Copeland, that someone was trying to kill her, and that she had to reach her father in Wisconsin. The next thing I knew, two women showed up, armed to the teeth, and threatened to kill me if I didn't keep my mouth shut."

"What did they want?" Young asked.

"They wanted the woman. But then there were shots outside and they decided to stay put." Toni had been waiting for a reaction from Young or Senarighi that would indicate they knew she was lying. But it didn't come. Evidently there was no bug on her houseboat, or whoever had manned it had been taken out by the CIA. It was incredible, here in the United States. It was worse than the cowboys and Indians she'd believed in as a little girl.

"Are they American?" Senarighi asked.

Toni looked at him. "The one spoke English. I don't know, maybe she's American. Maybe not." Toni laughed disparagingly. "Tell me, is it the Russians again? You must have a very big bed for all of them to hide under it."

"How'd you get out of there?" Senarighi asked, ignoring her comment.

"I just ran. They shot at me, I think."

"What about the other woman?"

"I don't know. She's very frightened that they're going to kill her."

Young hurried back up to his car, where his chauffeur was waiting for him, the engine running, and got in the backseat.

"Back to the office, Mr. Young?" the man asked.

"No, we'll stick around here for a while yet," Young said. He telephoned Ed Wilder at Bureau headquarters in the Hoover Building, and was connected immediately.

"What's the situation down there, Allen?" the FBI director asked.

Young explained it to him in less than two minutes. "I don't know about Miss Wagner, maybe we've got her all wrong, though I still doubt it, but I think we'd better call in the team."

"I agree," Wilder said. "I'll have them there within the hour."

"We'll stand by in the meantime. The situation seems to have stabilized."

"Watch yourself," Wilder said, and rang off. The unit he would call was the Bureau's elite Hostage Rescue Team.

Young looked up into the sky. The overcast seemed thicker, and the falling snow heavier than before. If the team could not use helicopters, it would come by road. Whatever, he felt better that they were on the way. Above all, he wanted no one hurt here.

Sweeney could hardly believe his ears. It was as if his worst fears had materialized this morning. The heartburn in his gut deepened to the molten-metal stage. Drury, back at Langley with the team, had just explained the fiasco to him.

"Did you check back, Bob?" Sweeney asked. "Did you at least make a flyby?"

"The snow had reduced visibility, but we got close enough to see that the Bureau was pouring a lot of assets into the marina. With that muscle the situation shouldn't get out of hand."

"What does Adkins have to say about it?"

"He wants you back here as soon as possible."

"Goddammit, Bob, what the hell is he going to do about those two girls? We're not going to leave them like that. You said yourself that something had evidently gone wrong inside the houseboat."

"Take it easy," Drury warned.

"If I have to blow the whistle myself, I'll do it."

"You're out of line, Richard," Drury shouted. "Push it,

and I'll have your ass. This is coming from the top, and I do mean the top. You know what's at stake."

"Sorry," Sweeney said. "But we can't leave those girls in the lurch."

"Nor will we, you have my word on it," Drury said. "The chopper and pilot are standing by for you at operations. Oh, and another thing you'd better think about on the way up. We just learned that Toni Wagner, Raya Nechiporenko, was released by the Bureau this morning. There's a real possibility she's at the houseboat as well."

"Christ," Sweeney groaned. It definitely was not what he wanted to hear.

Senarighi used the keypad on his walkie-talkie to tie into the local telephone system, and he dialed the houseboat's number. Niven and Harding had been gassed, and they were on the way to the hospital now. In the meantime they'd been replaced in the surveillance unit. So far there'd been no sounds from within the houseboat except for some movement. Whoever the three women were, they were saying nothing.

The telephone rang and Senarighi looked up at Joslow, who was listening in. Joslow's specialty in the Bureau was as a hostage negotiator. He wasn't the best, but he was near the top. Senarighi had a lot of confidence in the man. If they would talk.

On the fifth ring, the line was disconnected.

"Someone inside pulled the plug," Joslow said.

"Shit," Senarighi swore.

Everyone agreed that the situation was getting completely out of hand and something would have to be done about it immediately. The problem was that no one was able to agree on exactly what should or could be done.

The President agreed to see Vaughan and the CIA's general counsel, Morris Segal, immediately. When they arrived they were met by the President's special counsel, Charles Fritsch.

It was a job that Charles Colson had filled during the Nixon years. No one had forgotten.

"Bring me up to date, General," the President told Vaughan. "I don't want to see anybody get hurt."

"Neither do I, Mr. President," Vaughan said. "But we're very close now to proving Tyson's innocence."

"Or his guilt," Fritsch suggested. He was a ruddy, outdoorsy-looking man who ten years ago, when he was in his mid-thirties, had successfully climbed K2, the second-highest mountain in the world. He was an enigma in Washington. Not many people knew much about him, except that he had the President's ear.

"Or that," Vaughan conceded. "But if we interfere now with what the Bureau is trying to do, we might blow our chances."

The President sat back in his chair and shook his head. "I'm listening."

Vaughan and Segal exchanged a glance. "This is how we see the present situation. The Bureau believed that Tyson's mistress, a woman who identifies herself as Toni Wagner, was in actuality a Russian agent. At the very least she was exchanging sexual favors with Tyson for information. At worst she and Tyson were working together. In other words, Tyson was an agent for the KGB."

"You said *believed*, General," Fritsch said.

"Miss Wagner was arrested by the Bureau last week, but she was released this morning. So far as we have been able to determine, no charges have been filed against her, and the Bureau even apologized."

"I didn't hear about this," the President snapped peevishly.

"No, sir, neither had I," Fritsch replied.

"Miss Wagner returned to her houseboat this morning," Vaughan continued. "In the meantime a Russian woman named Marina Demin, who claimed that she had been the mistress of a high-ranking Russian government official, entered our embassy and asked for political asylum. She told my people about a plot to bring down a member of your staff, Mr. President."

"Tyson?" the President asked.

Vaughan nodded. "She said that her father, a teacher at the University of Wisconsin, had something to do with it. Something to do with Tyson's past. And that if we brought her here, she would identify him for us."

"Is she here in Washington?" Fritsch asked.

"Yes," Vaughan said. "But not in our custody. She slipped from a safe house last night and came directly to Miss Wagner's houseboat."

The President and Fritsch were both rocked by this news. "What does it mean?" the President asked.

Vaughan sat forward. "Mr. President, we think that Toni Wagner will probably identify Tyson as a traitor. And we think further that Miss Demin came here to identify someone who will be connected with the KGB. Someone who will admit that Tyson is working for them. These two women, we believe, are two elements in a very sophisticated plot to bring Tyson down."

"Why?" Fritsch asked sharply.

"I don't know. But it'd be my guess that Tyson knows something that the Russians are afraid of."

The President's eyebrows knit. "What are you saying, General?"

"I think that Tyson, probably back in his college days, may have gotten himself involved with the wrong element. Possibly the KGB. It's something I think he's long since forgotten about, but it's something I think the KGB means to use against him, along with Miss Wagner's testimony."

"Unbelievable," the President said softly.

"Yes, Mr. President, I agree with you," Vaughan said. "Nonetheless, we can think of no other reason that the Demin woman went immediately to the houseboat."

"What now?" the President asked.

"The FBI has called in its Hostage Rescue Team. They should be on-site within the hour."

Fritsch's eyes widened. "You're monitoring FBI radio broadcasts?"

Vaughan said nothing, and the moment passed.

"We believe that Toni Wagner and Marina Demin are holding two agents we sent to recapture the Demin woman. We want the Bureau's team to rescue them. But, Mr. President, I'm asking that you telephone Ed Wilder now and order the team *not* to use deadly force in their rescue."

"Our people would be at a grave disadvantage," the President said. "Some of them could get shot, killed."

"Yes, sir," Vaughan said.

"You are fully aware of what you're asking?"

Vaughan nodded. "Yes, I am, Mr. President. What's at stake is nothing less than your national security adviser."

"Nothing less than the security of the White House, if I may add, Mr. President," Segal said ponderously.

"What about afterward?"

"The Russians will make the next move, Mr. President. If they want Al Tyson badly enough, which we believe they do, they'll move."

Still the President hesitated, until finally he picked up his telephone. "Get me Ed Wilder at the Bureau."

The news media had finally arrived, along with several dozen curious passersby, some of whom had boats in the marina. The District Police had also been alerted and the Bureau had pressed them into service as perimeter control.

Toni Wagner had been taken up to the office, which was being used as a central clearinghouse and communications center. She'd been shuffled off to the side, given a sweater and a cup of coffee and a young Bureau agent to keep an eye on her.

Young was in overall charge of the situation, with Senarighi and Joslow as his seconds-in-command. A bullhorn had been brought out, but Young had vetoed its use after a hasty conference with the Hostage Rescue Team leader, Donald Wood, now en route by helicopter from Andrew Air Force Base with his people.

"We'll use that as a distraction just before we go in," Wood had explained. "Unless you think the situation is inherently unstable at this moment."

"No, everything is quiet on the houseboat," Young had said on the telephone just two meters from where Toni sat sipping her coffee.

"We have an ETA your position in thirteen minutes," Wood shouted over the noise in the helicopter.

"We're standing by," Young said, and he hung up the phone. He glanced over at Toni, the expression on his face blank, and then turned and left.

"I have to go to the bathroom," Toni Wagner said, standing up.

Her watchdog, whom she figured wasn't older than twenty-five or twenty-six, jumped up. "What?"

"Bathroom. I have to pee, you know. Would you like to come watch?"

The kid's face turned a little red, but he shook his head. "I'll wait here."

"Do that," Toni said, and she went down the short corridor and into the women's room, the kid watching her every move.

Inside was a pay telephone. She'd taken a couple of quarters out of her purse on the chance that she could get in here, and on the chance that the Bureau had not blocked the lines.

She got a tone and dialed her contact. The number was answered on the first ring. "Is Uncle Harold back?"

"Where are you?" Igor Lubiako asked, obviously recognizing her voice.

Toni quickly explained her circumstances. "Can you get me out of here?"

"*Nyet*. But listen carefully, Raya, this is what you must do, and when it's over we'll meet in Moscow. In the spring, I think."

23

EVERYTHING SEEMED TO BE MOVING WITH THE SPEED OF LIGHT, yet it had been more than an hour since Sweeney had gotten word at the Farm that something had gone wrong with the operation. He stood now across from Drury and Adkins in the deputy director's office at Langley, trying to digest exactly what was being thrown at him.

"The President himself called Wilder and ordered the Bureau's people to use no deadly force down there," Adkins was saying. "It puts their people at a disadvantage if Marina Demin opens fire, but they're professionals. They'll do as they're told."

"It's not Marina I'm worried about. It's the other woman, Raya Nechiporenko." Sweeney had been thinking about her as Drury had suggested, all the way up from the Farm.

"That situation may have changed as well," Adkins said. "We just got word that she's off the boat."

"Have we got someone down there?"

Drury nodded. "He's posing as a newspaper reporter. We

figured we had to do something in a hurry before the situation got completely out of hand."

"I can't believe that I'm hearing what I'm hearing," Sweeney said.

"What do you recommend?" Adkins asked.

"Call Wilder right now and tell him what's going on, goddammit. We've got two people out on a limb. What the hell are we going to do if someone gets hurt?"

"That's not your responsibility, Richard."

"We're going to leave them . . ."

"For the Bureau's Hostage Rescue Team to pull them out," Adkins said. "Once that happens we'll step in."

Sweeney started to protest, but Adkins held him off.

"Let me finish, Richard," he said. "Once the situation has been stabilized, once we're certain that no one is going to start a shooting war, we'll step in and explain what we have."

"In the meantime the Russians will almost certainly make their move to discredit Tyson," Drury put in.

Sweeney looked at him as if he were seeing the assistant deputy director for the first time. The man was a weasel. The thought came unbidden into Sweeney's head. "Then let's get Tyson involved ourselves."

"Don't be a fool," Drury said.

"Hold on," Adkins broke in. "Richard may have something."

"Instead of waiting for the Russians to make their move, which I think they'd be foolish to do now, let's force the issue. Let's lean on Tyson and see which way he jumps. At the very least it may make the Russians nervous enough to make a mistake."

Adkins looked at Sweeney for a very long time. "You don't like them very much, do you?" he said finally.

"It's not a matter of like or dislike, Dick. It's always been a matter of trust. Still is."

Toni Wagner was definitely frightened. She did not have to pretend for the FBI's benefit. Her tenure in the United States was ending. Probably she would spend a few months in prison, but then, as Igor had suggested, he and she would meet again in Moscow in the spring. It was a nice thought, unless someone got hurt.

Win or lose, she told herself, coming out of the ladies' room, her work here would soon be over. Very soon.

Young was still on the telephone. She caught his eye and motioned for him. He put a hand over the mouthpiece.

"What?"

"I'm afraid somebody's going to get hurt in there," Toni said. "I don't want to see that happen. Nobody does."

The other agents in the room had stopped what they were doing, and they were looking at Toni. Young said something into the phone and hung up.

"My real name is Raya Nechiporenko, and I work for the KGB," Toni said.

Young's eyes widened. "Somebody fetch Sandy Senarighi, tell him to get up here on the double. I want everyone else out of here."

"Mr. Young, the team will be here any minute," an agent called from across the room.

"I want to see the team leader as soon as they touch down. Now, get the hell out of here. Everybody."

Toni sat down, and when everyone was gone, Young came over and perched on the edge of a desk. "Did I hear you correctly, Miss . . . Nechiporenko?"

"Yes," Toni said. "I have been a spy in this country for two years."

"What was your mission?"

"To spy on Alfred Tyson, and turn him if possible."

"Have you been successful?"

Toni looked away for a moment. She could feel her heart hammering in her chest, and her stomach felt very hollow. "Not very," she whispered.

"I don't understand," Young said. "Can you be a little more specific?"

Toni looked up at him, her eyes filling. "I seduced him, but I never got anything from him of any consequence."

"What do you mean by that?"

"I mean nothing more than I said."

"And you expect me to believe you?" Young asked. "Why the sudden change of heart? What do you hope to gain?"

"That girl down there on my houseboat, I think she is working for the KGB too, here to take over with Tyson where I failed. She's young, she may be desperate."

"Is she armed?"

"Yes, she says she has a bomb."

"Who are the two women?"

"I don't know. Maybe KGB, I don't know, it's all so confusing. There may be a faction fight going on between certain people here and others in Moscow. Nobody is saying much."

"Why tell me this now?" Young demanded.

"Because I was ordered to do so, you fool," Toni spat.

"What are you talking about . . . ?"

"In the ladies' room, there is a telephone."

Young looked toward the corridor. "Jesus Christ."

"The KGB does not do violence in the United States. Just as the CIA does not do violence in our country. It is the way it is. No one wants to start a war, tiny or large. All we want is information." She threw her head back defiantly. "It is no different with the United States. You spy, we spy. All of us, we just want to make sure of our own safety."

"Tell that to my two dead agents," Young said, shaking his head in amazement at what she was saying, when Senarighi came in.

"What's up?"

"Everything has changed," Young said. "And I do mean everything."

Judy Tietz and Sarah Yesler lay so that they were facing each other on the floor, their noses about ten inches apart. Sarah's back was toward the middle of the saloon, but Judy could see Marina Demin. Judy, who was the younger and less experienced of the two, was frightened, but Sarah had whispered a few words of encouragement to her that Marina

Demin had apparently not heard. But Judy had, and she'd seemed to draw some comfort. They were in a difficult situation, Sarah understood. Raya Nechiporenko had seemed and acted like a pro, but this one was obviously an amateur. She had both pistols, and she had the remote-control triggering device for the plastique that was supposedly aboard somewhere. If fifty kilos of Semtex were to blow, there wouldn't be enough pieces to bury in a coffin. It was not a pleasant thought. Nor was the thought that at this moment there were probably dozens of Bureau agents and uniformed cops outside watching this place. She hoped no one out there had an itchy trigger finger. But what worried her the most was what Raya Nechiporenko might be doing, or saying.

For several seconds Marina Demin had no idea what it was she was hearing. But something was happening outside. Some machinery, getting louder and louder, presumably approaching the boat basin. Then she had it. A helicopter, perhaps more than one helicopter.

Raya had warned her about this, but now that it was starting to happen, she didn't know if she could do as she'd been told. She was very frightened of being shot to death.

Marina got up from where she'd been waiting on the couch, a pistol in her one hand and the detonator in the other. The younger, more slightly built of the two women on the floor was looking up at her. Marina motioned for the woman to turn her head the other way, then went to the window and cautiously looked outside.

Her heart skipped a beat. She didn't want to believe what she was seeing. The boat basin was filled with cars and trucks and vans, behind each of which were men, a lot of them. Perhaps a hundred.

Over by the office she could just make out the rear of an ambulance, and up the road she could see the rotating lights of several police vehicles.

In a clearing to the east, three helicopters were touching down, the wildly blowing snow kicked up by their rotors obliterating them from view finally, but she could still hear them.

Marina turned back. The huskier woman had turned around and was looking up. Their eyes met and locked for a second or two until Marina raised the pistol with a shaking hand and pointed it at the woman, who, after a long moment, turned away.

Yeb vas, Marina thought in Russian. Fuck you. But she couldn't see how this was going to work out.

Donald Wood, special agent in charge of the Hostage Rescue Team's Baker Unit, looked like an accountant, and spoke softly, almost diffidently. He and his executive officer, Special Agent Jack Shirley, a very large, very black man, came up to the marina office on the run, the twenty-two men they'd brought with them staying with the choppers for the moment.

"What is the exact situation here, sir?" Wood asked.

Young and Senarighi quickly told the team leader everything they knew, leaving out nothing except the fact that Toni Wagner had been under arrest until early this morning.

Wood turned his gray eyes to her. "Who is holding whom hostage aboard the boat, ma'am?"

"I don't know," Toni answered.

"I see. Well, ma'am, tell me what you do know about the situation as you left it."

"Two women came aboard with weapons. They wanted to take away the other woman."

"Who identified herself as Janice Copeland, but whom you believe to be working for the KGB."

"Yes."

"What next?"

"There are explosives aboard."

"Who told you that?"

"Janice Copeland."

"She has the detonator?"

"Yes."

"All right, ma'am. What happened next?"

"The two women who came aboard were looking at Janice Copeland, and I just ran to the door, yanked it open, and got out."

"Then one of the two newcomers fired the single shot?" Wood asked.

"I don't know."

"But so far as you know, Janice Copeland was armed with nothing other than the detonator?"

"That's correct."

Wood nodded. "I see," he said. "Can you draw me a picture of the layout of your houseboat?"

"Yes . . ." Toni said, but Senarighi stepped forward. "I'll do it."

Wood turned his almost sleepy gaze to him. "You have been aboard?"

"Yes. This woman's actual name is Nechiporenko. She is a KGB agent."

"I see," Wood said, apparently unimpressed. "I will also need a complete map of the marina and the surrounding water."

Anatoli Kaplin was released from Lefortovo Prison around 5:30 P.M. There was no one to offer him any explanations, no one to drive him home. Instead of bringing dinner, his street clothes had been returned to him in his cell, and he had quickly gotten dressed. Twenty minutes later a young guard had unlocked his cell and had escorted him to the front door of the fortress.

The early evening was dark, and very cold, and the slam of the door behind him promised a return visit soon.

"Either that or my nine ounces," Kaplin mumbled to himself as he pulled down the wool cap they'd given him (his long hair and beard had been completely shaved off) and shuffled painfully down the street to the Metro station on the corner.

When he'd been arrested, he had had nearly three hundred rubles in his pocket. But the *pizdas* had robbed most of it, leaving him with less than fifty rubles. Enough for the subway, and perhaps some soup, bread, and a beer or two. Not much more.

He breathed deeply of Moscow's midwinter air: a combination of nose-numbing cold and the acrid odors produced by the burning of low-grade coal. Kaplin had read somewhere recently that the latter was the smell of the old East Bloc.

At the entrance to the Metro station, and still within sight of Lefortovo, he fished a two-kopek coin out of his pocket, dropped it into the slot of the pay phone, and dialed a number. As he waited for the connection to be made, he turned around so that he could look back the way he had come.

"Good evening," a woman said. "You have reached the embassy of the United States of America. How may I help you?"

"I wish to speak with Richard Sweeney. My name is Kaplin."

Tyson wasn't at his office. Sweeney reached him by phone at his Georgetown home.

"I don't believe I know you, Mr. Sweeney."

"I work for the Central Intelligence Agency, Mr. Tyson. I just recently returned from Moscow with a young woman by the name of Marina Demin. I was wondering if I could drop by your house this morning to have a word with you."

Tyson was silent for a long time. When he finally spoke, his voice was rough, and it came from the back of his throat, as if he were having a hard time swallowing. "Ah, that would be fine with me. This morning, that is. Do you have the address?"

"Yes, sir," Sweeney said.

Sweeney had been told to expect FBI surveillance units on Tyson, but if they were around, they were good, because he saw no one.

Tyson, dressed in a business suit and tie, answered the door. He looked as if he hadn't slept in days. "You're Sweeney?"

"Yes, sir," Sweeney said, showing his identification. "I think it would be better if we talked in my car."

The suggestion startled the man, but he nodded after a moment. "Just let me get my coat."

Sweeney went back to his car, an Agency-issue Chevrolet Cavalier, and Tyson joined him a minute later. He pulled away from the curb and headed west on R Street toward Wisconsin Avenue, which was finally being plowed.

"Where are we going?"

"Just around the block. We believe that your home is under electronic surveillance."

Tyson nodded heavily. "I expected as much. Was it your people who dropped off that crazy message about the Bureau?"

"Yes, sir," Sweeney said. "And it's true. But what we don't understand is the role Marina Demin is playing in this apparent plot to destroy your career."

Tyson just shook his head.

"She claims that her father is a teacher at the University of Wisconsin, and that he is being used by the KGB somehow. Do you know anything about this, sir? Has this man contacted you?"

Sweeney wasn't certain, but he thought he saw a look of relief momentarily cross Tyson's eyes.

"No, I don't know anything about it. Is this Russian woman still here in Washington, or has the Agency taken her to Wisconsin?"

"She's here, but it's one of the reasons I came to see you. She's involved at this very moment in a hostage situation aboard Toni Wagner's houseboat in the Columbia Island Marina. Miss Demin never mentioned your name specifically, but when she showed up there . . . well, we naturally had to ask you about it."

Now Tyson was deeply shaken. It seemed as if he were shrinking into his clothes. "Everyone in Washington knows about my private life," he said bleakly.

"I'm sorry, sir, but we must know if you can help us."

"Take me home," Tyson said, looking up. "I have nothing further to say to you. Take me home immediately."

"We'll go in by water," Wood told them. They were gathered around the map of the marina and surrounding area, and the floor plan of the houseboat that Senarighi had sketched for them. Raya Nechiporenko had also made a sketch. It matched Senarighi's.

"The moment your people try to board the boat, the three people in there will feel the motion," Senarighi pointed out.

"That's right. Unless their attention is diverted."

"They'd still feel it," Senarighi insisted.

"No," Wood said. "Our distraction will be Miss Nechiporenko, if she is willing to do it."

Everyone looked over at her.

"I don't think that's such a good idea," Young protested.

"Pardon me, but with weapons and explosives aboard, we're going to need all the help we can get."

"What have you got in mind?" Young asked.

"I want to send her back down there, just to talk. The moment she steps aboard the boat, she'll stumble so that she'll move around a lot. At that instant the signal will be given for my people to climb aboard. The people inside will be distracted in two ways: by Miss Nechiporenko's presence and by the motion of the boat that she will cause."

"I'll do it," Raya said from across the room.

"You haven't been asked," Young said over his shoulder.

"What, do you think I want to see someone get hurt down there? I want to be kicked out of this country and sent home, I don't want to spend time in your prisons for being a part of murder."

Wood turned his apparently dispassionate gaze to her. "If you tried to warn them, you would be taken out."

"I value my own life too," Raya said. "I'm a spy, not a kamikaze."

Wood thought about it a moment, then nodded. "Are you telling me that you are willing to help?"

"Yes."

Wood turned to his exec. "Get them ready."

"Yes, sir," Shirley snapped, and he left.

Sarah Yesler was taking the chance that Marina Demin would push the detonator button if she was backed into a corner. But Sarah reasoned that by now the Bureau would have reestablished its bugs on the houseboat, and would be listening to everything that was going on here. She also figured that there was a very good possibility the CIA would wait for the Bureau's Hostage Rescue Team (who had undoubtedly shown up aboard those helicopters) to effect a rescue before stepping in.

Sarah did not want to get shot and killed in the heat of the attempt. She had to take the risk now of letting them know she and Judy were Americans.

She raised her head and looked over at Marina, who nearly jumped off the couch. The woman motioned with the pistol for Sarah to lie back down.

"I have to take a piss, goddammit," Sarah said. "Cut us a little slack, would you?"

"What the hell was that?" Special Agent DuPris asked, holding the earphones tighter against his head.

"Wasn't a Russian said that," his partner, Special Agent Lowrey, replied. He got on the radio to the command post in the marina office across the channel. If the one woman was Russian, then it was a safe bet the other two were Americans. And by the sounds of it they were the ones being held hostage.

The Hostage Rescue Team helicopter touched down behind a line of trees screening it from the road and curious passersby, although because of the snow, there still wasn't much traffic. Washington was apparently staying home.

Jack Shirley and his five team members jumped down from the chopper and hurried through the snow to the channel, where they would enter the water at a point nearly four hundred yards northwest of the houseboat. They were dressed in black wet suits, and instead of the much bulkier scuba gear, they used self-contained oxygen rebreathing equipment which left no trail of bubbles. The only two disadvantages of the Navy equipment was that it could not be safely used below twenty-five feet, and on oxygen the divers would feel the cold much more intensely than they would on compressed air.

The rest of the team was standing by across the channel in the marina, some of them in or near the helicopters, several aboard boats on either side of the houseboat, and more behind a large panel van that had been pulled into position twenty-five yards directly above the houseboat in case their only option turned out to be a frontal attack. They were dressed in white winter camouflage clothing, and carried a variety of high-powered rifles and suppressed .22 automatics.

It was very cold. Snow was falling at an angle, blown by a sharp wind that brought the chill factor down to zero or below. There were even whitecaps within the narrow confines of the channel. Many more days like this and the water would freeze. Either the boats in the marina would have to be pulled or bubblers would have to be installed to prevent ice from damaging hulls.

Shirley was an ex–Navy UDT man. The worst thing ever said about him was that he was "one tough sonofabitch in a fight." Shirley even looked mean, with a fullback's physique, a gymnast's agility, and an apparently permanent scowl. His wife, who at five feet tipped the scales at barely one hundred pounds, sometimes called him "every WASP's worst nightmare." In actuality he was a professional cop with three daughters who adored him, and was in the choir at their church. There wasn't a mean bone in his body.

They formed two teams of three men, each man linked by rope. Shirley took the lead team, and making certain their equipment was in working order, silently entered the water, submerging to a depth of ten feet.

Taking a compass course of nearly 090 degrees, Shirley lead his team across the one hundred fifty yards to the opposite side of the channel and the first of the boats and docks just below the Lyndon B. Johnson Memorial, still more than three hundred yards from the houseboat. They were taking no chances that they would be spotted by someone aboard.

Reaching the first pilings in a little less than three minutes, Shirley and his people waited for the second team to arrive, which they did ten seconds later.

The channel was pitch-black, but not nearly as cold as on the surface. There was no wind-chill factor, of course, and since the water was not frozen it was above thirty-two degrees. There were some compensations after all, Shirley thought, though not many of them in this job, except the feeling that you were doing some good.

Following the line of docks to the southeast, they came eight minutes later to the relatively flat-bottomed hull of the houseboat, which they positively identified from beneath the surface of the water by the three wires leading from the bugs the Bureau had placed on the hull.

Shirley gave the sign to wait, and slowly surfaced next to the hull near the aft quarter of the boat. The freezing-cold wind and snow immediately numbed the exposed portions of his flesh around his face mask and mouth.

He spat out his mouthpiece and spoke very softly into his communications radio. "Baker one, in position."

"Copy, Baker one," a voice said into his ear. "Stand by, we've got an update for you."

"Roger."

"Jack, we're changing the timetable slightly." Wood's voice was in Shirley's ear. "I want you to surface at T plus forty minutes."

Shirley looked at his diver's watch. T plus forty was eight minutes from now, three behind schedule.

"Action to commence on my signal at T plus forty-two. Copy?"

"Roger, wilco," Shirley said. He put his mouthpiece back in and slowly sank back to where his people were waiting. He wrote the brief message in grease pencil on his plastic slate, handed it around, and settled back to wait the eight minutes, which was a very long time under water with little to do except think about killing someone—or getting killed.

Sarah, her ear pressed to the floor, heard a very slight noise from a direction she thought was beneath the houseboat. Divers, she asked herself, or was she merely so hyped she was hearing rats in the cellar? If the Bureau's Hostage Rescue Team was going to try for a rescue, it would make sense for them to come in from the channel side. Under the water. Wait for a signal, then clamber aboard. But they'd need a diversion. She didn't think it would take much to frighten Marina Demin into pushing the detonator button.

"I still have to go to the bathroom," Sarah said, raising her head.

Marina Demin motioned wildly for her to keep quiet.

"I don't care if you shoot me, for chrissake, I gotta take a pee."

"Shut up, shut up, or I swear I will push this button," Marina shouted.

Special Agent Lowrey got on the radio again to the command post in the marina office. "You'd better listen to this."

"More from the houseboat?" the radio operator asked.

"Yeah, we've got it on tape this time."

"I'll get Sandy," the radioman said, and a half minute later Senarighi was on the channel.

"What have you got, Stu?"

"Listen to this," Lowrey said, and he patched a replay of the exchange between the two women aboard the houseboat.

Young was on the telephone with the Bureau director. "I tried to talk him out of it," Wilder said. "But the Man is standing firm."

"We can't operate this way," Young protested. "It's suicide. I can't ask my people to go in with that restriction. They might just as well leave their weapons behind."

"No one is saying that." Wilder backed him down. "The

President said only that 'excessive' force was not to be used."

Young held himself in check. "What you're telling me, sir, is that my people may use deadly force in order to protect their own lives and the lives of any hostages?"

There was a slight hesitation. "I'm saying that your team may not use excessive force. Do you understand that?"

It was unlike Wilder. It was as if the man were trying to protect his own skin.

"No, sir, I'm afraid I do not," Young said. "My people may go in there armed?"

"Yes."

"They may shoot . . . to kill . . . to save their own lives or the lives of any hostages?"

"Yes," Wilder said. "But only to save lives."

"I understand, Mr. Director," Young said. He hung up and motioned for Wood to come over.

The FBI was undoubtedly monitoring their conversations aboard the houseboat. Toni had instructed her what to do in case she couldn't keep the two women absolutely quiet. "It is a play we're producing here."

"A dangerous one," Marina had whispered back.

"You will have to improvise. But it won't be for very long, I promise you. There is no bomb connected to the detonator. And I have managed to unload both pistols without those two seeing me. So if you do exactly as I say, you will not get hurt."

Raya wanted her to become an actor, and Ivan had said that she would carry his banner. She didn't know if she was capable of either.

She looked out the window. The helicopter that had taken off still had not returned. It was snowing harder now. Their attack would happen soon, she felt.

Turning, she went back to the couch, where she laid down the detonator and picked up the other pistol. "You won't get hurt if you keep your mouth shut and do exactly as *we* say,"

Marina told the two women. "If you say another word, you will die."

"Now what the hell?" DuPris asked, looking over at his partner.

Lowrey was shaking his head. He rewound the tape and replayed the last two transmissions. When he was finished he was still shaking his head. "If the first one was American, who the hell was this one?"

"Maybe the first one is Russian."

"Then her idiomatic English is damned good," Lowrey said, and he called the command post again.

Wood looked at Young with little or no expression on his face, or even in his eyes, though his lips were compressed. "I'll pass along Director Wilder's message to my people," he said.

He took a notebook and pen out of his pocket and handed them to Young.

"I'd like you to put that in writing, sir," he said.

"What are you talking about?" Young asked. "This is nothing more than standard operating procedure for your people. To kill only in the event the agent's or the hostage's life is in danger."

"We're not talking about that exactly now, sir," Wood said unflinchingly.

Young held his eye for a second or two, but then he nodded. "You're right," he said, and he sat down and began writing out the instructions he'd received from Wilder.

Senarighi called Wood over to the communications post set up in the corner. "You'd better listen to this. Might change a few things, though I don't know what the hell to make of it for sure."

Shirley and his five people surfaced, taking great care not to touch the hull of the houseboat. They were somewhat protected from the wind in the lee of the boat, but the air was extremely cold. Spitting out his mouthpiece, Shirley spoke softly. "Baker one ready."

"Stand by, Baker one," the communications operator said, and a second later Wood was on.

"There's a big problem coming your way, Jack."

Shirley was inured to such messages, they all were. Very few operations of this nature ever went without a hitch. "Go ahead."

"No excessive force unless your people or the hostage are in immediate danger," Wood said.

Shirley's eyes narrowed slightly. "Roger."

"Now the tough part. We're not sure at this point who is holding whom hostage. But it splits out two against one, all women."

Shirley digested that information. Three women, at least two pistols and one detonator. He and his people had spent the last eight minutes going over the hull of the houseboat for any sign of the explosives. They'd found nothing other than the Bureau bugs.

"What about our diversion?" he asked.

"In place and ready to roll."

"Roger, we're ready."

"Good luck, Jack," Wood said.

Shirley didn't bother responding, and he and his people pulled off their rebreathing equipment and swim fins so that they would have more freedom of movement. Fortunately the Kevlar vests they wore beneath their wet suits were light enough not to seriously hinder them either in the water or out.

"Get me Bob Vaughan," Wilder told his secretary, and he sat back in his chair and looked out his office window. It was snowing again, and the wind had kicked up. This situation was getting out of hand. Young had just called and told him about what they were hearing from the houseboat. It didn't make sense.

"Sir, Mr. Vaughan is not at his office, shall I try him at home?"

"Yes, Maggie, please. Do whatever it takes, but I must speak with him immediately."

"Go," Wood told Raya Nechiporenko, and without looking back she stepped around the end of the van and hurried quickly through the snow down to the dock. She hesitated for just a moment, feeling the eyes and the guns on her back, before walking out onto the dock, and then she stepped aboard the houseboat, stumbling and falling to her knees.

Marina Demin was away from the window when the houseboat suddenly rocked, so she did not see what was happening outside. But she definitely understood that someone had come aboard and that the rescue attempt Raya had talked about was happening now.

"You will save your life, and the life of this mission, if you do exactly as I say," Raya had told her. But it was so difficult to keep it all straight in her head. She was frightened, and her heart pounded so hard her chest hurt.

Sarah and Judy had felt the movement too. It was their intention to get past the armed woman to the detonator, which they considered to be a much greater threat than the two pistols.

They jumped up, but instead of shooting, as they had expected the woman to do, she tossed both pistols to them and collapsed in a heap on the floor.

"Go." Wood's radio message came at the same moment Raya Nechiporenko had stumbled onto the houseboat.

"Roger," Shirley radioed back, and he and his five people scrambled up onto the low deck, careful to make no noise and to keep the boat's movement to an absolute minimum.

Shirley and two men hurried forward while the other three went aft. They would come in through a bedroom window and act as backup if needed. If the houseboat were to blow they might have a chance of survival in the water.

All the windows on the northwest side of the boat wer

tightly curtained, allowing no sight line into the boat's main saloon. But they'd spotted that fact from the air.

"In position. Window is unlocked. Repeat, unlocked." Shirley's co–team leader aft radioed.

"Proceed," Shirley called back. He came to the front of the houseboat and peeked around the corner just as Raya Nechiporenko was picking herself up. She glanced over at him, her eyes widening slightly. But then she stepped back.

Sarah Yesler heard something from the back of the houseboat and suddenly felt a very cold draft. Someone had opened a back window.

She and Judy had both grabbed the pistols from the floor, and now she had a split second of intuition that something terribly wrong was about to happen, when the front door of the houseboat crashed open, and the largest black man she'd ever come face-to-face with barged through, at least two other figures directly behind him.

Shirley absorbed the scene in one practiced instant, rolling right, allowing his team members to enter the houseboat behind him. One woman was facedown on the floor, her hands empty in plain sight. The other two women were on their feet, both of them armed.

The slighter of the two was looking directly at Shirley. She started to say something in surprise as her gun hand came up. Shirley shot her twice, both bullets hitting her torso and driving her backward off her feet.

Sarah Yesler, the second woman, tried to raise her hands as she shouted "CIA!" but both men who'd come behind the black man fired simultaneously, hitting her in the torso at least five times, killing her before she fell to the floor.

Shirley scrambled to the third woman, lying facedown on the floor, and pulled her over to see if she was all right. Her eyes were nearly popping out of their sockets, her complexion deathly pale. But she was alive and conscious.

One of the team who'd come from the back bedroom swung around the corner, and spotting the detonating device lying on the couch, scooped it up.

"Detonator is secure," he radioed.

"Two bad guys down, hostage is secure." Shirley picked Marina Demin up as if she were a toy and headed for the door. "Houseboat is secure, I'm coming out, I'm coming out!"

"Mother of God," one of Senarighi's people said softly twenty minutes later. He was holding the pistols they'd taken from the two dead women.

Senarighi came over. There were agents everywhere. They were just starting to sort through the mess. The bodies had been taken away, and the lone survivor had been hustled by helicopter back into the city.

"What have you got, Hal?"

"These guns. They're not loaded, Sandy."

"Shit," Senarighi said, and he turned and left the houseboat in a dead run.

24

ALLEN YOUNG HAD NEVER BEEN SO DEEPLY SHAKEN IN HIS entire life. He, Wood, Shirley, Senarighi, and two other FBI special agents stood facing each other aboard the houseboat. The bodies of the two women had been removed by ambulance, and so far the media had been stalled.

"Her name was Sarah Yesler," Gordon Overstreet, one of the special agents, was saying. "I went to school with her."

"She's definitely with the Agency?" Senarighi asked. "No chance for error here, Gordy?"

Overstreet was a tall, rawboned man of about forty. He was a late bloomer. Most men his age had been promoted to a desk somewhere or as a field office chief. He still worked the field out of the Washington office.

"It's been five years, but I'd know her anywhere," he said. "We sort of had a thing for a while. She wanted the Agency, and she got it."

"That's for sure," Senarighi replied, not meaning it to sound as cynical as it did.

Young gave him a sharp look.

"Sorry, Mr. Young, but this should never have happened. Not in a million years. What the hell were they trying to accomplish here? It was the Agency that took out Natalie and Bill on this side and our people in the sound van, making it look as if the Russians were responsible. But why?"

"They were trying to protect Tyson for some reason." Young let it slip, and he immediately realized his error. Not everyone here was cleared for the operation. He looked at them all. "If I hear that repeated by anyone at any time, I will personally have his balls. Clear, gentlemen?"

Everyone nodded except for Wood and Shirley, who kept clenching and unclenching his big fists. He looked like a dark volcano on the verge of exploding. All during their discussion no one except his boss had dared stand near him.

"No, Mr. Young, it is not clear," Wood said softly.

"All right, people, let's go," Senarighi said, hustling his men off the houseboat.

"I'm going to the director on this, with or without you," Wood said when the others were gone.

"It's none of your concern from this point," Young said.

"If need be, we will hold a news conference right here at the marina, now," Wood said evenly. "Your choice, sir. But this will not be swept under the carpet. Two of our own people were recently gunned down in front of Mr. Tyson's home, and now this. I want to know what my people are involved with."

"Very well," Young said after a long hesitation. "Very well."

Sweeney watched Tyson hurry up the snow-covered walk and enter his house. There was no telling which way the man was going to jump, but jump he would, and very soon.

It was essential that they get Marina Demin to ID her father in Wisconsin, who would in turn presumably clear up at least a part of this mystery. So far Tyson had done nothing wrong, nothing that could be construed as suspicious, except take as a mistress a woman who worked for the KGB. That was th stuff of scandal, not necessarily the stuff of an espionage trial.

Still there was something just outside the range of Sweeney's understanding, something that he could feel but not quite grasp, that was bothersome. Something didn't add up. Raya Nechiporenko evidently worked for Ivan Kiselev. And Marina Demin, who said she'd overheard the major talking, had run to the Nechiporenko woman's houseboat. Wasn't the message clear?

No, Sweeney decided, pulling away from the curb. The message was anything but clear. There was something else.

His pager beeped and he pulled over to a phone booth five blocks away on M Street. The snow was coming down very heavily now, making driving increasingly difficult.

He got Drury on the phone. "Where are you?" the assistant DDO asked.

"Georgetown. I just left Tyson. I'm on my way over to the marina . . ."

"Negative," Drury snapped. "Adkins wants you back here ASAP."

"What's happened, Bob?"

"Plenty. Where are you calling from?"

"A phone booth. It's secure."

"Your madman, Kaplin, was sprung from Lefortovo. He tried to call you at the embassy. Rodgers told him you were gone, but he insists he talk with you. It's a message you must have, he said. Life or death."

"All right," Sweeney said, thinking ahead. "Did he·leave a contact number?"

"No, but he said he'd call back at twenty-two hundred hours Moscow time. Gives you about two hours to get back out here."

"I'll stop at the marina first . . ."

"No," Drury said flatly.

"What?"

Drury hesitated. "It's over," he said guardedly.

"What happened out there?" Sweeney demanded. He had the feeling that he was going to hear something terrible.

"There were some shootings. Some fatalities."

"Sarah and Judy?"

"We don't know for sure . . ."

"Talk to me, Bob," Sweeney demanded menacingly.

"We don't know for sure . . . but we think so."

"Christ. What about Marina Demin and Raya Nechiporenko?"

"The Bureau has them."

"I'm on my way in," Sweeney said, and he crashed the telephone back on its hook.

"Where are these two Russian women now . . . the second one is Russian as well, isn't she?" Wilder asked

Young, Wood, and Shirley sat across the desk from him in his office.

"She's identified herself as Marina Demin. She and Miss Nechiporenko are downstairs at the moment with Senarighi and the others."

"What have we gotten from her?"

"Nothing so far," Young said. "But five minutes ago we got what surveillance thinks is a pretty good confirmation from a wiretap source."

Wilder held up a hand to stop him. "What about a positive identification on the two fatalities?"

"Sarah Yesler and Judy Tietz, CIA Technical Services Division. Their prints are on file. It came up from the computer just before we arrived."

They could see Wilder working out the ramifications of what he was being told. It was monstrous. None of them felt good about it.

"Their weapons were unloaded," Young said. "We found the bullets under the cushions of the couch in the main saloon. And the bomb was nonexistent. The detonator was an ordinary television remote-control device."

"Then the two downstairs are responsible," Wilder said, holding his anger in check.

"No, sir," Wood broke in. "I am responsible. My people shot and killed them, and we will have to live with it. But we were not given the proper information. Pardon me, sir, but somebody fucked up on this project. A lot of somebodies. But I'm sure there'll be blame enough to go around."

Wilder picked up his telephone and dialed his secretary. "Get me General Vaughan at Langley," he said. "And, Maggie . . . if they say he's not there, and cannot be reached, tell them I'll phone the President."

Wilder put his phone down.

"Sir, my people would like some answers here," Wood said.

"You'll get them in time. At the moment we're involved with an extremely sensitive investigation."

"Concerning Albert Tyson."

Wilder and Young exchanged a glance. "Where did you hear that?" Wilder demanded.

"I let it slip," Young admitted. "The heat of the moment."

"I see," Wilder said carefully. "What is it you think you have the right to know?"

"Miss Nechiporenko has admitted that she works for the KGB, and now we are being told that the woman we rescued is also a Russian, and that the two of them have some involvement with Mr. Tyson. What involvement?"

"This is a counterespionage operation," Wilder said.

Wood waited.

"We believe that Mr. Tyson may be supplying national security information to the Russian government. One of the women has been his mistress for some months now."

"Who?"

"Miss Nechiporenko."

"And the other?"

Wilder shook his head and looked at Young. "What did we get from the wiretap?"

"I think it's best if we wait to discuss it."

"No," Wilder said. "We have a wiretap on Tyson's home," he explained to Wood.

Young looked definitely uncomfortable. "The CIA brought Marina Demin over from Moscow."

The news was stunning to Wilder, and it was suddenly very

obvious that he regretted including Wood in this conversation.

"I took the same oath as you did, Mr. Director," Wood said impassively.

"Anything else?" Wilder asked.

Young shook his head. "Except that Richard Sweeney, who my people tell me is chief of CIA operations in Moscow, was the one who brought the woman over. He was the one who called Tyson. Apparently they were going to meet this morning. We've got nothing further than that as yet."

Wilder picked up his telephone. "What about my call, Maggie?"

"General Vaughan is speaking with the President at this moment. His secretary said as soon as he gets off he will call."

"Call them back," Wilder said. "We'll hold."

"I didn't think you were going to make it in today," the President said as Tyson came in. "Some storm, huh?"

"The roads are pretty bad," Tyson said. "But I've got a pile of *nothing* work on my desk that grows faster than I can deal with it."

"Delegate it."

"Everyone seems to have disappeared on me. No one wants to make a decision. No one wants to stick his neck out. It's like election year."

The President, who'd been staring out the bowed windows at the increasing snow, chuckled bleakly and turned around. It was a couple of minutes after one in the afternoon but was dark outside. Two days ago Washington had surpassed its all-time-record snowfall. The snow had been falling even heavier since.

"Reminds me of Christmases in Maine."

"I had some like this as a kid," Tyson said. "I have that Syrian report you wanted to see."

"In a moment, Al," the President said. "Coffee?"

"No thanks, I just finished lunch."

"We've got a problem," the President said bluntly. "It's

your problem, but it's mine too, since you're my national security adviser at the moment."

Tyson said nothing, but he sat down when the President motioned for him to do so. The President perched on the edge of his desk.

"Bob Vaughan and Ed Wilder are coming over at two, and the four of us are going to sit down and hash this thing out."

"I don't know what you're talking about, Mr. President."

"Yes, you do. But believe me, you have friends. You're not alone."

Tyson had to look away. He was shaking. "I don't . . . know what's happening to me. All of a sudden everything is somehow . . . different. I can't . . ."

"I want you to pull yourself together, because you're going to have to face some very serious charges," the President said. "The FBI has gathered evidence that you've been sleeping with a woman named Toni Wagner."

Tyson started to say something, but held himself in.

The President nodded. "This woman has been identified as Raya Nechiporenko, an agent of the KGB. I'm relieving you, for the moment, as my national security adviser, but I'm not abandoning you. At this point these are only accusations. There have not been, nor will there be for the moment, any legal charges brought against you, because the Central Intelligence Agency believes that you may be the object of a Russian plot to discredit you. It has something to do with a young woman named Marina Demin."

Tyson held his silence.

"Do you understand what I'm telling you?"

"Yes, Mr. President," Tyson mumbled.

"Unfortunately there have been some deaths because of this. Two of them FBI agents, and two more this morning who worked for the CIA. I still can't believe it."

Tyson was shaking his head.

"I have to know what is happening, Al. You can understand this. Bob Harms gives you top marks; so do a lot of other people. But I can't ignore what seems to be valid evidence."

Tyson just looked at the President.

"Christ, Al, fight back. Tell the bastards they're barking up the wrong tree."

"The meeting is at two?"

"Yes," the President said after a moment.

"This has . . . sorta taken my breath away, Mr. President, if you know what I mean. I've spent a lot of years in government service to end up like . . . this."

"I understand, Al."

"I'd like to go back to my office. I need to gather my thoughts."

"Talk to me, Al."

"I need to go."

"Talk to me."

"It's a lie, Mr. President. I swear to God, I'm a loyal American."

Privet had taken a few of his things out of the safe house and checked into a hotel under a different name. In Moscow such a thing would not have been possible, but here no one even checked identification cards as long as cash was paid for the room.

He had seen enough at the Columbia Island Marina to be convinced that either this operation was dirty from top to bottom or something else, much deeper, much more subtle, perhaps even sinister, was happening. He really didn't care which it was because from this point on he would distance himself from his controllers.

Privet had not actually received word that he was to assassinate Tyson, but there could no longer be any doubt in his mind that it would have to be done, and very soon. The FBI was watching Tyson's every move, and now the CIA, from what he'd been able to gather, was involved. A somewhat befuddled Lydia Lubiako had let that slip when they'd talked.

Standing at the window, sipping a cup of tea with a lemon wedge, and watching the continuing snow, he waited for the afternoon to pass and the night to fall. Then he would go to work, finally.

Young entered the soaring nave of the National Cathedral a little before 2:00 P.M., fifteen minutes late because of the difficult driving conditions. He climbed the stairs to the balcony and hesitated for only a moment before going up the steeply slanting aisle to where Dick Adkins was waiting for him. The church was neutral ground.

They shook hands and Young sat down.

"If anyone is keeping score, it's tied at two all between us, with only one bad guy down," Adkins said gruffly.

"What the hell were your people doing there in the first place?" Young flared up, but he kept his voice down. "If there'd been any liaison, they wouldn't have been killed. Do you fucking people know what's going on?"

"Tyson is innocent," Adkins shot back. "It's a goddamned Russian plot to bring him down."

"He's screwing a KGB case officer, has been for months. We have the evidence, and we have the woman in custody. She's admitted it."

Adkins shook his head. "Look, Allen, we're both cops. You know the score as well as I do. Both of us are interested in the same thing, no matter how we go about it, and no matter whose turf we find ourselves on. Four of our people have lost their lives under tragic circumstances. Let's put an end to it now."

"From now on it becomes a joint operation," Young said, relieved. "The Agency takes care of Moscow, the Bureau runs Washington. But we communicate."

"It's a two-way street," Adkins said.

"Yes."

"What about Marina Demin? She says that her father is a teacher at the University of Wisconsin and that he's been forced by the KGB into involving himself with this Tyson operation."

"We're talking to her now," Young said. "Send one of

your people over and we'll go through the testimony we've already gotten from her, and from Raya Nechiporenko."

Adkins nodded. "I'll send over Major Kiselev's file, but I'm warning you, Allen, that it's slim pickings."

"What about Dick Sweeney?"

"What about him?" Adkins asked cautiously.

"He brought Marina Demin over, and he's approached Tyson about her. We'd like to talk to him."

Adkins thought about it for a moment, but then nodded. "Fair enough," he said. "He'll act as our liaison for the moment."

"Good."

Marina Demin had told them that she'd been ordered to defect to the CIA in Moscow with a story about a plot to bring down a senior U.S. government official. Once she was in this country, she was to escape and call a certain number (listed, they found, to a nonexistent address in Bethesda), which she did. She'd been given instructions to go immediately to the houseboat, where she would get further instructions.

Senarighi was with her in the interrogation room while a sketch artist was drawing her father's face under her direction.

"He has something to do with this KGB plot, but you don't know exactly what, is that correct?" Senarighi asked.

"Yes," Marina Demin said.

"Your mother is dead, but you know your father's face from her descriptions of him, and from a few photographs you saw years ago?"

She nodded. "They were college students here in the United States. My mother worked for the KGB."

"But not your father . . ." Senarighi said, but then he stopped in midsentence, his breath catching in his throat.

The sketch artist was holding up the completed drawing. "Is that your father?" he asked. "I've aged him to match what he might look like today."

"Oh, yes," Marina cried excitedly. "Yes, that's him. I would know him anywhere."

"Excuse me," Senarighi mumbled, and he left the room in a rush.

"What's the matter?" Mamedov, the Russian translator, asked in the corridor.

"That picture," Senarighi shouted over his shoulder as he raced for the elevator.

Sweeney's mind was filled with a dozen different possibilities as he took the elevator down to communications, where a secure link would be made with the U.S. Embassy in Moscow. It was coming up on 2:00 P.M. Washington time, or 10:00 P.M. in Moscow, when Kaplin had said he would call again. Vaughan would be meeting with Ed Wilder, Al Tyson, and the President in the Oval Office, and, as Adkins said, "It's possible everything will change afterward." In the meantime the DDO had hammered out a cooperative agreement between the Bureau and the Company.

"Since they're holding Marina Demin, along with this other Russian woman, and since Marina is your project, I want you to act as liaison to the Bureau for us," Adkins had ordered him.

"No rest for the wicked, huh, Ernie?" Kay had told him when he'd called to let her know he would not be able to make it in time for dinner at the hotel.

"Worse than that. How are you holding up?"

"Okay," Kay said. "Has that got anything to do with that . . . incident at the Columbia Island Marina this morning?"

"Is it on the news already?"

"Every channel."

"Yes," Sweeney told his wife, even though he knew he was breaking security regulations. But he'd never held back from her, unless it was something that might hurt her.

"Keep your head down," she'd said.

"Will do."

He used the red phone in one of the small conference rooms. The operator told him the encrypted link would be completed in a half minute. The call would be recorded, of course, but Sweeney had brought a pad of paper and pencils, along with the files on Kaplin and the others in the now defunct MOHAWK network.

Kaplin had been released from Lefortovo, according to the flash from Rodgers, which made the man suspect at the very least. The KGB did not release its prisoners without some gain in mind. Even these days.

But Kaplin had simply been too good a source to ignore even now.

Rodgers came on the line. "Dick, that you?"

"Hello, Roy. How's the weather?"

Rodgers laughed. "Apparently not as bad as Washington's . . . Wait." The line fell silent for a moment. "It's him. I'll switch over now. He sounds wired to the max, Dick, watch yourself."

Kaplin was on a second later. Encrypted phone links were regenerative, so the reception was perfectly clear. "Richard?"

"I'm here, Anatoli. What is it you want?" Sweeney asked directly. There was no use wondering if Kaplin was calling from a secure phone. It wouldn't make much difference.

"They just released us from Lefortovo," Kaplin said. He sounded weak, very strung-out. "Me and Larissa. I am going to see her now. Do you understand?"

Rodgers hadn't known about Larissa Dolya's release. She would have to be pulled out of Moscow immediately before it became impossible. She and Kaplin would undoubtedly be arrested again. The KGB was just fishing with them now. Using them as bait.

"Yes, Anatoli, I understand. Congratulations. But be careful."

"Listen, you *pizda*, you don't understand shit, see? Just listen to me for once."

"I'm listening."

"I'm going to see Larissa and the others. We are going to make a name for ourselves."

Sweeney's gut instantly tightened. What the hell were they

planning? "Anatoli, don't do anything stupid. Maybe we can help you."

"Bullshit, we will help ourselves. She is our country, the *Rodina*. You will see, and so will the world. But I have to warn you about two things, Richard. That little girl of yours, Marina, she is lying. She never was Mikhail's mistress. Do you understand? She works for the KGB!"

"Yes, I understand that."

"And the KGB has a spy either in the CIA or in your National Security Agency. Do you hear me? It is someone who has the capability of reading our computer transmissions over telephone lines. This one is very important, Richard . . ."

Kaplin was gone. A second later Rodgers was back. "We lost him."

"Did you get all that?" Sweeney asked.

"I sure did, but what was he talking about? Do you know anything about this from your end?"

"No, not unless Adkins is on to it."

"Could be a bluff to get more attention."

"I don't think so, Roy. But I'll check it out from here. In the meantime see what you can find out. I don't know what the hell he's up to, but if you can find out in time to stop him, I think you'd be saving some lives."

"Will do," Rodgers said. "Watch yourself."

"You too."

Wilder and Vaughan showed up at the White House within a minute of each other and they were ushered into the Oval Office by the President's appointments secretary. It was just 2:00 P.M., and the President's mood was dark.

"Before I call Al in here, you two are going to get your stories straight," the President said. He pointed to the door. "The media smells blood. First two Bureau agents are gunned down in Georgetown, and now they've found out that the latest two casualties worked for the CIA. They want to know, and rightfully so, what the hell is going on."

"Mr. President . . ." Wilder said.

"Just a minute, Ed." The President cut him off. "The CIA has no business conducting operations on American soil. That's one question we're going to have to answer right off the bat. The second question is why the Bureau killed those two women. If either of you two gentlemen have answers that are going to satisfy the American public, and especially the Democratic Congress, I'd like to hear them. In the meantime the Agency believes Al Tyson to be the object of a KGB plot to discredit him, while the Bureau believes Al Tyson may be a traitor."

"That may have changed, Mr. President," Wilder said. He took a police artist sketch from his attaché case and handed it across. "This is a drawing made from Marina Demin's description of her . . . father."

"Good Lord in heaven," the President said, studying the sketch for a long moment. He handed it to Vaughan, who looked at it.

The President picked up his telephone. "I'll get Al in here."

Valentin Grigoriev slammed the car phone back on its hook. "Central Telephone has no tap on this phone box."

"It's something Kaplin might know," Yevgeni Andreyev said, hunched over the wheel.

How was a man supposed to do his job if his hands were unnecessarily tied behind his back? Grigoriev asked himself. They'd been following Kaplin ever since his release from Lefortovo. The first thing the man had done was call someone from a phone box less than one block from the prison. Incredible as it seemed, the phone had not been tapped. So they'd been out in the cold.

In the past few hours, Kaplin had made three other telephone calls, plus this one, from four different phone boxes around Moscow. Not one of them had been on Central Telephone's register of ordinary surveillance locations. It was more than coincidence.

"That sonofabitch is up to something," Grigoriev said, grinding his teeth.

"He hasn't done anything illegal yet," Andreyev pointed out.

"He will. I'll make sure he does. And then I'll kill the bastard myself, if need be."

Privet had changed his mind again. Perhaps it was the weather, he told himself, or perhaps it was simply because he was operating in the United States for the first time in his career that he was spooked. But he could not stay put. He got the feeling that something was catching up with him.

The good operatives are known for their tradecraft. In some instances what an operative does, and how he handles himself on assignment in the field, become a signature. The tradecraft of the very best operative, however, leaves nothing but the objective behind.

Blend in and you will be saved. That particular Westernism had come directly from the American CIA in Italy. It fit, so a KGB officer who'd heard it in Rome, and had later retired to teach at School One, had added it to the lexicon for officer-trainees.

Privet's specialty had always been one of blending in. Leaving the safe house that had been set up for him in Georgetown, he had blended in as a tourist registered in a Washington hotel.

But, he reasoned, if he were to barge into Tyson's house this evening, the FBI surveillance units would hear everything and cut off any chance he might have of escaping.

And escape he meant to do. By shuttle to Montreal from the Baltimore-Washington Airport, which according to the television news was scheduled to reopen sometime late this afternoon or early this evening, and then to Europe, where he would lose himself for the time being.

But if he showed up in broad daylight, posing as someone perhaps unexpected, but unchallengeable, he could wait until Tyson showed up, kill him silently, and make his escape by merely walking out the door and leaving the neighborhood on foot.

So far as he'd been able to learn, the Tysons did not

employ any house staff, nor did Albert Tyson, in his role as assistant national security adviser, routinely use the services of a Secret Service bodyguard or chauffeur, though he did so on occasion.

It was a risk Privet was willing to take. He had no doubt that he could successfully handle one or two such men if the need arose.

Tyson himself would most likely be at his office all day. There was only a slight possibility that he would be home this afternoon. If he was, Privet would kill him immediately and make his escape earlier than planned.

If Tyson was gone, but his wife was at home, which Privet thought was more likely than not, he would gain entry to the house and, picking his time and method, would kill her in such a fashion that the FBI surveillance officers would not know what had happened. He would remain in the house, part of the background noise, until Tyson did return, kill him silently, and make his escape as planned.

He was already feeling the first faint stirrings of sexual pleasure just working out the possibilities. Within twenty-four hours he would be sitting on a veranda someplace warm, sipping a cool drink and thinking with satisfaction about what he'd done here this day.

Cabs were being delayed as long as two hours because of the storm, and Privet wanted to save his rental car for the drive up to the airport, impossible if the FBI surveillance units at Tyson's home got its description. So he was forced to walk the three or four kilometers over to Georgetown. He entered Montrose Park where it adjoined Oak Hill Cemetery a block and a half east of Tyson's house, and worked his way west. Because of the tree cover, many of the paved paths were not badly clogged with snow, nor was the weather particularly cold. In Moscow this sort of day, at this time of year, would mean temperatures well below zero . . . Fahrenheit as well as Celsius. Definitely not the sort of day for a long walk.

"You will not make the kill until I give the word," Lydia

Lubiako had told him. She was frightened. "This is absolutely essential."

"What is it you are not telling me?" he asked. She'd been holding something back from him. They all had.

"Nothing that you need know . . . yet. When the time comes."

But if he waited, he felt his chances of successfully making his escape would be sharply reduced, so he had decided to do it now. He didn't intend on becoming a martyr for a cause, and a government, that were all but dead and buried.

He spotted the television camera trained on Tyson's home across the street in the park, and a second on a light pole. He figured there would be others, hopefully none of them indoors. It was another risk.

Leaving the park, and knowing that everything he would do from this point on would be monitored either visually or aurally, Privet crossed the street, hurried up the walk to Tyson's home, mounted the front steps, and rang the doorbell.

A half minute later Kit Tyson, wearing a smart gray wool skirt and matching cashmere sweater, answered the door. "May I help you?"

"Yes, ma'am," Privet said in a broad Texas accent. He held up his CIA identification card. "Wonderin' if I could come in and have a word or two with you."

Kit's eyes widened slightly, and then a look of sadness crossed her features. She stepped back. "Won't you come in, please?"

The direct line from the President's office buzzed, and Tyson snatched up the telephone. "Yes, Mr. President."

"They're here, Al. Would you join us?"

Tyson had been taking Tums all day, but it still felt as if he'd swallowed a gallon of hydrochloric acid. "Be right in." He hung up the phone, got his jacket, and hurried out.

In the corridor he hesitated for a long second or two, his heart thumping wildly. Most of the nonessential staff had not shown up for work. The White House seemed almost deserted.

Instead of turning right, toward the Oval Office, Tyson turned left and hurried down the corridor to the stairs, emerging from the White House and rushing across to where he'd parked his car.

"He's disappeared," Lydia Lubiako shouted. She sounded on the verge of collapse.

Truskin held the phone so tightly his knuckles turned white. "Where are you calling from?"

"The safe house, you fool. He's not here. I think he means to kill Tyson sometime today, or tonight."

"It's too soon. The . . . package hasn't been passed to Tyson. The meeting hasn't been set up."

"Well, I don't think we're going to be able to do it now. Everything has changed. Of course you've heard what happened at the houseboat."

Truskin tried to think it out. Somehow they were going to have to salvage this operation. If not they'd all be arrested and shot for treason.

"Stop him," he said.

"What?" the woman shouted.

"It's the only way."

She started to protest, but he held her off.

"We might still be able to salvage the operation. But we're going to have to work together."

"You idiot, do you realize what will happen to us if that document falls into the wrong hands?"

"Yes," Truskin said. He was just as frightened as she sounded. "But do you realize what will happen if we don't succeed?"

25

KAPLIN GOT OFF THE METRO TRAIN AT THE OKTYABRSKAYA Station and took the escalator up to street level near the Warsaw Hotel. At this point he was less than two blocks from Gor'kiy Park. On the street he pulled up his coat collar and headed over to the safe-house apartment building that Sweeney had brought him to what seemed like years ago.

The KGB *pizdas* were following him, he was sure of it, even though he hadn't spotted them. Then again he hadn't looked for them. No reason for it. They were back there as certainly as the sun would rise in the morning, even over Moscow.

Which was good. He wanted them to follow him this far. He wanted them to see what he was doing so openly. He was hiding nothing for the moment, except for the phone calls.

But soon, he thought smiling, they would understand what sort of man Anatoli Stepanovich was. And they would be eternally sorry they'd ever fucked with him.

The pricks at Lefortovo had not taken his keys, so he let himself into the building and trudged up to the second floor

where a dull yellow light shone beneath the door to Larissa
Dolya's apartment. He stood for a long time listening to the
ordinary night sounds of the building. No one had moved into
the cold apartment above, so it was silent. But from below he
could hear a radio or television playing, and from within
Larissa's apartment he thought he might be hearing her sobs.

She was a crier. From the day he'd met her on the stairs
she'd cried. It made him want to wrap her in his big arms and
hold her so tightly that no one or nothing could ever harm her.

But he was too late for that now. The sonsabitches had hurt
her badly. She'd been wounded so horribly that she would
never recover. She would never be the young woman of
promise he'd met that day. That was all gone out of her. The
bastards had tortured it out of her, and what remnants there
were they had cut out with the surgeon's scalpel.

At length he knocked softly at her door, and the crying
stopped. After a moment he could hear her shuffling slowly
to the door and then it was opened and she stood there in a
floppy sweater, dirty jeans, and thick wool socks on her feet.
Nothing registered in her eyes when she realized who it was.

"Hello," Kaplin said, and she stepped aside so that he
could come in.

Without a word he got her boots, and sitting her down on
the shabby couch, put them on her feet and laced them. Next
he got her coat and hat and scarf and dressed her for the
outside.

"We'll go to my apartment in the city. It's very warm
there, you'll see," he said for the benefit of the microphones
that the KGB had surely installed.

He had tried to telephone his KGB directorate chief this
evening, but the man was gone and no one knew where to
reach him. Kaplin had merely wanted to confirm something
he already suspected: that he was a dead man, a nonperson.
He did not exist.

Well, that would change, he thought.

He put Larissa's mittens on and then looked deeply into her
eyes before he kissed her. But there was nothing: no

response, barely even life. They'd even succeeded in cutting most of that out of her body and mind.

Switching off the light, he guided her downstairs, and outside they walked the several blocks to Gor'kiy Park. It was a few minutes before eleven and the park would be closing soon, but there were still a few people around, and music still played at the skating pond.

The pavilions were closed, as were the Ferris wheel and nearly everything else in the park. Some of the lights had even been switched off, leaving much of the park in darkness.

Well away from the skating rink, Kaplin suddenly veered left, and he and Larissa plunged into the woods, lost to the darkness in five or ten meters.

It was extremely painful to move fast, yet Kaplin hurried as quickly as possible, dragging Larissa with him. Once from somewhere well behind them he thought he heard someone shouting, as if one pursuer to another, but then he lost the sound to his own labored breathing.

They came out of the park behind the City Clinical Hospital, and without the slightest resistance, Larissa let herself be led to a waiting ambulance.

The rear door swung open, and Kaplin helped her inside and climbed up after her. Two other men were aboard, the driver and a second person in the front seat.

"Were you followed?" one of them asked.

"Yes. Get the fuck out of here," Kaplin said.

KGB Director Yuri Novikov's long black Chaika limousine pulled up behind the Russian Federation Parliament Building a few minutes after ten. His two bodyguards immediately jumped out, surveyed their surroundings for a long moment or two—only a pair of Red Army guards were stationed at the entry—then opened the car door.

General Ryazanov got out first, his uniform crisp, and stepped respectfully aside as Novikov climbed out. Without a word the two men entered the building.

As early as a few months ago, the KGB director was the

number two most powerful man in Russia behind Mikhail Gorbachev. All that had changed, of course. Now Boris Yeltsin was at the apex of a new pyramid of power, and the KGB director had become, in many respects, nothing more than a lapdog . . . still very powerful, but not like the old days.

The Komitet's strength had been cut from an all-time high of a half million people just before the coup, to less than a third of that—almost the entire internal security force either being eliminated altogether or being transferred to the Interior Ministry.

Even its overseas divisions had been sharply pared because of increasing shortages of hard Western currencies, which, since the ruble was worthless outside of Russia, were needed to finance extraterritorial operations.

"Lean and mean." Novikov had preached a bit of Westernism to his staff.

Upstairs, he and Ryazanov left their coats, hats, and gloves in an anteroom and entered a small dining room. Boris Yeltsin and a half dozen of his closest aides were gathered around a sideboard on which was laid out champagne, iced vodkas, and platters heaped with pickles, fish, caviar, eggs, sour onions, blinis, and a dozen other delicacies. Meeting like this over a late-night supper and drinks to discuss policy had been common since the days of the czars.

What was uncommon this evening was the summons of the KGB director by the Russian president. But, then, power had shifted, and continued to shift, dramatically since the Kremlin coup.

"Yuri Vasilevich, just on time as usual," Yeltsin said, turning.

"A half minute early," Novikov said dryly, and some of the others laughed.

No one said a word to Ryazanov, nor did they even acknowledge his presence.

"If you will excuse me, I promise not to delay your supper too long," Yeltsin told the others, and he led Novikov and Ryazanov across the long, narrow room and out a door at the rear, into a much smaller office that served on occasion as a private conference chamber.

"We have a problem, the three of us," Yeltsin began directly. "One that will have to be addressed immediately."

"I am sure that General Ryazanov will cooperate with us," Novikov said.

Ryazanov had been called out from a dinner party at his apartment by the KGB director without a word of explanation. But none had been needed. He nodded.

"It is the matter of the budget. And Russia's good name abroad."

"We cannot afford further budget cuts, Mr. President," Ryazanov said. At least he would defend himself and the Komitet, even if that fool Novikov would not. "The West has not stopped spying on us. On the contrary. If anything, the United States has stepped up its efforts against us because of the closely held belief that we have become dangerously unstable."

Yeltsin showed no expression. "Your work is important. But we have become a nation of laws that no one is above. Isn't that what August nineteenth proved?"

Ryazanov said nothing.

"I am speaking here of accountability."

"To whom, Mr. President?"

"To the government."

"And, respectfully, Mr. President, who is the government?"

Yeltsin stepped menacingly closer. "Do not toy with me, Comrade General. Suffice it to say, the Komitet is not in charge. Those days are finished. You may aid, you may advise, but you may not decide policy."

"That is completely beyond the scope of my office," Ryazanov said, understanding that he might be in even deeper trouble than he'd imagined.

"Until now," Yeltsin contradicted bluntly, and he continued before Ryazanov could respond. "No need to deny this, I have gathered the proof. Nor need you worry that I will have you removed . . . yet. You serve the *Rodina* well."

"Proof of what, Mr. President?"

"The diversion of funds. Of Western currencies, from Intourist and other Russian government agencies to the KGB. Specifically to finance unauthorized operations abroad."

"I don't know what you're talking about," Ryazanov said, but it was as if someone had kicked him in the gut. How was it possible for Yeltsin, or anyone else outside of a very select few men Ryazanov had handpicked, to know the entire story?

"You do, and I will have your acknowledgment along with your promise to stop, this evening, or I will see to your dismissal, and your trial for high treason."

"Then you must be more specific with your charges, Mr. President."

"Very well. For the past three months a special investigative unit working under the direction of Konstantin Malakhov, at Director Novikov's bidding, has been busy sifting through the financial records of a number of government agencies, including the Komitet."

"I heard nothing of this," Ryazanov said to Novikov.

"No," the KGB chief replied, smiling faintly. "The work was done by computer from an office here in Moscow, but away from any other government agencies."

Ryazanov could hardly believe what he was hearing. Kiselev had promised him that Tinker had been eliminated.

"Discrepancies were found in the budgets of Intourist, the Ministry of Agriculture, and at least seven heavy-equipment factories."

"Such inefficiencies are common . . ."

"All such monies involved foreign trade, therefore foreign currencies. The same amounts in each case were traced to the KGB's Finance Directorate, and from there to your First Directorate operations abroad."

"Impossible."

"For us to break into your computer system? The sign of the rose, I believe, was their first big hurdle. After that, however, the investigation is said to have proceeded smoothly."

Ryazanov felt a deep sense of frustration and even shame that everything he had worked for—and it had all been for a *Rodina* that was disintegrating from within—was gone. He'd been outwitted by men he considered beneath him. Where was the justice?

"Homeward Bound, whatever it really is, will stop immediately," Yeltsin said coldly.

"We mustn't stop spying . . ."

"No, we mustn't. You have Source KHAIRULLA. Develop other such sources. But the age of blackmail and assassination is over. In this instance, Comrade General, your life depends on it. Treason is punishable by death, as you well know."

"It may not be possible to withdraw . . ."

"Then you will simply have to do the impossible," Yeltsin said, smiling as he took Novikov's arm, and they joined the others in the dining room.

A short, dark-complexioned man came for Sweeney in the lobby of the Hoover Building, introducing himself as Sandy Senarighi, special agent in charge of the Tyson investigation.

"I'll be your contact here at the Bureau," Senarighi said. He signed Sweeney in and they took the elevator down two floors.

"You're the one who came to Langley last week to ask about Raya Nechiporenko," Sweeney said.

"At least you've done your homework. Now, if you'll cooperate like the nice man I've been told you are, everything will be fine."

"I'm not the enemy," Sweeney said.

"No. But you and your chums give honest cops a bad name."

"Worse than Hoover?"

Senarighi's jaw tightened. Not only had the Bureau lost two people in this investigation, it was dealing with the shame of having killed two friendlies. "Walk softly over there," Drury had cautioned him.

"I was told to cooperate with you, Mr. Sweeney, and I will. I hope you will do likewise. Now, what is it you want here?"

"The truth," Sweeney said. "And I don't give a fuck who it hurts or helps, my bosses or yours."

"Fair enough," Senarighi said, and they went down the corridor to a small conference room in which a slide projector and screen had been set up.

"I'd like to speak with Marina Demin. You're holding her and Raya Nechiporenko here or at a safe house?"

"Here," Senarighi said. "But first tell me about Miss Demin, and about a KGB officer by the name of Ivan Kiselev. I understand you're the expert."

Sweeney took off his overcoat and dropped it over the back of a chair, then opened his attaché case and began removing files and photographs.

"Time is of the essence here, Mr. Senarighi, so I would like to finish as quickly as possible. The situation, as I see it, is definitely unstable."

"You think that the shit is about to hit the fan, Mr. Sweeney?"

Sweeney looked at him and nodded. "Yes, as a matter of fact I do."

"So do I," Senarighi said.

Tyson stood at a window in the Watergate apartment holding one of Toni Wagner's scarves to his nose, her scent still strong. He'd found the scarf stuck by static electricity to the back of the closet door in the master bedroom. Everything else was gone. It meant she had help. A controller. A handler.

After all, it was difficult to move yourself out when you were being held in jail.

Marina Demin was Joseph's daughter, and now the KGB was trying to use her against him. To embarrass him? Kit would understand, he would make her see, but the President apparently was having trouble understanding what had happened so many years ago.

The Marina Demin Tyson remembered had been about the same age, maybe a little younger, but she had known things at a level that was very much different from Kit, and even different from Toni. Kit was reserved, midwestern conservative, while Toni was professional, a prostitute in her sexual expertise. But Marina had been passionate and understanding, appreciative of the slightest thing you did for her, and patient, almost as if she were a teacher sent to instruct you on how to love, to relax, to let go without becoming crazy.

With Kit there was love and friendship, and even comfort knowing that there would be continuity. With Toni there had been excitement and danger. She'd been forbidden fruit.

But with Marina there had been the feeling at the end of a long sigh. The feeling that she was quenching a thirst that you never knew you had, but instinctively felt was there, somewhere.

First loves, he'd read, were the most memorable. First loves lasted forever, if only in the mind.

In the end, though, Kit was the only one who could understand. She would know what to do. She would help him.

He went to the telephone, picked it up, and dialed his home number.

Privet had been mesmerized by Kit Tyson. She was so completely American, yet so diffident, he was charmed. But he was a professional and he realized that he had only two options: Either he had to leave before Tyson arrived, or he had to kill the woman. If he waited too long, and Tyson returned home, it would be nearly impossible to control the killing of two people so that no suspicions would be raised by the Bureau's surveillance people.

"My husband is in some sort of trouble, isn't he?" Kit Tyson had asked directly.

"There are some people who would like to think so," Privet had answered.

"But not you."

Privet shrugged, looking at the objects in the living room. A dozen places, more, in which to conceal a microphone.

"Then why are you here? What do you want? You people can't be serious."

"Actually I'm here to help, Mrs. Tyson."

"Then let me call my husband."

"Actually I wanted to speak with you."

"I think not," Kit had said, rising. "I'll call Al."

"You are aware, I assume, that your husband's mistress has been arrested by the Federal Bureau of Investigation."

The air seemed to go out of Kit. She sat down. Her lower lip began to quiver.

"I'm sorry to bring this up, Mrs. Tyson, but the problem is with her, not your husband."

"I don't understand," Kit said, finding her voice after a moment or two.

"The woman. She's a Russian spy."

Kit closed her eyes.

"I'm sorry, Mrs. Tyson, I thought you knew."

"I didn't," she said, getting up. "Excuse me, please. For just a minute." She turned and left the room.

Privet got up and followed her, careful to make absolutely no noise. In the stair hall, he had to step back until she disappeared down the corridor on the second floor, and then he went up, hesitating just at the top before continuing.

The bedroom door at the end of the short hall was ajar, and Privet flattened himself against the wall so that he could just see inside. The odor of vomit was sharp. Kit had crossed the room and entered the bathroom, but she'd left the door open behind her. The water was running in the vanity sink and she was bent over, splashing her face.

After a while she placed a wet washcloth on the back of her neck and came back into the bedroom. Privet didn't move.

She was distraught, but she was trying desperately to pull herself together as she paced back and forth. She had soiled the front of her sweater and her skirt, but at first she didn't notice. She was sobbing softly, and shaking her head in shock. She simply couldn't believe what was happening to her. Privet had seen the same look on some of his victims. Disbelief. This is not happening to me. It cannot be happening.

She stopped in midstride and looked down at herself. Throwing down the washcloth, she peeled off her sweater, tossed it aside, then unzipped her skirt and stepped out of it.

Privet felt like a voyeur, but then he'd always believed that two people can have no relationship more intimate than a killer and his victim. He felt his penis grow hard as Kit went into the bathroom, where she started the shower, then took off her bra and stepped out of her panties.

It was time for her to die.

Opening the shower door, Kit tested the water with her hand, adjusted it, and then stepped inside, closing the glass door behind her.

Privet stepped into the bedroom. He took off his jacket and was about to lay it down when the telephone rang, and he froze.

The telephone, on the nightstand beside the bed, rang again, and Kit, her eyes closed, her face filled with soap, slid back the shower door and reached for a towel.

Privet turned and left the room, again remaining just out in the corridor.

It was sometime after one in the morning when the ambulance bearing Kaplin, Larissa Dolya, and the others entered an old factory building ten kilometers northeast of the city center. Even Kaplin didn't know exactly where they were, although he thought he'd recognized Eutuziaslov Road, which was the highway to Gor'kiy. Gremiakin had elected this place months ago when they'd decided that the group would need a contingency plan.

"If we are discovered, and there is time to do something before our arrests, then I say we go all the way," Kaplin had told them.

They agreed, but it was Gremiakin who, with his KGB

School One training and connections, had come up with the stunning solution.

"We wouldn't survive such an action." Mukhin sounded the only note of caution.

"Probably not," Kaplin had replied. "But we understood that possibility from the moment we first began to have our doubts. When we crossed over that line, we ceased being invisible. If we're discovered we will have no other choice."

The driver and another man riding shotgun were part of Gremiakin's team of what he called "bullyboys" from the school. No one knew how he came up with them, but they were former KGB field officers who'd been pulled in for duty as teachers. Their loyalties were unquestionably to Gremiakin, and no longer the Komitet. Kaplin thought of them as renegades. Useful if they could be kept under control, but dangerous nonetheless.

Now, of course, the lives of everyone in the group depended upon Gremiakin and his bullyboys.

Near the center of the factory building they went up a broad ramp to the second floor, and the driver switched off the ambulance's headlights and came to a stop. They sat in the nearly absolute darkness for a full two minutes before the front and rear doors were yanked open and strong lights were shined in their eyes.

Larissa reared back against Kaplin, and she cried out. "It's all right," Kaplin cooed. "We came in clean," he called toward the light.

"Sergei?" someone asked.

"We're clean," the driver answered.

The lights were turned aside and several pairs of hands helped Larissa and Kaplin out of the back of the ambulance, then led them across the broad space toward the rear. Larissa clung tightly to Kaplin. She was extremely frightened, and at one point he had to support her entire weight.

Kaplin had not been to this place, but Gremiakin had told him and the others about it. "If the need arises, it will suit."

Well, Kaplin thought grimly, the need had arisen.

Gremiakin was waiting for them in what had apparently

once been the factory's cafeteria and kitchen area. Four tables were loaded with a variety of weapons and ammunition, among them AK-47 assault rifles, pistols, hand grenades, two grenade launchers, and three antitank weapons with a dozen rockets each.

Gremiakin came across the big room to them and carefully hugged Kaplin, kissing him on the lips. When they parted he looked critically at his old friend. "You look like shit. The bastards must have really stuck it to you."

"It'll be a while before I impress the girls that way."

Gremiakin nodded knowingly. Everyone in the KGB knew what went on in some interrogation cells. The sadists and perverts were still a part of the business, all the denials to the contrary.

"Then it's time to do it another way," Gremiakin said, eyeing Larissa. "How are you feeling, my dear?"

She was still leaning against Kaplin for support. "Not so good," she said softly.

"Maybe we should leave her out of this, Anatoli."

Kaplin shook his head. "They'll never leave her alone. She's a dead woman no matter what. At least this way we might have a chance . . ."

"Don't say it."

Kaplin hesitated, but then sighed tiredly. "Where are the others?"

"Vitali and Mikhail are coming in together. They should be here within the hour. With us, plus my six bullyboys, it makes eleven."

"Mikhail and Vitali will be our hostages," Kaplin said. "An assistant foreign affairs adviser to the President, and a KGB counterintelligence officer, will get their attention."

"So will we," Gremiakin said. "Now, come have something to eat and I will show you what weapons we've managed to steal."

"I don't see the gas masks or the food and water supplies."

"Already loaded aboard the truck."

Kaplin looked around the room. "Where are your boys?"

"On lookout."

"Before we get started I want to meet them," Kaplin said. "All of them."

Gremiakin nodded. "They want to meet you too, Anatoli."

"She's probably sleeping," Rodgers said.

Seagren was driving a two-door Lada with Estonian plates that he'd bought earlier in the day from one of the dealers just off the outer ring road near the Riga Station in Dzerzhinsky for fifteen thousand rubles. Everything worked, though the muffler was a little loud, and the inside of the car smelled like exhaust. There were no lights in any of the apartments as they slowly cruised past Larissa Dolya's building.

"Either that or she's gone out again," Seagren said, turning the corner at the end of the block. Back here there was absolutely no traffic at this hour. If a Militia cop came along, they would stick out like a sore thumb.

"She wouldn't be that dumb. Not after what she's undoubtedly been through."

"They had her long enough to do plenty," Seagren agreed. "And Lefortovo is no rest camp."

"Then she's there."

"Not if that crazy bastard Kaplin has already made his move. Shit, there's no telling what he might do, but it's a safe bet he's sucked her in."

"She's better than that."

Seagren smiled to himself. "I wouldn't count too heavily on it, Roy," he said. "But it's your call. What do you want to do?"

"We're not going to leave her. Make another pass. If it's still clear, you can let me off and I'll go up to make sure."

The car was packed and ready to make the same trip to Tallinn that Sweeney had made with Marina Demin. But Seagren had seemed almost nonchalant about the operation almost as if he didn't really think it would happen. Nor had he seemed very surprised that there were no lights from Larissa's apartment. Rodgers had been almost too preoccupied with his own thoughts to notice Seagren's odd behavior but when he finally did he put it down to a case of the jitters. Everyone reacted differently to stress.

"Don't worry about it, Bill. If something goes down, I want you to bail out immediately."

"What about you?"

"I'll stay put until we can get a van over here from the embassy."

"Are you carrying a piece?" Seagren asked as he turned the corner back onto Dobryninskiy 1 Pereulok.

"Yes."

"Well, just watch yourself. Won't do anybody any good if you start a shooting war over this little girl."

"She's one of us," Rodgers said.

"Yeah."

Nothing moved in either direction on the broad avenue. Seagren slowed the car to a bare crawl in front of the apartment building, and as soon as Rodgers was clear he took off into the darkness.

Rodgers sprinted across the sidewalk and into the deeper shadows of the building's doorway, where he remained. The Lada's taillights disappeared around the corner, leaving him utterly alone in the night, with an oddly unsettled, distant sensation. He'd felt the same thing once as a kid, deer hunting in northern Maine. It was before sunrise, when the deep forest was at its darkest, and he was alone, hidden in a clump of bushes on a hill looking down into a broad valley. He could hear wind rushing through the trees below, but nothing else, and a tremendous sense of loneliness came over him. It was as if he'd just learned that all of civilization had ceased to exist for some reason, and he was the only person left on the earth. At times Moscow engendered that feeling.

Letting himself in with the duplicate of the key they'd given Larissa Dolya, Rodgers paused again for several seconds at the foot of the stairs as he listened for a sound, any sound, from within one of the apartments. But the building was silent, and dark. It could have been that no one lived here, except that they knew the building supervisor was the babushka on the first floor. She'd be sleeping now.

Rodgers took out his pistol, a .9-millimeter Beretta, switched the safety off, but then immediately switched the safety back on and stuffed the gun back into his shoulder holster, feeling faintly foolish. He was acting like an old woman.

Careful to make no noise, he took the stairs two at a time to the second floor, where he listened at Larissa's door. The apartment was quiet. She was sleeping. Or gone.

Using the duplicate of the apartment key, he opened the door and stepped inside. For a second or two Rodgers stood just within the door. The apartment consisted of only one room. In the dim light filtering in from outside he could see that she was gone, and that her coat was missing too. A few articles of clothing were folded on a shelf, and her cardboard suitcase sat on the floor in the corner.

Back out in the corridor, Rodgers hurried silently up to the third floor. Kaplin's apartment door was open, and it only took a moment to confirm that no one was inside.

Wherever they were at this hour, Rodgers had the feeling the two of them were together. And it wasn't a very good feeling, he decided as he hurried back downstairs and outside.

Rodgers was stopped by a pair of Militia officers in front of the embassy and had to show his papers. The cops were armed and suspicious. It was too late for Americans to be walking around Moscow, diplomatic officers or not.

Two marine guards had come to the door and were watching. They were not authorized to use force, but they knew exactly who and what Rodgers was. If anything went down, one of them could at least run some interference while the other called for help.

The original plan was for Seagren to have left Moscow immediately with the girl. That had changed, of course. He was parking the car now in a safe spot a few blocks away and would be showing up within the next twenty minutes.

"Thank you, sir," one of the Militia officers said, handing back his passport.

Rodgers was nonplussed for just a moment, but then he turned and entered the embassy.

"Everything okay, sir?" one of the marines asked.

"Just fine," Rodgers said. He'd expected at least a question or two, but they'd asked him nothing. "Mr. Seagren should be showing up here within the next fifteen or twenty minutes. Keep an eye out for him."

"Will do, sir."

Rodgers checked with the OD on the second floor for any messages—there were none—then went downstairs to communications, where the last of the overnight reports were going out to Langley. SOP required that Moscow's night cables arrive at Langley each day no later than 6:00 P.M. Washington time, which was 2:00 A.M. in Moscow.

He quickly wrote out a brief message outlining their failure to locate Larissa Dolya and get her out of the country, and handed it through the slot to one of the night operators.

"I want this sent as a bulletin to Sweeney."

"His traffic is being directed through Mr. Drury's office, sir," the clerk, a young, heavy-set woman said.

"Fine, just make sure this gets out immediately."

"Yes, sir."

Petr Zazyadko opened the security window that looked out onto the loading platform of GUM, the state department store. Someone had been ringing the buzzer for the last ten minutes, all through the end of his lunch hour, and he was irritated.

"It's about time, you bastard," a heavy-set man in rough workmen's coveralls shouted. A large canvas-covered truck was backed up to the loading dock.

"What do you want?" Zazyadko shouted back.

"Winter boots," the workman said. He held the bills of lading up to the window. "I want to get them unloaded and go home."

It was a damned odd time of the night for such a delivery to be made—for any delivery to be made here—but then these days anything was possible. And there was no denying that there was a shortage of boots.

"All right," Zazyadko said. "Just a second." He closed the security window, then unlocked the main service door and slid it open. "Did you bring someone to help you unload?"

"I thought you could help."

"Fuck you," Zazyadko said good-naturedly, but he had nothing better to do. "Here, give me those bills and I'll lend a hand."

The workman handed him the sheaf of papers and then went back and flipped open the canvas flap at the rear of the truck. Gremiakin and two of his bullyboys, AK-47s in hand, jumped out onto the loading dock. Zazyadko stepped back.

"Nobody is going to hurt you if you cooperate," Gremiakin said, taking the night watchman aside.

"Is this a robbery?"

"No," Gremiakin said. Kaplin and the others climbed out of the truck, and the young men began quickly unloading the weapons, Zazyadko's eyes growing wider as he realized what he was seeing.

"Who else is here with you tonight?" Gremiakin asked.

"No one."

"You're alone?"

"Yes."

"The papers you were given are not bills of lading. They're much more important than that. I want you to take them immediately to the Militia headquarters and turn them over to the officer in charge. Tell them what you saw and heard here, and tell them that if everyone remains calm, there will be no killings. Do you have that?"

Zazyadko nodded. "What do you want? This is just a department store."

"Do as you're told," Gremiakin said. He stepped aside. "Now get out of here."

"What about my coat . . ."

"Leave it," Gremiakin said, and the man turned and sprinted across the loading dock, down the stairs, and around the corner onto Drovezd Sapunova.

"Ten minutes," Gremiakin said, and he looked around as Kaplin and the young woman stopped to stare up at the sky as if for the last time.

An extremely frustrated Grigoriev and his partner, Andreyev, were heading back to the Lubyanka when they heard the first of the sirens toward Red Square. He switched over to the Militia's tactical frequency, which was filled with a babble of excited voices.

"Sounds like they've got a revolution on their hands," Andreyev said, pulling through the gate into the courtyard. "It's the fucking black marketeers having another shootout."

"Maybe not," Grigoriev said, trying to make sense of the dozens of radio transmissions.

Andreyev parked in their slot, shut off the car's headlights, and started to switch off the ignition, but Grigoriev stopped him.

"Wait. I thought I heard Vitali Boyarov's name."

Andreyev shrugged.

"Special Service Two. One of our people." Grigoriev switched to the KGB's city communications frequency. "City, two-seven-one-zero."

"Twenty-seven ten, go."

"We're picking up something strange on the Militia tactical frequency. Are you indicating any troubles?"

"We're just receiving word of an apparent hostage situation, but we've got no confirmation."

"I thought I heard Captain Boyarov's name mentioned. Special Service Two."

"That's what we're getting. Boyarov, along with Colonel Gremiakin and Captain Kaplin, may be involved."

Grigoriev's gut tightened. "City, did you say Kaplin? Anatoli Stepanovich?"

"That's what we have so far."

"Where are they? Sheremetyevo?"

"GUM."

"What?"

"GUM. They've supposedly got weapons . . ."

Grigoriev switched back to the Militia's tactical frequency as Andreyev turned on the headlights and backed out of their parking slot. He slammed the car in gear and peeled out across the courtyard and through the main gate.

Three minutes ago Grigoriev had been tired and frustrated. His investigation had come to a dead end, and in the morning he would have had to face an unsympathetic Colonel Vilkov. But now he'd been handed a reprieve, practically on a silver platter.

Andreyev shot across the nearly deserted square and raced down October 25th Street.

"I knew that crazy bastard wasn't through," Grigoriev said.

"It belongs to the Militia now."

"No way in hell, Yevgeni. Kaplin is ours, now and forever. I own the son of a bitch!"

"If he sees either of us, he'll open fire."

Grigoriev laughed. "And so will we. I have no sympathy for him or his little whore. They're traitors, and I've spent my life fighting them. I'm not going to stop now."

"I'm not saying that . . ."

"Then find me the on-site commander. I want in before the Militia fucks it up."

"To do what, Valentin?"

"Dig him out, or kill him. Frankly I don't care which."

GUM, housed in a large building across Red Square from Lenin's Tomb and the Kremlin, was actually a Russian version of a shopping mall. Along a central hall, rising three stories and topped by curved iron skylights, dozens of shops were housed behind ornately carved brick façades. Filigreed iron railings ran along the second-floor walkway. And an arched bridge of similar ironwork crossed the hall at the third level.

Standing alone in the gloom on the bridge, listening to the gathering sirens outside, Kaplin could see the front and rear entrances to the building. Gremiakin had stationed one heavily armed man at each. As a fortress, of course, the big department store was practically indefensible. But by now the Militia would have gotten the information that they were holding two very important men as hostages. As long as no one got crazy and tried to storm the building, they'd be all right for a little while.

Beyond that, Kaplin was having a difficult time seeing where it would lead. Change was what they wanted, what they'd wanted from the beginning. But they were not willing to wait forever, nor were they willing to endure the deepening chaos that gripped the country. Unless the economy turned around soon, the military or some other faction would try again to take over. This time they might succeed, and it would be a disaster, not only for the Soviet people but for the rest of the world as well.

Gremiakin appeared below, and looked up, spotting Kaplin. "They've been notified," he called up, his voice echoing in the big hall.

"All of them?" Kaplin shouted.

"Yes. Most of them thought it was some kind of joke. But I got their attention. Where is the little girl?"

"Sleeping up here."

"Well, it won't be long now and there'll be plenty for us to do."

"If the Militia lets us talk to them."

"If not it'll be a bloodbath, and we'll get our point across anyway."

It took Yuri Truskin twenty-five minutes using his *Rezident*'s one-time cipher pad to decrypt Director Novikov's for-your-eyes-only flash message. Homeward Bound was to be terminated at once, no matter the cost in lost assets. That the order had not come from General Ryazanov or Kiselev, the architects of the scheme, told Truskin nearly as much as the terse message which had come via burst transmission off their *Kolya II* communications satellite. He was relieved, though pulling everyone out was going to be next to impossible. It would be a long time before their operations here could return to normal.

The unwritten message, of course, was to keep Source KHAIRULLA insulated at all costs, which made the cancellation of Homeward Bound even more difficult than it already was.

Pocketing the decrypted message, Truskin left his office and went down to the office that the Lubiakos were sharing at the end of the corridor. But the rooms were dark, no one was there.

Going back to his own office, he telephoned the Lubiakos' apartment upstairs, but there was no answer. Next he dialed the embassy operator. "This is Truskin. I'm trying to find the Lubiakos."

"Madame Lubiako left the embassy at sixteen hundred hours and has not returned yet, Comrade Truskin," the male operator said.

"And her brother?"

"He is here. Shall I try his apartment?"

"No, that won't be necessary," Truskin said, hanging up. He left his office and took the stairs up to the third floor, using the service corridor to reach the rear section of the embassy building, where most of the apartments were located.

He knocked at the Lubiakos' door, but when there was no answer, he let himself in with his master key.

Igor Lubiako was in the front bedroom packing his single suitcase. He looked up when Truskin appeared in the doorway. "It's you."

"You didn't answer your phone."

"No need to," Lubiako said. "I figured it was probably you, and that you'd show up here sooner or later."

"Where are you going?"

"Home."

"I thought you were in the middle of an operation," Truskin said without surprise. He'd learned in his career not to be surprised by much.

Lubiako stopped what he was doing and looked up. "You will be getting a message from Center very soon telling you to terminate Homeward Bound."

"How do you know this?"

"Because I've already received mine."

"There was nothing in communications."

"By telephone, from the major."

Now Truskin was surprised. "On an open line?"

"In code and through an intermediary. You've used the method yourself, I'm sure."

"But only in an extreme emergency, when no other form of communication is considered secure . . ." Truskin let it trail off.

"Yes," Lubiako said. "You have already received your orders. From whom, if I may ask?"

"Novikov."

Lubiako nodded. "Then you understand just how serious this is."

Truskin glanced toward Lydia's bedroom. "Where is your sister?"

A look of concern crossed Lubiako's face. "She's not back yet."

"I know. She left the embassy a couple of hours ago. Where'd she go?"

"To give Privet his stand-down orders."

"I'll be glad when that bastard is gone," Truskin said. "I didn't think we still used people like that."

"It doesn't happen very often."

"Maybe she needs help."

Lubiako was shaking his head. "She told me to stay out of it. She said she would handle him."

"What about Raya Nechiporenko and the other one, from Moscow?"

"I don't know. I wasn't told a thing about them, except that it would be worked out. The FBI is holding them now, and no one knows how that'll turn out."

"In the meantime I inherit the mess."

"You still have assets."

"Yes," Truskin said thoughtfully. "As soon as Lydia shows up I want to see both of you in my office."

"We're taking the Montreal flight from Dulles this evening, if the airport stays open."

"My office, before you go," Truskin said. "And bring the document with you."

Lubiako was startled. "I thought Lydia gave it to you."

"No."

"That means it's still in her possession."

"Out on the street?" Truskin shouted in disbelief. "She took it out of here . . . now, of all times?"

Lubiako was shaking his head. "I don't know what she's trying to do."

"Kill us all, that's what," Truskin said.

Kit had sounded very strange on the telephone. Tyson had remained at the Watergate apartment for a little while after he'd talked to her, trying to work out in his mind what was going to happen next. Oddly, it seemed safe here even though the place belonged to a Russian spy. The thought was incredible to him. And now he looked back with shame and even embarrassment at what they'd done together. How had he been so naive? How had he allowed himself to be so easily led?

But she'd been exciting. Being around her had stirred his blood, made him feel as if he were living on some dangerous edge. She had provided him with a stimulation that had been lacking in his life for a very long time.

At what cost?

Leaving a few minutes later, it took him nearly half an hour because of the snow to drive the dozen or so blocks to his home. Already it was dark, and Washington seemed like a city on another planet, or like a city in Siberia. He shivered.

The lights were on in his living room and everything looked normal. But Kit's voice had sounded . . . strangled. As if the words were choking in her throat.

Something was wrong. And on the way over he'd just about convinced himself that somehow she knew about Toni, and he wondered how he would ever face that sort of a disaster piled on top of everything else.

It wouldn't be long before the Bureau came for him. Not now that the President was directly involved.

He let himself in. "Kit," he called as he took off his overcoat and hung it in the closet.

Jerry Wilson, the Bureau surveillance shift chief, picked up his telephone and dialed his supervisor's number downtown.

"This is Wilson. Tyson just showed up."

"Good. Is his wife's guest still there?"

"He's CIA, I think," Wilson said, listening with one earphone to what was going on in Tyson's home down the block. "Yes, he's still there."

"We have two units rolling. Stand by."

"Will do," Wilson said.

26

KIT TYSON PICKED UP THE TELEPHONE WITH A SHAKING HAND on the third ring just as her husband let himself in and shouted her name from downstairs.

She started to call out, but Privet motioned with his pistol for her not to do so. Someone was on the telephone. Privet could hear the voice but not the words from where he stood across the bedroom.

"Privet?" Kit said into the phone, confused. "I don't know who you're talking about."

Tyson called her name again, and this time his voice was faint, as if he'd gone into the kitchen at the back of the house.

"What? What are you saying?" Kit asked, looking fearfully at the assassin. "I don't know any Privet."

Tyson's telephone call earlier had saved her life. When she'd hung up she'd been totally distraught. She'd received some news that was so stunning it was nearly destroying her.

Privet had entered her bedroom, and before she'd had a chance to cry out, he had pulled her back into the bathroom, where he turned on the water in the shower and the sink and flushed the toilet. The noises would help blot out their voices, make the words difficult to pick out, except after computer analysis, which would take time.

"Who was that on the telephone?" he had whispered urgently to her.

For a moment she couldn't catch her breath. Privet had jammed the barrel of his pistol against the side of her head, and her eyes were nearly bugging out.

"Who was it?"

"My husband."

"What did he say?"

"He's coming home. He's in . . . trouble."

"What kind of trouble?"

"Oh, God, I don't know. But he's not a spy."

Spy? What did that mean? He had allowed her to put on a robe, but they remained in the bedroom so that he could watch the street. He'd seen Tyson drive up, but he had not expected this telephone call now. Who knew he was here, and who knew his Privet work name except someone from the embassy?

Privet was across the room in three strides, and he snatched the telephone from Kit. They had used his work name to call this number, which was almost certainly being monitored by the FBI.

"What?" he said, forcing himself to keep calm.

"Do you know who this is?" Lydia Lubiako's voice was on the phone. She sounded unhinged.

"Yes."

"Homeward Bound has been compromised. The operation is to be terminated immediately."

"On whose authority?" Privet demanded.

Tyson was on the stairs now, and he called Kit's name again. Kit started to move toward the door, but Privet raised his pistol, cocked the hammer, and pointed it at her head. She stopped.

"The highest authority," Lydia Lubiako said. "Everyone is leaving. Get out while you still can."

"That may be impossible."

"Listen to me, you bastard, you don't know what's been happening. You were never meant to get away. My orders were to kill you once Tyson made delivery. I was to leave your body for them to find."

"What was Tyson supposed to deliver? And to whom?"

"A document I brought with me from Moscow. It was written on White House stationery, taking the blame for the August coup. Tyson was blaming his own country, and he was going to hand the document over to a *Washington Post* reporter. Don't you see what would have happened? We would have come out as heroes of the *Rodina*."

Tyson was coming upstairs.

Privet could hardly believe his ears, and yet what she was saying had the ring of truth. He'd felt it in what Truskin and some of the other pricks had said to him . . . more in how they had treated him. He was to have been sacrificed.

"Why are you telling me this now?"

"Because I'm taking the document with me. I'm defecting."

Tyson was just out in the corridor. "Kit?"

"Get out of there . . ." Lydia Lubiako shouted.

Privet put the phone down and turned his pistol toward the door as Tyson came around the corner.

Sweeney and Senarighi were seated in a small waiting area adjacent to the interrogation rooms where they'd been speaking with Raya Nechiporenko and Marina Demin. During the long afternoon, Sweeney had learned about the sketch of Marina Demin's father. She had admitted that she had never known Mukhin, and that she worked for the KGB, but she had steadfastly maintained her story that her only job was to come here and identify her father.

"Has she been shown recent photographs?" Sweeney asked. The sketch had come as a complete surprise to him.

"Not yet. Ed Wilder went to the President with this, of course. But I've gotten no word on that meeting as yet."

"The business about her father being a teacher in Wisconsin was a lie?"

"We're checking on it. We sent some people out to look

around. Tyson met with someone last week at a restaurant while he was having dinner with his wife. Whoever the man was, he passed Tyson a note or a card, and afterward he jumped in a car with Raya Nechiporenko."

"What did she say about it?"

"We haven't asked her. Not yet. Not until we know the answer."

"But this," Sweeney said, glancing down at the police artist's sketch. "It's incredible."

"Yes, isn't it?" Senarighi agreed. "We were hoping that you might be able to tell us what's going on. This is a Russian plot, apparently orchestrated by Major Kiselev. He's got two women involved, one of whom is Tyson's mistress, and the other who claims to be his . . ."

"Who claims to be his daughter, according to this sketch."

"It's Tyson, all right. I don't think there's much doubt about it. The question is whether she's telling the truth, or this is just another element of Kiselev's plot. You listened to both of them, and you spent time coming out of Russia with Miss Demin. You tell me."

"Apparently they came here to bring Tyson down," Sweeney said. "Which means he's innocent."

"Perhaps innocent of being a paid agent of Russia, but certainly not innocent of having a mistress who was. And if Miss Demin is his daughter, then he had a sexual liaison with another Russian spy when he was in college."

Sweeney nodded.

"And another question: Just who the hell is this teacher in Wisconsin she keeps talking about? What's he got to do with anything?"

"My God, who the hell are you?" Tyson asked, pulling up short.

"He says he works for the CIA, but I think he works for the Russians," Kit said in a breathless rush.

For just an instant Privet was left wondering how she had guessed the truth, but then he realized that Lydia could not hide her Russian accent. Kit Tyson was sharp.

"I came to kill you, Mr. Tyson, but my orders were a mistake," Privet said, knowing that everything he said here in this manner would be picked up by the Bureau.

Both Tyson and his wife were staggered. "But why?" Tyson asked.

"It doesn't matter. As I said, my orders were a mistake." Privet was thinking ahead to how he was going to get out of here and out of the country. Time, he decided, was of the essence.

"Then go," Tyson said.

"I don't think it will be that easy. The FBI is listening to everything we say. By now they will have units on their way here to arrest me."

"Just go," Kit screeched. "Leave us alone. What are you doing here in the first place? Just go back to your own people."

"That is my intention, Mrs. Tyson. But you and your husband are going to have to accompany me to ensure my safe passage."

Special Agent Wilson got on the phone again to his supervisor in the Hoover Building.

"This is Wilson. He's Russian. The guy in there with Mrs. Tyson is a fucking Russian."

"What?"

"Tyson showed up, and the guy admitted that he was sent here to kill him, but that it was a mistake and now he needs to get out of the country. And he means to use the Tysons as hostages. Somebody called just a minute ago and talked to him. Told him that Operation Homeward Bound was a bust, and to get the hell out. She said something about a document on White House stationery that was blaming us for the Kremlin coup last August. She said she was going to defect with it."

"The caller was Russian?"

"I'd bet my Corvette on it. She called him Privet."

"All right, hold tight. Help is on the way."

"What if they bug out . . . ?" Wilson asked, but the line was dead.

Senarighi slammed the telephone on its cradle and raced down the corridor to where Sweeney was watching Marina Demin through the one-way glass. He seemed fascinated by her.

"The shit you were worried about has just hit the fan," the Bureau agent shouted.

Sweeney turned around.

"We've got to go," Senarighi said, starting toward the elevator.

"Where?" Sweeney demanded, falling in behind him.

"Tyson's house." Senarighi hit the call button. "He's there along with a Russian assassin who was sent to kill him. Our surveillance unit picked it up."

"Now? He's there now?" Sweeney asked, trying to work this out in his head. First the girls and now this. What the hell was Kiselev trying to do?

"Yes, but the assassin's orders were evidently changed. Something about Homeward Bound, and some fake document. At any rate he's going to try to get the hell out of the country using Tyson and his wife as shields."

"Either that or it's part of the operation."

"What?" Senarighi asked. The elevator doors slid open.

"A last-ditch effort to throw suspicion off Tyson. And if all else fails, get him out of the country."

"I don't believe it," Senarighi said, holding the elevator door.

"Get the girl," Sweeney said. "She claims Tyson is her father. We'll take her out there and confront him. See what happens."

"Hold the elevator," Senarighi said, and he sprinted back to the interrogation rooms.

"Geronimo surveillance, this is unit seventeen. We're just coming around the corner of R Street from the east. What's the status in there?" Tom Parker radioed. His partner, Charles Goode, was driving.

"You're the first on scene, seventeen. But watch yourself, the bad guy is about to bug out," Wilson radioed from the surveillance unit set up in the Dumbarton Oaks Research Library.

"Is he armed?"

"Presumably, seventeen. Sounds like he's going to use Geronimo and Geronimo's wife as hostages. We have more units en route."

Kit Tyson got dressed, and Privet herded her and her husband downstairs to the living room, where he pulled on his overcoat.

"Where is your car parked?" he asked Tyson.

"In the driveway. But what do you think you're going to do?"

"Leave the country," Privet said, glancing out the window but still holding his pistol on Tyson and his wife.

"It won't work. The FBI is following me. They'll be all over this place any minute."

A gray Toyota van pulled up and blocked the street about sixty or seventy meters to the east. No one got out.

"You can't simply jump in a car and drive to Russia, or anywhere else where you'll be safe, for that matter."

"That's true," Privet said. "Mrs. Tyson, you will drive. I'll want you to go west, on R Street, toward Wisconsin Avenue. I'll give you other instructions en route."

"En route to where?" Tyson asked.

"We'll keep together out the front door," Privet said. "I don't want to hurt either of you, but I will do whatever is necessary to save my own life and make good my escape. Do you both understand this? Clearly?"

Kit shivered, but then she nodded.

"Mrs. Tyson, you first, please, behind the wheel. Mr Tyson, you will sit in the front beside your wife. I'll sit in the rear." Privet motioned them toward the front door, and after a hesitation, they moved.

*   *   *

"Here they come," Parker said. He got on the radio. "Geronimo surveillance, unit seventeen. Geronimo, his wife, and the third party just stepped out of the house."

"We show them on camera, seventeen. Your orders are to follow them, but take no other action. You got that, Tom?"

"Seventeen, this is two," Senarighi radioed. They were on Pennsylvania Avenue heading up to Washington Circle.

"Roger, two."

"What car are they taking?"

"They're just getting into Geronimo's car. I don't see any other vehicle . . . Hold it."

Senarighi and Sweeney exchanged glances. Marina sat between them, her complexion pale.

"Right, the lady is driving, Geronimo is in the front seat, and Privet is in the back."

"Did they spot you?"

"Yes."

"Tyson has probably got a phone in his car," Sweeney said. "Can we monitor his calls from here?"

"Yes," Senarighi said. "But where the hell does he think he's taking them?"

"All right, surveillance, here they go," Parker radioed. "Looks like they're heading west on R Street."

"Geronimo surveillance, this is unit two."

"Go ahead, two."

"I'm switching to Tactical Channel three. I want you to patch our monitor of Geronimo's car telephone over to me."

"Will do," Wilson radioed, and Senarighi switched channels.

"What have you got in mind?" he asked Sweeney.

"I don't know, yet. But that Russian didn't run off half-cocked. I'd bet anything he's got something in mind."

A dial tone came from the speaker, and someone punched up a seven-digit telephone number.

"That's him," Senarighi said.

The call went through and was answered on the second ring. "Operations, Captain Bergstrom."

"Del, this is Al Tyson."

"Mr. Tyson, good afternoon, sir."

"How's the field looking?"

"Not so hot, but serviceable. Don't tell me you've got to get somewhere."

" 'Fraid so. There'll only be three of us, so seven-seven-echo should be fine."

"Ah, yes, sir. What's your destination?"

"Reykjavík."

"Operations where?" Sweeney asked.

"Andrews Air Force Base," Senarighi said, hauling the car around in a U-turn and heading back the way they'd come.

"I tell you that I personally know at least two of those bastards in there," Grigoriev was saying to Militia Captain Leonid Solyakov, the on-site commander for the moment.

More Militia units were streaming into Red Square and the streets on the other three sides of the big department store. The scene was unreal. It reminded Grigoriev of pictures he'd seen during the purges of the thirties. A real manhunt.

"What are you telling me, Lieutenant? That you want to go in there and order them out so convincingly that they will gladly follow you like little sheep back to Lefortovo?" The captain was a tough-minded, tough-looking man who'd already spent eighteen years on the force. He'd seen too much in his day to be overly impressed by the Komitet, and especially not by a forty-year-old lieutenant.

"That's exactly what I'm telling you, Captain. I *own* those two."

"Don't be so sure," Captain Solyakov said, looking across at the front entrance of GUM. "You saw their list of weapons and their hostages."

"They're not hostages, they're co-conspirators," Grigoriev lied, not knowing he'd inadvertently guessed the truth.

"Then you'll get yourself killed."

"My worry, not yours."

Solyakov shook his head in amazement. "Will you take your partner with you?"

"Of course," Grigoriev said, glancing at Andreyev, who nodded uncertainly.

"Then be my guest, Comrade Grigoriev."

Grigoriev took out his pistol, checked the load and the safety catch, then stuffed it down the front of his trousers. After a moment Andreyev did the same. When they were patted down, the pistols might be missed.

"We'll bring them out . . . one way or the other," he said to the Militia captain, and then he and Andreyev, holding their hands in plain sight above their heads, started across the broad square to the department store.

Fedor Miroshnichenko watched for a moment to make certain there were only two of them coming across the square and then he looked over his shoulder. "We've got two plainclothes coming in. Hands over their heads."

Gremiakin stood within the shadows of the doorway to a leather goods shop twenty meters down the central corridor. The door to the shop was open, and from his position he could keep an eye on the front and rear entrances, and Kaplin on the bridge, and at the same time have immediate access to the telephone just inside. That was, of course, until someone bright remembered the telephones and cut them off.

"Do you recognize either of them?" Gremiakin asked, stepping out.

"Too far."

"Armed?"

"Nothing visible."

Gremiakin looked up at Kaplin. "Warn the others up there. It might be a diversion."

Kaplin disappeared across the bridge. Two of Gremiakin's bullyboys were watching the roof. The other two, watching the central corridor from the second floor, would have heard the exchange below.

"If all they want to do is talk, we'll talk," Gremiakin called softly in the darkness.

"They might want to see our prisoners."

"We'll negotiate that. Any sign of the media?"

"Not yet."

After he had warned the two men watching the roof, Kaplin hurried back to the telephone switchboard room on the third floor, where Larissa Dolya waited with Mukhin and Boyarov. The only door to the room was thick steel, almost as secure as a bank vault door. Telephones were as important as gold.

"There are two people coming across the square toward us," he told them. Larissa was starting to recover, but she was still very pale and extremely nervous.

"The Western press or television?" Mukhin asked. He was a heavy-set man with thick white hair.

"Not yet."

"Shit, I recognize one of those pricks, now," Miroshnichenko swore. He turned again to Gremiakin. "He's a One man, name of Grigoriev. Oldest fucking lieutenant over there."

Kaplin had come back to the bridge. "Grigoriev?" he bellowed. "Did you say Grigoriev?"

"Was he the one, Anatoli?" Gremiakin called up.

"Yes. Let the *pizda* in. I'm coming down."

"Stay there," Gremiakin shouted, but Kaplin was already gone.

"Do you want me to kill the bastards?" Miroshnichenko asked.

"No. Let them in," Gremiakin replied, switching his AK-47's safety catch to the off position.

Grigoriev got the impression of someone or something very large standing just within the main entrance to the department store, and he had a little premonition that he might be walking to his death. But he shook it off and yanked open one of the doors, and stepped inside the central corridor, Andreyev right behind him.

"That's far enough," someone said from the darkness to his right, and Grigoriev started to turn, when something shoved Andreyev into him with tremendous force, causing him to stumble and fall to his knees.

They waited on Pennsylvania Avenue in front of the U.S. Information Agency, Senarighi figuring that if Privet was heading toward Andrews Air Force Base, they would have to pass this way.

The surveillance post in Georgetown had picked up on the telephone call as well, and had come to the same conclusion. Base Security had been notified that a hostage situation was coming their way, and several Bureau units had already been dispatched. "But keep them out of sight," Sweeney had warned. "There's no telling what this Russian is going to do if he's confronted by what he perceives as a no-win situation."

"Unit two, this is seventeen. Geronimo and party just passed the Four Seasons Hotel. They are definitely heading down Pennsylvania."

"Roger, copy," Senarighi radioed.

"Unit two, headquarters. We've got that information for you."

"Go ahead," Senarighi responded. He was watching in the rearview mirror for Tyson's gray Mercedes sedan to show up.

"Geronimo ordered the C21 readied for him. That's the VIP Learjet. It's on the apron right now, with the crew standing by."

"Destination?" Sweeney asked, and Senarighi relayed the question.

"It's confirmed. Reykjavík, Iceland. Flying time four hours, and once Privet is there he's home free. The Icelanders cooperate with the Russians as much as they do us, even though we've got military bases up there."

"Then we don't let them get that far," Sweeney said.

"Might be tough to do if you don't want to risk Tyson or his wife."

Sweeney looked back at Marina. "We'll see," he said. "That is, if you're up to it."

She nodded uncertainly. "I don't want anyone else to get hurt . . ."

"Don't say that," Senarighi warned.

"All right, here they come."

Sweeney jumped out of the car and helped Marina out. The snow had begun to slow down, but the temperature was dropping. She was shivering violently.

Tyson's Mercedes was a half block away when Sweeney led an unresisting Marina around the front of the car to the street side.

He waited for two cabs to pass and then stepped out away from the car with her. At the last moment she raised her right hand, as Sweeney had instructed her to do, and the Mercedes passed, Tyson looking out at them from the passenger side in the front, his eyes wide, his mouth open.

It was her standing on the street with that man. God in heaven, he'd been instantly transported back thirty years to Kent State, and Marina. Lovely, understanding, warm, and patient Marina.

So Joseph had been telling him the truth that night at the Rive Gauche. She had come all the way from Russia to see him. Not to see her father, Joseph. It wasn't Joseph back there with her.

"We've picked up another tail," Privet was saying in the backseat, but Tyson was barely hearing him.

Marina's face, what he'd been able to see of it as they had passed, was the same as her mother's. There'd been no doubt in his mind, even in that brief glance, who she was. But there'd been nothing of Joseph in her. Nor had Joseph given him any explanation, other than the message that she was coming to the United States.

Joseph had given his wife . . .

Or had he? Marina had been a free spirit in those days when "free spirit" seemed to mean something to nearly everybody. He'd once tried to kid her about it, since she was Russian, but she'd gotten angry. "What, don't you think we have poets in the Soviet Union? Do you think they all work for the state? You think they are not free here?" She hit a fist against her own chest. "You don't understand."

Tyson turned in his seat to see if he could still catch a glimpse of her, but they'd already gone too far, and Privet was asking him something. The words flowed around him; he could hear what the man was saying, but it made no sense whatsoever.

Marina, the daughter, had come to the United States to see who . . . ?

Her father, it suddenly came to Tyson. She'd come this far to see her father. Not Joseph, though Joseph may have had a hand in getting her here. She'd not come to see Joseph.

Tyson turned that thought over with amazement. Marina Demin, the girl who had come here to the United States from Russia, was his daughter. Conceived on the campus of Kent State. Joseph had been cuckolded by his wife, by the state, and now by this girl.

They'd passed the White House, and Kit turned right on 15th Street and then left on E Street past the National Theater, where she picked up Pennsylvania Avenue again, the Capitol complex nine blocks straight ahead.

Kit had been glancing over at him, a look of concern mingled with fear. "What is it?" she asked. "What's the matter?"

Tyson looked at her. What to say? How to explain after all these years, and especially after what had gone on . . . what he had caused to go on between him and Toni? He had not been able to finish his letter to Debbie because he'd felt so guilty.

Now what?

"You know that girl back there?" Privet asked.

Tyson glanced back at him and then turned again to his wife. "Yes," he said. "I do."

"Who is she?" Privet asked, and it sounded to Tyson as if the Russian knew the answer.

"What girl?" Kit asked. "What are you talking about?"

"The girl standing at the side of the street. Just before the White House," Tyson explained.

Kit shook her head. She'd evidently not noticed.

"She's a Russian, and she came here, or was sent here, to see me."

"Why?"

"I think they wanted me to become a spy for them."

"Why her, Al? Why did they send that girl? What is she to you? Another mistress? How many do you have? Or should I say, how many *more* do you have?"

How to tell her? Tyson asked himself.

"Who is she?" Kit screeched.

"My daughter," Tyson replied.

Grigoriev got to his feet as Kaplin emerged into the central corridor, but his eyes were drawn to Gremiakin, who stood much nearer. He could hardly believe it. The man was an executive secretary of the KGB's School One. Trusted. Well respected. A power.

"Comrade Gremiakin?" he said. "Are you unharmed . . . ?" Grigoriev suddenly realized that Gremiakin was holding an AK-47. It dawned on him that the man wasn't a prisoner here. In fact, he was one of the conspirators, and that realization staggered him.

"Search them for weapons or transmitting devices," Gremiakin said.

One of the bullyboys had come down from the second floor and he watched the activity on Red Square from the front door as Miroshnichenko quickly patted down Grigoriev first, and then Andreyev. He missed the weapons stuffed down the fronts of their trousers, but then he'd never been a One man. Grigoriev suddenly regained some of his confidence.

Miroshnichenko stepped aside. "They're clean," he said.

Kaplin stepped up, an intense, almost maniacal grin on his craggy face.

"We've come to take you back, traitor Kaplin," Grigoriev said harshly. "You and your whore. As for these others, I don't care what happens to them, but you are my prisoners."

Kaplin smashed his fist into Grigoriev's face without warning, sending the man sprawling flat on his back, his legs spread. Without hesitation, Kaplin stepped forward and kicked the downed man in the groin with every gram of his strength.

Kaplin's steel-toed boot had driven the pistol into Grigoriev's pelvis, cracking it. He had never realized how intensely pain could dominate a body. He did not think about the prisoners on whom he had inflicted pain; he thought only about his own, searing, screeching agony that rebounded from his groin to his armpits, and then upward to his head, threatening to blow off the back of his skull.

He was retching, and each time he spasmed his pain spiked, and he truly wished at those moments that he were dead.

Kaplin hauled him off the floor and shook him like a rag doll.

"If you fall down, comrade interrogator, I will crush your balls like you crushed mine," Kaplin's voice came in Grigoriev's ear.

Gradually he became aware that there were others standing around him, besides Kaplin. Andreyev, Gremiakin, and the one who had searched him. They were watching him, tense, expectant expressions on their faces. They wanted him to fall down.

Kaplin let go, and Grigoriev staggered back a pace on rubbery legs, but then regained his balance. "Fuck you, traitor. When you're back in Lefortovo, which you will be soon, you'll be sorry you ever laid a hand on your betters."

"Come," Kaplin said, almost gently now, taking Grigoriev by the arm. "There is someone upstairs who would like to see you, and although there may not be a hose up there, we'll figure out something."

"Anatoli . . ." Gremiakin warned.

Kaplin turned toward the man. "Don't interfere. This one is mine, and Larissa's."

* * *

Kaplin could barely contain his own anger, not only toward Grigoriev and the system that still allowed men like him to flourish, but at himself as well, for the depth of his own cruelty. He was reminded of a peasant proverb his grandmother had used to describe Russians, high or low. Wash a pig as much as you like, she said. It goes right back to the mud.

It made him stop for a moment to wonder if Grigoriev's hate for a person he considered to be a traitor justified his cruelty as completely as Kaplin's hate for the torturer justified his own evil intent. It didn't matter. The strongest were the most just, and now it was his turn.

"Go with them, Fedor," Gremiakin said.

Miroshnichenko followed Kaplin, who had to help Grigoriev up the stairs to the third floor, then along the interior corridor to the telephone switchboard room.

Boyarov had been standing in the doorway, and Grigoriev was rocked by the presence of yet another high-ranking KGB officer. But he said nothing.

Inside, Mukhin and Larissa Dolya had been talking. She looked up, her expression blank for a long time, but suddenly her eyes widened when she realized who stood there. She jumped up, knocking over her glass of tea.

"At least one of you bastards knows enough to show a little respect for the proper authority," Grigoriev said.

Kaplin shoved him headlong into the room, driving him once more to his knees.

Sweeney and Marina climbed back in the car and Senarighi was rolling even before the door was closed. Tyson's Mercedes had already turned the corner by the Treasury and was out of sight for the moment.

Marina was shaking even more violently than before, her eyes moist, her lips moving as if she were trying to say something.

"Did you see the look on his face?" Senarighi asked. "He spotted her, all right. Not only that, he recognized her."

"Did you recognize him?" Sweeney asked.

Marina looked up and nodded. "He's my father," she said in a small voice. "What is he doing here in Washington? What is going to happen?"

"I don't know for sure, but we're going to try to catch up with him, and I'll want you to say something to him."

"Say what?" Marina asked.

"Whatever Major Kiselev sent you here to say," Sweeney said.

Kit Tyson was in shock, her driving wooden, automatic. She refused to look at her husband, and he didn't know what else to say to her if she did. His explanation would come out hollow. He'd been a radical in college. A communist for a short time. He had slept with the Russian wife of a radical student leader, and she'd had his child, who'd evidently come to America to try to turn him.

They passed the Peace Monument in front of the Capitol and headed left around the circular drive, traffic picking up a little.

He'd dedicated his life to service to his country because he'd truly believed the road to survival was through peaceful negotiation and not war. Now he was being asked what it would take for him to betray his country, if not that ideal.

In some respects he had already betrayed his country through his relationship with Toni Wagner. He certainly had betrayed Kit, and he'd definitely betrayed the President.

What now?

He wasn't sure, but he did know that he would not get on any plane with a self-professed assassin.

"Larissa Dolya has surfaced, and we've got big trouble," David Zuckerman told Rodgers as they entered the embassy screened room.

Tony Havlachek, the embassy's general counsel and expert in Russian law, was waiting for them, his hair mussed as if he'd just gotten out of bed, which considering the late hour, he probably had.

"Where is she?" Rodgers asked.

"GUM, along with just about everybody in Sweeney's MOHAWK network," Zuckerman said. "The ambassador has been notified, but you're going to have to authorize a flash to Langley."

"What the hell is going on, David? Give it to me straight."

"I don't have all the answers yet. But twenty minutes ago we got a call at Spasso House from Stuart Rittenhouse, CBS television, wanting to know what we knew about some sort of a terrorist attack on GUM, which made no sense to me until he started naming names. MOHAWK names, plus Larissa Dolya's."

"Kaplin?"

Zuckerman nodded. "Evidently Rittenhouse got a call from the terrorists who've taken over the department store, and are going to hold it until they can speak with representatives from as many of the Western media as possible. I guess they called everybody."

"Have you any idea what's going on?" Havlachek asked.

"No," Rodgers said. "I'll send off the flash, and then get over there myself."

"Be careful, Roy, this is supposedly a Russian matter. There are no Americans inside, if Miss Dolya's cover is intact."

"Maybe not, but our news people will be on the scene, so it'll be in our interest to be there as well."

"Oh, by the way, have you seen Bill Seagren?" Zuckerman asked.

"Should be in his apartment."

"I checked, he's not there. In fact, he's nowhere in the embassy."

"He probably got word and went over there on his own," Rodgers said on the way out, but that explanation made no sense to him whatsoever.

A dark rage engulfed Grigoriev. He was in a veritable den of traitors. And they had dared to manhandle him in retaliation for his actions at Lefortovo. But he'd been doin his duty: investigating treason. He could not be faulted for that.

He managed to pull the Makarov pistol from inside his trousers, pain coming at him in waves. Switching the safety catch off, and cocking the hammer, he rolled over. Kaplin was off to his left, but Miroshnichenko's bulky form filled the doorway.

Grigoriev fired four times in rapid succession, all four shots hitting Miroshnichenko in the torso, and driving the man back out into the corridor.

He started to switch his aim, when Kaplin kicked his gun hand, dislodging the pistol, which discharged when it hit the floor. Larissa Dolya cried out sharply.

Kaplin grabbed the front of Grigoriev's coat and bodily hauled him off the floor, tossing him up against the switchboard as if he were a toy.

This time the pain exploded in his head, but through the haze that seemed to cover his eyes he could see that the woman had been hit in the chest by the accidental shot. A spreading patch of blood stained the front of her sweater.

Mukhin was helping the girl, and Boyarov was shouting something from out in the corridor, but Kaplin was like a madman. He kept coming and coming, smashing Grigoriev's body against the switchboard.

"The whore will die here," Grigoriev croaked.

Kaplin dragged him away from the switchboard and hauled him out into the corridor, shoving Boyarov aside. Someone was coming up the corridor in a dead run.

Kaplin turned in the opposite direction and, half dragging, half carrying Grigoriev, hurried ten meters to an archway that opened onto the gracefully arcing footbridge that spanned the central corridor.

"Anatoli," someone called from below, his voice echoing hollowly.

"You'll all die in here," Grigoriev croaked. "Too bad, because, you know, I wanted to fuck that little whore of yours."

Kaplin was insane. "Chekist bastard," he shouted, and he

picked Grigoriev off his feet and flung him head first over the railing.

Grigoriev could not believe what was happening to him, but he had only a second or two in which to ponder his mistakes before the unyielding marble floor suddenly rushed up to meet his face.

Major Kiselev showed his KGB identification booklet to the perimeter Militiamen, and worked his way over to the on-site commander's Moskvich parked directly across from GUM's main doors.

A man had just emerged from the department store, his hands over his head, and he rushed across the sixty or seventy meters of open ground.

Kiselev held back for a moment. "Who is that?" he asked the Militiaman standing next to him.

"KGB. He and another one went inside ten minutes ago. No telling what happened to his partner."

"Something important is happening over there, Major," General Ryazanov told him on the telephone. "Contain the situation at all costs. The stakes are very high. You understand."

"Yes," Kiselev said. "I understand, Comrade General."

Mukhin had been Homeward Bound's weak link on two accounts. In the first place, he'd told the traitor Kaplin that he had no knowledge of Marina Demin, and in the second, it was he who had supplied Yeltsin's special investigative unit with the necessary passwords to break into the Komitet's computer system.

One disaster piled atop the other. Blood was being spilled. Kiselev wanted to make sure none of it was his.

"They killed him! They killed him!" the KGB officer was shouting.

Kiselev pulled out his identification booklet again, and pushed forward to where the Militia on-site commander and his people had gathered around the KGB officer. The commander's name tag read "Solyakov."

"Captain, I'm KGB Major Kiselev. I am taking charge here," Kiselev said.

Solyakov turned, looked at Kiselev's face and then his identification booklet. "Be my guest, Comrade Major. Already one of your fools has gotten himself killed."

"What happened in there?" Kiselev demanded.

Andreyev was shaken, but he knew enough to understand that if Kiselev was involved, this must be very important. He told them exactly what had happened so far as he knew it.

"There were gunshots, and shortly afterward Kaplin threw your partner's body over the rail?" Kiselev asked.

"No, Comrade Major. Not Valentin's *body*. He was alive, awake even. I saw the look on his face when he hit the floor."

Even the Militia captain was impressed. "What do they want?" he asked.

"They've called the Western news media. They said they will kill the hostages unless they are allowed to talk to the television and newspaper people."

"No," Kiselev snapped.

Solyakov looked at him. "What?"

"First of all there are no hostages."

"They say they're holding Minister Mikhail Mukhin and one of your people, Colonel Vitali Boyarov."

"Both of those men are under investigation for treason," Kiselev replied. "They are plotters. They want to bring down President Yeltsin. Even kill him. It's worse than August."

The captain held back some remark.

"They will not be allowed to talk to anyone," Kiselev said. "Telephone them, tell them they must surrender immediately. Then cut off the phones and the electricity, and send your men in."

"Send my men in?" Captain Solyakov asked.

"Yes. To bring the traitors out, or kill them. Frankly, I don't care which."

"They have weapons."

"I'm sure they do."

"And you will lead this charge, Comrade Major?"

"Of course," Kiselev said. "And you, Comrade Captain, will be at my side."

Miroshnichenko was dead, but Larissa Dolya was all right for the moment, although she had lost a lot of blood. The stray bullet, which had ricocheted off the switchboard, had become distorted and had torn a fairly large hole in her left shoulder. So far as they could tell, it had missed her lung and any major artery, but it had done a lot of tissue and muscle damage.

Kaplin was seeing spots in front of his eyes as he looked over Boyarov's shoulder. The man worked to staunch the flow of blood from her wound. She smiled up at him.

"Anatoli . . . ?" she said, when a line on the switchboard buzzed.

Kaplin got to it before Mukhin could, and he picked up the phone. "*Da.*"

"This is the Militia. We have you surrounded, and you now have sixty seconds in which to come out, unarmed, with your hands over your heads. Do you understand this?"

"Fuck your mother," Kaplin swore, and he slammed down the telephone. "They're coming for us," he told the others, then hurried back out to the bridge to warn everyone else.

Contain the situation at all costs. The general's words came back to Kiselev as he flattened himself against the wall one meter from GUM's front entrance. Solyakov had pulled up on the other side. They both carried satchel charges.

The periphery of the square had filled with people. Many of them, the Militia had reported, were Western news-media reporters, photographers, and cameramen. The traitors inside GUM had apparently notified every non-Russian in Moscow about what was happening here.

It was becoming increasingly difficult for the Militia to control them. But the general wanted the situation contained, which meant the Western press had to be kept out, and what fighting was necessary was to be confined within the department store, and was to be done in the shortest possible time and with the minimum possible force.

As Captain Solyakov said: "Three instructions completely opposite of each other."

A dozen Militiamen, equipped with riot gear and bullet-proof vests, and armed with a mix of riot guns, automatic weapons, and tear gas launchers, were lined up behind Kiselev on one side of the main doors, and behind Solyakov on the other side.

A similar force waited at the rear of the building, and marksmen had been sent to the roofs of the adjacent buildings, including Lenin's Tomb directly across the square.

Kiselev nodded to Solyakov, and in unison they both switched their satchel charge timers to four seconds, but Kiselev held his release button as Solyakov rolled around the corner, tossed his bag up against the door, and rolled back.

The explosive went off with a sharp bang, blowing open the front door.

Kiselev released his timer, rolled around the corner, and tossed the bag through the opening.

Gremiakin's bullyboy at the front door was killed in the first explosion, the front of his body cut to ribbons by flying glass, steel, and pieces of concrete. Gremiakin himself, realizing that a second explosion would come on the heels of the first, had just managed to pull back into the shop when it happened, the force of it knocking him off his feet.

Someone began shooting from the second floor, and a split second later more automatic weapon fire came from above on the bridge.

He would have bet almost anything that the Militia wouldn't have gone this far this fast. Someone else was behind the attack, and it had to be KGB.

"There they are," Senarighi said as they came around the back side of the Capitol building. Tyson's Mercedes was just turning down one of the curving driveways to Independence Avenue which led past the Library of Congress to Pennsylvania Avenue. The car was moving erratically all over the road, as if the tires were getting no traction.

"Something's wrong," Sweeney said. "Fall back a little, let's give them some room."

Senarighi slowed down as the Mercedes shot out onto Independence in front of a yellow cab. There was no chance to avoid a collision. The cab smashed into the Mercedes' right rear fender, sending the car spinning on the icy street.

Senarighi pulled to a stop, skidding sideways half out onto the avenue, as the Mercedes plowed into a snowbank blocking the broad sidewalk up to the library.

Both front doors popped open. Tyson jumped out one side and his wife got out on the other.

Sweeney scrambled out, drawing his pistol and, hunching over, started across the avenue. "Get down! Get down!" he shouted.

Kit Tyson looked his way and pulled up short, but Tyson turned and sprinted up toward the library's loading docks.

The rear door of the Mercedes popped open, and Privet jumped out. He fired two shots at Sweeney, who dove facedown in the street, and then raced around the corner and down the ramp after Tyson.

The assassin was interested in only one target: the assistant national security adviser, and not the wife. It was Tyson's only hope as he tore open the service door and paused just long enough to make sure Privet was behind him, before plunging into the labyrinth of the Library of Congress.

Tyson had been here only twice before. He was counting on the likelihood that the assassin had never been here, and that whoever was following them—probably the FBI—would make it in time to effect a rescue.

If nothing else, however, he'd drawn Privet away from Kit. It was something.

Sweeney hauled Kit Tyson to her feet and hustled her back to the car, where Senarighi was already on the radio asking for backup.

"Are you all right?" Sweeney asked her.

She was half hysterical, crying something about a daughter. It was difficult to make sense of anything she was saying.

Senarighi stopped in midspeech, releasing the microphone button. "Daughter?" he asked Sweeney.

"What do you mean, Mrs. Tyson? Whose daughter? Where?"

Kit Tyson looked up into Sweeney's eyes, hers filled with tears, then looked over at Marina Demin still seated in the car. "Her," she said.

"What about her?"

Kit Tyson looked back into Sweeney's eyes. "She is my husband's daughter."

"How do you know?" Sweeney asked. "Who told you?"

"He did. My husband told me."

"Stay with her," Sweeney told Senarighi. "He's admitted it, which means he's innocent, and Privet will have to kill him." He turned and headed across the street in a dead run, Senarighi shouting something.

Kiselev's operation had been delicate and deadly. He'd planned, by using Raya Nechiporenko and Marina Demin . . . who were to do nothing but tell the truth . . . to try to discredit Tyson in the eyes of the American authorities. They were to do it in such a way that the CIA and FBI would believe that Tyson was the victim of a Russian plot to turn him.

But that was only one part of an operation they were apparently calling Homeward Bound. The two women's real mission was to unhinge Tyson to the degree that he would, in one rash moment, agree to cooperate with them by handing over some forged document to a *Washington Post* reporter. That document purported to prove that the American government had contributed somehow to the August 19th Kremlin coup by secretly supporting the conspirators while openly supporting Gorbachev.

Senarighi had outlined everything Special Agent Wilson had overheard in Privet's telephone conversation with his control officer.

Of course Tyson could not be counted on to become a permanent agent for the KGB hard-liners, who'd meant to use this triumph to regain some of the power they had lost, so Privet was to have assassinated the assistant national security adviser as soon as the document was in the hands of the press. Privet, in turn, was to be killed, leaving no loose ends.

But something had gone wrong, possibly in Moscow, and the operation had been called off.

Privet was a desperate man. Under a death sentence at home, he was apparently lashing out at anything that stood in his way of escape. Tyson was his prime target.

Sweeney yanked open the service door and entered the library. He stood just within the loading area for a second, catching his breath and trying to listen for the other two men.

The library was open, but there wouldn't be many people here because of the weather.

Then Sweeney spotted the wet footprints across the loading area and into a rear corridor. Tyson and Privet had both tracked in snow on their shoes.

The room was vast, it seemed to go on forever, and yet the space seemed intimate because of the hundreds of thousands of books crammed onto the shelves. Privet took out his .22 automatic pistol, screwed the can silencer onto the end of the barrel, and followed Tyson's footprints into the maze.

He was getting an erection, and his blood was beginning to sing. He'd been too long in America, too long on this one assignment. It was time now for him to make the kill and then get away.

In his idle time over the past few days he'd studied maps and booklets on Washington. Twenty meters from here was the entrance to the tunnel that ran under First Street to the Capitol building. He would make his escape from there.

There was an underground passageway between the library and the Capitol complex. Tyson had been in it once a couple of years ago, but he'd been with a group of congressmen and hadn't paid much attention. Now he was turned around; he no longer knew which direction was toward the east down here. In fact, he no longer knew the way back to the stairs he had come down.

If he could reach either the tunnel or the stairs, he might be able to sneak past Privet and get out. But he was going to have to get lucky, and soon.

He stopped at the end of the row and cautiously peered around the corner both ways down the broader corridor. No one was here. On a normal day there would be library clerks removing or returning books, but the weather had apparently stopped returns and orders.

If he survived this ordeal, what would he say to the President? How would he even be able to face the man? There would be a public trial. Disgrace. Christ, where had it gone wrong? At what point had his conceit ruined his ability to think rationally?

Making sure the corridor was still clear, Tyson hurriedly stepped across into the next row, as something made a book jump on the shelf about head height just behind him. He turned and looked back.

One of the books on the shelf had been pushed farther back. He stood flat-footed staring at it. In the dim light he could make out a small hole in the spine of the book. A bullet hole! Privet!

Spinning on his heel, Tyson raced to the end of the row, turned left down a narrow aisle, then right again down another row.

He stopped short and held his breath to listen. There were footsteps behind him, off to the left, for just a second, and then they stopped.

Privet was right behind him. But how?

Tyson looked down, suddenly realizing that his feet were wet. He'd left tracks. He took off his shoes and then hurried silently to the end of the row and started right, when something very hot and very sharp penetrated his left arm just above his elbow. There was no pain, but his hand went instantly numb, and he dropped his shoes.

He'd been shot. Blood started to ooze from the wound.

He fell back into the row he'd just come out of as a bullet ricocheted off the metal bookshelves inches away from him.

Christ, Privet was right there.

Tyson turned and ran headlong down the row, skidding to the right in the aisle and immediately left again down the next row, crashing into a roll-about cart filled with books.

Tyson was in trouble. He was bleeding and he had crashed into something. Privet could hear the man grunting like a pig that knows it is about to be killed and gutted.

Taking his time now—Tyson was still thrashing around, trying to extricate himself from whatever he'd crashed into—Privet stepped out into the aisle and followed the trail of blood.

The wet footsteps finally petered out, and Sweeney ranged in a zigzag pattern through the seemingly endless rows of aisles of floor-to-ceiling bookstacks. He stopped every ten or fifteen seconds to listen for a sound, any sound that might indicate Privet or Tyson was nearby. He carried his .9-millimeter Beretta automatic, the safety off, the hammer cocked.

When the crash came, it was close and off to his left. Sweeney turned directly and hurried down the aisle in that direction, taking great care to make as little noise as possible.

His heart was hammering and his mouth was dry, and when Privet stepped out into the aisle barely fifteen feet away, Sweeney nearly shot him.

The Russian could have been anyone: a bureaucrat, a tourist, a clerk, one of a hundred thousand exactly like him. But this one stopped at the intersection between two rows and raised his pistol.

"Privet," Sweeney shouted, raising his own gun.

The Russian spun around in surprise. For an instant it was clear he could not make a decision, but then his gun hand started to come around.

"No," Sweeney shouted, and a moment later he fired three shots. The first caught Privet in the left side, spinning him around; the second hit him in the chest; and the third slammed into his forehead, blowing out the back of his head as he fell.

Gremiakin ejected the spent clip from his AK-47 and slapped his last into place as the heavy thump of still another explosion came from the rear of the department store. The bastards had blown the back door. He couldn't remember which of his men was back there, but it was a safe bet he was dead by now. As they would all be soon. If only the Western press and television reporters had shown up.

Holding the assault rifle out in front of him, Gremiakin pointed it around the corner and squeezed off a burst. Someone cried out in pain.

Returning fire slammed into the stone beside the doorway in which Gremiakin crouched, sending sharp chips flying into his face and eyes, blood spurting down his forehead and obliterating his vision.

"Bastards," he shouted at the top of his lungs, and leaped out into the central corridor, firing toward the main doors as he moved.

At least fifteen bullets slammed into his legs, his head, and his neck, knocking him out of his shoes, killing him before he stopped falling.

Kaplin just managed to get off the bridge a second after Gremiakin had gone down, when an explosion lifted its center section two meters straight up, and it began to tumble and fall. The force from the blast had also blown a huge hole in the skylights, glass flying everywhere.

Back at the opening, he fired the last of his ammunition down into the central corridor, and then fell back.

It was over now. None of them had believed they would survive this night. But if it got Western attention, then they would have succeeded.

The sound of the battle below him in the corridor was intense. The Militia, the KGB, the Army, whoever it was, knew their business, and were not fooling around.

Pushing himself away from the wall he'd been leaning against, he went back to the switchboard room.

The instant the firing stopped from the bridge archway on the third floor, Kiselev moved out from under the protection of the shop doorway and scanned the second and third levels on the northwest side of the central corridor.

Solyakov, who'd turned out to be a damned good fighter, did the same on the other side.

They'd each lost three men. So far, Kiselev added in his head. So far.

There was a short burst of firing from above, inside the building somewhere, probably from the troops who'd come in through the back. They'd radioed that they'd put down two hostiles and were working their way up to the third floor.

The building fell silent.

Solyakov looked at Kiselev with a questioning shrug. There was a movement above.

Kiselev swung his assault rifle in that direction. Second floor. Someone in the doorway of a shop. A man. Unarmed, his hands over his head. He stepped out onto the walkway.

For a moment Kiselev looked up at the man. Then he squeezed the AK-47's trigger, driving the traitor backward into the glass storefront in a spray of blood.

Larissa was alone in the switchboard room, huddled in the corner. She was shivering.

"Where are the others?" he asked her.

She looked up and shook her head, unable to speak.

The firing had stopped. It meant everyone else was either dead or captured. If they were taken alive, they would be sent back to Lefortovo. Kaplin knew that he could not handle that. Not now. Not ever again. Neither could Larissa. They had nothing left to give, no strength with which to endure.

"Come, little one, it's time to leave," Kaplin said, gently helping her to her feet.

Outside in the corridor he could hear someone coming,

boots loud on the wooden floors. He turned the other way and he and Larissa shuffled painfully away.

"Clear up here," Solyakov's walkie-talkie blared.

"Any survivors among the hostiles?" the Militia captain radioed back. He was slightly sick to his stomach. This carnage had been unnecessary.

"No, Comrade Captain. There are no survivors."

Solyakov looked at Kiselev, who seemed smugly satisfied. "There, it is done."

Kiselev started to nod as a very strong white light suddenly illuminated the interior of the central corridor.

"What the fuck . . ." He spun on his heel as more lights came on, and dozens of people streamed through the broad opening blasted in the storefront.

"Major Kiselev," a man shouted from behind the lights. "Major Kiselev, can you tell us what has happened here?"

"What is this?" Kiselev roared. "Who are these people?"

"Dan Boyer, ABC News," the man shouted.

27

SWEENEY PICKED UP A TELEPHONE ON THE WALL AT THE END OF the stacks where Tyson had gone down, and dialed Drury's number at Langley.

He'd stuffed his handkerchief inside Tyson's shirt sleeve to staunch the flow of blood, and helped the man to the table and chair near the phone.

"It'll be all right now, Mr. Tyson," Sweeney told him. "Privet is dead."

While Sweeney waited for his call to go through, he looked over at Tyson, who was watching him.

"It was you," Tyson said.

"Me?"

"At the side of the road with . . ."

"Your daughter?" Sweeney said. "Yes, sir, it was me."

"What's she like . . . ?" Tyson asked, but Drury was on the line, and Sweeney turned his attention away.

"Where the hell are you, Richard?" Drury asked. "Christ, the Bureau is all over our asses."

"I'm at the Library of Congress," Sweeney said. "With Tyson and one dead Russian assassin."

"Son of a bitch," Drury said after a slight hesitation.

"You can say that again. What I'm going to need is some help. Tyson's been wounded in the arm, and I don't want him to go into shock on me. Besides, there's no telling if any of the opposition is around. I'm about done in on gunfights, if you know what I mean."

"What about the Bureau?"

"Out front for the moment, but I don't think it'll be long before they get down here."

"Help is on its way, Richard. Just hang on. And for God's sake, don't lose Tyson."

"No," Sweeney said, and he hung up. Tyson was still looking at him.

"What's she like?" Tyson asked.

"Very Russian, Mr. Tyson," Sweeney replied. "Very Russian."

A Company helicopter touched down on the Capitol grounds across the street from the library about the same time the ambulance and a half dozen FBI units showed up.

Adkins climbed down from the chopper, and keeping low, hurried out from under the rotor blades and got into the backseat of Young's chauffeur-driven limousine.

"Tyson is innocent," Adkins said without greeting the FBI man.

"So it would seem," Young agreed. "At least innocent of actually being a spy. But he showed damned poor judgment in his choice of mistresses. A Russian in the sixties and another now."

"So he's out as national security adviser. From what I'm told, the President's friend Charles Gleason has agreed to come over from Reston to take the job."

"Not soon enough."

The ambulance attendants hustled into the library with a stretcher.

"Where do we go next?" Adkins asked.

"The President isn't happy and neither is Wilder."

"Nor is Vaughan. But the question stands, where do we go from here?" Adkins said.

"Well, to start with, there's no question about Tyson returning to any sort of government service."

"Agreed. But we wouldn't like to see this come to trial."

"We?" Young asked pointedly, but Adkins didn't answer. "No, a trial would be counterproductive. But then they were successful, to a point."

"If their object was to bring Tyson down, then yes, they were," Adkins said.

"That other, with the forged White House memo, wouldn't have worked. No one would have swallowed it."

"Lydia Lubiako showed up on our doorstep, you know, with the memo. It's crude, but it might have worked. There're enough people out there who'd love another conspiracy theory. Hell, they're still questioning the Warren Commission report on Kennedy's assassination."

"It's the name of the game . . ." Young said, but Adkins cut him off.

"No game. Real people get killed, real people's lives get all shot to hell. In the meantime it's still us and the Russians with gun barrels hidden now, but still pointed at each other's heads, and our fingers on the nuclear triggers. So, we spy, and they spy. We just hope it doesn't get out of hand too often."

"Like this time?"

"Like this time," Adkins agreed.

Sweeney came up with the ambulance attendants, bearing Tyson on the wheeled stretcher. Senarighi was waiting with Kit Tyson and Marina Demin. Neither of them had said a word to each other.

Kit let out a little cry and broke away from Senarighi, rushing to her husband's side. "They said you were shot, but they wouldn't let me come down to be with you."

Tyson smiled wanly. His complexion was pale. "It's al right now," he said.

"Are you sure?" she asked. She looked up at Sweeney. "Is he going to be all right?"

"Your husband was shot in the arm, Mrs. Tyson. He'll be just fine. But he has to go to the hospital."

"I'll ride in the ambulance with him," Kit said.

"Fine," Sweeney told her.

She turned to look over at Marina Demin. "If you want to come along, you may."

Marina shook her head.

"He's your father."

Marina turned, looked at Senarighi, and then climbed back in the car.

Captain Solyakov watched as ambulance attendants began removing the first of the bodies the back way through the loading dock area. After the first confused minutes when Western journalists and cameramen seemed to be everywhere, the Militia had managed to restore some semblance of order. Now a police line had been set up ten meters from the front doors, beyond which no civilian was allowed to come. A public relations officer, from Militia Headquarters, had taken charge outside.

Kiselev had disappeared almost immediately. And no one had seen him since. Which was too bad, Solyakov thought bitterly. It would have been good to have the major here to share in the spotlight, and the glory.

"Still no luck finding them, Comrade Captain," Lieutenant Petr Zhurkov said. He was second in command.

Solyakov turned to him. "Get the building engineer down here with blueprints. They could not have simply walked off. It means they're still here somewhere. Hiding in some little hole or corner."

"Maybe the list they released was in error. Maybe they were lying."

"Not about that, I think. Just do as I say."

"Yes, sir," Zhurkov said.

28

THERE WAS DARKNESS EVERYWHERE, AND WETNESS. THE walls were slimy with dampness, and there was a ferocious odor of rot and death.

Larissa had managed with some help to get all the way down into a subbasement beneath the big department store. But at that point she had collapsed and Kaplin had had to carry her like a baby in his arms. He feared now that she was dead.

There were dozens of underground rivers in Moscow and the city's subterranean structure was honeycombed with storm sewers and arched watercourses through which many of the rivers were channeled. In the spring and through much of the summer all the underground tunnels were filled with raging torrents of water. But by fall and winter many of them were dry or nearly dry. Many of them, not all.

Kaplin had gotten lucky with his choice. Down a steel-runged ladder five meters beneath GUM's subbasement he'd had five choices: five different branches of one tunnel. He chose the one he thought ran east or slightly northeast, in the general direction of the American Embassy, nearly three kilometers away, and more important, the one that ran *away* from the Moscow River. He hadn't survived this long only to drown.

Kaplin was convinced that the tunnel was gradually rising. He hadn't been able to see anything, but he felt it in his legs, in the extra effort it took to walk, and in the fact that the tunnel seemed to be getting drier. Now he was sure that he was beginning to be able to see, to just make out a very dim grayness ahead, and he picked up his pace.

Larissa moaned and a big smile broke out on his face. She was alive! "It's all right now, little one," he cooed. "Soon we will be warm and dry."

What little light there was came fifty meters later down a shaft that led five meters or so straight up to the street. Holding Larissa with one hand, Kaplin awkwardly climbed the ladder using his other, and at the top heaved the heavy manhole cover open with his shoulder.

They had come up in the middle of a very broad boulevard, a large building directly across. For a moment Kaplin didn't recognize anything, until he turned around. Behind him was a broad park, beyond which the east walls of the Kremlin rose into the night sky. It was the Alexander Gardens. They'd crossed completely under Red Square and the Kremlin, and were on the other side.

Kaplin climbed the rest of the way out of the storm sewer, replaced the manhole cover, and hurried a half block down to the Metro station. There was absolutely no traffic at this hour, though he could still hear sirens from the other side of the Kremlin. The authorities would be searching for him and Larissa at GUM.

It was too late at night for the Metro trains to be running, but the upper part of the entryway was open. Kaplin propped Larissa against the wall and used the pay phone to call the American Embassy.

"This is Anatoli Kaplin. I need some help immediately," he told the operator.

"One moment, please," the woman said.

A couple of seconds later a man came on the phone. "This is Bill Seagren. Exactly where are you?"

Kaplin didn't know the name, but he was beyond caring now. He told Seagren where he and Larissa were and how they'd got there.

"Don't move, I'll be right over," Seagren said, and the connection was broken.

After his wounds were tended to at Bethesda Hospital, Tyson was to be flown down to the Farm at Camp Peary for his debriefing, which the experts figured could last several months.

Marina Demin had refused to see her father, and although there was sentiment that she should be kept in the United States, and in fact be placed on trial for her part in the plot against Tyson, Vaughan ordered that she be returned to Moscow immediately, with or without her consent.

Kit Tyson was not giving up on her husband. She phoned their daughter at Kent State, who promised to be on the very first plane to Washington.

"There's somebody outside who'd like to have a word with you, Mr. Tyson," one of the Bureau guards said.

"Who is it?" Tyson asked. He was being kept under observation at the hospital for twenty-four hours.

"Roland Clark."

Tyson looked up at his wife. "I'll see him," he said. "But you'd better wait outside."

"I'll be right there if you need me," Kit said, and she left, but the Bureau agent remained.

Clark came in. "How you doing, Mr. Tyson?" he asked. It was hard to read his expression, but he didn't seem angry.

"Sorry I disappointed you," Tyson said.

"If you had told me, I might have been able to help. As it was I had to keep my own head down. They were watching me too."

"There wasn't anything to tell you, or much for you to do until it was too late. I screwed up, and they took advantage of it, that's all."

"We all screw up one time or another," Clark said. "And when this is over, maybe we'll have a drink together, sir."

"Maybe," Tyson said.

"I'll be there."

"Thanks."

Dr. Thomas Heller stood on a chair in the basement of his Middleton home, a stout rope tied around his neck. It was secured to a steel beam overhead. There was no chance of its breaking or coming loose.

He'd been used all these years, and he'd been discarded. At any rate, the great socialist experiment had lasted barely seventy years, and had failed.

He stepped off the chair, knocking it over, and in a minute and a half he was unconscious.

"How did you get out of there?" Seagren asked.

"Do you know me . . . us?" Kaplin asked. "How?"

"I work with Sweeney."

"I was expecting him. Where is he? Why isn't he here?"

"He's in the States. He went home. So I was sent to help you."

Kaplin nodded. It was about what he'd expected. "Well, you're going to have to get this one back to the States too. She's American, she belongs there."

Larissa looked up at him, only barely comprehending what he was saying.

"How long have you known?" Seagren asked. He, too, was surprised.

"From the beginning, you idiot," Kaplin said. "Do you think the KGB employs fools?"

"No," Seagren said. "But it employs traitors." He pulled out a silenced pistol and cocked the trigger.

Larissa stiffened and tried to cry out, but it only came as a whimper. Kaplin shook his head. "Fuck your mother," he said. "You can't trust anybody in this world."

"It's not worth dying for, Bill," someone said from the stairs above.

Seagren started to turn.

"Don't make us shoot you."

"Roy?" Seagren asked.

"It's me," Rodgers said. "Put your gun down, and keep your hands in sight."

Seagren did as he was told. When he'd straightened up he raised his hands. "How did you guess?"

"We've been watching you for a while now," Rodgers said, coming down the stairs. "Actually Dick Sweeney had his doubts and ordered a loose surveillance."

"I never spotted them."

"No," Rodgers said.

Seagren looked over at Kaplin and shrugged. "You're right," he said. "I guess you *can't* trust anybody in this world."

Major Kiselev came to attention in front of General Ryazanov's desk, and saluted. The general returned the salute after a long second or two.

"I have read your report, Comrade Major. Have you anything further to add?"

"Yes, sir. I believe we need to make an effort to have Comrades Nechiporenko and Demin brought home."

"The Americans will offer a trade. Unless Mr. Tyson raises an objection . . . which he is hardly in a position to do at this time . . . there should be no problems."

"Considering that Marinka is not actually his daughter, no, sir, I see no problems either."

"There is no chance of Tyson's rehabilitation?"

"None whatsoever, Comrade General. Our operation is an unqualified success, so long as Director Novikov doesn't find out."

"With care," the general cautioned. "Charles Gleason has not yet been confirmed by the Senate as the next national security adviser."

"He will be," Kiselev said. "And when he is in, we will have our Source KHAIRULLA within the CIA to run him. We will have won."

"But not everything."

"Sir?"

"You're forgetting the two survivors from the debacle at GUM. They reached the American Embassy, and your source there was shot to death."

"Only a minor loss, Comrade General, compared to what we will gain in Washington."

"But a loss nonetheless," the general said. "See that it does not spread."

"Source KHAIRULLA has been instructed to lay low for a while. And his source within the National Security Agency has had an automobile accident. A fatal accident."

"I see. Then perhaps we have won, after all."

The afternoon was overcast, very cold and windy, snow sculpted into long sweeps across the highways. Working mostly on a hunch, Sweeney had driven over to the Reston office of Charles Gleason, arriving in time to follow the man down to a coffee shop just outside of town.

Someone within the CIA or NSA was working for the Russians, according to Kaplin. And now that Tyson had been brought down, Gleason would become the next national security adviser to the President. It made a sort of twisted sense to Sweeney, but only if Gleason were also working for the Russians.

A long shot, but there'd been enough things in this business that hadn't added up in his mind to make him extremely wary of any pat solution.

If Gleason were working for the Russians, he would undoubtedly have a control officer. The traitor in the CIA?

Sweeney was of half a mind to turn his suspicions over to Adkins and let someone else do the investigation. He didn't know if he actually wanted to know who the traitor was.

A gray Thunderbird came off the highway and immediately turned into the coffee shop's driveway. From across the street Sweeney could hardly believe his eyes. He knew the car. He knew who was driving it. And now he knew the identity of the traitor within the CIA.

The car pulled up and parked, and a square-shouldered man got out, looked around, and then entered the coffee shop.

Sweeney drove across to the coffee shop and parked next to the Thunderbird. Still he hesitated for a long few seconds. What if he was wrong? What if they were simply old friends?

He transferred his pistol from his shoulder holster to his coat pocket, then got out of the car and went into the restaurant.

One person was seated at the counter, and the only other customers were the two men in a back booth. Sweeney went back to them.

Charles Gleason looked up, puzzled at first, but then a look of alarm spread across his face.

Bob Drury, whom Nancy Perigorde and Gleason had known as Dr. Hamilton, turned around, an expression of incredulity changing slowly to one of resignation.

Sweeney slid into the booth next to Gleason. "Hello, Bob."

Drury nodded. "You brought backup?"

"Across the street," Sweeney lied.

Again Drury nodded. He looked at Gleason, then back. "How did you find out?"

"We had someone watching the KGB, who told us about the computer hacker in Moscow. Only way they could have known was from someone on this side."

"MOHAWK network?"

"At least it was worth something."

Drury thought for a moment or two. "But that would have brought you only to the NSA. We don't have the capability to read phone lines in Moscow."

"Tyson is out," Sweeney said. "Dr. Gleason here is the next logical choice for national security adviser."

"So you figured that if he was part of the plot, he'd have a control officer."

"But you came as a surprise," Sweeney said.

"Now what?"

"If you run, I'll shoot you," Sweeney said matter-of-factly.

A slight smile played at the corners of Drury's mouth. "No use my trying to bribe you."

Sweeney shook his head.

"Or trying to pull out my gun and have a shootout here."

"There've been enough bodies, don't you think?"

Drury sighed deeply. "You're right, of course, Richard." He smiled and shook his head. "It would have been grand, though. Think about it: a national security adviser to the President of the United States . . . a spy for Russia."

"Maybe next time," Sweeney said.

"Maybe there won't be a next time, for us."

—— EPILOGUE ——

IT WAS VERY LATE EVENING. SWEENEY AND KAY LAY IN EACH other's arms in front of the roaring fire at their Chesapeake house, listening to the wind howl outside. The normal ninety-minute drive had taken them twice that long because of the weather, but it was worth the effort.

They were drinking wine after making love on the fur rug, and Sweeney couldn't remember a time when he'd been happier.

"That was nice," Kay said.

"I'm glad you approve. I wish everything I did came out so well."

Kay looked up at him. "Want to talk about it?"

He shook his head after a moment. "Nope. I'm the spy who came in from the cold."

"No kidding?"

"No kidding," he said. He put down his wineglass, took hers and put it aside, and then gently forced her back down on the rug. "How about double or nothing?"

"Ernie . . ." she said, but then there was no further reason to talk.